PRAISE FOR THE GRAY MAN NOVELS

"Never has an assassin been rendered so real yet so deadly. Strikes with the impact of a bullet to the chest. . . . Not to be missed."

—*New York Times* bestselling author James Rollins

"Hard, fast, and unflinching—exactly what a thriller should be."

—#1 *New York Times* bestselling author Lee Child

"Excellent. . . . Greaney seamlessly adjusts focus between the timelines, jumping from one exhilarating roller-coaster ride to the other. Spy and military thriller fans will be well pleased." —*Publishers Weekly* (starred review)

"Writing as smooth as stainless-steel and a hero as mean as razor-wire . . . *The Gray Man* glitters like a blade in an alley."

—*New York Times* bestselling author David Stone

"The latest in the Gray Man series continues to demonstrate why Greaney belongs in the upper echelon of special-ops thriller authors."

—*Booklist* (starred review)

"The action is almost nonstop, with nice twists right to the end. . . . This is good, Clancy-esque entertainment." —*Kirkus Reviews*

"Mark Greaney continues his dominant run." —The Real Book Spy

BURNER

+

MARK GREANEY

BERKLEY
NEW YORK

BERKLEY
An imprint of Penguin Random House LLC
penguinrandomhouse.com

ISBN: 9780593548127

The Library of Congress has catalogued the Berkley hardcover edition of
this title as follows:

Names: Greaney, Mark, author.
Title: Burner / Mark Greaney.
Description: New York : Berkley, [2023] | Series: The gray man; 12
Identifiers: LCCN 2022041612 (print) | LCCN 2022041613 (ebook) |
ISBN 9780593548103 (hardcover) | ISBN 9780593548110 (ebook)
Classification: LCC PS3607.R4285 B87 2023 (print) |
LCC PS3607.R4285 (ebook) | DDC 813/.6—dc23
LC record available at https://lccn.loc.gov/2022041612
LC ebook record available at https://lccn.loc.gov/2022041613

Berkley hardcover edition / February 2023
Berkley trade paperback edition / August 2023

Printed in the United States of America
1st Printing

Interior art: Black-and-white Paris map © Nicole Renna / Shutterstock.com
Book design by Kelly Lipovich

Slava Ukrayini

We know they are lying.
They know they are lying.
They know that we know that they are lying.
We know that they know that we know that they know
they are lying.
And still... they continue to lie.

—ALEKSANDR SOLZHENITSYN

CHARACTERS

COURTLAND "COURT" GENTRY: aka Violator, aka Six, aka the Gray Man; freelance intelligence asset; former CIA contract officer; former CIA Special Activities Division (Ground Branch) paramilitary operations officer

VITALI PESKOV: president of the Russian Federation

EDDISON JOHN: attorney-at-law, Castries, Saint Lucia

DANIIL SPANOV: director of the Security Council, Russian Federation

IGOR KRUPKIN: Russian financial planner

ALEXANDER VELESKY: banker for Brucker Söhne Holdings, Zurich, Switzerland

LUKA RUDENKO: CIA code name Matador; podpolkovnik (major), GRU (Russian military intelligence), Unit 29155

ULAN BAKIYEV: starshina (first sergeant), GRU (Russian military intelligence), Unit 29155

EZRA ALTMAN: American forensic accountant

PETRO MOZGOVOY: intelligence officer, Donetsk People's Republic Security Service Battalion

HENRY CALVIN: attorney, Hartley, Hill, and Prescott, LLC, New York City

SEBASTIAN DREXLER: Swiss freelance intelligence asset

ANGELA LACY: senior operations officer, Directorate of Operations, CIA

SUZANNE BREWER: special assistant to the deputy director for operations, CIA

JAY KIRBY: Director, CIA

ZOYA ZAKHAROVA: code name Banshee; freelance intelligence asset; former SVR (Russian foreign intelligence) operative; former CIA contract asset

BRUCKER SÖHNE HOLDINGS: Zurich-based Swiss private bank

GARNIER ET MOREAU CIE.: Geneva-based Swiss private bank

DPR: Donetsk People's Republic; pro-Russian eastern Ukrainian separatist region

DPR SSB: Donetsk People's Republic Security Service Battalion; intelligence service of the DPR

BURNER

These Russians weren't fucking around tonight.

One dozen men were arrayed on the 281-foot mega yacht, all armed with new polymer-framed AK-12 rifles, two-thousand-lumen tactical flashlights, and communications gear that kept them in contact with one another wherever they were positioned on or around the huge watercraft. The *Lyra Drakos* stood at anchor, far out in English Harbour off the island of Antigua in the eastern Caribbean, and the sentries on board scanned the black water with their bright beams, made regular radio checks with the night watch on the bridge, and kept themselves amped up through the dark hours with coffee, cigarettes, energy drinks, and speed.

In addition to the expansive nighttime deck watch, three more armed men slowly circled the vessel in a twenty-seven-foot tender with a 250-horsepower engine. And below the surface, yet another pair patrolled underwater in wet suits, dive gear, and sea scooters: handheld devices with enclosed propellers that pulled them along at up to 2.5 miles per hour. These men carried flashlights, spearguns on their backs, and long knives strapped to their thighs.

The men and women on board the yacht had been at this high level of readiness for nearly two weeks, and it was grueling work, but the man paying the guards' salaries compensated them well.

The owner of the yacht and his security detail were ramped up like this because of two separate incidents the previous month in Asia. Three and a half weeks earlier, a 96-meter ship called *Pura Vida* sank off the Maldives in the Indian Ocean. The boat had been linked to a Russian oligarch who had somehow managed to avoid having his offshore property confiscated like most of his fellow billionaire countrymen after the invasion of Ukraine began a year earlier. The cause of the sinking had not been revealed by local authorities, but most of the Russians with boats still in their possession presumed it to be sabotage.

Their assumptions seemed assured just nine days later when a second vessel, a 104-meter yacht with two helicopter landing pads owned by a byzantine collection of shell corporations and trusts but ultimately the property of the impossibly wealthy internal security chief of the Russian president, suffered the same fate in Dubai, sinking to the bottom of Jebel Ali, the largest human-made harbor in the world.

No one had been killed or even injured in either incident, but the destruction of the property itself was more than enough to have the remaining oligarchs with ships afloat both incensed and on alert.

The fear here in Antigua, understandably, was that the *Lyra Drakos* would end up in the bottom of the bay like the ships in the Maldives and Dubai incidents. The *Lyra* was a Greek-named vessel registered in the Seychelles to a front company in the UK belonging to a shell in Cyprus that was owned by a blind trust in Hong Kong that itself was owned by another blind trust in Panama. But she was, ultimately and in truth, the property of Constantine Pasternak, a sixty-three-year-old billionaire from Saint Petersburg and the former minister of natural resources and environment of the Russian Federation.

The *Lyra Drakos* was not as ostentatious as many of the other mega yachts that had been owned by wealthy Russians and seized after the invasion of Ukraine began. With a price tag of 120 million USD and an annual operating cost of just over ten million dollars, she was half the size and a fourth the cost of some of the biggest vessels on the sea. Still, she was currently listed as the 105th largest yacht in the world, and though Constantine Pasternak had hidden his ownership well, he suspected his ship might eventually be a target of whoever was sabotaging Russian-owned property.

All had been quiet in the mega yacht world for two weeks now, but Pasternak and the few men like him who still owned anything that hadn't been seized or sunk had thrown all their guests off their vessels and then replenished them with well-trained and heavily armed goons. This was survival mode now, and everyone was just waiting either to be hit or, preferably, to catch some group in the act of trying.

Hence the *Lyra Drakos* was anchored a full kilometer away from any other vessel in the harbor here in Antigua, and constantly patrolled both above and below the waterline. The soft mood lighting that normally ringed the ship had been replaced with glaring floods. The security crew was made up of men from Stravinsky, a Russian military contracting firm, and divers kept their watch, making sure no explosives were attached to the hull of Pasternak's last remaining prized possession outside the Russian Federation.

These men were former special forces members and they were prepared to repel any attack, and the events in Dubai and the Maldives had only honed their attention to a finer point.

The seventeen security assets on duty tonight presented an incredibly imposing show of force to any would-be aggressor, and to a man, they were utterly and unshakably confident of one thing.

Nobody . . . *nobody* . . . was going to come here and fuck with Constantine Pasternak tonight.

Court Gentry had come here to fuck with Constantine Pasternak tonight.

He knelt on the sandy ocean floor, fifty-six feet below the waterline and behind a cluster of six-foot-tall barrel sponges, peering through his night vision monocular. Five-foot-long tarpons circled him languidly, casually interested in the strange creature who'd encroached on their nighttime feeding grounds.

Soon Court flipped his underwater night observation device up away from his mask and squinted into the bright lights around the *Lyra Drakos* above him and just thirty yards to the north.

He'd spotted the divers the night before on his first visit to his target location, and again ten minutes ago, immediately after arriving this evening. The men were too far away for him to see them in any detail, but their lights sweeping against the hull of the yacht as they patrolled independently were unmistakable. They were two in number, just as there had been last night, and Court was doing his best to study their protocols, though he knew he couldn't wait around for long. His bottom time at sixty feet was less than twenty minutes; after that, he'd run the risk of decompression sickness as he headed back to the surface.

Last night he'd been ready to act but decided there was too much security to go forward without a better understanding of their patterns of movement, so he'd returned to his own boat, ready to reboot for another attempt this evening.

Court's sinking of the *Pura Vida* in the Maldives three and a half weeks ago had proved to be a relatively easy task. The boat's security practices seemed to be focused on the surface, and coming up below it and placing three small magnetic charges in critical areas had been no great feat.

The attack in Dubai had been a more difficult job. The *Ormurin Langi* was a larger vessel, and after the Maldives incident, word was out in the community that someone was gunning for the oligarchs' big toys. The owner of the *Ormurin* had upgraded his security; speedboats patrolled the water around the vessel, and underwater cameras had been placed fore and aft. Still, Court managed to avoid the cameras using his night vision monocular, and he minimized tipping anyone off above the waterline to his presence by diving with a Dräger RBD 5000 rebreather as part of his gear, effectively eliminating any bubbles escaping and rising upwards to the surface.

He'd placed three charges on the *Ormurin Langi*, same as with the *Pura Vida*, and he cleared the area forty-five minutes before the small but critically placed detonations erupted, damaging the mega yacht and ultimately sending it to the floor of the bay some thirteen hours later.

Now Court was here, on the other side of the world, and just as he'd imagined, security seemed exponentially more robust around this vessel.

The enemy was adapting to his tactics, that was clear, but Court wasn't worried.

He'd adapt right the fuck back.

Courtland Gentry was American, a former CIA officer, and then a former CIA asset—a contract agent. Now he worked freelance intelligence jobs, only taking contracts he thought to be principled.

He'd been living on his boat down here in the Caribbean, hoping for some action that would leave him feeling like he'd made a difference in this increasingly cold, black world. He was contacted on the dark web by an expat Ukrainian oligarch named Andrei Melnyk, who had escaped the war and now lived in Romania. Melnyk was a thug and a crook, Court had no doubt, but Court worked for thugs and crooks as a matter of course when he believed the mission to be righteous, and the job the Ukrainian offered him seemed both doable and noble, so he accepted.

Melnyk boasted access to one thing Court needed: intelligence product. The Ukrainian oligarch had contacts in the world of international finance who could connect the dots along the way between wealthy Russians and their property in the West.

Now Court worked for Melnyk, ridding the Earth of the last of the vanity luxury belongings of the criminal Russians who served as the enemy of the Ukrainian's homeland as well as his competition in business.

Court Gentry, in short, had become a professional saboteur.

Currently, the Ukrainian's list named nine yachts. They were all uninsured because of the threats of them being seized by governments, and the vessels' Russian owners had been uncovered via high-level forensic accounting. Six more boats after this one meant steady work for Court Gentry, and once he brought down the *Lyra Drakos*, he had plans to lay low here in the Caribbean for a week or two before heading down to Port of Spain in Trinidad and Tobago and sinking a seventy-two-meter vessel moored there that was owned by the deputy prime minister of Belarus.

Court suffered no illusions that he was changing the world with any of this. This was simply inconveniencing and pissing off some very bad people who had been party to unspeakable crimes against humanity.

He'd much rather be in Crimea or Moscow or Saint Petersburg or Minsk or wherever-the-fuck, shoving stilettos or ice picks or screwdrivers or two-handed swords between the ribs of these bastards—*all* of these bastards. But his Ukrainian benefactor was a money man who employed money men. He only knew how to follow the money. He did not possess the intelligence capacity, the logistics, or the connections to put Court within reach of anyone of military or intelligence value within Russia or its satellites.

Simply destroying some rich dickhead's water toy felt like weak sauce to

Court, but it was *something*, and as far as he was concerned, this work was nevertheless an honorable endeavor.

He checked the computer on his wrist and told himself he'd better get to it. He didn't expect any problems on his ascent, and as long as he could see the two flashlight beams on the hull, he thought he'd have no trouble avoiding the divers while working around a vessel nearly the length of a football field.

He lifted a mesh bag containing three limpet mines from where it had been lying on the sand next to him. Each mine weighed twelve pounds, and he reattached the bag to his buoyancy control device, then added some air from his tank into his jacket. Slowly he began to lift off the ocean floor, the air in the jacket more than making up for the addition of the thirty-six pounds.

He ascended slowly, closing on the yacht at its stern, his eyes shifting back and forth towards the two moving lights he saw bouncing off the hull of the *Lyra Drakos*. He hadn't gotten a good look at the divers; he'd only seen their shadows and silhouettes, but he could imagine they would be carrying either spearguns or Russian APSs, gas-powered underwater submachine guns that fired 5.66-millimeter rounds through unrifled barrels.

Court was armed only with a pair of knives: a six-inch serrated stainless steel Mares fixed-blade dagger in a sheath on the chest of his BCD, and a three-and-a-half-inch titanium ScubaPro Mako with a tanto tip, this strapped to his calf. He *couldn't* get into any shootouts tonight and didn't *want* to get in any knife fights down here under the waves, so he told himself remaining covert would be key.

At thirty-five feet he heard the buzzing sound of an outboard motor churning above him; he looked up and picked out a large tender lazily sweeping around the stern and heading up the starboard side.

The motorboat in the water was not his concern; it was the divers. But still, he liked his chances. The divers' job wouldn't be to scan the black water in all directions for aggressors; it would be to keep an eye on the hull to make sure no devices had been attached. It took each man over ten minutes to circle the vessel, and since they were more or less equidistant, he knew he had five good minutes at each location to place a mine.

At seventeen feet below the surface, he reached out and put his hand on the hull at the stern, just in front of the massive propeller, and he reached into the bag to grab the first limpet. The mine operated with an electromagnet, so he placed it carefully on the aluminum hull and then initiated a secure connection between the weapon and the target. He checked around again for the divers' flashlights and saw that they were shining on the port and starboard sides but more than halfway up the length of the hull, so he carefully put his hand on the tab connected to the limpet mine's chemical fuse.

Then he took a couple of calming breaths, using the moment to think about his situation.

For his attacks in the Maldives and in Dubai he'd set his fuses for one hour, but after coming here last night and seeing the divers actively searching for mines, he'd trimmed them down so that they would detonate after only twelve minutes.

With a twelve-minute fuse, even if the mines were detected, it was highly unlikely the divers would be able to remove or disable them before it was too late.

Court hadn't killed or even injured anyone on the first two attacks, but tonight he knew it was likely that at least a couple of assholes would lose their lives, and he really didn't give a shit.

These guys worked for Russian oligarchs, crooked beneficiaries of a monstrous regime with targets on their heads.

Fuck these divers, Court told himself as he pulled the tab.

He left the first limpet and advanced forward under the hull, using the small keel at the center as a shield by moving to port to hide from a sweeping light on the starboard side, then ducking under the keel again to hide himself from the light on the port side. It was slow going; while there was a pattern to the divers' movements, they weren't perfectly synchronized, so he had to concentrate fully.

When the starboard-side diver made his way back towards the stern, Court himself went under the keel to starboard and quickly attached the limpet on the hull just below the surface, swimming up the side just after the diver passed, heading aft. Court's operating theory was that it would be five minutes before the diver on the port side made it around here, and once he did, there was a good chance he would miss something almost at the waterline, since he'd be mainly scanning lower down the yacht's seventeen-foot draft.

With two limpets attached and their fuses initiated, he swam back to port and in the direction of the bow. He could see the port-side diver's light sweeping, but he'd lost sight of the light from the man at the stern now. He assumed that either the diver back there had gone to the surface to communicate with men on deck, or else his light just wasn't visible from where Court was positioned below the hull.

Placement of this last device, Court knew, could be lower in the water than the mine on the starboard side, because by the time the man made it up here within thirty feet of the bow, the first mine would have detonated. At that point, anyone in the water this close would be not only severely concussed but much more focused on getting the hell out of the way of any subsequent blasts than trying to disarm any remaining mines.

Court placed the third limpet, pulled the fuse tab, then looked down to his dive computer. It had been over eight minutes since he'd triggered the first mine's fuse; it would take him a full minute of swimming to ensure that he was clear of the blast radius, so he had less than three minutes to get himself out of here.

He inverted his body in the water and kicked, descending to go back under the keel and then to continue down to the ocean floor and swim away as fast as possible.

He passed under the keel; he was twenty feet below the surface under the hull in the dark area the deck lighting didn't reach when, from out of nowhere, a bright white beam flashed him in the eyes.

Court was blinded and stunned by the light instantly, but despite the sudden danger and disorientation, he retained awareness of the fact that he had only two minutes and forty-five seconds to get his ass the hell out of there before the mines began to blow.

TWO

Instinctively Court spun away from the bright beam. The light would be in the hand of a man with a weapon, and since Court couldn't tell how far away his opponent was, he worried he'd get shot if he didn't put something between himself and an attack.

As soon as his back was to the light, he felt and heard a powerful *clang* off his equipment behind him. From the sound it seemed as if a spear had hit his steel tank and glanced off.

Court knew the shooter would need time to reload his speargun, so he kicked as hard as he could out in front of him, sending himself backwards in the direction of the danger with his tank still between him and the threat.

As he did this, he drew the big knife on his chest and, when he collided with a man under the hull, he immediately spun around and slashed out.

His blade made no contact with his enemy, but the diver's light spun in the water and began to fall away.

Still partially blinded from getting zapped in the eyes, Court lunged forward with his blade now, stabbing out, but the other diver had himself kicked away to put some distance between the two of them, and Court missed his mark again.

There was so little light here under the hull, and his retinas were still recovering from the sharp beam that had flared them, so Court knew he wasn't much of an effective fighter at the moment. He reached up and pulled down his night vision monocular, assuming this would give him the advantage he needed, but once he looked through the narrow forty-degree tube, he saw not only the diver racing towards him with a long knife but also a night vision system over the man's eyes.

Shit. These guys had better kit than he'd planned on.

Through his narrow monocular he couldn't see the knife coming at him from the diver's right, but he anticipated the strike and lurched his head back. The blade scratched against Court's mask, meaning it would have sliced open his face had he been a tenth of a second slower.

Court lunged out with his own knife again, but he'd moved too far back for a counterstrike.

The American tried to kick away, to make some space until he could find the knife swinging back and forth at him at the end of the other man's arm, but before he could do so, the Russian diver kicked forward and slashed again, and Court felt a tugging impact on the right side of his face.

A shot of seawater down Court's throat told him the blade had pierced the hose on his Dräger rebreather. He fought panic, lunged forward, and wrapped up the enemy with his arms, letting his own knife drop from his left hand so that it would be free to find and control the enemy's weapon.

He held his breath as the two men struggled. His night vision monocular took a knock from the other diver's regulator, dislodging it from his head and sending it towards the ocean floor.

Court's world went black, but then, as he got his gloved hand around the right wrist of his opponent, his world lit up again, brighter than before. He could see the diver inches from his face, the knife he held extended away from his body, Court's severed hose pouring bubbles up the right side of his face.

Court had wanted visibility, but now that he had it, he knew this wasn't good news. This meant someone else, presumably the other diver who'd been patrolling the hull, had been alerted to his presence here and was headed this way.

The other diver would have a weapon as well as a light, and Court's bad situation just became worse.

And as he fought to rip the mask off the diver he was locked in a death grip with, he had the presence of mind to also worry about the fact that the mines were going to start blowing on the ship above him in about two minutes.

The Russian grappling with him thirty feet underwater was surprisingly strong and skilled. He pushed Court's hand off easily as the American tried ripping away his enemy's mask. Court used his left hand now to reach down for his emergency backup regulator, also attached to his tank and stored on the front right side of his buoyancy control device.

He grabbed the emergency regulator—called the octopus—out of his BCD, and he shoved it into his mouth, but just as he did this, the diver he was wrapped up with reached behind his own back and handed his knife off from his right hand to his left hand behind his tank. Court felt the man's arms go behind him, and he figured out what was happening, so he hurriedly wrapped his legs around the diver's waist and leaned back and away.

His adversary's knife shot in from the left now, and it sliced right through the hose of his octopus.

Once again Court inhaled seawater and gagged.

As the diver stabbed out a second time with his left hand, Court contorted away but grabbed the man's left wrist with his right hand. With his left hand he pulled his enemy's octopus off the right side of his chest and shoved it into his own mouth, then Court began sharing air with the man desperately trying to kill him.

The Russian diver hugged himself tight around Court's body. As the men thrashed and spun in the dark water, a spaghetti-like maze of equipment only bonded them more. The American felt their dive rigs getting wrapped up together: hoses, buckles, even Court's loose pressure gauge console threading under his enemy's regulator hose.

The American could barely maneuver, and he couldn't try to swim away, because he needed the air in the tank on the other man's back to stay alive.

The light shining on them from behind Court brightened as the other diver closed in, and Court knew the man would have likely already shot him with his speargun if he hadn't been worried about missing and hitting his colleague.

The diver in Court's face head-butted him, opening the seal on Court's mask enough for it to fill with seawater. Court didn't have a free hand to fix it; his right was now clutching his enemy's left to control the knife, and his left was fighting with the other man's right hand, which was still trying to yank off Court's mask or pull back the octopus.

One minute till boom, Court told himself as he struggled.

He shut his eyes to keep out the salty seawater, and he knew he had seconds to get out of this, or he was a dead man.

With his options so limited, the idea that suddenly came to him didn't get a lot of examination before he began its implementation. With his arm wrapped in the Russian's regulator hose at the man's right shoulder, Court let go of the man's wrist, then reached to the tank on the Russian's back and began turning the valve knob. He was shutting off his opponent's oxygen supply, but in so doing he was also shutting off his own. He took one deep breath as the tank closed, just before the Russian managed to pull back his octopus with his newly freed hand.

The other diver understood his predicament as soon as he tried to take a breath but instead registered the terrifyingly sudden lack of air, and he instantly began working to get his valve reopened. This was a two-handed job for the person wearing the gear, so he let go of Court and kicked back, trying to create some space to work safely in.

Court quickly lifted the bottom of his mask and blew out through his nose before sealing it again to his face, clearing it of seawater. Now he could see; the Russian closing behind him with the flashlight had lowered his beam for a moment. Court took that as a sign that the man was readying a weapon to fire. He swam towards his nearer opponent, the diver frantically hefting his tank with his left hand from below and reaching for the valve knob up behind his right ear.

But Court was on him before he could reopen the tank. In one sweeping motion, the American asset reached down to his ankle, pulled his three-and-a-half-inch titanium Mako knife, and stabbed the man up under his chin, sending the tip of the blade into his cervical spine.

Court let go of the knife hilt and used both hands to spin the dying man around, and just as he put the diver between himself and the flashlight's beam, a barbed steel spear fired by the other diver impaled the Russian through the intestines.

Court pulled the regulator out of the dying man's mouth, shoved it into his own, then hurriedly turned the knob on the tank to reopen the oxygen flow.

As the man died, his body hung there in the water, and Court got behind it, then began pushing it forward towards the flashlight's beam.

And then the first mine detonated at the stern of the *Lyra Dracos*. The charge, while big enough to blow a two-meter-wide chunk out of the hull, was too far away from where the two divers were to do more than rattle their eardrums and shake up their insides.

Nevertheless, the detonation did have one very positive effect for Court. The flashlight pointing at him swept hurriedly in the opposite direction, and he could see the other diver swimming away from the ship as fast as his fins would take him. The man still had a speargun on him, but Court didn't think he was going to waste time reloading it and chasing Court down, since he would have no way of knowing how many mines were locked onto this ship or how long it would be before the next one blew.

Court was about forty feet below the surface now, and he held tight to the dead diver by his tank valve knob and began swimming away, trying to create distance between himself and the yacht. As he swam, however, he multitasked by removing the diving gear from the corpse, then switched out the gear strapped to his own body, since both of his regulators were inoperable thanks to the Russian's knife.

He even took the mask off his victim so he would have the night vision tube, and then, when he had everything he needed from the dead Russian, he pulled the Mako out of the dead man's neck, then let his body drift away.

Court continued kicking. The big tender was directly above him; they were probably readying more divers to come down here and help their mates, but Court had no plans to wait around to greet them.

He swam to the south as fast as he could, slowly ascending along the way to preserve what little air was left in the Russian's tank.

Twenty minutes later, well after the detonation of the three mines and simultaneous to the call on board the *Lyra Drakos* for everyone to abandon ship, a lone figure emerged from the black water at Nelson's Dockyard Marina, coming up between a pair of pleasure craft tied in adjoining slips.

Court looked around to make sure there was no one out at four in the morning, then climbed up the stern ladder of a forty-six-foot sailboat, all the diving gear—both his and that which he'd borrowed—left behind on the sandy bottom of the marina right below the slip.

It took one minute to remove the lines from the dock, and in another minute he was standing at the helm under the dodger, stripped out of his wet suit and wearing only black swim trunks, seawater still dripping from his body.

Blood on his right arm told him the Russian's knife had managed to slit him through his wet suit and nick him just below the shoulder, but it didn't hurt, and there wasn't enough blood to worry about, so he ignored the wound.

He fired the engine of his motorized sailboat and reversed slowly out of the slip, then turned the wheel till he was facing to the south, away from the marina. He increased speed and began turning to starboard, to the west, then picked his binoculars off the helm and brought them to his eyes.

Off to the southeast he could make out the *Lyra Drakos*; it was listing to starboard already, and the lifeboats had been launched. He saw no fire, but Court knew the little limpet mines would bring the boat down over a few hours; they hadn't been designed to blow the ship to smithereens.

Still, it would be a complete loss for Constantine Pasternak, and that made Court smile a little as he headed west around the island, with his ultimate destination his temporary home, nine hours' sailing time to the north.

THREE

Alex Velesky sat alone, eyes fixed on the frozen darkness beyond the light around him, his body racked with implacable dread.

A car door had just opened and then shut on Neumarkt, just twenty meters up an alleyway in front of him. The man he'd come to meet had arrived, and Alex had no idea if he was ready to deal with this bullshit or not.

Wet snowflakes blew through the empty side streets in Zurich's Altstadt; cobblestones shone slick with ice, reflecting the radiance of gas lamps. This was the old city: narrow, winding streets lined with medieval cathedrals, squares, and colorful stone buildings buttressed against one another, many of which dated from the fourteenth century. The Altstadt absolutely bustled in the summer, but late on a Thursday night in mid-January, the few tourists in town now slept ensconced in the warmth of their hotel rooms.

Shortly before midnight, thirty-five-year-old Zurich resident Alex Velesky sat alone at a plastic table in the walled back garden of a shuttered bistro, protected from the precipitation by a clear plastic awning hanging over a trellis, and only partially warmed by a long wool coat and a gas heater.

Five minutes ago, the chill had bothered him, but now sweat formed on his forehead as he sat perfectly still, staring into the black beyond the lights around him.

It's business, just business, he told himself again and again as the hollow echo of approaching footsteps grew in the alleyway. *You don't have to like it, you just have to shut your mouth and do your fucking job.*

He wished to be anywhere but here. He wished to be at home watching television; he wished to be with his old friends playing hockey or going out to dinner; he wished to be with his family, his beautiful baby nephew in his arms and his worries far away from here, far away from a clandestine meeting in a cold back alley with a man Alex barely knew.

A man Alex utterly loathed.

He pushed his long-dead dreams of happiness away, and with a trembling hand, he poured two glasses of Ornellaia from the bottle opened and then left on the table by the waiter shortly before he'd locked up the restaurant for the night. The establishment was actually located across the tiny square on Neumarkt, and it was closed now, the waiter having left his one guest alone in back of a neighboring building, against house rules, after rolling over a gas heater and securing a two-hundred-euro tip. Alex had promised to turn off the heater when he finished his wine and left the tiny courtyard, but he'd mentioned nothing of a secret meeting with a business associate from abroad.

A figure came into view at the edge of the lights now, and Velesky put the bottle down, then forced a phony smile on his clean-shaven face. He rose, his knees quivering almost as much as his hands.

The new arrival was tall and beefy, with a bushy mustache and silver hair that blew untidily in the late evening's breeze. Though Alex knew the man was in his early fifties, he appeared much older, shockingly so.

Alex kept the smile frozen on his face as he reached out and shook the older man's hand. Their eyes met, but then Velesky looked away quickly. Though he was not a violent man, Alex wanted to slam his fists into the bastard in front of him until his face turned to pulp, and he felt certain his utter malevolence would show through the windows of his soul.

But he wasn't here to kill anyone. He was here with the presumed objective of making a lot of money for his employers, and though it sickened him to do so, he planned on being nothing more this evening than a good company man.

Let's just get this shit over with.

Alex Velesky had known Igor Krupkin for years, albeit only in a professional sense. Velesky was associate deputy director of digital assets trading at a venerable Swiss private bank called Brucker Söhne Holdings, and Krupkin was a Russian financial planner who had steered billions of dollars of his clients' money to Velesky's firm over the past decade, much of it through Bitcoin and other cryptos. But Krupkin normally dealt with those several rungs higher up the ladder than Velesky, and this was but one reason the thirty-five-year-old banker was trepidatious about being called to a meeting late at night with the man from Moscow.

Krupkin spoke English with a heavy Russian accent. "You told no one?"

Velesky shook his head. In a measured tone he said, "You asked me to keep it quiet. Even from my bank. That's what I did."

Seemingly satisfied, Krupkin reached into his jacket and pulled out a pack of cigarettes.

Velesky hid his seething revulsion and tried his best to sell the pleasantries. "Have a good flight?"

Krupkin sat roughly and lit a Golden Yava Classic. He shook his head as he waved away smoke. "Airplanes, trains, cars. Moscow to Belgrade, Belgrade to Budapest, Budapest to Zurich. Not the best twenty hours of my life, no."

Velesky cocked his head as he sat down. "Why the circuitous route? You have dual citizenship, if I remember correctly. You could have made it with only one layover."

Krupkin smoked, then downed a third of his glass of the Italian red without a proper toast. He didn't answer directly; instead he said, "I have something to give you."

"The bank is always at your service," Velesky replied, a well-practiced line that used to mean something to him. But now his words were hollow. *Nothing* meant *anything* to him these days. Alex was a man on autopilot, the residual momentum of his past life propelling him forward through the present and towards the abyss certain to be his future.

When Krupkin did not speak immediately, Velesky felt discomfort in the dead air and snapped back into gear to fill it. "But . . . I am . . . I'm quite frankly confused about the reason for this meeting. You're in the most capable hands at our firm with Herr Thomas Brucker himself, and I don't normally meet with clients outside of the bank.

"So . . . why did you call *me*?"

"Do you believe in serendipity?"

It was a strange non sequitur. "I'm sorry?"

"We've known one another for a decade. I've always liked you, Alexander. For this reason, it couldn't be anyone else but you."

Alex Velesky's stomach roiled. It was true, he had known the man for a decade; vaguely, anyway. They'd met at Davos and at dinner parties here in Zurich or down in Zug or over in Basel. The Russian had always been warm and friendly, but now Alex determined Krupkin to have a uniquely punchable face.

Alex shook off the violent fantasies and got down to it. "What do you have that you *had* to give to me?"

The older man looked around, making sure they were still alone, then took something from his wool coat and handed it over to the younger man.

Alex took it. "An iPhone?"

Krupkin nodded. "There's no mobile service or Internet on it. I even removed the radio transmitter, so there should be no danger of tracking. It's just, essentially, a portable hard drive with some unique features."

Alex said, "It's loaded with cryptocurrency, I assume? There are easier ways to transfer that out of Russia to me, even these days."

"It's not crypto," Krupkin said.

"Then . . . what is it?"

The Russian just stared at Velesky for a long moment, then stamped out his cigarette, drank more of the wine. Without looking at the man across the table now, he said, "You are Ukrainian."

This came out of left field, and Alex Velesky felt bile burn in his stomach. He sat up straighter. He balled his hands into fists under the table, the cuffs of his Turnbull & Asser white cotton dress shirt strained at his forearms. Rubbing his hands together quickly and stifling his emotions, his voice cracked as he replied. "I . . . yeah, I am."

Krupkin instantly switched into Russian. "Dual citizenship with Switzerland, just like me, but you are Ukrainian, and I am Russian."

Velesky never spoke Russian these days, but he'd grown up with it along with Ukrainian. He himself slipped into the language, though it was the last thing in the world he wanted to do tonight. "What does the nation of my birth have to do—"

Krupkin interrupted. "You are Ukrainian," he said for the third time, "an expert in private banking data and . . . *delicate* . . . accounts, as well as your bank's leading expert on cryptocurrency. You are perfect for my needs, the only man in Switzerland I trust with the information that is on that phone."

Information?

Krupkin shrugged, refilled his glass, and looked around quickly. "I didn't know if I'd make it here tonight. They already know what I did, so they'll be close behind me." With a heave of his shoulders, he said, "I had to take measures in case I was captured before I met with you, so I sent an identical phone to an attorney in the Caribbean." He added, "He's an honest man, I think. Too honest for my liking, but that's neither here nor there. But . . . he's missing two attributes that you possess, so I am putting the vast majority of my faith in you." He pointed a thick finger at Alex's heart.

"*Faith?* What are you—"

"You have the access that he does not possess, and you have one other thing he does not possess."

"What is that?"

"Motivation. I trust *you* to do what needs to be done, Alex."

"You barely know me."

Krupkin looked around again. "I know two things about you, and that's enough. One, as I said, you come from Ukraine. From Staryi Krym, just north of Mariupol."

Velesky's heart pounded now.

The Russian leaned forward. "And two . . . I know that they're all gone. All four of them."

The Swiss-Ukrainian closed his eyes now. Rage gave way to pain, and then pain mutated into shame. Tears fought to force their way out through his closed eyelids.

The Russian spoke more softly now. "Your mother and your father. Your sister, Oksana. Your infant nephew, Dymtrus. All dead."

Velesky's eyes opened slowly, Krupkin's visage blurry through the tears. Why was this motherfucking Russian prick invoking the names of his dead nephew, his dead sister? He tried to speak, but no words came. He was on the verge of crying when Krupkin added, "Unspeakable crimes."

Velesky looked off into the snowy night now. Any pretense of a normal business meeting was gone, so his demeanor had changed accordingly. "What the fuck do you want from me, Krupkin?"

FOUR

The silver-haired Russian seemed to take no offense. "I want you to open that phone. The password is 'Dymtrus.' It has a two-terabyte hard drive, and it is nearly full."

Velesky continued to sweat as he stared into the night. "Full of . . . of *what*?"

"Secrets," Krupkin said as he lit a fresh Yava.

"Secrets?" Alex was confused.

The Russian blew fresh smoke. "State secrets. A blueprint, a daisy chain, if you will, showing how Russian national wealth is funneled through one man in Moscow, and then from him to dozens of shell companies across Russia. It's all mapped out for you." He paused, then said, "The data shows how all of this wealth has been routed into Brucker Söhne via cryptocurrency transfers."

Krupkin reached out and touched the phone with the hand holding the cigarette. "It's money Russian intelligence sends to its accounts in the West, where it is then doled out to its agents, its officers, the recipients of its bribes. It's used to pay for safe houses and weapons, for private armies and law firms, for corrupt government officials and for police. It's used for who knows what, but it's used by Russia for illegal Russian interests around the world."

Alex's mouth dropped open.

This was extraordinary. Russian oligarchs, especially those closely tied to the State, went to astonishingly great lengths to hide their offshore wealth. Velesky knew that Krupkin handled the money of some of the most notorious oligarchs in Russia, high-ranking state officials and mafia goons who'd raped the nation and then squirreled away their money abroad.

The very men who had kept President Vitali Peskov in power as he pummeled Ukraine over the past year.

But to compile this data, to link it to Russia's intelligence services and to sneak it out of the country to hand it off to a foreigner—this was an incredible undertaking, and certainly something that would get the man across the table from him killed.

Alex's body shook more now. He didn't dare reach for his wine, lest he reveal his emotions. He just asked, "Why?"

"Use that information, Alex. Show the world who's on the take from Russian intelligence, show them who is attacking the West . . . the West that doesn't even acknowledge that it's being attacked."

"I'm a banker, Herr Krupkin. I'm not a journalist, or an intelligence agent, or any—"

"Journalists and intelligence agencies can't do anything with the information in the files on that phone. It takes someone with access to transactions at your bank. Yes, my information shows how much was transferred into the accounts by Russian intelligence, and there are scans of signed documents and audio files proving who sent what to Brucker Söhne, but it doesn't show where the money went *after* that. My information is all but worthless without the records from inside your bank. *You* have the power to get in there, to go through the numbered accounts, to find the actual names of the owners and tie this to the information I'm giving you. If you unravel it, you can expose the path of every single ruble from the Kremlin to the criminals abroad."

Velesky cocked his head. "How do you know all this?"

"Because the person at the top of the entire operation is Daniil Spanov. Do you know who that is?"

Velesky admitted he did not.

"He's the director of the Security Council. Former Russian military intelligence, former head of the GRU. He works and lives in the shadows, but he's President Peskov's right-hand man.

"I've been working for Daniil Spanov for four years, exclusively, as he funnels money out of Russia to pay off foreign assets around the world. I am the single financial conduit between Russian intelligence and Brucker Söhne, and almost *all* of the money goes right through your bank, Alex."

Krupkin smoked a moment in silence, then said, "The power to stop it all is now in your hands."

There was confusion, fear, the remnants of anger, in Velesky's voice. "Why are you doing this?"

Krupkin took another drag, and while doing so, he seemed to ponder the question, as if for the first time. Finally, he said, "If you look at me and think I'm too old, have done too many bad things to suddenly grow a conscience, I would have to say I agree with you. But everything my nation built over thirty years since the end of the Soviet Union, it was all pissed away by the madman in charge, and I now know I have no future."

He hesitated, then said, "No future, but I can still have a legacy." He pointed to the iPhone. "*That's* my legacy."

Velesky slowly shook his head. "No. There's something else. You're giving up your life for this, and you know it. There *must* be another motivation."

The Russian's bushy eyebrows rose; he seemed impressed at Alex's powers of deduction. Then the eyes below the brows went glassy. Tears formed quickly. He sipped wine with the hand holding the cigarette, then he said, "My son . . . Yuri. He was a major in the 11th Guards Air Assault Brigade. Deputy commander of a reconnaissance battalion. Deployed to Ukraine last spring." Krupkin waved his hand again. "Far away from Mariupol. In Makariv, west of Kiev."

Velesky sat there, silently hoping this story ended with the death of this motherfucker's piece-of-shit son.

"He was injured," Krupkin said. "Not severely. A broken leg and lacerations. Shrapnel from a mortar, I'm told. He was taken to a field hospital, treated there. He called me, he seemed stable. He told me he was being transported to Belarus, then would be flown to a hospital in Russia.

"No new information came to me for four days, and then I got a call. My boy had died of his wounds." Krupkin added, "In Ukraine. He never made it back over the border to Belarus, much less Russia."

Velesky took his own glass of wine and drank deeply. He didn't care that his hands shook visibly.

"We got his body back after a month, had a funeral. It nearly killed his mother. I was heartbroken, but life went on. For nine months . . . for nine months, I heard nothing more. Then a captain in his unit emailed, asked if he could meet me for tea in Moscow." Krupkin pointed at Velesky. "*There* I heard the truth."

"What truth?"

"The field hospital that treated his wounds was using medicine and bandages and equipment that dated back to 1983. From the Afghan War! Antibiotics that had expired decades ago were applied, bandages from the time of Andropov were used. Pain pills for my boy's agony were older than he was.

"And, to top it off, all the trucks used to transport the wounded in the region had rotten tires that failed after no more than one hundred kilometers, so he sat on a gurney in a field hospital until he drew his last breath."

Velesky did well to stifle a cruel laugh.

Krupkin did not notice. "I didn't want to believe, but the captain had taken pictures of my boy, photos showing the expiry dates on the fucking medieval equipment they were using on him." Krupkin shrugged. "I looked into purchases made for the medical forces of the 11th Guards myself. How could this be? Military spending has been increasing year after year after year. We should have the best care for our soldiers."

Krupkin puffed and blew smoke, then coughed. Finally, he said, "Graft. The money had been stolen, bit by bit, year by year, by the siloviki, the connected men in the military and intelligence circles who surround President Peskov. Money for field hospitals ended up buying yachts and whores, country homes in England, skyscrapers in New York, racehorses in Kentucky, and Formula One cars in Germany."

The older Russian looked off into the night now. "I could say 'they' killed my boy, and they did. But 'they' had a lot of help." He made fresh eye contact with Velesky. "Help from me. I've been moving money out of Russia for twenty-five years, money that the State allocated for critical military and social needs, but money that functionaries of the State took for themselves. I killed Yuri, as certain as the Ukrainian soldier who dropped the mortar in the tube that shredded his legs."

Velesky didn't know what to say, but he understood Krupkin's motivations now.

The Russian continued. "Four years ago, I started working for Spanov. Billions of dollars, and I got the impression almost immediately it wasn't all going to real estate in Malta or Miami . . . it was moving into the West for operational purposes."

Alex knew nothing about intelligence work. He only knew crypto and private banking, and though he wouldn't admit this even to himself, he knew how to launder money.

Russia was a kleptocratic political system, and it would only work with outside enablers. Alex Velesky had been one of those enablers since he got out of college, and it was all he knew.

The heavyset man said, "Over two decades ago, we Russians gave up liberty for security, and that was a disaster, both for us and the world around us. Now the world around us has had enough, and the end is here." He smiled a little, his first time doing so. "I am a rat leaping off a sinking ship, but I'm bringing the captain's log along with me, just to make sure the crew can't sail away on a lifeboat as if they were the victims."

Velesky waved the phone in his hand. "So . . . now, with this information, *I* am a target?"

"Just as your family in Mariupol was a target last year." Krupkin took another drag and blew smoke.

Velesky shut his eyes tight again. He thought about hockey, his only reference for violence, and he thought about skating all the way across the ice and body-checking this bastard into the boards, face-first. With menace in his voice, he said, "I *really* need you to stop bringing up my family."

Krupkin replied, "Pashalusta." *Sorry.* He then said, "The difference is . . . *you* stand a chance, Alex."

The Swiss-Ukrainian opened his eyes slowly. "What do I do?"

"You *know* what you have to do. You have to take all the information to Altman."

Alex lurched back in his chair, reacting as if he'd been punched in his face. "Altman? You've got to be kidding."

"Ezra Altman is the best forensic accountant working on sanctioned Russian wealth transfers in the world. He's got Brucker Söhne in his sights, and he alone has built the database of offshore accounts that will be the key to unraveling all this."

"Yeah," Alex said, "and he's been trying to have me arrested by Interpol for three fucking years!"

"When you give him what you have, believe me, you won't be of interest to him any longer. This is so much bigger than you. So much bigger than me.

"Take it to Altman." Krupkin held a finger up. "Take it, *physically*, to him. The data on that phone can't be copied or transferred. You try to do that, and you'll encrypt everything. That was how my phones and computers were set up by the GRU for my use with Spanov and his people. I could move data only between them, nowhere else, or the data would evaporate into a code I could not break.

"The physical device has to be taken to Ezra Altman in New York, and it should be taken by you, with the Brucker Söhne data you will steal from your bank's computer."

Alex's head reeled with the implications of it all.

Krupkin continued. "But you'll have to work fast. I threw my pursuers off with the trip to Belgrade, but surely they already know what I took, and they'll figure out where I went with it soon enough."

Velesky nodded slightly.

"And there's something else. You know about the summit in New York next week?"

The banker did know about the summit. Everyone in his office was talking about it, even if he refused to get involved in the conversations. Over a dozen Western nations would be meeting in the city to sign accords petitioning the World Trade Organization to return most-favored-nation trade status to Russia, something they'd taken away a year before. The recent cease-fire in Ukraine, although shaky and potentially temporary, had immediately caused countries feeling the pain of no Russian oil or gas exports or other trade to call for a resumption of relations, and the cease-fire, in Velesky's estimation, was being used for political cover for a West that wanted to get back to business, damn the Ukrainians and their suffering.

It all made Alex sick. Russian war crimes were still occurring in the eastern fourth of his nation, specifically in Donetsk Oblast, where he was from. A high-level summit with the foreign minister of Russia and other world leaders in New York City was a slap in the face to his people, to his own flesh and blood. The prospect that all would be forgiven and forgotten for economic gain in the West was an entirely different level of disgrace.

Velesky felt nauseated, but when Igor Krupkin stood suddenly, he recovered and followed him up. "Where will you go?"

The older man just looked around. "Where *can* I go? Nowhere." He sighed. "No matter. I quite like it here. I think I'll just find a hotel, go have a late dinner, and wait around till they come for me." He cocked his head, looking at Velesky. "Do you suppose it will hurt?"

Alex Velesky knew nothing about such things, but common sense told him that the moment the GRU caught up with Krupkin, it would, indeed, hurt very much.

The Russian reached out and put a hand on Alex's shoulder, startling the Ukrainian with the gentle gesture. He said, "First thing tomorrow, go to work, get copies of transaction activity. Every numbered account in the file. Take it from your bank and take that, and my phone, to New York. Do this for Oksana and Dymtrus. Do it for your parents, for yourself." He shrugged. "Do it for my Yuri. He wasn't a bad boy. He just believed in a cause that was shit, because people like me turned a blind eye to criminality in the name of nationalism."

Krupkin pointed again, the last of his cigarette dangling from his mouth as he talked. "Just like me, you're tainted by taking money from criminals. Trust me, it feels good to do something to wash off a little of that stain. Forget about your country. You aren't working for your nation now." With a rueful smile he said, "You are working to salvage your very soul."

He looked around, as if worried he was being listened to. "And do it before the accords are signed in New York and the sanctions are lifted. If this information gets out into the world, it would destroy Russia's attempts to rebuild their reputation as an honest partner."

"The summit is in four days," Alex said softly.

"Then you'd better get moving. Your eternal salvation is at stake, if you believe in such things."

Alex *did* believe in such things, once upon a time, but his faith had been severely strained.

Krupkin turned away, then called out as he began walking back towards the alleyway. "Good luck, Alex. You can make a difference if you're smart and fast and ruthless."

Velesky was smart, this he knew. He wasn't sure if he possessed the other two qualities Krupkin mentioned.

And then the Russian was gone.

Alex sat alone again, but everything felt different now.

After a full minute's hesitation, his brain almost shutting down after the influx of information and emotion that had just assaulted it, he slipped the phone into his jacket pocket, gulped the last of the wine, turned off the heater, then left the courtyard.

His life had ended almost a year earlier when his family members had been taken from him. He'd been a shell of a man ever since. But now his life seemed to be abruptly changing a second time. He wasn't happy . . . he imagined he'd never be happy again.

But he *was* reinvigorated, charged with a mission, a chance to do something.

For many years, he'd used his talents to help the Kremlin and the devils who worked there, and now he would use those same talents to bring the devils down.

FIVE

The forty-six-foot ketch rocked gently in the bay off the western side of Virgin Gorda, a few hundred yards offshore of one of the largest of the British Virgin Islands. The old boat wasn't anything special to look at, virtually indistinguishable from many other similar-sized single-hulled craft in the water here.

It was a 1977 model that could stand an overhaul, but the white hull and sails kept it from sticking out in a crowd. Even the vessel's name, *Serenity*, was the most commonly registered name for a private sailboat.

The man standing on the bow of the *Serenity* was himself similarly forgettable. In khaki board shorts, a white wide-brimmed hat, and sunglasses, his feet and chest bare, he looked like any other thirtysomething Caucasian boat captain as he raised his binoculars and oriented them toward a seventy-two-foot catamaran at full sail behind him, still a quarter mile away but approaching rapidly.

The binos stayed on the boat for thirty seconds, and then they lowered as the man on the smaller ketch scanned 360 degrees, looked over a twin-engine turboprop aircraft as it rose into the warm sky from the airport at Beef Island, examined the rock-and-scrub-brush-covered shoreline to his north and the sleepy marina to his east, and then quickly assessed a couple more smaller catamarans running under engine power into Saint Thomas Bay.

But soon his glass was back to his eyes, and he had returned his attention to the approaching seventy-two-footer. He saw a captain at the helm, a woman seated beside him, but he saw no one else on deck.

The man with the binoculars quickly assessed that a catamaran of that size could hold twenty or so fully kitted men hidden belowdecks, and the speed at which the big craft closed on his smaller anchored vessel remained a cause for concern.

He backed up a few feet in the direction of his helm, but he kept his eyes on the closing threat.

The big cat began to slow, and then it veered to starboard. When the vessel had completed its turn to the south, the captain of the ketch saw kids on the rear deck of the larger vessel, a mom in a bikini, a deckhand passing out drinks.

This boat was no threat to him. Another false alarm.

Courtland Gentry finally lowered his binoculars, satisfied that the boat approaching on his stern wasn't filled to the gills with a team of CIA Special Activities Center Ground Branch paramilitary operations officers, ready to board the *Serenity* and put a bullet in his brain.

Gentry was paranoid, but not without reason. The world was full of people who wanted him dead. From Mexican cartels to Chinese intelligence officers, from German private military corporations to dictators, despots, and human trafficking organizations.

And the CIA. Always the fucking CIA.

If the threat this afternoon had been real, then Court had a plan. He liked to tell himself he had a plan for everything. If the catamaran had made it to within two hundred meters, he would have armed himself with the old MP5K submachine pistol he kept hidden under his berth below, and he would have cinched one of his three bug-out bags to his chest.

At one hundred meters he would have lowered the Falcon rigid-hulled inflatable tender, fired the engine, and raced to the nearest shoreline.

The bug-out bag had burner phones, a handgun and ammo, cash, clothes, medical gear, and a couple of passports that might do in a pinch, as well as food and a water purification device that would allow him to live for days in the weeds and scrub if he had to. There were small swim fins and a mask-and-snorkel set in case he had to sneak out and commandeer a boat on the water.

Ultimately he'd make his way to Road Town on Beef Island, where he kept a tiny seaplane gassed and ready in a marina, and he'd use this to make his escape.

He was ready for trouble, especially after sinking the *Lyra Drakos* down in Antigua two nights earlier, but so far all had been quiet.

He'd spent today waiting for word from his benefactor about his next target, but he'd not been idle. He'd done a little free diving and spearfishing for lionfish and other sustenance; he did push-ups on the deck, dips on the companionway down to the salon, and pull-ups on the main sail. He ran on the beach this morning at dawn, and he rock-climbed a cliff on Virgin Gorda at the water's edge this afternoon.

These islands were beautiful, comfortable, and seemingly safe, but he was alone, and that weighed on him like never before in his life.

He thought about visiting the bar in the marina, but that would entail risks, and he did his best to fight off his loneliness and stay disciplined regarding his personal security.

Paranoia was much more than a full-time job. It was a job that forced its employees to work nights and weekends, as well.

There was a solution to his loneliness, or at least he hoped there was. There was one woman on this planet who meant something to him, though he had no idea where she was. His objective in his life at present consisted of first sinking some dumb Russian boats and then finding Zoya Zakharova, seeing her face, speaking to her, explaining why he had to run so fucking far and so fucking fast, and begging her for forgiveness.

And maybe one more chance.

He looked at his watch, then at the setting sun. He told himself he'd have dinner and a drink at a quiet dockside bar here at the marina. They had a strong Internet signal, and he could sit there with a cold beer and thumb his phone, looking for hints of Zoya in the news or other open source intelligence.

And he would also look for her on the dark web.

Court had access to a site where freelance intelligence operatives offered their services and those needing to hire someone made their offers. Court wasn't in the market for the services of an operative, but each and every day he went on the site and looked over the solicitations of others in his field, hoping to see something that would lead him to believe Zoya Zakharova was the one putting up the cryptic contact information.

He had no knowledge that Zoya was working as an asset-for-hire like he was, but he thought it was possible. She was on the run, as was he, and he knew she could make good bank working for the shitheads who frequented the dark web.

He'd scan the new listings tonight, like he did every week or so, but he didn't expect today to be any different.

Going to the dockside bar would still be a lonely experience for him, even dining among others. But being in the middle of a little crowd would be better than lying on the deck of the *Serenity* and looking up into the stars for yet another night.

He decided he'd surveil the marina from afar until the last of the sun's glow left the sky, and then he'd head to the aft deck to lower his little RIB into the water.

Court Gentry—professional saboteur, private assassin, and international fugitive—brought the binos back to his eyes and scanned the marina.

SIX

The small and spartan fifth-floor apartment in the heart of Milan had one thing going for it: it was just a few quiet blocks away from the beautiful Piazza del Duomo, the gargantuan gothic cathedral there, the miles and miles of winding streets full of shopping around it. But the sole occupant of the flat on Via Morigi wasn't availing herself of the heart of Milan tonight. It was January, cold both inside the flat and out, and the dirty floor-to-ceiling windows were covered with dusty floor-to-ceiling drapes to hold in some of the warmth of the tiny electric heater.

Though there was a cheap sofa and a couple of plastic chairs in the living room, the woman living in the apartment sat on the floor, a smartphone in her hand, her eyes glazed with sadness and with drink.

Empty cardboard pizza boxes from the restaurant downstairs, empty foam cups, their ice long melted and their straws jutting up, and empty vodka and wine bottles adorned the laminate coffee table next to her.

Zoya Zakharova didn't think of herself as an alcoholic, but if she took the time to ruminate over it at all, she would have had to acknowledge that she'd been drunk for virtually every waking moment of the past three days.

But she didn't care. She didn't care about much of anything. She watched TV, looked at her phone, slept, drank, and ate food delivered to her door, passing money through the mail slot so that the delivery person wouldn't see her face.

The bottle of vodka on the floor between her splayed legs was Contari, an Italian brand, and different in taste from the good Russian vodkas like Imperia and Stoli Gold that she preferred. But Zoya wasn't reviewing it, she was drinking it, and the Contari seemed to work much the same as Russian vodkas.

She took another swig, then placed the bottle back between her legs.

This was depression; she was self-aware enough to see it, even if she wasn't going to do anything about it. She had no purpose, no mission, no objective. She worked as a freelance intelligence asset, but the few jobs she'd taken over the past several months had been soulless, and they'd only contributed to her despair.

Criminal-versus-criminal shit, with Zoya planting bugs, stealing documents, even hijacking a truck full of luxury cars stolen in Germany to be sold in Moldova, then delivering the goods not back to their rightful owners but instead to a rival gang of car thieves in Bucharest.

This wasn't anything that she believed in. To her, this was just mindless busywork a trained monkey could perform.

And yet still she was somehow managing to fuck up this easy gig.

Her phone hadn't rung in weeks because the two most recent times she'd received a call out, she'd been unconscious in bed. Her handler, a Frenchman named Broussard, had let her know the last time they spoke that he was tired of her shit.

She didn't blame him. She was tired of her shit, too.

She thought about Court now, as she always did when her blood alcohol level soared. She was pissed off at him half the time and searching the depths of her heart to acknowledge that she was in love with him the other half.

At present her thoughts about him were positive, but this only led to deeper sadness. A good man had walked out on her. She saw no reason for this other than the possibility that she was not a good woman.

And she had other evidence to support this hypothesis.

Namely, she was Russian.

A former operative in SVR, foreign intelligence, trained to lie and cheat and manipulate, trained to steal and to kill. She'd defected to the U.S. two years earlier; she had no more ties with the Russian government, but that hardly mattered to her. She was still Russian, and her nation was now a pariah.

No one was more disgusted by the actions of Moscow than Zoya; she felt sickened by all that had taken place in the last year.

She spent hours each day doom-scrolling social media, using fake accounts and searching through distributed virtual private networks to avoid detection, not that her own personal security was much on her mind these days. On Twitter she read story after story of the war, watched videos of the horrors. She read between the lines about Russian troop movements and intelligence operations, occasionally realizing she knew some of the players.

A general she admired as a child when he was a captain in her father's unit had been killed in Kherson. An FSB man she remembered from a training class in Moscow had been captured in Poland. A unit of Spetsnaz Alpha Group, men she had worked with on and off for years in her role as an SVR operative, had been credibly accused of war crimes, delivering Syrian troops into villages and setting them loose upon civilians while the Russians stood back and watched.

It was all so goddamned insane. She'd had no idea the nation of her birth would, *could*, do anything this horrible on this scale, and it sickened her to the point of utter demoralization.

And the fact that all signs indicated they would get away with it depressed her more. The summit in the United States and then the vote in the Security Council and in the WTO. It was theater, as far as she was concerned. A way to return to business as usual between Russia and the West.

As if tens of thousands of men, women, and children had not been systematically slaughtered by Moscow, to say nothing of the millions forced from their homes or subjected to rule by their oppressors.

She closed her drooping eyelids and tears dripped onto her cheeks. She laid her head back against the seat of the sofa and dropped her phone on the floor next to her as she struggled to reach the vodka bottle without looking.

And then her phone rang.

Her eyes opened; she wiped her cheeks with the forearms of her sweater, then picked the device up off the floor. Though she was a Russian national, she answered in English with a vaguely midwestern American accent, her voice scratchy from not having spoken at all in many days. "Yeah?"

The man on the other end of the line spoke English, as well, but with a decidedly French accent. He was older, into his forties, she imagined, though she'd never met him. "Transit?"

It was her handler, Broussard, calling her by her code name.

"Yes, Trompette, it's me." His call sign was "trumpet" in French, and by saying it through the phone, she affirmed her identity.

"Are you in service?" The man's tone expressed no small measure of doubt.

She fought off a wave of nausea brought on by heavy drinking and fast food. After only a short delay, she said, "Of course. Totally."

"A situation has come up."

"Where?"

"Zurich."

She rubbed her eyes hard now, looked over her shoulder, and tried to focus on the clock in the tiny kitchenette behind her, but she couldn't make it out. "When?"

"I need you there now. *Right now.*"

Zoya wondered if she could even stand up. She'd managed to make it to the bathroom an hour or so earlier, but she'd probably downed three more shots since then.

The man on the other end said, "Might be two . . . three days' work. A bank in Zurich had a data breach today. Our client is a bank in Geneva who wants the Zurich branch's pilfered data. They are asking us to find the employee who stole the files in Zurich and babysit him so that no one else can get the information before they do. That's all."

No one contracted Zoya for babysitting services. Still, this sounded a little more interesting than the things she'd previously been hired to do, and it sounded a lot more interesting than sitting here looking at Twitter or watching bad TV in a language she hadn't studied in years.

She was still trying to figure out how she was going to pull herself to her feet, to say nothing of getting to Zurich and then executing a recovery and protection mission in her condition, when the man spoke again.

"You know what? Forget it. I don't sense any enthusiasm from you. I have a man in Frankfurt who can handle it. You are closer, but he's more reliable. Get some sleep, you sound like shit."

"Broussard!" Zoya barked out, almost frantically. "*Wait*. No. I can be there."

"How soon?"

She had a car, a four-door Opel, but she was in absolutely no condition to drive it.

"I'll get on the first train. Be there before dawn."

"Why not take a car?"

"It's . . . it's a long story." She paused, then said, "I'm intoxicated."

"That's actually a pretty short story, isn't it?"

She sniffed and rubbed her eyes, desperate to regain at least a portion of her wits. "I can do it. I . . . I *need* to do it."

She heard Broussard tapping keys. After a moment, he said, "There's a late train leaving Milano Centrale in twenty-six minutes. Three hours twenty minutes to Zurich. You are either on *that* train or I'm calling Frankfurt."

Zoya made it to her knees, scooted back against the sofa, then sat down on it. Forcing her eyes to open wide, she flipped on a table lamp, bringing light other than the television or her phone to the room for the first time in over a week.

After clearing her throat, she said, "I'll see you in Zurich."

"You most definitely won't. I don't do fieldwork."

"Right." If she'd been anywhere close to sober, she would have realized that.

The man hesitated; she worried he was about to call her off. Instead, he said, "I'll send instructions to your box. There's a ticking clock. You'll need to hit the ground running." Then he added, "Others will be after this man and his information. Be ready for anything."

Zoya was most definitely *not* ready for anything, but she acknowledged, and ended the call, then used her hands to steady herself as she moved behind the sofa, then stumbled into the little kitchen. Opening the pantry, she reached into the back corner, past a mop and a broom, and pulled out a garbage bag full of towels. Throwing this onto the floor behind her, she went back in and hefted a black backpack that had been hidden there in the corner.

Stumbling back into the living room, struggling with the pack and her precarious equilibrium, she returned to the coffee table and dropped the bag next to it.

Twenty-six minutes till the train leaves, she told herself. The station was fifteen minutes away. *Eleven minutes.* A five-minute walk through the station to her platform. *Six minutes.*

Five to be safe. She had to leave her apartment in five minutes.

But instead of slinging her pack over a shoulder and heading for the door, she sat back down on the hardwood floor.

She unzipped a small pouch on the top of the pack by the carry handle and removed a plastic vial. Hurriedly she opened it and poured out the contents onto the table in front of her.

She sniffed hard to clear as much congestion out of her sinuses as possible, pulled a soda straw from a fast-food cup, then blew through it to ensure there wasn't any liquid left inside.

She used the straw to push the powder into two equal lines on the table in front of her.

After a long sigh, she leaned forward, slipped the straw into her right nostril, and quickly and efficiently snorted two lines of coke.

Three minutes.

The powder burned, her eyes watered more, and she started to cry.

She tossed the straw, zipped the pouch on her bag closed again, then fought her way back to her feet, more tears streaming down her face.

The coke hit her like a bolt of lightning a few seconds later. It felt more like anxiety than energy. It didn't sober her, but it certainly awakened her, and her crying stopped as the new sensation took over.

In the kitchen she poured herself a glass of water from the tap, something no self-respecting Italian would ever do, and she drank it down. She downed a second glass while leaning against the sink, and then a third.

One minute.

She hit the bathroom, urinated quickly, then shot across her little living room, snatching up her thick black down coat. She put it on, then pulled a black watch cap over her dark brown hair. She hadn't worn makeup in months, and she knew the big coat and her heeled boots would make her look like a man from any distance.

Good, she thought. She was a master of disguise, and she could alter her appearance even more while on the train to Zurich.

She grabbed her keys and purse by the door, then exited, locking up behind her.

Heading down the hall for the stairs, she told herself she wasn't in any condition for this, though she had no idea what she'd be asked to do in the next few hours. Nevertheless, she convinced herself she'd shake it off on the train to the north.

She *had* to. Zoya wanted to feel alive again, to matter again, to respect herself again.

The war, the booze, Court Gentry: they had *all* taken a vicious toll on her psyche.

Zurich wouldn't save her, but it would keep her away from the flat on Via Morigi for a couple of days, and she knew that, more than anything, she needed to get out of the house and back into the game.

SEVEN

Twenty-four hours after Russian financial advisor Igor Krupkin handed over a mobile phone to a man in Zurich's Old Town, the middle-aged Russian lay dead on a cold concrete floor in a horse trailer factory in the town of Embrach, just north of the city proper.

He'd been stripped to his underwear, his body battered and sliced and burned, and four of the five men standing around and looking down at him were worried that his death would get them in serious trouble with their boss.

The fifth man standing on the factory floor did not share the misgivings of the others.

The other men were private military contractors from Russia, brought in because they were as merciless as they were available.

But even though the fifth man was Russian, as well, Luka Rudenko wasn't a mercenary.

He was something else entirely.

The other men wore leather jackets, they had shaved heads and beards, and their arms were wrapped with tattoos. Rudenko, in contrast, wore a cream-colored cable-knit sweater, Tom Ford jeans, and a Burberry peacoat. His hair was short and blond and spiked, and he looked simultaneously older and healthier than the other four. He was just over forty; his broad shoulders and muscular build showed him to be exceptionally formidable physically.

Rudenko had only arrived minutes ago, long after the beating had begun and just moments before an already mortally wounded Krupkin drew his last breath.

The instant he'd arrived, Rudenko realized he only had seconds to get information out of the man before he died, so he pulled his Steyr A2 pistol, screwed on a long suppressor, aimed at a stack of trailer tires against the wall, and fired six rounds from the weapon.

As the Russian contractors near him swiveled their own guns around in surprise, frantically searching for threats, Rudenko took the white-hot suppressor of his pistol and pressed it against the side of Krupkin's face. Another three rounds through the gun a minute later, an application of the hot steel to Krupkin's privates, and the dying man began talking, his voice raspy due to his lungs being labored with pressure from the blood pouring out of the damaged veins inside him.

Krupkin talked and talked, and then the confession ended.

Internal bleeding was the COD in Rudenko's professional opinion.

The life had left Krupkin's body just two minutes earlier; Rudenko stood there impassively while the four younger tough guys freaked out, thinking it likely they would be in hot water for his death.

And then the door to the factory opened, and a new man entered.

He approached slowly across the large, mostly barren factory floor; he was brown haired and in his late forties, handsome and healthy looking, although he walked with the aid of a cane, favoring his right leg.

The new arrival regarded the Russian security men and the dead body, and then he finally looked to Rudenko. In English he said, "Follow me."

While the bearded contractors stood wringing their bloody hands, still worried about beating a man to death when they were only supposed to rough him up, Rudenko and the man with the cane walked a dozen meters away. Here the older man continued speaking English, his Swiss accent obvious.

"Spanov sold you to me by saying you're the best of the best. But your orders were to keep him alive until I got here."

"I didn't kill him. *Those* dumb fucks did. I just arrived from Helsinki."

The older man let it go. "Tell me you got *something* out of him."

There was no indication of pride or satisfaction in Luka's answer. Just cold delivery. "I got everything."

"Enlighten me."

"Krupkin somehow created a blueprint of banking transfers out of Russian intelligence coffers and into the West."

"How?"

Rudenko shrugged. "He was a financial conduit for Russian intelligence. The man who made Kremlin money look like regular old boring oligarch money when he sent it out of the country."

The older man sniffed. "I suppose that's why the chief of the Russian Security Council called and offered me a private plane to get me back here from the Azores and a blank check to fill out as I wished."

Rudenko said nothing.

The Swiss man added, "If we fix this problem for him, quickly and quietly, I'm sure he'll reward you, as well."

Rudenko sniffed. "I don't want a blank check, I want a promotion."

"He told me you were a major."

"I am, and I want to be a lieutenant colonel."

The man with a cane cocked his head. "That's all? Why?"

"My director is in Moscow in his top-floor office, while I'm here in Switzerland with a bunch of shithead military rejects burning a man's nuts off. Does that answer your question?"

Now the Swiss man chuckled. "You want your boss's desk?"

Luka Rudenko shook his head as he looked back to the body across the room. "I want *a* desk."

The man followed his gaze. "Very well. What did Krupkin say he did with his file?"

"Yesterday he had a mobile phone with the encrypted data on it couriered to a man on the island of Saint Lucia, in the Caribbean. It will arrive there later today, local time."

"What man?"

"His name is Eddison John. He's a lawyer, apparently."

The older man nodded. "He works in offshore banking. He's helped Russians launder billions of dollars. He served as a straw man for decades, putting his name on property owned by oligarchs, but he lost his zeal when the war started. Won't touch Russian accounts anymore." He thought a moment. "I imagine John will be well protected, but getting to him shouldn't be any problem. Anything else?"

"Yes. Krupkin gave another mobile phone to a man here in Zurich."

"*What* man in Zurich?"

"A banker named Alexander Velesky."

The older man's eyes narrowed and looked off; it was clear he wasn't familiar with the name.

Luka remarked about the tell. "Spanov told me you know everyone worth knowing here."

"I thought I did, but I don't know a Velesky."

"According to Krupkin, he works in crypto at an investment bank called Brucker Söhne Holdings."

"Shit," the older man said now. More softly, he said "shit" again.

Sebastian Drexler did, in fact, pride himself on knowing everyone worth knowing in this nation, and although he didn't know the name the Russian had just given him, he most definitely knew the man's bank. "Shit," he said a third time. "When did Velesky get the phone?"

"Last night."

"Twenty-four hours ago." He gave off a smile, but he wasn't happy at all. "All hell's going to break loose. My guess is the file from Russia will match up nicely to transaction data at Brucker Söhne." He thought over the ramifications. "Spanov will be displeased to learn this."

Rudenko took it a step further. "Spanov will burn down Zurich to get that data back."

The older man said, "I guess your desk in Moscow will have to wait. What else?"

"Velesky lives in a flat in Oberdorf, in the Old Town. He's our target now?"

Drexler said, "If Velesky has a brain, he won't be at his home, but we have to start somewhere. Take these guys, check it out."

Luka looked over at the men still standing over the body. "I take it they're private contractors?"

"Stravinsky," Drexler said as an answer. "Mercs. They were the first men Spanov could get here. They'd been working in Serbia when he called them today."

"I don't like Stravinsky guys. They're cowboys. Undisciplined."

Drexler didn't even look back over his shoulder to regard them himself. "Well, then, it's good we have you here to keep them in line."

The Russian with the spiked blond hair didn't seem appeased by this, so Drexler added, "Daniil Spanov gave me operational control over them, which means he will have them killed if they don't do exactly as I order them to do." With a faint smile he said, "Believe me, they are more highly motivated to succeed than either of us are."

Luka said, "Speak for yourself." He barked something in Russian, and the four men followed him out the door of the warehouse, where they piled into two vehicles.

Sebastian Drexler hobbled out to his own car, a BMW 5 Series, and sat down roughly behind the wheel. Rubbing his leg a moment to stanch a bit of the pain there, he fired up the engine, but his mind remained on his knee.

He couldn't help but think about his knee, because it hurt all of the time.

Sebastian Drexler was a fixer for hire, used primarily by Swiss financial institutions on extremely delicate matters. Not long ago he'd become a consultant for the Syrian government, until that job ended badly when the Syrian president was assassinated, the president's wife was killed right in front of Drexler, and then Drexler himself was shot through the kneecap by the rogue hit man known the world over as the Gray Man.

Drexler had made it out alive, however, albeit with a permanently wrecked knee, and now he was back at work, in this case taking a crucial assignment to retrieve compromising material circulated by one of the most well-connected financial consultants in Moscow.

The well-connected financial consultant now lay dead in the factory in Drexler's rearview, and as he drove through the night, he wondered what his next step should be.

It had taken Drexler just a couple of hours to find Krupkin at the Dolder Grand hotel, from where Spanov's goons took him to a location Drexler had secured north of the city.

Drexler himself had gone to his suite at the Storchen Zurich, in the Old

Town, manning his phones with his team of technicians, speaking with Spanov multiple times, and working on getting one more asset to the scene.

Spanov made it happen immediately. Luka Rudenko was a forty-one-year-old operative in the GRU, Russian military intelligence, but Rudenko was special for another reason. His parents had moved to Helsinki in the 1980s, and he'd lived the first fifteen years of his life in Finland.

Luka could pass as a Finn, and he'd used this throughout his career to avoid scrutiny when operating in Western Europe.

Drexler knew Luka would have incredible skills and no conscience whatsoever, and he was happy to have him to augment his sketchy force of rough-and-tumble private military contractors.

The Swiss man knew that Spanov could get whatever official resources he needed to recover the two iPhones full of data. Russia was, in Drexler's opinion, just a big gas station run by gangsters, and other than the Russian president and his most inner circle, there was no one more powerful than Daniil Spanov.

The information Krupkin had snuck out of Moscow could, quite literally, cripple hundreds of Russian intelligence operations in the West and reveal their crimes to the world. To avoid this, Drexler had to get the data back from a man here in Zurich, and he had to get an identical copy of the data back from a man in the Caribbean.

He had the identities of both men, but *they* had a head start.

It was going to be a difficult mission, to be sure, but no one hired Drexler for the easy, clean jobs.

He drove in the direction of his hotel, ready to spend the nighttime hours working with his team here in the city and calling his contacts developed over decades of operating in the deep shadows of dirty banking.

EIGHT

The sun had just touched the horizon line when Court Gentry emerged from the salon of his sailboat and stood on his deck in bare feet, shorts, a plain white T-shirt, and a baseball cap. His clean-shaven face was tan from the sun here in the British Virgin Islands, his brown eyes hidden behind sunglasses he wouldn't need for long. He lifted his binoculars, ready to take one more long, slow scan of the marina area here in Virgin Gorda before slipping into his sandals and taking his little rigid-hulled inflatable boat to shore to have dinner at a bar and grill one block inland.

But his binoculars never made it up to his eyes. The sound of a small boat rumbling in the water came from his right, from farther to the south of the bay, and he turned to look.

A wooden-hulled skiff with an outboard motor moved leisurely over the placid water, heading his way. Its bow was full of boxes and crates of produce and other items, and cases of beer and soft drinks and booze were stacked just aft of this.

These vending boats could be found on the water everywhere in the Caribbean; on board would be a salesperson/captain who offered food, drinks, sundries, and the like to the leisure boats moored in the marina. Their prices would be higher than in the stores on land, but these boats peddled convenience. It was much easier to buy a case of beer or a bag of ice off someone who came right alongside a vessel than it was to go ashore and look for supplies.

Court found nothing threatening about this at all. He could see a couple of people in the back who both appeared to be locals, and all the groceries and other essentials he'd expect to find filling the deck.

"Hey, man!" a cheerful young captain called out, one hand controlling his outboard while he waved with the other. He wore shorts and no shirt, his sinewy body showing Court he had spent his life heavily engaged in manual labor.

Next to him at the stern sat an extremely attractive Black woman, perhaps a decade older than the captain, dressed in a faded pink T-shirt and off-white jeans. She smiled pleasantly and waved, as well.

Court quickly decided he'd buy a case of Cooper Island Lager, a local brand, and a crate of eggs if these two had any for sale.

He reached for his wallet and walked to the edge of his deck. The captain threw a line out and Court caught it.

"You guys are working late today," Court said as he tied the line off on a cleat on the deck.

The captain answered in a thick local dialect when he saw the man's wallet. "If you want to buy something, I'm happy to sell it, man, but I'm done working for today. I'm just here as a taxi service right now."

Court cocked his head. *Taxi service?*

The Black woman stood up from her seat at the stern. "Good afternoon," she said with no hint of anything other than an American accent. "Hope you don't mind . . . I asked this gentleman for a lift. Wondering if I could come aboard and talk to you about chartering your boat."

Court slipped his wallet back into his shorts and looked her over, the pistol wedged in the small of his back suddenly comforting, if not comfortable.

"I don't take charters, ma'am."

"I'll make it worth your while. Let's just talk about it before you say no. All I ask is ten minutes of your time, and then maybe a lift in your dinghy back to shore."

And then she did something that in his nearly twenty years as an intelligence operative he'd never seen anyone do. She winked at him. It wasn't done provocatively; rather, it was surreptitious, as if she were imploring him to play along.

He sensed no danger from her, but he also had enough experience to know that he could be dead wrong and she could be some sort of a threat.

The captain of the boat looked back and forth at both of them, sensing some unease from the white man now. But finally Court said, "You're welcome aboard, ma'am."

The woman pulled out a couple of bills from her pocket and handed them to the skiff captain, and then she hefted a small leather backpack from the deck and slung it over her shoulder.

Court stepped back a few feet as she boarded.

Soon she climbed onto the deck, the skiff was released, and the captain cruised away with another wave of his hand as Court's head moved as if on a swivel, looking all around for more obvious threats to materialize.

She started to speak, but Court put a finger to his mouth, watching the wooden boat leave. When it was fifty yards or so away, he turned his attention back to her.

The woman standing on the deck with Court seemed relaxed, perfectly at ease, and this made no sense to him. She was clearly on the job; this wasn't about a charter. She'd been sent here by someone with a message or a threat or an offer of employment, of this he had no doubt. But if this were the case, he felt certain she would know all about him and the fact that he was an incredibly dangerous individual.

The woman extended a hand.

"Angela Lacy. Pleased to meet you."

Court took her hand, shook it once. "Nice to meet you." And then his voice lowered. "Just so we understand each other, know this. If you reach a hand into your backpack, I'll slit your fucking throat."

Her eyes widened in surprise and terror. "*What?*"

Court didn't know what was going on, and this made his defenses kick into high gear. He pulled her by her wrist, spun her around, and pushed her down face-first against the low cockpit dodger.

His Benchmade knife was open now, in his left hand and against her neck.

The woman's body began to shake, but she said, "Calm the fuck down, dude."

He pulled the pack off her back, unzipped it with his right hand, and dumped the contents out onto the deck.

A phone, a charger, lipstick, and a few other odds and ends. No weapon, no obvious intelligence tradecraft paraphernalia other than the phone, which was all anyone really needed.

While he was looking everything over, she stammered, "I'm . . . I'm a friend."

He didn't look up. "I don't have any friends."

Next he frisked her quickly from head to toe. Finding nothing of note, he said, "Go down to the salon. Sit at the chart table."

Her voice unsteady, she said, "I don't know what that is."

"The bench by the radios."

She climbed down the companionway and, still shaking, sat down on a bench next to the marine radios and navigation equipment built into the wall there. Court followed, leaving the contents of her bag on the deck, but he stayed on the second stair on the tiny companionway so he could both keep an eye outside the boat and see her down inside the salon.

He said, "All I want to hear right now is who sent you and why."

Her voice quivered. It seemed to Court as if she had been completely taken off guard by his actions. "I . . . I was sent to speak with you. I was . . . just told where to go and what boat you were on. I . . . I don't know anything about you, and I'm certainly no threat." She added, "We're on the same team."

Court's eyes narrowed. "Tell me, Lacy. What team are we on?"

"The company, of course."

This meant CIA.

Court drew his pistol from behind his back. His entire body went tense, and he looked out over the water again, almost certain he'd find an American Navy Cyclone-class patrol boat barreling down on him. He scanned all compass points, but there was no Navy.

"Six," the woman said now, invoking his old call sign within the Agency's Special Activities Division. "Put the gun down. *Please*. I don't know what you think you're—"

"Who, *specifically*, sent you?"

She stared at the pistol; it was down at his side. "The special assistant to the DDO."

"Name?"

She furrowed her eyebrows, seemingly taken aback that he had to ask this question. "Suzanne Brewer."

Well, shit. Suzanne Brewer had been Court's handler when he ran in a sub-rosa Agency outfit called Poison Apple. That program ended a year ago, as far as Court knew, anyway, and he had every reason to believe the CIA was out to kill him . . . again. Court had never trusted Brewer for many reasons, but one of those reasons was that Zoya Zakharova had told him Brewer tried to shoot him in the head in Scotland. He didn't know if Zoya was right or wrong about this, but the fact that Brewer served as a high-ranking employee of an organization that had targeted him for termination didn't exactly make Angela Lacy look like anything other than a threat at present.

Lacy was still visibly shaken by what was going on, but she cleared her throat and said, "She wants to talk to you."

"I bet she fucking does."

The woman on the couch by the radios looked confused. "I was sent here to put you on the phone with her, and to await further instructions after that. That's all."

"You're D/O, too?" The Directorate of Operations was the CIA's action arm. If Brewer was a high-ranking D/O official, Court assumed Lacy to be from the same directorate within the Agency.

"Yes. I'm a senior operations officer. Used to be a case officer, same as you."

Court had never been a case officer in his life. He'd been hired into CIA as a special programs asset, and then he was moved laterally to become a Special Activities Division paramilitary officer, and he hadn't worked for the CIA officially for many years. He'd done denied contract work for them in Poison Apple, in between periods of time when they were actively trying to kill him, but Angela Lacy seemed to know none of this.

Court wondered what bullshit Brewer had fed this poor woman before sending her down here alone and into mortal danger.

He shook away the question and asked, "How did you find me?"

She cocked her head now. Something about this entire affair didn't compute with her, that much was obvious from her expression. Finally, she said, "*Find* you? I . . . I didn't know you were lost."

"Are you joking?"

She shook her head, then blotted her eyes with her wrist, one at a time. She'd been scared, but now she was beginning to just look annoyed. As if she was realizing she'd been sent into a situation without proper information, and that was *not* the way she liked to operate. "Look, I was in Miami this morning . . . on vacation. Brewer called me, told me to get my ass to Virgin Gorda and stand by. A few hours later she directed me to the marina and gave me the name of your boat. My instructions were to make contact, then call her and hand you my phone." Angrily now, she said, "That's it! I show up and you're treating me like a hostile."

"How did she know where I was?"

Lacy rolled her eyes. "I just told you, I don't have a clue. All she said was you were a non-official cover officer and to call you Six. I didn't know anything about you being off reservation, missing, in hiding"—she looked around at the boat—"whatever this bullshit is that's going on here."

This frustrated Court, even though the woman appeared to be telling the truth. "If you don't know anything, why did she send you?"

This she thought over a moment. In a softer tone, she said, "I don't know. Maybe because I'm female. Less threatening."

"You've obviously never met another female," Court said, half under his breath.

This was all bad news to him. Brewer knew where he was, clearly, which meant he couldn't stick around. But the fact that teams of killers had not shown up to do him in already told him there was something else at play here.

"I'll talk to Brewer, but I'm not going to do it here. I'll get out of the marina, on open water, and do it from there." He added, "I want to see anybody coming my way."

"You're really paranoid, aren't you?"

"That's what all the people trying to kill me keep saying."

It was clear to Court that this young woman from the CIA thought him to be utterly insane, and she had no idea why some senior Agency exec would be associated with him, even if only to connect on a phone call.

But Court didn't care what Lacy thought. He was operating out of a pre-ternatural desire for survival. "I'm going to zip-tie you so I can deal with the boat."

She shook her head now. "*What?* Look, man, that's totally unnecessary."

"Maybe you're right," Court said, "but I'm doing it anyway." He reached into a drawer for some zip ties, and Lacy reluctantly stuck her hands out in front of her.

"Nope," he said. "Behind your back."

"Asshole," she said, but when he said nothing, she eventually did as instructed.

As he tightened the plastic around her wrists, he said, "I'm just the ass-hole who was minding his own business till you showed up. If you need to be pissed at somebody, be pissed at Brewer for sending you."

She didn't miss a beat. "I have the capacity to be pissed at two people at the same time."

"Fair enough," Court replied, but once her wrists were securely bound, he headed up to the deck to pull the anchor.

NINE

Alex Velesky ran through the night, his heart seeming to swell in his chest at the same rate that the lactic acid coursing through him increased the burning in his legs. But he ignored both the pain in his extremities and the potential cardiac event, and he pumped his arms harder and harder and sped up.

He was exhausted, but his utter desperation more than made up for his athletic shortcomings right now.

Alex had gone to the office today, but he'd changed out of his work clothes as soon as he'd gotten home, exchanging his Brioni blue tonal plaid wool-silk suit for faded brown corduroys and a black knit sweater, along with a pair of $1,500 Nike basketball shoes that now spanked hard and fast on a wet and icy cobblestone alleyway that sloped down through the Altstadt in the direction of the Limmat River.

He made it another fifty meters at this speed and then he slowed to skid around a turn to the left, after which he picked up the pace again. Racing under a gas lamp and down another steep hill, he cussed at himself in German.

"Was zum Teufel hast du denn gemacht, Depp?" *What the hell have you done, idiot?*

The two men were still on his tail; he could hear their own shoes striking the pavement, and from the increasing volume of their footfalls echoing off the buildings around him, he could tell the men were closing fast. He hadn't seen any weapons, only a recognition from the pair standing across the tiny dark street as he left his apartment building, and then, when he began walking away from them, they pushed off the wall they'd been leaning against and slowly followed.

He'd watched them in the window reflection of a chocolate confectioners' shop; they were forty meters back and their hands were in their pockets, but their gaits seemed purposeful and intense. They were thick, big, bearded; they wore caps and heavy coats, and they ignored the icy air as they moved under the gas lamps lining the alleys.

Alex wasn't trained to pick up surveillance, but it didn't take an expert to see that these two didn't fit in at all.

He'd made it to a corner, negotiated the turn in a relaxed stride, and then immediately took off in a run.

He went a full block before looking back over his shoulder, and when he did so, he saw the two coming around the turn behind him, then racing in his direction. He didn't know who the two men were, but he had no problem guessing what they wanted.

They were after the phone given to him the night before by Igor Krupkin.

The banker wasn't much of a runner, but he found himself uniquely motivated as he sprinted through the Altstadt, hurtling downhill.

Alex had the phone on him right now, zipped in a pocket of his coat, and this weighed heavily on him as he fled. The phone was a hot potato that he didn't want to be holding, but he couldn't make himself toss it in a lake or in the trash.

Last night, after his meeting with Krupkin, he went home and lay in his apartment, staring at the ceiling while the snow fell outside, trying to formulate some sort of a plan, some course of action to honor his family.

It was revenge he was after, and once he gave in to the desire for revenge, it was literally all he could think about.

Today at work, just before lunch, he had a course of action in mind and was prepared to launch it, and just *after* lunch, he began its implementation. He copied troves of Brucker Söhne Holdings account transaction files onto a Seagate drive the size of a hardback book, arcane digital recordings diagramming the secret movement of billions of dollars from hundreds of shell corporations.

Alex didn't have Krupkin's intel about the accounts—that was still on the phone and he hadn't accessed it—so he swept up everything that involved cryptocurrency transfers from Hydra and RuTor, Russian dark web crypto sites that Krupkin had used to funnel money into Brucker Söhne. There would be tens of thousands of transactions that had nothing to do with the data Krupkin had told him was on the iPhone, and it would take an expert and some time to match the Russian data to the Swiss data to have a clear picture on where the Russian intelligence services were spending money in the West.

Covertly copying files was an incredibly unsettling feeling to the heretofore obedient and loyal bank employee. He'd spent one hour and nineteen excruciating minutes in his office pulling records and transferring them to the hard drive, all the while expecting the phone to ring or the door to fly open.

Alex had known at the time he was copying the files that the IT department at Brucker Söhne would receive a real-time alert that someone was in the process of accessing confidential records, but he felt that once they saw Alex's log-in credentials, they would think nothing of it. There were perhaps a half-dozen people at the bank who could go anywhere in the system, and Alex had earned that right through a decade of diligent service and the fact that his delicate work had made a fortune for the bank.

Everyone at the bank knew he was Ukrainian, and they all knew he'd lost his sister, parents, and newborn nephew the year before. But in the months since, no one, not *once*, not *ever*, had expressed any misgivings about having him continue working with Russian clients.

Money was lord at the bank, not nations, not borders, not family. Velesky had been a good worker bee in the siphoning of riches from Russia, and there was no hint he wouldn't continue to remain a good worker bee in the future.

Alex Velesky could, quite simply, go anywhere he wanted in the Brucker Söhne system without any suspicion, though that didn't mean he wouldn't eventually be found out. System checks would be done by bank security, usually at the beginning of the week; they would see that the data had been downloaded from his computer to a device, and then, Velesky knew, they would be on him like hellfire.

But today was Friday, so he wasn't overly worried about internal security at his bank.

After stealing the files, he finished out his workday, and then he came home and locked himself in his opulent flat. He made dinner and ate alone, then changed clothes and sat down at his own computer.

First he created a new website on the dark web, a tactic he used to transfer extremely confidential data when dealing with his most mysterious clients. He uploaded the Brucker Söhne Holdings data from the hard drive to the site, and then he destroyed the hard drive with a hammer and took the remnants directly down to the recycling bin on the first floor, tossing them below some cardboard boxes.

The incriminating data was now out of his hands, on a website inaccessible to anyone who didn't possess a twenty-three-digit string of random numbers, letters, and symbols. He'd written down the randomly created address on a small sheet of paper, then folded it and put it in an envelope.

He thought about mailing it to himself, care of his final destination, a hotel in New York City.

But finally he decided against this. He could be captured by whoever would be looking for Krupkin's phone, and if that happened, the piece of mail would sit impotently at the hotel, presumably forever. Even if someone opened it, they wouldn't know what to do with the numbers.

Around one in the morning, Alex figured out a solution to his quandary. He decided instead to send the letter directly to Ezra Altman. Altman ran a New York–based forensic accounting firm that worked on white-collar criminal complaints against Swiss banks. In the past few years he'd had Brucker Söhne in his sights, especially when it came to defying sanctions and hiding Russian wealth.

Altman saw Velesky as a villain, but now Velesky saw Altman as his only hope.

Alex looked up Altman's office address, wrote it on the envelope, and put his own name and return address on it.

Before sealing it, he took out another sheet of paper, and on it he wrote:

Mr. Altman. Soon after you receive this, I will be calling on you personally at your office, using the pseudonym Pavel Chyrkov, under the ruse that I need help getting my inherited jewelry back from a bank in Bern. I hope you will grant me a meeting to discuss this material, and other material in my possession. I will come alone, and I am no threat to you. I only ask for your time to speak about this urgent matter. Please speak to no one about this, because by the time I arrive in America, I am sure I will have interested parties pursuing me.

Alex knew that when Ezra Altman found this small and innocuous-looking letter in his daily mail a few days from now, he would glance to see who it was from, and as soon as he saw the name Velesky, he would rip it open frantically.

Just as Alex only knew this man by reputation, this man knew Alex by *his* reputation, and he wouldn't hesitate to see what he'd sent him.

And when Altman read the note, Alex hoped he would agree to any meeting with Pavel Chyrkov, a name he'd pulled from the first name of the goalie on his hockey team and the last name of one of his favorite defenders on another amateur club.

After affixing the correct postage to the envelope, Alex went downstairs around two a.m., and came outside to walk down the street to look for a mailbox, not wanting to put it in the mail slot in his own building in case he was somehow discovered before the mailman picked it up and his pursuers thought to check his outgoing mail.

Alex had had no reason to believe anyone was after him, either for stealing his own company files or for accepting the phone with the data from Russia the night before, but since first thing this morning, he couldn't shake the distinct feeling of eyes on him, tracking him every step of the way.

And now he knew without question that he'd been right. The men in pursuit kept gaining on him; he could see through reflections without having to turn around and look, and he was certain it was just a matter of time before they overtook him, found his envelope and the phone in his jacket pocket, and put a quick end to the threat he posed to Russia.

He skidded around a building, and right in front of him he saw a bright yellow post box affixed to a wall on Weite Gasse. At a run he pulled the letter containing the dark web address out of his jacket and crammed it in the slot, nearly breaking his hand in the metal box as he did so.

He'd made it halfway up the block when the men chasing him raced around the corner from behind and saw him again, and even though they were just twenty meters or so back, he felt confident he'd managed to mail the letter without them detecting it.

Now he wanted to dump the phone, but he didn't know how to do this while ensuring he'd be able to find it later.

A minute later he skidded onto the sidewalk running along Theaterstrasse, his legs and lungs in agony from the exertion, and as soon as he did so, a car pulled up next to him, appearing from behind him, rolling along at the speed at which he was running.

"Alex! Alex! Hurry! Get in!"

A middle-aged man waved out the driver's-side window of a VW Golf. He'd spoken English, he sounded like an American, and he looked absolutely nothing like the pair after him now.

The VW motored along at the same speed Alex ran, and the man stared at him imploringly. "Get in the damn car!"

Alex kept running. Through the stabbing pain of labored breath, he said, "Why?"

"I can protect you."

"I don't know you."

"I'm from the U.S. embassy, and right now, we're your only chance."

"Who . . . who are they?" he asked, but before the American could respond, a shot rang out from behind. The round struck a metal lamppost just meters away, and sparks flew in all directions.

"Scheisse!" Alex shouted, and he ran in front of the car, then around to the passenger side.

The American had already reached over and opened the door, and Alex leapt into the rolling VW.

Looking in the passenger-side mirror, he saw that the pair of men had closed to just a few meters behind the VW before it began racing off. Both of them slowed to aim their pistols, but the American driver stomped on the gas, then skidded at high speed around a turn slick with snowfall, and the men chasing him didn't get a shot off before he was out of their view.

Velesky sat there in a state of both exhaustion and shock, spending several seconds trying to catch his breath as the car raced by the Zurich Opera House.

The man behind the wheel gave him only a brief moment before initiating the conversation. "Those fuckers mean business. I didn't figure they'd start shooting so quickly. I tallied four guys back there watching your place. Looked like they'd been there all evening, waiting for you to leave."

"Who are they?" he asked again.

Matter-of-factly the American said, "Russians. I'm guessing mob guys, but they could be contractors. Probably came up from Serbia, but who knows?"

Just as Alex had suspected, this wasn't about the files he'd stolen from work today. This was about Krupkin's mobile. He rubbed his face in his hands, suddenly unable to accept the gravity of his predicament.

"Who are you?" he asked the driver.

"I told you. I'm from the—"

"I mean, what's your name?"

The American said, "You can call me Dale."

Alex nodded, still gasping for air. He felt his calves tightening, verging on full-on cramps. The VW drove south through mostly empty streets this late at night. "The embassy. Does that mean you're from the CIA or something like that?"

"That doesn't matter right now."

"I'll take that as a yes," Alex said, and he rubbed his face again. This bad situation was going downhill by the second.

Dale turned to him now and said, "What did you stick in the mailbox back there?"

And just like that, his predicament left the hill entirely and launched out over a cliff.

TEN

"What?" Alex was sure he'd croaked it out unconvincingly.

"Saw you do it," Dale said as he raced along the eastern bank of the Limmat River. "The mailman won't pick it up till tomorrow, so as soon as I have you secured, I'll get some colleagues to bust the box off the wall and go through it." He shrugged. "You might as well just go ahead and tell me what you shoved in there."

Velesky looked out the window. *Shit.* He didn't know who he could trust, but he definitely did *not* trust American intelligence. He'd probably find himself in prison in the United States before he managed to do anything to negatively impact the monsters in the Kremlin.

When Alex did not respond, Dale said, "Look, man. Those four guys? They're just the tip of the big-assed iceberg in your path. They want Krupkin's data. There will be dozens of Russian mafia or spooks on the way here by now. Whatever you just mailed was so important you didn't want to be caught with it, so I know it has to do with what Krupkin passed you last night."

The letter did not, in fact, have anything directly to do with what Krupkin gave him, but he wasn't going to say anything else until he came up with a plan.

Dale was about to speak again when his phone rang on the center console. He snatched it up, listened, cussed, then hung up. He flashed a fresh look at Velesky now. "Shit, man. You *really* screwed the pooch."

"Screwed . . . the . . . What does *that* mean?"

"My people just found out that Brucker Söhne is hunting you down, as well. You downloaded confidential records from your bank, and now *that* information is out in the wild, along with Krupkin's data. Are you just *trying* to get killed?"

Shit again. Alex stared out the windshield, exhausted and despondent. His daylong dream of bringing truth to power and punishing the Kremlin for killing his loved ones was falling apart before his eyes.

Before he could say anything, Dale said, "Trust me. You have no idea the shitstorm you've opened up now. Brucker Söhne has some of the dirtiest money on Earth flowing through it, and every bad actor involved is going to want to retrieve what you took."

Dale looked him over. "You want to give me that data? Believe me, you're safer without it."

The phone with Krupkin's data was in the front right pocket of Alex's coat, but he made no move to reach for it.

The VW made another turn, this time onto Bellerivestrasse. Dale pushed down harder on the gas, keeping his eyes on the road while he talked. Lake Zurich was still on their right; on the left was a continuous row of lakeside shops and cafés, parking lots, and smaller roads that headed east. There was no traffic at all this late at night; it appeared as if the two men had the city to themselves.

Dale said, "I figure Krupkin's files relate to accounts at your bank, you got the account records today, and you're going to try to match them up. We can work together, man, that's exactly the information my government is after. If it's money you want—"

"It's not about money. It is about my family. All I care about is—"

Alex stopped talking suddenly. He was facing the CIA man who was behind the wheel and looking out the windshield in front of him, so Alex was the only one of the two of them who saw a black four-door Mercedes streaking out of a parking lot to the left of their vehicle and barreling right down on them at high speed.

Dale turned to Alex to see why he'd gone quiet, but Alex screamed, "Watch out!"

Dale tensed up, but he didn't have time to turn his head, and he never saw the oncoming vehicle. The Mercedes sedan slammed directly into the driver's-side door; it crumpled in on Dale as Alex went flying to the left, slamming hard against the driver.

Airbags fired all around as the VW Golf lurched to the right under incredible violence and broken glass, skidding on its wheels. It ran off the road, slammed into a concrete entrance to the Zurich underground railway, and then finally came to rest.

More glass crackled as it gave way around Alex. The radiator hissed and steamed and the engine smoked.

His head spinning, the feeling of the grit of glass and other debris in his eyes, Alex Velesky moved his head around. The left side of his forehead hurt; he had no idea what he'd hit it against, but he shook away the haze and looked over to see that Dale was still alive. Blood drained from the American's mouth and nose, and he seemed at least partially pinned into his seat by twisted metal, but he slowly lifted his head and looked around.

Alex was still too disoriented to do more than gaze on, but Dale apparently saw something outside through the vapor pouring from under the hood, and he scrambled to get his hand under his jacket. He pulled out a pistol—Alex didn't know why—but before he could raise it, a loud but muted thud barked somewhere out in the night, and the windshield, already spiderwebbed from the impact with the sideswiping Mercedes, exploded inwards in front of the driver's side.

Dale was shot through his right cheekbone. Brain matter splattered the wrecked headliner and door, dripping down on the still man and the limp airbags all but covering his body.

The American's pistol clanked to the floorboard between his feet, and Alex screamed, certain he would be next.

But there was no more shooting. Instead, a man with short, spiked blond hair appeared in his passenger-side window. He yanked on the door, which had bent from the impact with the concrete wall of the subway entrance, and eventually managed to wrench it open.

He held a stainless steel pistol with a silencer in his right hand.

As Alex sat frozen, the man reached across him with his free hand, unfastened his seat belt, pulled him out of the wreckage, and shuffled him on unsteady legs towards the damaged Mercedes.

A gray Toyota Camry sedan screeched to a halt behind the scene of the accident, and four men poured out. And though Alex could not be certain, he thought that among them were the pair who had chased him from his apartment. They shouted something in Russian to the man who held on to Alex by the collar of his down jacket, and then the blond man turned and yanked the banker away from the Mercedes and towards the Toyota.

Alex Velesky was shoved into the passenger seat of the vehicle; the blond man pushed one of the Russians out of his way as he walked around the front and climbed behind the wheel. He put the car in gear and launched forward, around the wreckage and to the south, soon turning away from the lake and heading east.

Certain he had a concussion, and with no idea who had him now, other than the fact that the man who *did* have him now had apparently just murdered an American CIA officer, Alex fought waves of panic-induced nausea. He was nearly hyperventilating, but the man next to him ignored his condition and spoke to him in English.

"Where is the phone?" His accent was Russian, and Velesky knew he was a dead man.

But he did not answer.

"You *will* talk. Just like Krupkin." He turned to Alex now. "And then you *will* die, just like Krupkin."

Velesky shuddered. Krupkin had already been found and killed.

"Who are you?" he asked.

"I need the phone," the man repeated. "And I need to ensure it is the correct phone."

Alex rubbed his eyes under his glasses. The debris was clearing out slowly, but still they stung. "And I asked who you were."

The man behind the wheel pointed his pistol at Alex's head now. He answered the banker's question with "I am going to count to one, and then I am going to shoot you."

"Okay! Okay!"

Velesky reached into his coat, pulled out the iPhone Krupkin had given him the night before, and handed it over.

The driver took it with a nod, then pocketed it, but he kept his weapon's barrel pointed at Alex's torso.

Neither man spoke now. Alex picked at his wounds, and the driver looked ahead; the Toyota drove on through the night, police cars racing past them towards reports of a two-car crash near the lake.

ELEVEN

It was past eight p.m. in the British Virgin Islands when Court Gentry dropped anchor in North Bay of Great Dog Island, a small, uninhabited rock just west of the large island of Virgin Gorda. There were no other boats in sight now, and Court had turned off all the mast and deck lights, so the *Serenity* bobbed there in the warm evening air, the rhythmic beats of water gently lapping against the hull the only sounds to be heard.

Angela Lacy remained zip-tied on the settee in the salon, so when Court was finished securing the boat, he climbed back down the companionway, then cut her bindings free.

Sarcastically, she said, "You sure about that? How do you know my hands aren't registered as lethal weapons?"

Court lifted his T-shirt, revealing the butt of his Glock pistol, now jammed into the waistband of his shorts at his appendix. "I *don't*, which is why I will shoot you through the eye if you make any sudden moves."

"You're a NOC," Lacy said, pronouncing it like "knock" and referring to CIA non-official cover officers. "I've met NOCs who were wound pretty tight, but none of them were anything like you."

Court ignored her. He wasn't here to make conversation or friends; he was here to find out what the fuck Suzanne Brewer wanted from him.

He grabbed Lacy's backpack with the phone inside, then handed it to her and sat down at a little dinette across from the settee.

The woman from the CIA eyed him angrily as she retrieved her phone, dialed a number, then activated the speaker function.

It rang twice, then was answered by a voice Court knew all too well.

"Brewer."

"It's Lacy. Lima, Lima, X-ray, four, four, nine, seven, Alpha."

"Iden confirmed."

"I have Six," Lacy said as she looked back up to Court.

Before Brewer could speak, Court snatched the phone out of Lacy's hand and turned off the speaker function, then left the woman in the salon and climbed up onto the deck. This afforded him a 360-degree view under the clear evening skies washed in an orange sunset.

After checking the water for divers on both sides of the boat, he whispered angrily into the phone. "What the hell's wrong with you?"

"What are you talking about?"

"This woman you sent. She has no idea who I am or *what* I am, does she?"

Brewer was unrepentant. "I needed someone unaware and unafraid. I needed someone who wouldn't scare you off from a distance, so we could have a discussion."

Court stood at the top of the companionway and looked back down into the salon at Lacy, then turned away so she couldn't hear. "You sent her because you knew I wouldn't blame her for whatever bullshit you were trying to rope me into."

Brewer added, "Is it a bad time for me to point out that my plan seems to have worked beautifully so far?"

This pissed him off, but he knew she was right. He'd have pegged anyone approaching him with caution. The fact that the woman thought she was just flying down alone to hand a phone to a run-of-the-mill operations officer made her successful in her approach.

Court let it go and asked, "How did you know I was down here?"

"We've been watching you."

"Bullshit," Court retorted with confidence. "I have a camera on my masthead, I can see for miles in any direction, and I haven't been followed by anyone."

"Oh, wow. You have a camera on your boat?"

"Damn right, I do."

"Gosh, that's impressive." She paused, then said, "Guess what, genius? I have a fucking constellation of *satellites* over your head."

Court's eyes couldn't help but look up into the evening sky now.

She said, "We figured it was probably you who sank the boat in the Maldives, and then we were sure it was you when you did the one in Dubai. We know you're working for the Ukrainian oligarch Andrei Melnyk, so it was then just a simple matter of tracking other boats his accountants had uncovered. The *Lyra Drakos* was one of four yachts we had our eyes on. When we heard it sank, we went back and looked at the sat coverage of the area."

Court knew what was coming next.

"Two hours before Constantine Pasternak's mega yacht sank, a little sailboat motored out of the bay, began heading north. We picked you up before you arrived in the BVIs, and I sent Lacy down before I even knew where you were mooring."

"Okay, you found me. But what's to stop me from throwing your errand girl into the water and then hauling ass out of here?"

"We've known exactly where you were for a day and a half. How many Ground Branch teams have HALO jumped onto your little schooner in that time, Violator? None? What does that tell you?"

His boat was a ketch, not a schooner, but he didn't correct her. Instead, he said, "What *does* it tell me?"

"That we aren't pursuing you." She paused a beat, then said, "We need you."

Court knew he was in jeopardy now that the Agency had found him, but he also knew that the manner in which he'd been approached meant there was, indeed, something they needed from him.

Before he could say anything, Brewer added, "Good work in Mumbai, by the way."

Court had done a freelance job in India many months earlier. Brewer had helped him with that, after a fashion. It was an acrimonious encounter that had, ultimately, led to a good result.

"I assume Mumbai was good for your career," he replied with no small amount of snark. Brewer had hardly been a hero that day, but Court assumed she would have taken a full helping of credit for the little that she *had* done.

She replied, "It didn't hurt. But I didn't call to talk about old victories. There's a new problem, and you're perfectly positioned to help us."

"I'm listening."

"A man down in Saint Lucia received a package this evening. Hand-couriered to him, all the way from Europe. We want it."

"What's the package?"

"We know it's data in some physical form, but we're not sure what form it's in. Might be a hard drive, a thumb drive, a laptop, a phone, something like that. Hell, it could be a suitcase full of paperwork. It came from Russia. Details of money transfers between the West and Russia, and between Russia and the West. That's really all we know."

"Who sent it?"

"Igor Krupkin. A Moscow-based financial advisor."

"Who's the recipient?"

"A man named Eddison John. He's a lawyer, involved in shady banking down there in the Caribbean."

"Why not send Lacy, or some case officer from down here?"

Brewer sighed again. "Lacy hasn't been in the field in years, and nobody down there has your experience. This is going to be a difficult black-bag job. Eddison John has a sizable security force on his property."

Court's eyes narrowed. "Not buying it. You've got dozens of people who can run high-threat black-bag ops. If you need me, there's another reason."

She sighed a little. "The Agency can't get their hands dirty when it comes to this man. He does some work with us. We have our own offshore accounts, as you know. John is one of many lawyers we use to establish our shells. The relationship needs to continue, and us sending Agency personnel down there to snatch this data won't be good for the relationship."

"If he works with you, why not just ask him to send it up to D.C.?"

"Because the data on the file, if he accesses it, might just make him aware of things we don't want him aware of."

Court said, "You just told me this data came from Russia."

"There are some data that directly involve the Agency's activities *in* Rus-

sia. We think the files snuck out of Moscow could be compromising for us."
She added, "That's all I'm prepared to say."

Court thought this over. "The information sent to Saint Lucia could
damage CIA ops ongoing in Russia?"

"From what I've been told, 'damage' is a less accurate word than, say,
'destroy.'"

"You guys must be involved in some dirty shit over there."

Brewer didn't miss a beat. "The dirtiest shit I've ever been involved in at
the Agency centered on you, so don't get too sanctimonious about the predicament the Agency finds itself in at the moment."

Court smiled a little at this, then turned serious again. "Why not send
me into Russia? I'm out in the cold now, working for Melnyk sinking boats
because I don't have the intel and support structure to get me inside Moscow,
where I can do some good."

By "doing some good," he meant killing some people, and Brewer would
know this.

"This would be a bad time to have you killing Russian government officials."

"You ever watch the news?" he asked. "There's no such thing as a bad
time to kill Russian government officials."

"Do *you* ever watch the news? Do you know about the summit in New
York?"

Court knew nothing about a summit. He sighed. "You've got to be kidding me."

"The Russian foreign minister and the U.S. secretary of state, along with
the foreign ministers of other Western nations, will meet in New York. Assuming Russia agrees to make the current cease-fire permanent, and assuming the World Trade Organization votes to let Russia regain most-favored-nation
status, then as far as the West is concerned, the war will be over."

"Do the Ukrainians get a vote?"

"No."

"So Russia wins the territory they've conquered," Court muttered.

Brewer sighed. "What do you want me to say? Of course it's bullshit. But
I'm not consulted on American foreign policy and international relations,

and last I heard, you aren't, either. There is nothing greater that you can do both for America and against Russia than acquiring Igor Krupkin's data and handing it over to us. Do this, Violator. Protect the Agency. Protect America."

He thought a moment, despondent about what he'd learned but also curious about his own status with the Agency. "So . . . I do this job, and then you start chasing me again?"

"We weren't chasing you. We were just looking into the yacht sinkings, and there you were. Look, once you do this for us, you're free to run away again, but maybe you won't want to. Maybe you'll want to stick around, do jobs for me from time to time."

"You're running Poison Apple?"

"There *is* no Poison Apple. I haven't heard from Anthem or Romantic; they haven't turned up anywhere we're looking on facial recog sweeps." She added, "Whatever they're up to, they're keeping a lower profile than the guy from Poison Apple who is flying around the world blowing up two-hundred-million-dollar boats."

Romantic was the code name for Zack Hightower, Court's former team leader and colleague. Anthem was Zoya Zakharova, the woman Court loved, the woman Court was desperate to find. If Brewer was telling the truth, if the CIA couldn't even locate Zoya, then his own chances of finding her were even worse than he'd feared.

He shook off the thought as Brewer continued. "Even though Poison Apple is gone, I *do* see value in employing assets not attached to the Agency. Like this job in Saint Lucia. There could be more work after that. Take-it-or-leave-it stuff. You decide."

Court didn't like or trust Brewer, but he was used to working with or for people he didn't like or trust in order to do work he felt was nevertheless honorable. As far as he was concerned, retrieving data that could undermine CIA ops in Russia sounded more important and impactful than him sinking another damn yacht.

"Okay," he said. "I'll go have a chat with Eddison John."

"Good. Angela will get you to Saint Lucia. You'll need to act quickly."

Court shook his head. "She'll give me all the intel you have, and then she'll get out of my way. I'll get myself down there."

"We don't have time for you to sail down to—"

"I'll be at the target before dawn. I'll act immediately, provided your intel is any good."

There was a long pause. "How do I know you won't just run? This may come as something of a surprise, but I'm having some difficulty buying that you're going to do what you say you are going to do if we let you out of our sight."

"You don't exactly exude credibility yourself, Brewer." He looked out over the water; a sailboat headed west, north of where he was now anchored. "Look. I don't trust you—I'm not an idiot—but I do believe that the mission, as explained to me, is important. I'll retrieve the data, but I'll do it my way."

Brewer let it go. "All right. Angela will be in Saint Lucia if you need her, but she won't be in your way. Put her back on the phone and I'll brief her."

"Brief her?" Court muttered. "She really has no clue about any of this, does she?"

"I'll rectify that and fold her into this operation. She'll stay remote, but honestly, that woman could use some dirt on her hands."

Working denied ops was part of the job in CIA operations, but most case officers and execs went their entire careers without touching anything too incriminating to implicate them in any sub-rosa acts.

Brewer was saying she wanted Lacy sullied by the same sorts of black operations that got Brewer's own hands so dirty.

Court didn't like it; he had nothing against the woman seated one deck down, and he knew firsthand how Brewer used people under her. But he had bigger fish to fry. If this mission really *could* protect CIA officers and agents, then that was more important than one midlevel exec's career path.

He went back down to the salon and handed Lacy the phone, then headed back up to the main deck to pull anchor. As he did this, he looked out at the dark night.

It was beautiful.

He liked it here.

He was going to miss it.

After only a few seconds to lament the end of his stay in the BVIs, he pulled the bow anchor, ready to motor west towards his aircraft at a marina on Beef Island, just an hour or so away.

TWELVE

Alex Velesky sat in the front passenger seat of the gray Toyota Camry holding his head, still pounding from the violent crash some ten minutes earlier. His nausea had subsided a little, and he thought over his situation.

Next to him and behind the wheel was the blond-haired Russian, who'd only asked a few questions of Alex and, when he didn't get any answers from him, calmly stated he would be tortured to death for information.

And then the man kept his focus on both the road and his vehicle's GPS.

Alex wasn't sure of much at the moment, but he was certain of one thing: he wasn't going to be tortured. He'd throw himself out of the car door at speed, facing near-certain death.

He'd never considered himself a brave man before, and he didn't consider himself one now; he just feared the pain he would undergo more than he feared breaking his neck leaping from a moving car.

But each time he thought about trying to bolt, it was as if the Russian man on his left sensed it. He pointed his pistol with his right hand while he drove with his left, and he pressed it against Alex's knee until Alex settled back down.

There was no way he could jump out of this car without being wounded in the process, so he just sat there, praying for an opportunity to fling himself out of the door.

It was clear to Alex that the Russian didn't know the city very well; the man made two wrong turns if his intention had been to flee the area, and in ten minutes he'd all but traveled in a large circle. Alex said nothing, but when they passed more orange and white police vans rushing to the area, the Russian began cussing to himself. He pulled over for a moment, held his gun to Alex's knee, and worked the navigation system on the Camry. Like Zurich itself, this obviously wasn't a car he was accustomed to, so this took a few minutes, but eventually they were back on the road.

Alex could now see on the Camry's screen that their ultimate destination was in Embrach, a village just to the north of Zurich.

He shook his head, still trying to clean out the cobwebs from the crash a few minutes back. As he did this, he noticed that for the first time in the past minute or so, the Camry was sharing the road with another vehicle. A white commercial van had turned onto Forchtstrasse in front of them, taking the left lane heading northwest while the car Alex traveled in was in the lane to the right. The spike-haired driver of the Camry sped up to pass the van on the inside, his right hand still holding the pistol that was now pointed at Alex's midsection.

"What's in Embrach?" Alex demanded, but there was no reply from the formidable-looking man.

They were more than halfway past the commercial van when the blond-haired driver suddenly turned his head to look back to his left—he'd seen something in his rearview, apparently—and then he moved the gun away from Alex to use his right hand on the steering wheel along with his left.

Alex had just registered that he was no longer being held at gunpoint and therefore might have a chance to leap out of the car when he realized why the driver suddenly seemed so alarmed. The commercial van on their left had jacked into their lane—and before the driver of the Camry could get out of the way, the van struck its left rear, and Alex Velesky felt the Camry skid to the right, completely out of control.

Alex crouched down and covered his head as the car spun out at sixty kilometers an hour; even through the fresh panic hitting him now, he was able to register that he was about to be in his second car crash in ten minutes, and the thought of this boggled his mind.

The Camry slammed sideways into the curb and flipped into the air. The airbags deployed all around, glass shattered, the driver slammed his head against his doorframe, and Alex desperately tried to cover his already injured head.

The sedan rolled over once, a violent scraping as the hood skidded on pavement for a few feet, and then it teetered back over onto its side. After more than a second seemingly in suspended animation, the car slammed back down on all four tires.

Alex was dazed again. The flipping, the noise, the broken metal and glass all around him—he couldn't understand how he was still alive.

Checking the driver, he saw that the Russian was either dead or unconscious; his head hung, and Alex saw blood on his broken window.

He looked out through the steam and smoke pouring from under the hood and saw that they were now facing south, pointing back in the direction from which they came.

He again rubbed his eyes, swishing around the fresh dust that had made its way under his eyelids.

And then it came to him: this was his chance. He had to get out of the car and make a run for it, now.

Just as he undid his seat belt and reached for the passenger-side door, however, the door was flung open, ripping the handle from his hand.

Someone stood just outside the car.

He threw up his hands to fend off an attack, but instead he heard a woman's voice.

"Hey! Hey!"

He lowered his hands and saw her through smoke and steam. The figure wore a black coat, a black knit cap, and glasses. Alex squinted to get a better look. It was a woman, and in her gloved right hand she held a black pistol. It wasn't pointed in his direction but was instead aimed at the unconscious man behind the wheel.

Alex just stared at her, utterly disoriented.

"Alexander Velesky?" the woman asked. Her accent sounded American, just as Dale's had a few minutes earlier.

She was *also* CIA?

From the north, a black Audi Q8 SUV raced into view, and Alex looked through the broken windshield at it; it was clearly heading towards the crash.

He didn't know if these were more Russians or any of the other groups of bad actors Dale had warned him about.

The woman shouted now. "Alex?"

He took his eyes off the approaching Audi SUV and looked at her again. "Who wants to know?"

"The only person around here who isn't trying to kill you."

He took her point. "I'm Alex," he answered back quickly.

The Audi skidded to a stop thirty meters away, positioning itself horizontally to the wrecked-out Camry. Alex saw the back window lowering.

The woman pulled him free of the wreckage without asking if he was injured, then lifted her pistol towards the man behind the wheel as if she was going to shoot him dead.

But before she could do so, gunshots cracked in the street. A man fired a handgun out the back window of the Q8 while three other men bailed, spreading out and searching for cover.

The woman ducked, yanked Alex lower to the ground, and pulled him towards the van that had just crashed into Alex's car.

"Wait!" he said. "My phone! My phone!" He hadn't even thought about grabbing it from the unconscious man when he'd been planning on running, but now that he remembered, he wasn't leaving this scene without it.

"Get another phone," the woman barked dismissively.

He fought against her, slowing his movement to the van. He decided he'd have to trust this woman if he was to get out of this alive. "No! The phone is what this is all about. The information on it. The man behind the wheel took it from me. It's in his jacket pocket."

She looked at him like she didn't have a clue what he was talking about, but she recovered quickly, then hustled Velesky into the front passenger seat of the van. Pointing a finger in his face, she shouted at him with intense authority. "Don't you fucking move!"

"Yes, ma'am."

Zoya Zakharova crouched as low to the ground as she could and then raced across the slick street to the driver's-side door of the Camry, desperate to keep the car between herself and the new arrivals to the scene.

She wasn't ready for this. She'd spent the last five hours trying to sober up and sharpen up, but if she was honest with herself, she had also spent much of those same five hours telling herself she could get through this operation this morning because it wouldn't be anything too taxing. A shady bank wanted records stolen from another shady bank; it hardly sounded like an endeavor that would have her stealing a van, pursuing a kidnapping victim, then wrecking him out, ducking bullets the moment she arrived on scene.

And yet here she was, opening the door of the wrecked Camry, her weapon out in front of her.

She saw blood on the blond-haired man's ear and neck; his eyes were closed and his head hung. He appeared dead.

The men from the Audi were now bounding in her direction; Zoya could hear their shouts to one another getting closer to her position, but they couldn't see her where she knelt at the driver's-side door.

She didn't want to give her location away by either firing on them or shooting the driver to make certain he was dead. Instead, she pressed her pistol against the driver's head with one hand and fished through his jacket with the other.

She found a phone, and then another. She pocketed them both.

As she crawled back out of the Camry, a fresh shot rang out, and it struck the roof of the car. The origin of fire told her that at least one of the men had flanked her around the back of the vehicle, but he remained in the dark behind a low wall.

She ran for the van she'd stolen just minutes earlier, extending her pistol behind her and squeezing off rounds as she went.

More gunshots chased her as she skittered around the front of the vehicle.

Once behind the wheel, she threw the transmission into reverse and accelerated backwards. This would send her right past the Audi in the street, but she was working under the assumption that the men would have left the vehicle to find her, and they likely would have swept around the Camry and not stood forty meters away at the Q8.

As she raced backwards past the enemy vehicle, a string of gunshots hit the side of the van, and one passed between Zoya and Alex, crafting a perfect circle in the front windshield.

Simultaneous to this, she reached across Alex with the pistol in her hand. It boomed, inches from the banker's face. She fired over and over at the Audi more than a dozen times. Two tires on the Audi went flat, and a man crouched next to it grabbed his leg and fell to the street.

Alex held his hands to his ears and screamed.

When her weapon was empty, Zoya concentrated on her driving, flipping off her headlights before turning backwards down a residential road and then flooring the big van out of view.

Once they'd made a turn that took them out of the line of fire, she executed a reverse 180, then shot off down the street at high speed.

It was quiet inside the van, but only for a few seconds. Then she held up both of the phones she'd taken from the man with the spiked blond hair.

"Which one?"

Clearly Velesky couldn't hear her.

She shouted at the top of her lungs, "Which one?"

"The one in your left hand," he finally replied.

Zoya put it in her coat pocket, then flung the other phone out the window of the speeding van.

Now she couldn't be tracked by the opposition tracing their own phone.

Then she rose up out of her seat a little to stick her head out the window of the van, and she began vomiting profusely as she drove.

Alex Velesky sat there, in silence and in awe, watching the woman driving through the darkness recover from her bout of sickness. Eventually she finished, then wiped her mouth and her forehead, not even looking his way, treating him at the moment as if he did not exist.

He used the time to shake his head to try to get his hearing back, and he wondered if he could leap out of *this* vehicle and back onto the street like he'd planned on doing with his Russian kidnapper.

The woman spit out the window now, clearing her mouth of the remainder of the puke, and then as she drove, she dropped the magazine from her pistol with one hand and put the weapon between her knees, the grip facing up. Alex watched her expertly draw another mag from inside her coat, then jam it into the magazine well, retake the grip with her right hand, and then push back the slide—again one-handed—by racking it on the steering wheel.

Her foot was all the way down on the gas as she reholstered.

Alex Velesky's brain did its best to fight through the adrenaline and confusion, and he spoke up through the haze of shock clouding his thoughts. "Are you . . . CIA?"

To his surprise, she answered. "No."

"You . . . work for the bank?"

The woman behind the wheel kept her eyes on the windshield in front of her. "Do I *look* like I work for a fucking bank?"

"Not really."

She shrugged now. "Somebody wanted me to collect you and hold on to you while they figure out what to do with you."

"You're talking about me like I'm a piece of luggage."

She shrugged. "You're my package. *That's* what you are."

"Can you tell me where we are going?"

"A safe place."

"Why?"

"So you can meet with some people."

"What people?"

"The investment bank in Geneva that hired me. They know you walked out of your own bank with highly sensitive material. They want that data." She patted the pocket where she'd put Alex's phone. "And I'm going to give it to them." She flashed her big eyes at him through her designer eyeglasses. "They want you, too. And I'm going to give *you* to them."

Alex realized this woman thought the phone contained the records from Brucker Söhne. But those records had been, in fact, uploaded onto an address on the dark web. The phone containing Krupkin's information about Russian foreign intelligence spending was in her pocket, but she'd given no indication she knew anything about Krupkin or his data at all.

"Why do they want the data?" he asked.

She looked in her rearview to make certain she wasn't being tailed. "Industrial espionage, I suppose. Your industry is money, and people will kill you to keep their financial affairs secret."

He muttered to himself, "This is insane."

The woman said, "I don't know what you're upset about. I just saved your ass, and the bank in Geneva is probably going to offer you a lot of money to help them understand the data you took."

For the first time, Alex Velesky yelled at the woman. "I'm not doing this for money!"

"Well, buddy, I am, so I'm going to do my job and bring you to the people who want to talk to you. We'll go to a safe house about a two-hour drive from here. Provided there are no security issues, the people from Geneva will arrive later today for a chat. You can ask *them* any other questions you might have."

"What if I don't want to chat with them?"

"I shot a guy back there who didn't want you to chat with them. *That's* what happens when you get in the way of me doing my job."

"I'm doing this because my family—"

The woman behind the wheel turned and pointed a finger at him. "Stop! Whatever your reason, I'm sure you care a lot about it. But here's the cold reality. I *don't*. I don't give a shit about you, or about what drives you.

"Believe me, Velesky . . . the less you tell me about you, the better it will be for both of us."

"But—"

"Let's sit in silence for a while."

"But I have—"

The woman opened her coat and put her hand on the grip of her pistol. "We aren't negotiating here."

Alex said nothing else.

The woman's face seemed to turn pale before his eyes, and she looked like she was about to vomit again, but she managed to keep the contents of her stomach down and her eyes on the road.

The commercial van, Alex Velesky's third conveyance in the past fifteen minutes, continued on to the east as police cars raced to the west, no doubt heading to the scene of another crash, this time with reported gunfire.

THIRTEEN

Shortly before six a.m., a man in a gray wool coat with a red knit cap pulled down far over his ears entered the lobby of the posh Storchen Zurich hotel on the banks of the Limmat River. He passed by a desk clerk without so much as a nod, and then headed unimpeded to the elevator bank.

A minute later, Luka Rudenko was led into a top-floor suite by a bearded cold-eyed Russian in his twenties and directed past two other serious-looking young men, one with tattoos visible on his neck, the other with a goatee carefully groomed to portray devilish menace. The man in the knit cap ignored them as he made his way across the room to the balcony doors.

It was just below freezing outside, but Sebastian Drexler stood alone on the balcony in a brown fleece pullover and gray slacks, his hands on his hips. His cane was nearby, but he had all his weight on his legs, as if he'd forgotten he was only partially ambulatory.

Luka stepped out onto the balcony as well, shut the door behind him, and pulled off his cap. He'd bandaged his ear, but blood had soaked through the white tape and gauze.

Drexler looked at him with no amount of sympathy. Instead, he said, "You've been unreachable for over two hours."

"My phone was taken." When Drexler's eyes widened, Luka waved a dismissive hand. "Nothing on it. I'm sure they dumped it anyway."

"What about Krupkin's phone?"

The Russian said, "I *had* Krupkin's phone. I *had* Velesky. Then we got hit."

Drexler looked back out over the river, towards the east side of town. He clearly knew this much already, having learned it from the Russians at the scene. "By who?" he asked.

"No clue."

Drexler said, "The men from Stravinsky who were following you say they only saw one man. They tried to stop him but didn't get there in time, and couldn't provide a physical description. One of the contractors was shot."

"I know." Now Luka was the one who showed no sympathy.

"Did you get a look at the attacker?" Drexler asked.

Luka pointed to the side of his head. It was black-and-blue at the temple, just above and in front of his bloody ear. "I didn't get a look at *anything* after we wrecked. The Stravinsky goons set the wrong address in their GPS. I got lost when I used their car to take Velesky. Had to start over, and that gave the people who attacked us time to set up.

"Then Stravinsky dragged me to their other car and got me out of there, and they had to take me to an all-night pharmacy because the idiots didn't even have a med kit with them."

"They said you disappeared after that."

"I wanted to go back to Velesky's apartment before the cops got to it, but I didn't want to do that with a bunch of tattooed mercs, so we parted ways."

Drexler just sighed and said, "In case you didn't know, you murdered a CIA officer tonight."

Luka Rudenko's reaction was muted. "Not the first time."

"The CIA will come at us hard for that."

This he responded to with nonchalance. "Then I guess it won't be the last time, either."

Although he did not admit it, Luka had *not* known that the man he'd shot was CIA. He'd had no idea who was driving Velesky away from his apartment, and he hadn't cared.

Drexler looked back out at the river. "You were brought in because of your reputation as cool and efficient. You were to make my job *easier*, not harder."

The Russian gazed down at the older man's crippled leg. "Maybe you should just do it all yourself. I can go back to Helsinki."

It was silent for several seconds, and then Drexler muttered, "Touché." Changing the subject, he said, "There's a Bombardier Global 6000 waiting for you at the airport."

"Saint Lucia?"

"Yes. You'll fly nine hours, arrive there by ten a.m. local. You'll retrieve the phone as soon as you get to Eddison John's mansion."

The Russian thought this over. "I need men with me in Saint Lucia, but I don't want *those* men." He jerked a finger towards the Russians in the living room.

"Those men will stay here and hunt down Velesky," Drexler said. "I will provide you with people in the Caribbean. They'll be there when you arrive."

Luka cocked his head. "*What* people?"

"I have contacts in all the major offshore banking nations. Don't worry, I'll assemble a crew. Weapons, as well."

Luka sniffed. "Spanov has deep pockets."

Drexler began heading over to talk to the Russians. "For now, he does. If we don't get that data back, then his pockets won't be so deep, and his life won't be so long."

Luka put his cap back on, covering his wound. "I'm going to my embassy to pick up some things and then I'll head to the airport. Tell the pilots I'll be there in an hour."

The Russian killer left the balcony, passing the mercenaries without a word as he headed for the door.

Sebastian Drexler remained on the balcony, standing in the cold a moment, dreading the call he was about to make. Security Council director Daniil Spanov would be furious that the operation wasn't tied off yet, but Drexler couldn't just ghost the man who was paying his salary.

He pulled out his phone and reluctantly pressed the buttons.

After waiting for the connection to be made, he spoke in English. "Director Spanov. Unfortunately, last night did not go as expected."

The Russian spoke in a grave tone. "Leave out no detail."

"We know who has Krupkin's devices. Two men, neither of whom are in our control at present, but we are working on accessing them both."

"Have I made it clear how important it is that the information is recovered and the compromise is removed?"

"Abundantly."

Spanov remained frustrated. "Your job was to secure this."

"And I'm doing my job, but I need more tools to do it."

There were a few dark breaths into the phone, and then the Russian said, "What are we talking about?"

Drexler was unequivocal. "More men. Better quality than the mercenaries you sent from Serbia yesterday."

"Be specific."

"The asset, Luka. I get the sense he is quite good, despite what happened this morning. I want more like him. *Exactly* like him." He added, "A lot of men."

The pause was short. "That can be arranged. Where do you need them?"

"I have all the resources I need in the Caribbean, so I just need men here, in Zurich. You get them to me today, you take away the men you sent yesterday, and I assure you that within twenty-four hours we will have both phones in our possession."

There was a long pause. Finally, Daniil Spanov said, "Are you familiar with Unit 29155 of the GRU?"

Drexler was, indeed, familiar.

"Yes."

"I'll make a call, have nine more of them to assist you by the end of the day."

Drexler hadn't known Rudenko was from 29155, the elite foreign assassination squad of Russian military intelligence. He held his breath a moment, realizing Spanov was now offering up an entire team of well-trained assassins to augment the one he already had on the mission.

If the GRU was sending a full squad of its most elite hitters to Zurich for this, then Drexler knew how important this was to Daniil Spanov.

The Swiss man decided to press his luck. "I need these assets under *my* command. I can't have them calling headquarters for approval every time I assign a duty."

Spanov said, "They will be under Rudenko; he's the highest rank. But Rudenko is under *your* direct command to use as you see fit." Spanov let out another breath into the phone, then said, "Don't make me regret this, Drexler. I am a desperate man at the moment, and desperate men can be volatile."

"Understood," Drexler said. "Give me the assets and I'll give you the results."

The call ended, and Drexler stood there, staring into the frigid dawn.

He couldn't believe it. He was about to run highly skilled Russian military intelligence assets on the streets of Europe. He was both thrilled and terrified of the prospect of this, but if he had to be honest with himself, he was mostly thrilled.

FOURTEEN

Three hundred feet above the choppy Caribbean Sea, a tiny all-white Progressive Aerodyne SeaRey aircraft was buffeted in light but persistent rain, heading to the east in the darkness towards the western shoreline of the island of Saint Lucia in the West Indies.

The SeaRey was designed for transporting no more than two people and a few suitcases, but Court Gentry was the lone soul on board, and in the passenger seat a medium-sized green pack was the only luggage.

And while the SeaRey was handy in that it could take off and land either in the water or on a runway, it was not built for long-distance travel. The roughly four hundred miles between the British Virgin Islands and Saint Lucia was virtually the maximum range for the little aircraft, and Court had worried during the four-hour middle-of-the-night flight that he might have to land to refuel somewhere, which meant he'd have to wait till the morning to take back to the air.

But now, just before five a.m. and still flying through complete darkness, the aircraft's fuel gauge told him he was virtually running on fumes, but his GPS told him he'd be landing within the next five minutes, having already set his final waypoint in a quiet bay picked out from his study of the area around his target location before takeoff.

He had the gas to get there, but he didn't have the gas to get away via the SeaRey after the fact.

He wasn't sure how he'd exfiltrate Saint Lucia. There were a ton of unknowns on this operation, but Court was confident he could access the target's property and the target himself. With security men, with cameras, with electric fencing, with whatever Eddison John had put in place to keep people out, Court knew he could find a way in.

He wasn't exactly thrilled about the fact that he needed to do it in daylight, but he had no choice. Every minute the data was in the possession of this shady lawyer was another minute he could access it, share it, do whatever the hell he wanted with it, and Suzanne Brewer was adamant that Court not let that happen.

He wore an earpiece under his noise-canceling headset that connected to his satellite phone, and it began chirping as he was finishing up his landing checklist. Court was a little annoyed to be getting a call right now, but he answered anyway, hoping to receive some last-minute intelligence on his mission.

"Yeah?"

"It's Brewer."

"Kind of in the middle of something at the moment."

"Whatever it is, it's not as important as this."

Court was traveling at seventy miles per hour just two hundred feet above the black water of the Caribbean Sea, descending quickly. This seemed pretty damn important, but he waited to see if Brewer could trump this urgency.

She said, "An ops officer from Zurich station was killed last night. We think it's related to what you are doing in Saint Lucia."

"How so?"

"There's a duplicate of the data you've been sent to retrieve. It was given to a banker in Zurich who then stole account records from his firm. We think his plan was to trace the money going into Russia to find out where it originated in the West. I don't have to remind you that tying any Agency black funds accounts going into Russia would expose and endanger a lot of operations, and a lot of agents."

"Shit," Court said. "And the guy who stole the banking info killed an Agency man trying to get it back?"

"No. The banker who stole the data is in the wind; we're looking for him now, but we don't think he was the killer."

"Okay," Court said. He backed his engines to idle; he was less than twenty feet over the surface of the calm but rainswept bay now, his concentration split between his phone call and his landing.

Brewer said, "Do you remember a GRU asset named Luka Ilyich Rudenko?"

"Doesn't ring a bell."

"His code name was Matador."

Court's eyebrows rose as he flared the aircraft. "He's 29155, right? A captain, back when I was active."

Brewer said, "He's a major now. He's worked South America, Asia, Middle East, Africa. Everywhere. Kind of like you." She sighed. "I chased him for years but never caught him."

"Kind of like me," Court said, now five feet from touchdown.

"Funny."

Court said, "And Matador killed the officer in Zurich?"

The seaplane touched down on the calm water, and Court kept his eyes on his instruments.

"Camera footage picked him up buying medical supplies from a twenty-four-hour pharmacy about thirty minutes after the incident. He was bleeding from the head. There was another car crash a few miles from the scene where the ops officer was killed. Bullet holes in the wrecked-out Toyota, evidence of two other vehicles that left the area. It's all related to the killing of our man, we think."

"GRU sent Matador to get the data?"

"We assume so. But the reason I told you about him is that we think he is now on his way to get the data from Eddison John."

Court's eyes widened. "Alone?"

"Also unknown. Lacy is looking over camera feeds in Zurich, trying to get a better picture of the situation. Matador *was* seen arriving alone at a hangar at the airport in Zurich, where it is assumed he boarded a private jet that left around six thirty a.m. local time. The jet's registry is murky, there was no flight plan filed, and its tracking is turned off. We picked it up flying southwest towards the Mediterranean, and it's a Global 6000, meaning it's got the range to get to Saint Lucia. We are proceeding on the assumption that Matador is on board and he's after the other copy of the missing data from Russia, which means he's on his way to you right now."

"How soon could he land?"

"Not before ten a.m. local. The airport is a forty-five-minute drive to Eddison John's residence, meaning Matador could be there no earlier than ten forty-five."

Court thought it over. "The Agency wants him dead?"

"We want the data. That is primary. Eliminating Matador is a secondary objective, but don't risk the primary to make it happen."

"Right," Court said as he began taxiing across the bay towards a small sandy beach. "I've got to go," he said.

"Angela will push any more information she gets your way."

Court hung up the phone and concentrated on the approaching shoreline. He extended the landing gear below the seaplane's floats and pushed the throttle a little more.

With Brewer's intelligence, this operation had just become more difficult, but it also increased in potential benefit to Court himself. If he bagged the man who'd killed an Agency officer, it might just go a long way to earning him some goodwill at Langley. Not with Brewer—she wasn't going to change—but perhaps with the CIA Director.

If Court got the job done in Saint Lucia, then, he reasoned, he might just win himself a new important ally at the Agency and in Washington, and that just might get the kill order against him rescinded.

There was a lot of hope involved in his plan—this Court acknowledged as the SeaRey climbed out of the ocean and up onto the beach. But it was a plan nonetheless, and Court could, at times, be optimistic.

He applied more power to move the aircraft to a shielded area surrounded by ten-foot-high boulders, and once he was happy with his positioning, he turned off the engine.

Thirty minutes later the skies had cleared, but Court had traveled only two hundred meters away from the hidden plane, having made his way slowly and carefully along the rocky volcanic shoreline towards the south. At this speed he wouldn't reach the target location for another two hours, but he intended to climb up from the shoreline and onto flatter ground above when he got to a steep trail just ahead.

He'd originally considered making a scuba insertion to the rear of the waterfront property but decided against it when he took a careful look at Google Maps. The estate was positioned at the edge of a one-hundred-foot-high cliff overlooking the churning water below. Court would have no trouble climbing one hundred feet of volcanic rock, but he could assume the currents would be incredibly high in the water, making the scuba insertion difficult before the climb even began.

It seemed to him the best course of action would be making an ingress from the land, climbing a fence, and approaching the main house on Eddison John's property from the north. As he picked his way along the water's edge, the occasional salty sea spray misting him as he walked and climbed over the rocks, his earpiece chirped again.

He didn't slow down as he answered. "Yeah?"

"It's Lacy."

"What's up?"

"I've spent the last few hours looking into the situation there on the ground in Saint Lucia. Normally I'd have someone at HQ helping me, but Brewer insisted that I keep this close hold." She paused. "I find that strange, don't you?"

Court's eyes scanned the rocks ahead, picking out a safe path. "I don't know what's strange anymore."

She seemed to think about this, then said, "I have blueprints to the residence, photos of the interior, details about the security posture, et cetera."

"Send me what you have."

"Texting it now."

"Good. Any more intel on who Matador has with him?"

Lacy said, "From cameras I was able to review at Zurich airport, it seemed as if he was the only passenger on the Bombardier. The pilot and copilot were the only crew. There was some equipment loaded, just some hardshell cases. We don't know if he has help there on the island, or if he has people coming from locations other than Zurich, or if he will act alone."

"I've looked over the property on Google Maps," Court said. "He'd be an idiot to come alone."

"So, *you're* an idiot?"

Court climbed up the side of a large boulder, careful to keep from cutting himself on the sharp and porous black volcanic rock. He said, "Trust me, if I had some guys, they'd all be here with me. Brewer wants this done with no Agency comebacks, so I've got to pull a solo op."

"Yeah, but don't forget, you have me."

"How could I forget?" He said it sarcastically. "No offense, but you won't be able to help me on this. I'll report in when I have something."

"I'm on the island already, preparing in case you run into trouble. I'll be standing by if you—"

"Stay the hell away, Lacy. Better for both of us." Lacy worked for Brewer, and this meant Court didn't trust her, even if she did come into this operation with no understanding of what was happening.

She was Brewer's underling, and that made her dangerous.

Court said, "Do you have anything else?"

Annoyed, Lacy replied, "Nothing else." And then, "Good luck."

Court disconnected the call.

Ten minutes later he sat in deep brush higher on a hill, still within sight of the ocean and several rocky outcroppings on the water's edge. He used an iPad with an encrypted app to look through the information Lacy had sent about the property, less than one mile to the south from where he now sat.

He wiped ocean spray off the screen from time to time and looked out to the sea to try to determine if heavy weather was on the way. There was enough light in the sky to see a fair distance, and he told himself the clouds would hold off the brightness of the sunrise for at least another hour.

Angela's intel on the property indicated there were seven guards on staff, and the perimeter was fenced. The main house was roughly ten thousand square feet—two stories tall with a walk-out basement—and the back garden sloped down to the cliff's edge he'd seen on Google Maps.

She'd also sent images inside the home from before Eddison John bought the property four years ago. Court flipped through them quickly, taking note of exits, sight lines, potential bottleneck areas.

Court kept looking over the interior, but when he flipped to the twelfth image, he stopped. It was an unfinished room, with a heavy steel door leading into an empty concrete cell-like space, perhaps ten feet by twelve feet. A room like this would be useful during hurricane season, Court imagined, but also damn near invaluable as a panic room.

He checked through other pictures and saw that the shelter appeared to be off the second-floor main bedroom, and he told himself this would be the first place John would go if there was any sign of trouble, either from him or from Matador.

He knew he had to hurry to get the job done before Matador arrived, so he stowed his iPad, rose to his feet, and then began walking up a rocky, thatch-covered hill through a cool and rainy early morning.

FIFTEEN

Zoya Zakharova looked out past the curtains and through the window, her view nothing but snowy pines and fields intersected by a long driveway, a black band on a steady incline that wound its way up to this private hillside ski chalet. Though below freezing, it was perfectly sunny, and Zoya's head wasn't ready for bright lights, so she wore polarized mirrored sunglasses to gaze out at the terrain.

Positioned just north of the town of Wengen, a fifteen-minute drive through the mountains south from Interlaken, this abandoned chalet was reasonably remote, as evidenced by the fact that Zoya spotted a cluster of small red deer at the tree line, languid as they rooted in the ankle-deep snow for food not forty meters from where she stood.

It was early afternoon, and she and Alex Velesky had already been here for hours. The heating wasn't working in the lodge, so she'd built a couple of fires in the fireplaces on the main floor, and a third smaller one in the second-floor bedroom where Alex now slept. She'd eaten rations from her pack, offering some to Velesky, who downed them greedily before falling asleep with one arm handcuffed to a bedpost.

Zoya was exhausted herself, suffering the aftereffects of the adrenaline of the rush to find Alex as well as the fight to liberate him, plus the fact that she hadn't slept in a day and a half.

And she needed a drink. Her body hurt from the activity and the daylight and the fact that she'd gone fifteen hours without any alcohol for the first time in many months.

She had a couple more vials of cocaine for quick energy in her bag, and she wondered if she should just go ahead and do a line to be ready for a long afternoon of very serious security work.

Then her phone buzzed, and the thought passed. She scooped it out of her black North Face down jacket and looked at the text she'd received.

Coming up the hill now.

She typed out a response. **Park twenty-five meters from entrance next to my van, get out, approach one at a time.** She grabbed the Uzi that had been sitting on a table next to the door, put the sling over her neck, and extended the collapsible stock.

She put her backpack on, as well, in case things didn't go as planned and she needed to get the hell out of here.

The group of red deer skittered away moments later, and Zoya saw a single black SUV making its way up the winding driveway. An older-model Range Rover, it eventually halted in front of the wooden chalet next to her van, just as Zoya had directed.

She stepped out onto the covered front porch, keeping herself shielded from the bright afternoon sun, and she stood there, her Uzi slung around her neck, her hands on the grip and foregrip and the barrel pointed in the low ready position.

Three men climbed out in all; they looked at her and they looked around, and then a bearded man in an unzipped ski jacket began approaching the chalet while the rest stood behind.

When he closed to within a few meters, he said, "Transit?"

She nodded.

"I'm Braunbaer."

Zoya spoke enough German to know that the man's code name was Brown Bear.

He opened his coat wider now and showed off an HK MP7, slung down to his waist.

"My sidearm is in my pack," he said, jerking a thumb towards a brown rucksack over his shoulder that was clearly laden with gear.

"Okay," she said, stepping to the side so that he could enter.

The man passed by her and looked around at the property. "This place is too big for four of us to cover effectively."

Zoya knew he was right; she'd been thinking the same thing since she'd arrived around dawn at the two-story, seven-thousand-square-foot building. "Trompette picked it, not me," she said, and Braunbaer just nodded, then waved the next man up.

The second arrival on the porch was Black, short and in good shape. Maybe thirty-five, he had eyes that told Zoya he'd been in some sort of military or paramilitary force for his entire adult life, if not before.

With a surprised smile that told Zoya these men had not been expecting to be working with a woman, the man said, "I'm Ifa."

She detected an African accent, east coast, perhaps Somalia, Ethiopia, or Eritrea, but she couldn't be sure. She had no idea what kind of code name Ifa was, nor did she really care.

"Pleased to meet you," the man said with a handshake that caused Zoya to awkwardly remove her hand from her weapon. "Parlez-vous français?"

"Oui," Zoya responded.

"Bon." In French he continued. "My English is not so good." He opened his jacket to reveal a folded-stock Benelli tactical shotgun hanging down from its two-point sling.

"Come on in," she said, and then he passed inside.

The third man was bigger, a little older, and she detected an immediate macho swagger to him. He looked at Zoya as if she were a selection on a dessert cart at a restaurant, and she furrowed her brow at this.

"I'm Bello," he said.

"Bello," she repeated. It meant "handsome" in Italian, and Zoya fought the urge to roll her eyes. He opened his jacket; a Beretta AR70/90 hung there, a high-quality Leupold scope on its top rail. Zoya liked the idea of having a bigger gun here in case they needed to defend this location from attack. The AR70/90 was the battle rifle of the Italian army, and it was accurate to much farther distances than either Braunbaer's HK, her Uzi, or Ifa's shotgun.

He extended his hand and she took it as she had with Ifa, but then he lifted her hand. His head came down in a bow, and he kissed her on her knuckles.

She let him do it but returned no warmth his way. He rose and smiled, keeping his eyes on hers as he passed.

She was on a mission to keep some dumb banker secure until some other dumb bankers came and took him away, and it looked to her like one of her colleagues was on a mission to get laid.

She shut, locked, then bolted the door, then hooked a wooden chair below the latch, providing a little more security to the front entrance.

Braunbaer was in the process of taking off his jacket and hat at the table near the entrance.

Zoya warned him, "The heater's not working. It's just the fireplaces."

The German sighed and kept his jacket on.

Ifa immediately headed to the fireplace here in the living room, grabbed a log lying on the hearth, and tossed it onto the flames. "I hate the cold," he said softly.

Bello mumbled, "Fucking Trompette."

In her handler's defense, Zoya said, "He needed a place fast, right between Zurich and Geneva. The bank down there is calling the shots. This isn't perfect, but it's just for a few more hours. We should be out of here tonight."

Braunbaer looked around some more. "Where's the package?"

"He's upstairs. Sleeping, I expect."

"You drug him?"

"Would have. Didn't have to. He'd apparently been up a couple days. I handcuffed his wrist to a bedpost. He's docile. I think he's still in a little shock."

Braunbaer said, "People can break out of cuffs."

"Not this guy," Zoya said distractedly, looking through wooden blinds out a front window to the drive.

Ifa turned away from the fire, still rubbing his hands together. "You think he'll try to escape?"

She shrugged. "He seems to want to be in the same place as the phone he had on him. He says it's holding the data. I have the phone, so I doubt he'll try to bolt." She shrugged. "Still . . . we need to keep an eye on him as well as on the perimeter."

Zoya's own phone rang, and she answered via her earpiece. It was Broussard, so she stepped into the kitchen.

She answered, "Transit."

Broussard said, "The men have arrived?"

"Yeah. Everything is fine."

"Bon. Did Braunbaer tell you yet?"

She cocked her head. "Tell me *what*?"

"You will report to him. *He's* in charge."

Zoya didn't like this at all. This was her op; these guys were just backup. "You were supposed to send me security *assistance. I'm* running this."

"You will do as you are told. You know better than I do that you're holding on by a thread. A few more hours with no access to a bar and you're going to be a mess. I'd send you home now, pay you for the excellent work you somehow managed to accomplish early this morning, but the bankers will be there by nineteen hundred hours, and I am holding out hope that you can keep it together till they come to retrieve Velesky and take him to Geneva."

Though offended, she felt a slight wash of relief come over her. With luck, she could be at a hotel in Interlaken by eight p.m., in the lobby bar downing her first of many vodkas on ice with a twist of lemon by 8:02.

She wasn't going to admit this to her handler, however.

"This is bullshit."

"You've done a good job. Finish up there and when Braunbaer releases you, go somewhere and get your mind right, because I will need you again."

Zoya let it go. "Seven p.m. for the meet, right?"

"That's correct. The bankers wanted to drive Velesky back to Geneva after dark. I assured them we had everything under control. What's the state of the package?"

"Under control," she replied flatly.

"Excellent. Give the phone with the stolen data to Braunbaer."

"This is bullshit," Zoya muttered again as she hung up the call, reached into her jacket, and pulled out Velesky's iPhone. She returned to the living room and handed it over to Braunbaer without a word.

The German mercenary pocketed the device, then pulled four walkie-talkies out of his backpack and handed them off to the group. After he did this, he looked to Zoya. "Wasn't my call to take over your op. Orders from the boss."

"Whatever," she said, and then she looked at him. "Clouds are supposed to move in by four p.m. It will be dark by five. I suggest we put two upstairs, two here. We'll need to keep watch on—"

The German turned away from her. "Ifa, you and Transit take the second floor. One of you in a window to the north, the other to the south. Alternate checks on the package . . . every fifteen minutes. Bello and I will be down here."

Bello said, "I brought some coffee, I'll get it brewed."

Braunbaer nodded, then tipped his head towards Zoya. "Bring her the first cup."

She didn't know how to read this; either he was saying Broussard had told him all about her, or else she just looked like death warmed over. Possibly both.

Or else he was just being chivalrous.

Zoya just nodded and headed for the stairs, telling herself she'd wait for the coffee, but she'd probably need that line of coke if she was going to have to spend four more hours looking out a window at trees and snow.

SIXTEEN

Court Gentry arrived at the northern-perimeter fence of the Saint Lucia property of Eddison John, attorney-at-law, as the clouds overhead burned off and the first rays of bright morning sunshine shone on the green ocean. He was well hidden in the thick foliage on the hillside, and after scanning the area a moment, he realized he could go around the fence instead of over it by advancing to the property's northwest corner, holding on to the last post before the cliffside, then swinging out and around onto the property, because no fencing ran along the sheer cliff itself.

This would mean he'd then have to cover fifty yards of the back garden to get to the main house, but there was impressive landscaping all around the steep hill between the property's edge and the home, and therefore plenty of opportunities to stay out of sight of sentries and cameras.

His plan was to slip by security and make it right up to his target. It was a Saturday morning. He imagined his target would be home, so he knew he had to separate the lawyer from his family to speak with him.

And then, when he had Eddison John alone, Court would be as menacing as possible, along with the promise that he was the nicest person John would come across as long as the Russian data was in his possession.

. . .

Twenty minutes later, Court was within sight of the two doors leading into a walk-out basement that functioned as a sublevel floor on the slope of the hill, directly below a bored-looking sentry on the main floor back deck and out of view, and he scanned the area in front of him, looking for both threats and opportunities.

Still fifteen or so yards away from either of the two basement entrances, he noticed a security camera positioned to catch anything moving across the rear garden or on the lower-level patio approaching the doors, so he lowered all the way to prone and skirted the camera's view by creeping slowly between rows of flowery landscaping.

On the other side of the row of greenery between himself and the basement was a covered patio: a few tables and chairs, a hot tub with a waterfall fountain running from it against the wall, and an outdoor shower.

But Court saw no way to avoid the camera's lens for the last ten yards as he closed on the basement entrances.

Still lying prone, he pulled off his pack, unzipped a side pocket, and retrieved a small black device.

He reached back into his pack and pulled out a six-inch-tall adjustable tripod, and this he screwed to the square device, then adjusted the angle slightly.

Crawling through a thick row of yellow-bloomed frangipani flowers at the edge of the patio, he pushed the device out in front of him, exposing it to the camera high on the wall, and then with his free hand he moved the flowers just enough to be able to see the device on the wall, staring back down at the patio. With his hand on the wand, he flipped a switch, and a bright green laser dot shone on the wall a few feet low and to the left of the camera.

He made one-handed adjustments to the tripod until he was sure the laser beam was hitting the camera's lens dead center, and then he backed out of the flowers, looked around to make sure no one was in view, and stood up.

The laser pointer would flare out the camera instantly, and although there was every reason to believe anyone monitoring the feed in real time would come and check on the device, he figured he'd have at least a minute to make his way into the building and put himself in a position to take control of the guard force.

Hummingbirds flitted in the air close by, making their way between the bright blooms all around as Court pressed on alongside the patio, passing the bubbling hot tub with the waterfall fountain and stepping into the outdoor shower, stopping at a smoked-glass door.

Court assumed this door would lead either to an indoor shower or directly into a bathroom, and he assumed it would be locked. He reached into his pack and retrieved his pick set, but after doing this, he tried the latch and it gave way.

Court stowed his pick set and drew his Glock 19, then silently opened the door. He found himself in an ornate shower stall, large enough to accommodate a half-dozen adults. He heard no noise in the adjoining bathroom, so he slipped in.

Country music was playing on an overhead stereo, and this surprised Court because he'd not expected the locals to be listening to twangy country, though he admitted to himself he didn't know much at all about the West Indies and their customs.

Slipping out of the bathroom and into a basement-level bedroom, he immediately discerned that this space was saved for guests. No one had used the bathroom in some time, the bed was made, and there were no clothes or other day-to-day items lying around.

With his pistol low in his hand, he cracked the bedroom door and found himself looking up a hallway that ran to a kitchen on his right and a staircase on his left.

The kitchen was as empty as the guest room, but the coffeemaker on the counter was halfway through brewing a pot, and there were cups and a few dirty dishes in the sink. Shifting his gun to the right, he saw a large den with magnificent views over the patio and the back lawn, and out to the ocean. High-end audiovisual equipment lined a wall, and a big wraparound sofa looked like it could accommodate ten people.

A large cross hung over the massive TV, and religious candles covered a table in a hall that led off the den.

Before Court had time to think about it, he heard a new noise coming over the sound of the country music piping through the house. The squeak of a chair, to his left, caused Court to spin his weapon in the direction of a hallway off the kitchen. There was an open doorway in the middle of the hall, and as he closed on it with stealth and peeked inside, he found it to be a small security room, just a desk with one large monitor on it. Camera feeds from around the property were broadcast on the screen. A man sat with his back to Court, his hand on his chin and his elbow on the table, an iPhone in his other hand that he was clearly more interested in than in doing his job. The whited-out image of the camera on the walk-out basement patio was in the upper right corner of the monitor, and the guard apparently hadn't even noticed it yet.

Court needed to capture the security guard, and he considered destroying the security equipment, but then he thought better of it. The GRU officer known by the CIA as Matador wouldn't arrive for another hour and a half, but he easily could have associates already in country, and Court might find himself with a need to defend this place.

Quickly he decided it would be smarter to turn off the security system rather than destroy it in case he needed visibility around the property.

Court backed up a few steps, holstered his weapon, then took off his black backpack. From it he removed some cordage and tape. Leaving the pack on the basement kitchen floor, he began moving forward again.

The bored security man was not going to be bored for much longer.

Eddison John drove his jet-black Lincoln Navigator along steep and winding Anse La Raye road, twisting his way back to his residence from Soufriere Evangelical Church. There were only a few clouds in the sky, and he could tell his beautiful island would be in for another absolutely beautiful day.

It was unfortunate, he thought, that he'd have to spend the majority of this perfect Saturday in his office.

Eddison had four children, aged nine months to fourteen years, and all of them were seated behind him now, making various noises. His two older boys passed a mobile phone back and forth sharing TikToks, his nearly eight-year-old daughter talked to her mom from the back seat about her upcoming birthday party, and Eddison's nine-month-old daughter loudly mimicked the Creole music playing over the radio.

The Navigator was a nice ride but not particularly well suited for taking on the narrow and winding roads here on the western side of the island. Seating-wise, it was perfect; it was the only vehicle he owned for driving his family of six around, but it was big and lumbering, and the Lincoln wasn't even in the top five of his favorite cars to drive.

John had an extensive automobile collection, worth well in excess of seven million USD. He loved to cruise alone or with his wife all over the island. The only downside to being a luxury-car owner here was the roads near his house, where it was difficult to ever get up to any real speed, and then for only a few seconds before he'd have to shift down and slow to a crawl to navigate his way up or down a steep hill or a hairpin turn.

Still, he normally took his Ferrari to work in the mornings, or sometimes his McLaren 720s Spider, his BMW i8 electric, or one of his two Porsches.

Saturday family drives to church for youth group and choir practice, and Sunday drives to church, however, were *always* in the big black Lincoln.

He pulled up to the entrance to his property, four acres of a beautifully landscaped decline that led to a cliff over the ocean, and stopped in front of the gate. Normally he just had to wait a second or two for whichever of his guards was monitoring the cameras to push a button to swing the gate open, but he sat patiently for thirty seconds and still the iron gate had not moved.

Slightly frustrated, he rolled down his window and punched his gate code into the box.

While he did this, his wife, Michaela, leaned closer to him. "What do we pay those guys for?"

Eddison nodded and shrugged. "It's Lewis, Toyon, and Toyon's brother today. Not exactly the A-team."

Michaela chuckled.

The gate opened, and soon he put his big SUV back into gear and rolled forward towards the massive detached garage to the south of the house, leaving the gate open behind them.

Once he had parked, Michaela took baby Elysha out of her car seat, William and Michael shot ahead to the front door, and Aisha continued talking to her mom about plans for her party.

Eddison John followed his family past his luxury cars, out of the garage, and towards the front door of the home. His boys and older daughter then all shot upstairs to their rooms, and Michaela put Elysha in the playpen in the den on the ground floor with no dispute from the toddler.

The man of the house decided to go upstairs to change out of his suit before heading into the office for a few hours, and Michaela began preparing lunch in the ground-floor kitchen.

As Eddison headed for the stairs, his wife called after him. "Eddie? Toyon isn't on the balcony."

Eddison waved his hand while he headed up towards the second floor. "The guys are probably in the gate house again, watching Australian cricket."

"Terrific," John's wife muttered, then repeated herself from earlier. "What do we pay them for?"

John wasn't as bothered as his wife. "It's Saturday," he said in reply.

At the top of the stairs, he went down a long hallway, passing the four kids' bedrooms before entering the main bedroom. Here he loosened his tie as he headed over to his walk-in closet.

Eddison John's closet was larger than the main bedroom in an average house, and he didn't have to share it with his wife because she had an equally large space on the other side of the bathroom, next to the hidden entrance to the panic room. Row upon row of suits, casual wear, shoes, and even some of his fishing gear lined the walls of John's personal wardrobe; a window at the back faced away from the ocean towards the front garden and then the street out front, and there were multiple seating options and a floor-length mirror against the wall.

He stepped in, then turned to drop his suit coat on a love seat against the wall.

But midmovement, he froze.

A white man sat on the love seat. He wore a backpack over one shoulder, a black T-shirt, and dark brown cotton/nylon pants, and he looked up at John with a casual expression on his clean-shaven face.

The Saint Lucian filled his lungs as if he were about to shout, but the stranger put his finger over his lips to silence him.

And then John looked down and saw the gun. The man's right hand was wrapped around a black pistol that rested on his knee.

Before he could speak, the white man spoke in an American accent. "Dude, your closet is bigger than my last apartment."

Eddison croaked out a hoarse question. "What . . . what *is* this?"

The man used the gun as a pointer, and he aimed it for the open door to the bedroom. "Shut that so we don't disturb anyone else."

John reached back and closed the closet door with a trembling hand. As he did this, he said, "I . . . I have armed security."

"You have *disarmed* security."

John blinked. Blinked again. "They're dead?"

The white man shook his head. "They've been restrained and placed in the attic. I told them if they make a sound, I'll shoot them in the face. They seemed agreeable."

"Who . . . are you?"

"That's up to you. I can be a slight inconvenience in your day . . ." The man paused. "Or I can be something else."

"What do you want?"

The white man looked at him as if the answer were obvious. "A package was hand-delivered to this address yesterday evening. I want it. That's *all* I want. Hand it over, and I disappear."

Eddison just stood there, his tie half off, his shaking hands at his sides. Perspiration appeared on his high forehead. When he spoke, he said, "My children, my wife . . . they are here."

"I know that." Again, the man casually pointed the gun at him for emphasis. "And *you* can keep them safe."

John's eyes widened; they were rimmed with tears suddenly, and then the muscles in his neck tensed. "You would hurt my family?"

"Not me," the American said. After another brief pause, he added, "I am not doom, but I *am* the harbinger of doom."

"What the devil is *that* supposed to mean?"

SEVENTEEN

Court Gentry again used the handgun to motion to a claw-foot upholstered stool just across from the love seat. "Let's talk."

The Saint Lucian moved to the stool and sat down.

"Are you armed?" Court asked.

"No, sir. The guards are armed, *were* armed, but I personally do not believe in guns."

Court chuckled softly, then adjusted the Glock on his knee to point directly at the man across from him. "It's *really* important that you believe in this one, okay?"

John nodded slowly as he looked down the weapon's barrel. "I do."

Satisfied, Court holstered his pistol under his T-shirt, leaned forward, and put his forearms on his knees. "I might not look like it, but I'm actually the friendliest, most agreeable person who's going to come asking for that package today."

The attorney said, "You *don't* look like it, no."

Court was impressed by the man's relative composure considering the circumstances, though he could register the lingering terror in John's eyes and the tension in the muscles of his neck. Court saw the cues; the man was dealing with a fight-or-flight reaction.

He spoke slowly and calmly to ease the man's panic. "First, how many security are here on the property?"

"Three."

Court nodded, satisfied that the man hadn't tried to lie to him. He then asked, "Why aren't there more?"

"Why should there be? I didn't know you were coming."

"With the arrival of that package from Russia, you should have been beefing up security, not giving them the weekend off."

John seemed confused. "Why? What's so special about a phone?"

Court hadn't known he was here to retrieve a phone specifically, but he gave no appearance of surprise. "You haven't looked at the data on it yet?"

Eddison John just shook his head.

Court took the man at his word, and found this to be good news. The fact that John didn't know what was on the device might well go a long way to keeping him and his family alive. Still, the American wasn't here to worry about the Johns' well-being; he was here to retrieve the package.

"A lot of people want that information," he said.

"Well, only one of them has come to my home to threaten me for it."

Court sighed, looked at his watch. "I'm not the only one. I'm just the *first* one. There's a guy on the way from Switzerland, and I'm pretty sure he won't come alone."

"Why Switzerland?"

"I have no idea. They didn't tell me."

"*They* don't tell you everything, do they?"

"Not even close. But *they* did say he could be here as early as ten forty-five. It's ten now. If you give me the phone you received, I'll secure you and your family in your panic room and release your guards."

"How do you know about my—"

Court ignored the question. "You can then call the local cops and wait for rescue. If we hurry, you might never have to deal with the guy on his way. Trust me . . . *that's* your best-case scenario."

John seemed unconvinced. He'd recovered somewhat from the prospect of being killed in his closet, and now he was the one asking questions. "Who are you?"

Court lied. "I'm from the bank."

"*What* bank?"

"A bank in the U.S. We have an interest in securing that data."

"Why did Krupkin send it to me?"

Court did show a little confusion now. "I assumed you knew why he sent it."

"I haven't spoken with that man in two years. I haven't done any business in Russia since the beginning of the war. I was very surprised to receive a package from him, and more surprised when it was just a plain mobile phone."

Court said, "Apparently neither one of us knows anything about that phone, except for the fact that somebody will be here within the hour to kill you for it, so we're just wasting time talking."

John was clearly a very intelligent man, and even though he was facing an armed intruder, he pushed back on what the American said. "You wouldn't have come here if you didn't know what was on the phone."

Court just said, "Something about bank wire transfers moving into and out of Russia. That's really all I know."

"That doesn't make sense. I used to set up daisy chains of offshore Caribbean companies for Krupkin. I helped him hide his clients' money. I was his man down here in the West Indies.

"But . . . since the war started, everyone in Russia, including Krupkin, knows I won't touch their blood money any longer." He waved a hand around the room, indicating his entire property. "I took a lot of money from them . . . but . . . but they are monsters."

Court didn't think *all* Russians were monsters. He was in love with a Russian, after all. But he wasn't going to enter into this debate.

He said, "Speculate later. Hand the phone over now."

Suddenly, the Saint Lucian's wife's voice came through the bedroom door. "Eddie? Your lunch is ready."

Court gave Eddison a threatening eye. After a nod, the lawyer replied loud enough to be heard out in the bedroom. "Great. Just changing. I'll be right down."

Court said, "This might be a good time for you to think about your family and not your career as a shady offshore banking lawyer."

Eddison John cocked his head. "You don't know anything about me, do you?"

Now Court was getting annoyed. He stood up, looming over Eddison. "I know you're a crooked straw man helping the Russians hide their wealth in the West, and I know I'm not leaving without the phone, and it looks like you aren't afraid of me *or* the man on his way." He put his hand on the grip of his gun. "I'm going to have to remedy that."

Before he could draw the weapon, however, Court caught something out of the corner of his eye, a flash of light outside the window. He pulled his weapon, kept his gun more or less on Eddison seated on the stool, and headed to look out at the street.

He'd sat here for twenty minutes while waiting for John and his family to come home, and he'd studied the area carefully while doing so. He had an excellent view of the road for fifty yards or so both to the north and to the south, and to the south, where there had been no activity, he now saw a pair of work trucks parked, not exactly in front of John's residence but on an incline in the road maybe forty yards from the driveway.

A reflection off the window of a truck door closing had caught his eye, and now he was fully focused on the vehicles. There were markings on the side, and Court had to grab his binoculars out of his backpack with one hand, the other still holding the Glock, to make them out. After a few seconds, he asked, "What does L-U-C-E-L-E-C mean?"

"LUCELEC." Eddison pronounced it as an acronym. "Lucia Electric. It's our public utility service. Why?"

Men stood around both vehicles wearing high-visibility vests, work helmets, and T-shirts, and carrying tool bags.

Court extended the binoculars to Eddison. "Take a look."

The Saint Lucian stood, took the optics, and peered through them out the closet window. He shrugged. "It's just a utility crew."

"They weren't there when you came home."

"They must have just arrived."

Court took the binos back and started looking the men over. There appeared to be at least five; they were Black men in their twenties and thirties and could easily be local utility workers. "Do these guys work on weekends?"

"It's the West Indies, man. Power goes out all the time. If the power is out in the neighborhood, then they show up . . . eventually."

He said, "The thing is, Eddison, I'm hearing enough shitty country music over your speakers to say that your power is *not* out."

Eddison John cocked his head. He was confused but not scared. "Yeah . . . you're right." He looked again. "But those men . . . they are Saint Lucians."

Court said, "The people after that phone have the money and the reach to order up a crew of goons down here."

Three more men appeared from the other side of one of the trucks. Eight in total, Court noted. "That's a lot of utility guys."

Eddison said nothing.

After a few seconds, Court lowered the binos and put his hand on Eddison John's shoulder. "That's them. They're early. Get the rest of your family up here, and I'll release your guards. If you try to double-cross me, I promise you, you won't have to wait for those guys to come in here and fuck you up. I'll do it myself."

Eddison John rushed for the door of the closet, frantic to get his wife and daughter upstairs into the panic room with the rest of his family before the men entered the house.

EIGHTEEN

Court looked again through his binos at the crew on the road. They were still forty yards from the driveway entrance, but now they were most definitely eyeing the big house.

And then, in unison, the men began walking down the hill in the direction of the driveway. He didn't see guns, but they carried tool bags over their shoulders, and Court didn't think it took much imagination to figure they'd have their firearms jammed in there.

His phone buzzed in his pocket, and he tapped his earpiece.

"Go."

It was Lacy. "Good news. It looks like Matador won't be there for a while."

"Explain."

"It's a forty-five-minute drive from the airport to you, and he should have landed five minutes ago, but instead his aircraft banked to the west, away from the airport. It's still in the air now."

Lacy thought she was delivering good news, but Court suddenly had a very bad feeling.

"Where is the plane?"

After a moment, she said, "It continued north along the coast of the island, and now it's banking to the east. Maybe he's going to land from the north."

Louder, Court said, "Where is he in relation to this property?"

Another pause, and then she responded with confusion. "That's weird. He's about to fly right over you."

Fuck, Court thought, because he suddenly understood everything that Lacy did not.

Major Luka Rudenko finished the last of the tangerine he'd been eating, wiped his hands on a cloth napkin, and then picked up the glass of orange juice in front of him, drinking it empty. Looking out the window of the Bombardier Global 6000 at the ocean just seven thousand feet below, he appeared to be nothing more than any bored commercial airline passenger, although he was in a high-end corporate jet, seated alone in the elegant cabin.

He absent-mindedly picked at the bandages on his left ear; the wound there itched a little, and the horrid bruise on the left side of his forehead had only deepened and darkened in the past twenty-four hours. Still, he'd taken no pain medicine, preferring to keep himself sharp for today's operation, not that he expected nearly as much trouble in Saint Lucia as he'd encountered in Switzerland.

Rudenko had been in the field for over ten years, and as comfortable as his present environs were, he wanted *out* of the field. Most of his work was not in the cabins of luxury private jets on his way to the Caribbean. No, serving as an officer in GRU's most elite team meant constant danger, often terrible conditions, and an uncertain future. GRU operational-level assets were still being sent into eastern Ukraine, now Russian-held territory but still very much in dispute, and vicious partisans there made every drive down the street a potential lethal encounter.

He'd known dozens of colleagues who had died in the last year alone.

Luka Rudenko was a damn fine assassin, but he'd done his time, and now he wanted the fruits of his labor.

GRU majors were low on the pecking order of the siloviki; the wealth of the nation was normally passed off to colonels and above, but a promotion from major to lieutenant colonel for Rudenko would mean more opportunity for the graft that was as common to the fabric of the nation as vodka and caviar. He could sock money away for his escape plan: not billions, but a million or two, for sure—a decent dacha on a decent lake somewhere, a new BMW instead of the Hyundai Solaris he now drove on those few trips back home to Khimki, the northern suburb of Moscow where he lived.

And he'd get his desk in Moscow, and this would get him out of the field before he was inevitably killed in the service of his nation.

He turned his thoughts away from his long-term plans as he picked at a croissant on the plate in front of him. He glanced up for the first time at the only other man in the cabin, the copilot of the flight, who stood up front by the main door and stared back at Luka anxiously.

Sweat drenched the armpits of the copilot's white uniform. He wore a wireless headset and a nylon cord hooked around his waist on one end, with the other end affixed to a metal grab bar in the little galley at the front of the aircraft.

The flight crew of this jet was from Macedonia, but the copilot spoke English to his single passenger. With obvious nerves in his voice, he said, "Sir . . . I am sorry to keep repeating myself . . . but you *must* prepare. We have less than one minute."

Luka did not respond. He finished the croissant and then casually rose from his cabin chair. His suppressed Steyr S9-A1 9-millimeter pistol was in a retention holster on his hip, and a long knife was strapped to his left thigh.

Standing in the aisle of the Bombardier now, he looked at the copilot at the main cabin door and gave him a curt nod. "Let's do this."

The copilot cocked his head. "Your . . . your parachute?"

Luka smiled a little; he was fucking with the copilot. Now he reached down to his right and grabbed an Aerodyne ZULU nine-cell parachute rig, stepped into it, and buckled himself in, all in less than twenty seconds. The copilot's nerves showed no sign of decreasing, however.

"I have to open the door, sir."

"Then open it already," Luka said, now grabbing a small black backpack and slinging it to his chest, wrapping a bungee cummerbund behind his back just below his chute and bringing it around to the front to Velcro it tightly to his body and the pack, securing it further.

The plane had been depressurized and the pilot had slowed to 110 knots, but even so, when the copilot pulled open the door, the sound of wind rushing by the hatch, along with the drone of the engines, was deafening inside the cabin.

Luka placed goggles over his eyes and moved forward towards the open hatch.

"Ten seconds," the copilot shouted, his back braced against the bulkhead behind him, one hand on the strap attached to him, his knees locked.

Luka crouched right next to him at the open door now, looked at the nearly terror-stricken man, and gave him a slight wink, then leapt out the hatch of the Bombardier and into the warm sunny sky. Buffeted by the 120-mile-per-hour winds, he hurtled towards Earth at maximum velocity.

After first getting his three older kids out of their rooms and into the hallway, Eddison John rushed downstairs to the den, calling for his wife as he did so. "Michaela? Michaela?"

He found her in the dining room, setting the table. Immediately she stopped what she was doing. "What's wrong?"

The lawyer scooped Elysha up from the floor of her playpen and shouted at his wife. "Panic room! Now. No time to explain!"

Michaela started for the stairs but then stopped. "The kids!"

"All upstairs. Go!"

Court continued to demand information from Angela Lacy as he saw the men in the front lawn drawing pistols from their tool belts, then ditching all extraneous gear in the yard. While they did this, the two LUCELEC trucks began rolling forward towards the house. "What's Matador's altitude?"

"Uh . . ." Lacy hesitated. "Seven thousand feet. He's over you right now."

"They depressurized the aircraft," Court said. The only reason the plane from Zurich would fly that low directly over the target was if Matador was planning on parachuting directly *onto* the target.

And if Matador was sailing out of the sky towards the house right now, that meant exponentially worse odds for the defenders of this place. From what he knew about the Russian assassin, he alone posed the same amount of danger as the eight local goons, if not more.

Lacy finally put the pieces together herself. "Wait . . . you don't think Matador would try to para—"

Court hung up on her, pulled a folding knife from his pocket, and flipped it open. He rushed out of the closet, then out of the bedroom. Turning right, away from the stairs and away from the three children standing there confused, he headed to the far end of the hall and opened a door, revealing an attic staircase. There, on the stairs just beyond the door, the three security men were bound, their hands behind their backs and their bodies taped together, and they were gagged with more duct tape.

They looked at him with terror, but as he began cutting them free, he knew the real danger they faced would be coming up the stairs in just moments.

Luka pulled his rip cord at seven hundred meters over the ocean; the canopy opened by five hundred, and then he grabbed the control lines and began steering towards the property on the cliffside in front of him.

He'd chosen the manicured back lawn as his landing zone. If he'd been alone, or if he had a good working relationship with the other men in this crew Drexler had arranged, he would have touched down right on the terracotta roof and made entry through a second-floor window.

But though the local hires had been told to expect a blond man parachuting in to help them, he sure as hell did not want to show up in the middle of the house without them knowing he was there.

The only way he had to deconflict with them was to approach from behind and enter the lower part of the building with stealth, then make his presence known from behind cover.

Luka landed expertly on the manicured rear lawn, released his harness with a single movement, and then drew his pistol and ran for the doors right in front of him on the patio. He'd make his way up from the basement, carefully, behind the attack on the first and second floors. With luck the locals would do the heavy lifting, and he'd have nothing to do today but retrieve the phone, ensure that the man who'd received it was dead, and then hitch a ride back to the airport with Drexler's locals.

. . .

While Court worked on releasing the three security officers, he spoke softly and quickly. Their mouths were taped shut, so he had something of a captive audience. "Listen to me. I'm on your side. You've got eight men approaching from downstairs. There's another guy around here somewhere. They'll all be armed, and they'll kill both you guys and the Johns, whether you fight back or not." Court shrugged a little as he worked. "Don't know about you, but *I'd* rather go down fighting."

The men appeared terrified, but Court was all business as he sliced through tape between their wrists and over their arms, and as he pulled the tape off the first man's mouth, the local said, "What the fuck is this about?"

"Your boss has enemies. You knew that when you took this job. If you call the police right now, how long till they get here?"

The man replied, "Twenty, maybe thirty minutes."

"Then forget the cops," Court said.

"Where are our guns?" the second man to have his tape removed asked.

As Court cut the last man's hands free, he said, "I'll give them to you when I know we're all on the same side. I'm putting the family in the panic room. You will position at the second-floor balcony and hold off the attack until I call for you, and then you can join them."

Michaela and Eddison made it back upstairs with the baby, and they stood with their bewildered children as Court and the three guards came running up the hall.

Gentry's pistol was out at the low ready in case one of the guards ignored his warning about the true threats approaching, and when Court made it to Eddison, he said, "Tell these guys to do what I say."

The attorney looked at his men, and at his family. "Whatever this man tells you to do, you will do. We are all in danger."

The sound of the front door being kicked in downstairs perfectly illustrated his remark.

Court opened the closet on his right, revealing the handguns he'd taken from the guards, lying on the floor. The three men leapt for them, frantic to get to the stairs before the attackers made it up here, and Court led the way back to the main bedroom as the John family trailed behind.

While the guards opened fire on the men trying to come up the stairs, and while the men coming up the stairs returned fire with pistols and pump shotguns, Court got all of Eddison's family, save for Eddison himself, into the panic room. It was ten feet by twelve, encased in steel, and there was a landline phone, bottled water, and a chemical toilet, and benches along the wall on both the left and the right. The three older kids sat on one side; they were still dressed in their church clothes, although the boys had removed their ties like their dad.

John's wife beckoned her husband in, while still keeping a suspicious eye on the stranger who seemed to be in charge at the moment.

"Eddie! Get in here."

"Sorry," Court said. "Your husband and I have some business first. Hang tight." He shut the door. It wouldn't lock without someone on the inside bolting it, but through the heavy steel door the family wouldn't hear the men's conversation outside, and they'd be protected from any stray gunfire.

As soon as the door was closed, Eddison looked nervously at the door to the bedroom. The gunfire was growing more intense by the second.

"What now?" he asked Court.

"The phone."

Sweat dripped from the bald-headed man's face. "I can't give it to you."

"The last guy who tried to hold on to that data is lying in a morgue in Zurich. You want to be on a slab in an hour?"

John took off his glasses and rubbed his eyes free of the perspiration draining into them. "No . . . I mean, I would give you the damn thing if I had it here."

"Where is it?"

"It's in Castries."

"What's Castries?"

"A town. Thirty minutes north. Where my office is."

"Bullshit," Court said. "The package was delivered *here*. Not to your office. It arrived last night."

"I didn't trust the phone. I thought it might be a trap."

BURNER 117

"A *trap*?"

"Yeah, loaded with malware to break into my own systems. People have tried it before. Russians, specifically. The Kremlin's been after me for the past year." He shook his head in disbelief. "My wife made me get bodyguards, but I didn't really think they'd come here to make trouble."

John continued. "An unsolicited communication device couriered here from Igor Krupkin? Fuck that, man. As soon as it showed up, I drove it to the office myself and put it in an air-gapped safe there. No radio waves can penetrate."

The shouts of men at the stairwell came through between the pops of gunfire. It was impossible to tell who was getting the upper hand, but Court assumed the eight attackers would overrun the three defenders before long.

"I was curious about what Krupkin sent me, of course, but I'm not a fool. I was going to go and look at it today, to try and decide what to do with it. I seriously considered dropping it in the bay, to be honest."

Court evaluated the man as truthful. "Give me the address and the code to the safe."

NINETEEN

Luka Rudenko entered the walk-in basement of the large property and cleared the area with his pistol quickly. There was a pool table in a den, a kitchen, some couches with video game consoles and kids' toys lying around, and beyond this was a hallway with doors leading off on both sides.

The Russian pushed forward; he assumed the stairs would be at the end of the hall, but he was growing increasingly concerned by the amount of gunfire upstairs. He'd fully expected the locals to encounter armed security, but it seemed as if the defenders of the property had been ready. It was no great surprise that Eddison John would expect trouble after receiving the phone from the Russian courier, but still . . . to Luka's practiced ear, the security men on the property were firing from a defended position, and the attackers were having a hard time getting the best of them.

He resigned himself to the fact that he'd have to go up there himself and start shooting, deconflicting with Drexler's local boys and then blasting it out with Eddison John's rent-a-cops.

He'd come prepared to do this. In addition to the Steyr pistol on his hip, in his backpack he carried a pair of fragmentation grenades and a pair of smoke grenades, as well as several extra magazines for his handgun.

He headed down the hallway towards the stairs, but on his way he cracked open each door he passed, checking to make sure John wasn't somewhere down here.

Upon checking a door on his left, he found a small security room, just a desk with some monitors, though everything was powered down for some reason.

Quickly, Luka shut himself in the room, sat at the desk, and turned the equipment back on via a switch on a power strip.

In seconds, the monitor in front of him began broadcasting camera images from around the property.

He reached for the mouse, clicked on one little screen and then another, enlarging them to get an accurate picture of the location and of the disposition of both friend and foe.

He saw two security men on a mezzanine over a family room, firing down at several attackers. There were bodies on the staircase; he didn't take the time to determine who they were, he just kept clicking on cameras for more visibility on the scene.

And then he stopped when he enlarged the camera feed from the upstairs main bedroom. A Black man in a white dress shirt and blue slacks was just standing there by his bed, agitated but unmoving, talking to a white man in a T-shirt with a backpack slung over his shoulder and a Glock pistol in his hand.

Quickly Luka realized the Black man was Eddison John, but he had no clue who the other person was. He was of average height, with dark brown hair, and athletically built though not particularly muscled. He didn't look like hired security; he didn't look like much of anything at all, but Luka noticed that even with the shooting going on nearby, the white man captured Eddison John's full attention.

He backed the video up a half minute or so, then hit play, reaching for the volume knob as he did so, because anyone having a conversation within fifteen meters of a gun battle *must* have been discussing something damn important.

The Russian watched and listened to John tell the American that the phone sent by Igor Krupkin was located in his office in Castries, and then he gave the location of the air-gapped safe it was housed in, and the combination, as well.

John mentioned that he'd not even reviewed the data yet.

This is too fucking easy, the Russian operative thought as he found a pen and an envelope and wrote all the information down on it.

He kept watching the video, but just when he was about to leave the room and head out to find a vehicle that would get him to John's office, the American upstairs demanded a car from the local attorney. John helpfully said he had a garage full of cars to choose from off the southern side of the house, and all the keys were kept in a lockbox on the wall with the combination 3-3-3-4.

Luka left the tiny basement security office with a satisfied smile on his face and avoided the fighting upstairs by retracing his steps back out the door to the rear of the property, where he immediately turned left and broke into a run.

The sound of gunfire had died down precipitously while Court and Eddison stood in the bedroom talking, and Court knew this probably meant the bad guys were going to be on them in seconds. At first he considered locking the rest of the family in the panic room while he took John along with him to his office, but he doubted he could get the man out of the property alive. The American had a plan, but it would be hard enough to execute it without bringing along an untrained partner.

He pulled open the panic room door and let John in; the attorney wrapped his arms around his wife and kids as he sat down. The whole family hugged and cried, but Court yelled at them.

"Lock the door!"

The shooting stopped completely, which told Court the three guards had likely been overrun, and he started to rush back for the walk-in closet and the window there, but just as he took his first step, the bedroom door opened.

Court raised his weapon but then lowered it. One of the guards stumbled in, clutching his stomach. He'd been shot; blood seeped through his fingers, but he was still on his feet.

In his other hand was a pistol, the slide locked back over an empty magazine. "They're coming!" the man grunted.

John had not yet sealed the door, so Court held it open while the security man lumbered by. "Just you left?" he asked the guard, who only nodded as he passed.

Eddison John took one last wide-eyed look at Court before he shut the door and latched the heavy bolt.

With the guard's proclamation that there were no more good guys alive on the landing, Court raised his pistol and began firing through the wall into the hallway as he ran towards Eddison's walk-in closet. After dumping several rounds, he shut the closet door as the bedroom door crashed open on the other side.

Court reloaded and then holstered his hot pistol, made it to the window and opened it, then climbed out, standing on a windowsill fifteen feet above manicured brush at the front of the Johns' home.

Quickly he knelt, grabbed the ledge, and scooted off, hung a second at full extension, and then dropped down onto the ground next to the bushes.

The massive garage was a freestanding building, impossible to miss forty yards away on his left as he faced the home, and he began running for it, first across the yard and then on the winding driveway that led between the garage and the road.

There were four garage doors; one was open, and as Court closed on it at a sprint, he peered into the darkness.

And then, right where his eyes were aimed, headlights switched on, their intense beams shining right back at him.

An engine revved, and a second later a red sports car all but flew out of the garage, directly towards Court.

He drew his pistol yet again, raised to aim it, but the speed of the oncoming vehicle was more than he'd bargained for. He fired off a shot as the barrel rose, striking the hood, but before he could level the gun and fire at the windshield, he realized he was going to be run down if he didn't get the hell out of the way. Instinctively he dove to his left, off the driveway and over a row of thorny bushes.

As he flew through the air, he saw that the car was a Ferrari, and he also saw a white man with blond hair and a chiseled jaw behind the wheel. Instantly he assumed this to be the Russian GRU agent code named Matador. The man was a cold-blooded killer; he'd murdered an Agency officer the day before in Switzerland, and Court knew the man would have no problem running him over now if he could.

Court hit the grass on the other side of the bushes, but something told him to keep going, to keep making distance from Matador's car, so he rolled three more times and then came up into a combat crouch.

The red Ferrari intentionally crashed into the bushes next to him, missing Court by four feet at most, but it did not slow. It skidded back to the left, flinging dirt and grass all over Court as it made it back onto the driveway, and then it raced out the open gate, squealing tires as it went to the left.

Left was north, and north was the direction of Eddison John's office.

Court ran as fast as he could for the garage, pulling his phone as he did so. He tapped a few numbers, then put the phone back in his pocket, holstered his pistol, and focused on his run.

Angela Lacy answered on the first ring, her voice coming through his earpiece.

He rushed his orders through labored breathing. "I have an address to give you. I need you to vector me there. I'm at the target property; I have to get to John's office in Castries before Matador does." He added, "He's got a sixty-second head start."

"You need me to come get you? I'm in Soufriere, to the south of you. I can—"

"I need you to do what I asked! Get me to the law office. Forty-nine Bridge Street."

Rushing, Lacy said, "Got it. Forty-nine Bridge, Castries. I'll get a route. Wait one."

Court found the key box open on the wall, then grabbed the first set of keys he saw. Pushing the button, he heard a beep, then turned to see the lights of a beautiful silver Porsche 911 Turbo blinking back at him.

"That'll work," he muttered to himself as he began running again.

He threw his backpack into the passenger seat of the open targa-top of the roadster, then leapt over the door and dropped behind the wheel. It was an older-model car, mid-1990s, he thought, but the engine turned over instantly and then roared like a lion as he stomped on the gas. He shifted into first and it lurched forward, squealing tires on the specially coated garage flooring.

Court raced out onto the driveway like a missile launch, only to see that one of the LUCELEC trucks had pulled into the gate and now blocked his path, approaching up the driveway directly between him and his only exit.

Instinctively, he jacked the wheel to the right, bounced through and over the same bushes Luka had just destroyed with the Ferrari, and skirted past the work truck.

He struggled to get the wheels back on the drive, and at first he over-corrected, hitting manicured landscape on the other side, but before he reached the gate he'd righted himself and he shot through, then stomped on the brakes and skidded to the left to follow the road to the north.

"Lacy, I need that route, *now*!"

"Head left out of the property!" she answered back quickly.

"Done! What's next?" he asked as he shifted into second gear.

"Just keep driving. You've got about ten miles on that road till you hit Castries. Where's Matador?"

"He's in front of me in a Ferrari. I'm in a Porsche, but I don't know which one is faster." Court wiped sweat from his eyes and peered through the windscreen of the tiny two-door.

"Wait," Angela said. "You are telling me that you're in a *car chase* with a Porsche and a Ferrari?"

"I'm not chasing *him*; I'm going for the phone. I've just got to get to it first somehow."

"I hate to tell you this, but you *are* chasing him. If Matador is in front of you, then he's probably on that same road. You'll have to go through him to get there first."

"Shit. Okay."

"What can I do to help?"

Court kept his eyes forward; he was all business now as he tried to control the 400-horsepower machine on the narrow and winding road. He could tell he was closing on the Russian GRU officer because as he hit a hairpin turn he could still see smoke in the air from the Ferrari's tires, and the black skid marks told Court that Matador knew how to drive and was pushing his powerful vehicle to its very limits.

"Get moving in this direction. I'll call you back when I get closer to town."

. . .

Luka steered the 2008 candy-apple red Ferrari F430 Scuderia through a descending turn that had him dropping down into first gear with the paddle shifter and tapping the brakes more than he'd like, but soon he was around the bend with a short stretch of straight road ahead. He floored the gas and shifted to second and then third, but then a small coupe pulled out of a gas station a hundred yards in front of him, forcing him to downshift again.

Looking in his rearview, he fully expected to see another sports car on his ass within seconds. The unknown American at the target location had shown incredible reaction time to avoid getting run over, and he'd been smart to keep moving farther from the drive in case the Ferrari tried to hit him on the lawn. He'd also been quick on the draw, and it was clear from the security camera footage that he was after the phone, same as Luka.

He didn't know exactly where he was going, so he slowed the car and tapped the address into his phone's map application now, holding the device with one hand and the steering wheel with the other as he whipped around the coupe and accelerated.

Once he had the route set, he saw that the app said he was twenty-four minutes away from John's office, but his phone wouldn't naturally assume he'd be driving a 500-horsepower race car, so Luka figured he could be there in fifteen.

Another glance in his rearview, and then the Russian sighed.

Whipping around the turn behind him was a silver Porsche. Even if he hadn't already seen it in John's garage, he would have known it was being driven by the American after the phone.

The Porsche was a couple hundred yards back, but soon it shot by the coupe Luka had just passed, skidded a little to avoid an oncoming taxi van, and then accelerated up the hill in the direction of the Ferrari.

Luka shifted into fourth now, but soon had to brake for another hairpin turn that sent him in the opposite direction. He turned until he was virtually facing his pursuer but on a higher portion of road that whipped around lava rock at the water's edge.

Smoke came from the silver Porsche's tires as the American decelerated into the turn, indicating to Luka that the unassuming-looking man had some amount of training in driving performance cars.

Still with one hand on the wheel, Luka called Drexler.

It took over twenty seconds for the call to go through, and during all this he swerved around slower-moving vehicles, alternately flooring it and applying the brakes to negotiate the bends in the road, benefiting from the paddles because, with a little effort, he could shift up or down without his one hand leaving the wheel.

While he waited, he flicked his eyes up into the rearview mirror to see the Porsche looming larger and larger behind him.

"Oui?" Drexler answered.

"The phone is at John's office, I'm ten minutes out, but an American at the original scene is in pursuit. He's after the phone, as well, and he's trying to get ahead of me."

"Who is he?"

"You tell me."

"I don't have a clue," Drexler said. "I just heard from the men at John's house. The four still alive, I mean. John and his family seem to have escaped."

"They're in a panic room on the second floor. Forget them; he hasn't accessed the phone so he doesn't know what's on it. Send those men to Castries. Forty-nine Bridge Street. I'll be gone by then, but if this American shows up after I do, they can deal with him."

Luka disconnected the call to Drexler without another word. The Swiss man was the commander of the overarching operation to regain control of the stolen data about Kremlin money moving into the West, not Luka himself, but right now, Luka was calling the shots. *He* was the asset on the ground, and he'd command Drexler until he achieved his objective.

He made yet another sharp turn, this time climbing up a switchback road away from the shoreline, and as soon as he straightened his wheels to keep climbing, a single brown goat stepped into his path. The bored-looking animal was unimpressed with the oncoming race car; it just ambled slowly along. The pavement was too narrow for Luka to avoid the goat, and the fiberglass Ferrari too brittle to just knock the two-hundred-pound animal out of the way without causing serious damage to the Ferrari's body, so the Russian was forced to slam on his brakes again, shifting back down to first in the process.

The goat continued slowly moving out of the way, and while he waited, Luka looked into his rearview to see the Porsche drifting around the turn, burning rubber and then straightening out and climbing, closing now to within one hundred meters.

Luka's pistol was in its thigh holster in easy reach, and he considered drawing it and firing out the back of the red two-door, but instead he waited another second for the animal in the road to move, and then he stood on the gas, just missing the goat on the right side. He accelerated from zero to fifty on a steep incline in just a matter of seconds.

The Porsche behind him had the momentum and the upper hand, however, and it closed confidently, only slowing when both vehicles neared another turn back to the north. They were still climbing up the winding road between tropical jungle and volcanic rock, the sea on their left when they headed north, the sea on their right when they headed south. After Luka made the next hairpin, he saw the climb continue on the tight road, with a sharp flora-covered cliff down a couple hundred yards on the left, and a sheer black wall of rock on his right reaching up to where the road switched back yet again above him.

The Porsche was no more than twenty-five yards back now, and Luka had seen the pistol in the man's hand on the security monitor earlier, so he knew that his adversary, whoever the fuck he was, was armed.

Luka also knew that both the car behind him and the gun behind him were in striking distance, but he was aware of one element in this that was decidedly in his favor. The Porsche was an older model; he was reasonably certain it would have a gearshift lever between the seats, as opposed to the paddle shifters Luka had on his steering wheel. The American needed both hands to drive on these winding, semicongested roads, whereas Luka could, with some difficulty, continue driving one-handed.

He unzipped his backpack in the passenger seat next to him and reached inside, a determined grin revealing itself on his face.

TWENTY

Court negotiated a hairpin turn with an adequately competent drift to the left, worrying all the while that he was shredding the Porsche's tires more and more with each of these rubber-stripping maneuvers. The Ferrari was thirty-five yards ahead of him now, and he shifted into second, then third, as he climbed the steep hill in pursuit.

Throughout the breakneck drive, while simultaneously worrying about a dozen different things, Court also spent brainpower wondering if Matador knew the combination to the safe at the office and, if so, how. He finally came to the uncomfortable conclusion that the GRU asset, who couldn't have been on Eddison John's property for more than a couple of minutes before rushing to get in a car to race towards the lawyer's office in Castries, had somehow heard the conversation between Eddison and Court in the upstairs bedroom.

It didn't take him long to suss out how this happened.

The security office. Matador had simply flipped the computer back on and found a camera with audio right there in the main bedroom.

Who the fuck puts cameras in their bedroom? Court thought, but then his mind returned to the problem at hand.

Court knew his primary objective was getting the phone, but he also knew there was no way around the Russian on these crazy ribbonlike roads, and he had no way of knowing if Matador had the resources to call others in Castries to have them go to the office and acquire the phone.

Court had to get to the office first, and to do this, he had to get Matador out of his way, both literally and figuratively.

He couldn't pull his weapon and continue to change gears on the manual-transmission car, so he decided he'd have to try to run the Ferrari off the road instead. He closed a little more to position himself for a PIT maneuver, but as he did so, he saw Matador's hand and arm appear out of the driver's-side window. He held something that he released, and a device the size of a baseball bounced in the road behind the Ferrari and just in front of the Porsche.

Even at these speeds, Court recognized it as a fragmentation grenade.

He jerked the Porsche to the right and then straightened back out, flooring it all the way, shooting closer to the slowing Ferrari.

In his rearview he saw a flash and then a cloud of black smoke, and he instantly heard the sound of a frag detonating.

Jesus Christ, he thought, but still he had no effective way to access and operate his handgun while driving the twenty-five-year-old Porsche.

He hoped like hell Matador had only brought a single grenade with him on this mission, and he continued closing, intending to strike the right rear quarter panel of the red Ferrari to spin the Russian assassin off the road at the next turn.

Tensing for the impact to come, he told himself he had to strike hard enough to have the desired effect to the other car, but not so hard that he either damaged his Porsche or barreled off the road himself into the palm trees or high brush or even off a damn cliff.

The Ferrari began to slow for the right turn; Court stayed on the gas, but when he was only fifteen feet or so from impact, he heard the unmistakable cracks of gunfire over the sound of his engine.

The rear window of the Ferrari spiderwebbed, Court's windshield took a round and then another, and Court was forced to slam on his brakes and duck down.

He skidded through the turn, stopping and stalling out in the grasses just off the road within a couple of feet of thick palm trees.

The Ferrari was already winding back up the hill to the south.

Court refired his engine and threw his car into reverse, then into first. He put the pedal to the floor and whipped around the turn to the south, then straightened out as he shifted into second.

For the next couple of minutes Court stayed on Matador's ass. Another grenade was dropped out the driver's-side window, but a lucky bounce for Court sent it off into the foliage on the left side of the road, and Matador had let the fuse cook off for just a hair too long, so the detonation was still fifteen yards ahead of Court's vehicle.

Together the two cars climbed higher, heading generally to the north but switching back to the south every few hundred yards, until Court saw a slightly less-sharp turn looming directly ahead of him. Beyond this was nothing but blue sky, indicating that just beyond the turn would be either a cliff or a steep hill, probably falling all the way back down to sea level and the water below.

Matador would have to slow for the turn, Court knew, and he decided to use this opportunity to strike the Ferrari from behind and knock both the car and the motherfucker behind the wheel off the mountainside.

He knew he couldn't fail to hit the Ferrari, or he himself would go off the side of the road. This tactic was almost as perilous for Court as it was for his intended victim, but since Matador was tossing grenades and Court couldn't even pull his sidearm, he saw no alternative.

He was thirty yards behind Matador as the Ferrari began to slow to make the turn to the right, but Court did not slow, and he closed quickly on the red vehicle from behind just as the Ferrari began its turn.

Fifteen yards from impact, Court braced himself, but just as he did so, he saw Matador's hand appear outside the vehicle for the third time. This time, however, he didn't drop something; instead he tossed it straight up into the air, and then his Ferrari skidded into a hard right turn.

As Court barreled down on the Ferrari's rear, he sensed movement on his right. A small canister dropped out of the sky through his open top, striking the roll bar before falling down and hitting his pack in the passenger seat.

It then bounced down on the floorboard.

It was a grenade.

Is this motherfucker made out of grenades?

He heard a pop and then a hiss. A thick cloud of red smoke spewed from the passenger-side floorboard, filling the cabin in seconds, and though Court was relieved the device wasn't a frag, he knew he was still in a hell of a lot of trouble.

And then Matador opened fire.

Court's windscreen cracked, glass peppered his face, and he shut his eyes to keep from being blinded. He ducked down to the left and, as he did this, he felt his Porsche deal a very glancing and inconsequential blow to the left rear end of the Ferrari.

Court was utterly astounded that Matador could negotiate a sharp turn at speed while firing accurately at a car behind him, but he didn't think about it for long. Instead, he just slammed on his brakes, desperate to remove the forward propulsion of his vehicle before he himself skidded off the road.

And in this endeavor, he failed. The kinetic energy that should have been absorbed by the impact was still in the car's momentum, and there was no way for him to stop.

As the candy-apple red Ferrari F430 Scuderia slewed right from the light impact and then completed the 180-degree turn to go higher up the hill, Court skidded sideways on screaming tires. He ran off the pavement on his left side, and then the Porsche 911 flipped.

The roll bar saved him from decapitation, but when the vehicle tumbled back over, right side up, it began sliding to the left, and then it rolled over the precipice beyond it.

Court ducked his head and hung on to the wheel for dear life, as the tiny car began crashing into thick palm trees sharply angled on a steep hillside, breaking limbs and trunks like they were twigs.

His body slammed hard to the left against the door and then banged towards the right, his head whipping around violently though his body was secured with his three-point seat belt. Red smoke continued billowing all around him.

He'd be a dead man without these trees, this he knew because as his car kept smashing and tumbling through them, the smoke grenade fell out and he caught a brief glimpse below through his cracked windscreen. The hillside was steep but not sheer, but even so, it was hundreds of yards of rocks and brush, all leading down to an ocean full of jagged boulders and roiling water.

If these palm trees weren't able to arrest his momentum, he'd tumble down into the volcanic rock at the seashore.

But with a final hard jolt, the Porsche came to rest, cradled in massive palm fronds. Green leaves almost as big as Court himself crowded the cabin around him.

He felt like he'd fallen down a flight of stairs. His seat belt had saved him, just as the trees had, but when all the noise and movement stopped, his head cleared enough for him to realize he was not out of danger.

Looking around carefully now, using a hand to move the big leaves out of the way, he could see the edge of the precipice above him by looking out the passenger-side window. He was only thirty feet below the road, though it had felt like he'd fallen much farther.

His neck hurt, he felt blood dripping down his back, and he had a feeling he was covered in contusions, but he considered himself lucky.

Until he looked back over his shoulder to get a better idea of his predicament, and the Porsche jostled in the trees. There was a cracking sound, and the car dropped a full foot before settling again.

Now he couldn't see anything but palm fronds. He was nestled in the treetops, green foliage pushing against every part of his head and upper torso, and the smell of the trees filled his nose along with the scent of burnt rubber and the residual fumes of the smoke grenade.

Court froze in place. Any movement whatsoever could send the car down through the trees, where it would impact with the hill and roll a couple dozen times before hitting the water.

Still, he was less worried about his own predicament than he was about the fact that he'd failed in his mission. Even if he found a way out of this, Luka would still get to the phone just a few minutes north of here well before he could.

He slowly and gingerly removed his phone from his waistband, tapped a key, and waited for Lacy to answer. His earpiece was gone, lost somewhere in the crash, as was his backpack full of gear, so he just carefully held the phone up to his ear.

"Six?" Angela said.

"It's me."

"What's going on?"

"I should say something cute like 'I'm just hanging out,' but to be honest, I'm stuck in a tree on a three-hundred-yard cliff face and it's pretty fucking terrifying."

"Why are you in a tree?"

"My car ran off the road."

"Up into a tree?"

"Pretty much. Tell me you are heading north."

She didn't answer immediately, showing Court that her focus wasn't on his well-being but on the mission instead.

"Where's Matador?"

Court sighed, then blew a swaying palm frond away from his mouth to talk. "I guess by now he's halfway to that phone."

"Shit." Lacy paused a beat, then said, "I can call the local police."

"Yeah, might as well. Give them the address to John's office. Tell them a Russian dude with blond hair is going to break into it in broad daylight. That might slow him down a little, though I imagine he'll be there and gone by the time the cops show up."

"Okay, I'm on the way to you."

Court sniffed and looked at the fronds all around him. "I don't know how you can help me."

"I have fifty feet of rope. Will that help?"

Court's eyebrows furrowed. "Why do you have fifty—"

The woman interrupted. "Because I'm not as useless as you thought I was. I'm still five minutes south of Eddison John's house, so I guess I'm fifteen minutes away from you. Can you hold on till I get there?"

"Holding on to something isn't going to do me a lot of good. I'll just sit here and hope I don't catch a strong breeze."

"Send me a ping on your exact location."

Court's eyebrows furrowed. "I don't know how to do that."

"What?" She was incredulous.

"I'm not really well practiced in the habit of giving out my location."

"Yeah, well, now that you're stuck in a tree, you might want to *get* in the habit." She explained the process of sending his location via his phone. Court did so, then told her again to call the cops.

"Got it," she said. "What will you be doing in the meantime?"

Court felt the palms sway again.

"Not a whole hell of a lot, Angela."

TWENTY-ONE

Major Luka Rudenko of the GRU took possession of Igor Krupkin's mobile phone shortly before noon.

He left the Ferrari on the street and vacated the neighborhood on foot moments later, just as police cars began rolling into view, and since Luka didn't know if the cops had his description, he avoided possible detection by dipping into a corner grocery store and leaving out a side entrance.

He took the sudden arrival of the cops as the work of Eddison John. The man had locked himself in his safe room and then, presumably, warned the Castries police about the American who would soon be raiding his office.

Thirty minutes after achieving his objective, Luka sat in the back of a taxi talking through his earpiece to Sebastian Drexler. He'd learned that the aircraft that had deposited him over the home of the attorney had landed without incident at Hewanorra International Airport, and it would be fueled and ready to leave as soon as Luka arrived.

With the phone in his possession, he was satisfied with his work, but Drexler informed him the job was not yet complete. "You'll come back to Zurich now. Alexander Velesky and the phone that Krupkin handed him here are still missing. We have an idea who has Velesky, but so far haven't learned where he's being held."

Luka rolled his eyes. He didn't mind the work—it beat fighting in

Ukraine or shanking some heavily guarded politician in Estonia—but he didn't like the fact that the people he had been working around had proved to be so incompetent. "Those Stravinsky idiots have had twenty hours. They're useless. We'll need to bring in new talent."

"I have a new set of Russian assets already working. Better than the last group."

"Who are they?"

"They are you."

Luka's eyebrows rose. "29155?"

"Correct, as well as other GRU support. But even though you are the highest-ranking officer on the mission, we're not in Russia, so I'm in charge."

"How are *you* in charge?"

"Call Spanov yourself and ask him that question."

Luka sniffed. "I'll pass. You're in charge."

Drexler said, "And the American you mentioned? Was he CIA? Is he still alive?"

"Yes, probably, and no. He's taken care of."

Drexler said, "The Agency is going to start getting annoyed that you are killing their officers, don't you think?"

"Call Spanov and ask him if I should have killed that guy or not."

"Touché. Spanov would turn America into a parking lot to get those files back."

Luka hung up the phone, occasionally looking back over his shoulder out the rear window of the taxi to make sure he wasn't being followed.

But as they neared the airport, he began thinking more about his situation. If the CIA was involved, they might well have been able to track his aircraft flying right over the target. They would see that it had landed, and they could be waiting for him to come back to it, either to engage him there or to track him in the air.

No, Luka realized he couldn't fly back to Europe on the aircraft Drexler had flown him to the Caribbean on.

He looked down at his phone and searched for international flights out of Saint Lucia this afternoon. He had documents that could get him any-where, so he just had to get out of here clean, and then work his way back to Zurich.

. . .

Eighteen minutes after spilling over a steep embankment and crashing into a tight cluster of palms, Court Gentry swayed with a gentle breeze, looking out the passenger-side window of the ruined Porsche 911. He'd meticulously torn away and dropped enough leaves and stalks in front of his face so he could see back up to the road, and through the swaying green fronds out of reach above him, he caught a glimpse of someone looking down from the top of the hill above.

He'd been on the phone with Lacy for the past several minutes, so he knew it would be her, though they hadn't quite figured out what to do next.

He didn't want to shout up to her; his vehicle's position here on its side in the treetops felt extraordinarily precarious still, so he spoke softly into his phone.

"Did you tie the rope off to your car?"

"Yes."

"What kind of knot?"

"I . . . I don't know. A knot. Tied to the trailer hitch. It's fine."

Court sighed. He was in no position to argue, and he doubted he had time to talk her through resecuring the line, so he instructed her to lower the rope.

The woman wore cargo pants and a tank top, and she didn't look physically able to do much more than lower the rope down to him. Fortunately for Court, however, that was all he needed. As the palms swayed, he said, "Don't throw it, lower it down. If you don't thread that right to me and it hits the car, then I'm going for a ride I don't want to take."

She nodded and began doing so, and while the end of the rope neared him, she spoke to him via her earpiece. "You shouldn't have passed on my help from the beginning. *We* might be holding that device instead of Matador."

Court knew he couldn't argue with the CIA officer's logic, but he also wasn't going to talk any more than necessary. He carefully crammed his phone back in his waistband without a reply, took the end of the rope with his right hand as soon as he could reach it, and gingerly reached down with his left to unfasten his seat belt.

The movement to get his belt off and then to tie the rope around his torso caused more disturbance than he would have liked, and before he was secure, the car began to slip to the left, deeper into the palm fronds.

Court grasped the rope with both hands quickly, squeezing with all his might, and the Porsche continued to slide down as the palms gave way.

He had just emerged out of the open targa-top when the car dropped suddenly out from under him, and then he was left dangling there in the fronds.

He didn't dare look down, but he heard the car fall twenty feet or so to the hillside, impacting with a sickening crunch, and then he heard it rolling over and over on its race down to sea level.

He looked up instead, and he saw Lacy standing there, looking past him and watching the car plummet a moment with rapt fascination.

After the crashing and smashing behind him ceased as the luxury automobile rolled off into the distance, Court shouted up to her. "That'll buff right out."

She looked at him like he was crazy, and then she yelled down, "Do you want me to pull you up with the SUV?"

Court thought a moment. "How good is your knot?"

Lacy disappeared from view above, but he could still hear her. "Let's find out."

"Shit," he mumbled.

Soon he began moving, lifting up and out of the trees, and then his feet made contact with the cliffside. He walked slowly up, letting the rope do most of the work.

Pain in his rib cage made him catch his breath. He'd broken ribs in the past, and the pain wasn't to that level, but he knew he'd be hurting for a while.

He still felt blood on his back, wetting his T-shirt, and another trickle on the back of his head. He assumed he'd cut his scalp as he'd done on his mid-back, but he prided himself on having an exceptionally hard head, so he wasn't overly worried.

With significant pain and moderate struggle, he made his way up to the road. Cars and trucks drove by, slowing to make their way around Lacy's rented Ford Escape, but no one seemed to realize a vehicle had plummeted over the side, so the traffic continued to move.

Court himself went to where the rope was attached to the SUV, and he saw that Lacy had tied a simple but effective clove hitch. As he untied it, he said, "I thought you were just some suit who rode a desk."

She didn't respond to this. Instead, they both climbed into the Escape, she behind the wheel and he in the front passenger seat, rubbing the back of his head and looking at the blood on his hand as he did so.

As she started the Escape, she said, "You think people who went to college can't tie knots? Wow." She fired up the engine. "You're kind of full of yourself, aren't you?"

Court didn't think he was full of himself. Especially now, after failing so badly here in the Caribbean. He just said, "Look, I'm sorry I misjudged you."

She began driving back down the hillside towards the south. She didn't respond to his contrition but said, "No point in going to Castries, is there?"

Court shook his head. "No."

"Then we go back to the airport. I have a G280 waiting to get us the hell out of here."

They began driving to the south, down the hill and back in the direction of Eddison John's property.

Court said, "I'll make my own way out of this, but I appreciate the lift."

Angela looked at him. "I don't think you have a say in the matter."

"I do, actually."

"Well, you'd better talk to Brewer."

"Brewer's not my boss, Angela."

The woman laughed aloud now. "She's not my boss, either, but she's my boss's boss's boss, and she works directly with the D/O, so I do what she says." She looked at Court. "Even when I don't want to. You do, too, I'm sure."

Lacy seemed to remain under the impression that Court was an active-duty NOC in the Directorate of Operations, but he said nothing more about his relationship with the CIA.

Court wanted a big bag of ice, a bed, and a beer right now. He did not want to talk to Suzanne Brewer, but he reluctantly took the phone when Angela dialed her number and handed it to him.

He opened with no preamble. "It did *not* go well."

"I already heard. I brought you in because I thought you could pull it off."

"Well, I guess you should have hired Matador. He's kind of a badass."

She changed gears. "We think he will return to Switzerland with the device. I want you to go there with Lacy."

Court looked over to the woman driving the SUV. She'd put on mirrored sunglasses and didn't even seem to be paying attention to his side of the phone conversation.

"Does *she* know this?"

"No, but *I'll* break it to her, not you."

"What do you want me to do?"

"I want the same thing I wanted yesterday. Get the phone."

"And Matador?"

"Kill Matador if, and only if, that doesn't interfere with your primary."

Court was glad he was going to get another crack at making this right. "I'll make my own way there."

"There's no time for that. You will take Agency transport."

"You keep forgetting that you're trying to kill me, don't you?"

"I'm not forgetting it. I'm moving past it to deal with a bigger problem than you. Get on the damn plane, Violator. We aren't enemies."

Court did not reply, so Brewer continued, "Look. Getting hold of this product will protect American assets and, with a little luck, it will also provide critical intelligence about Russian financial operations. This isn't sinking some rich men's water toys. This is making a difference."

He knew Brewer was right. He didn't like the idea of a summit and a slap on Russia's wrist after all they had done, but from what he'd been told, this *was* a vital mission, both *for* America and *against* Russia. And although he knew he could make it into Europe on his own, he also knew it would be so much faster to just climb on an Agency jet already here in Saint Lucia.

"Fine."

"Good. I'll get the latest intel from Zurich and call Lacy back in ten." And she hung up the phone.

Court handed the phone back to Angela, who continued driving along the winding roads Court had just covered in pursuit of Matador. Without looking his way, she said, "We're going to Zurich, aren't we?"

"Yeah." He turned to her. "Eddison John told me he did *not* work with the Russians. Not since the war. I don't know if he was telling the truth, but—"

"But," Lacy said, "Brewer might have been lying."

"Exactly."

The woman did not seem fazed. "Getting some bullshit story from your higher-ups comes with the territory."

Court nodded. "I'm just glad you aren't some Pollyanna who thinks we're always the good guys."

She laughed at this, then said, "I've worked in five duty stations since joining the Agency. We've done good things in every country, and we've fucked things up in every country, as well."

"Christians in Action," Court mumbled, using a pejorative term for the CIA.

"Yeah," she said, then turned to him. "I still believe in what we're doing, though." Court said nothing, and she nodded as she looked ahead again. "I get it. You're some disaffected, burned-out, jaded, hard-edged asset who doesn't believe in the mission any longer but keeps doing what he's doing because he doesn't know what the hell else to do."

This woman, Court realized, had more or less summed up his psyche in a single sentence.

But he pushed back a little. "I still *want* to believe. That keeps me going."

Lacy said, "I *need* you to believe in this op. We have a job, and we will do it. That's all there is to it." She paused, then said, "Fine. Don't trust Brewer. But *do* trust me. As long as you're working with the same aims as me and the mission, then I've got your back, Six."

"And what about you?" Court asked. "You don't sound like you're a naïve true believer, but you also don't strike me as someone ready to get their hands dirty."

She thought a moment before responding. "I'm a product of a military dad who saw some very bad things overseas and, through no fault of his own, brought them home to us. And I was a Black girl in public school in rural Mississippi, where I very much did *not* fit in."

"Mississippi?"

"Just outside Clarksdale. Doubt you even know where that is."

"I do not."

"Well, my dad was from there. My mom emigrated from Haiti in the 1980s; she served in the Peace Corps. My dad was in the Army; they met in Honduras. They married and had me, and then they went back to Mississippi. He ended up buying a farm that was once part of the largest plantation in the state. He was a descendant of slaves."

"Irony is awesome," Court said.

"I grew up on the family farm. Three hundred fifty acres. Mostly soybeans, but Dad has some hogs, as well. Worked my ass off.

"After college at Vanderbilt, I joined the Peace Corps myself, my mom's worldview rubbing off on me. I didn't accomplish much in two years there. I worked a couple places in Africa, built a few water pumps and some solar outhouses." She shrugged. "Wasn't exactly changing the world. Then I went home and got into Princeton, got a master's in public and international affairs.

"The Agency recruited me my last semester." She smiled. "Like the Peace Corps, I joined the CIA thinking I could make a difference."

"You made a difference to me. Pulled my ass out of a plummeting sports car."

She laughed a little. "Not originally what I had in mind." She looked out the window a moment. "To be honest, despite the work I do, I'm essentially a pacifist. I know the U.S. needs to project power, but I'm not going to be the one to shoot anybody."

Court shrugged. "Suits me. If we get into a jam where the only way out is a gun, then I'll do the shooting for the both of us. I don't need a killer. I need a good officer who's got my back. You've been around the block, and you know how to get an asset to commit to the mission."

"You mean you?"

Now he laughed a little, the sting of his wounds feeling the friction of the movement on the seat. "Let's go to Switzerland, Angela. I hear the weather's great in January."

Lacy said nothing as they continued on to the airport.

TWENTY-TWO

Suzanne Brewer stood in CIA Director Jay Kirby's outer office, ignoring the assistant who offered her a seat on the sofa to wait. She had too much pent-up nervous energy now, and she had to fight the urge to pace back and forth to dispel some of it, lest she reveal her mood to the critical eye of the woman watching her from behind the desk.

The news she had for the Director was all bad, obviously, but she had been working on ways to spin it for the past forty-five minutes and felt she was now as ready to take the heat as she'd ever be.

The executive assistant took a call from the phone on her desk and acknowledged, then hung up. "The Director will see you now."

Brewer passed directly through the double doors to the main office and stepped in to find Kirby standing behind his desk, a Yeti insulated coffee mug in his hand and a look of anticipation on his face. She met his gaze but gave away nothing, knowing she had to deal this blow delicately.

When she didn't speak upon entering, he said, "Have a seat, Suzanne."

She did as instructed, keeping her back ramrod straight, her butt on the edge of the chair, her files and iPad in her lap.

When Kirby sat down and just looked at her, saying nothing more, she took this as her cue.

"The asset I arranged in the Caribbean to retrieve the data from Eddison

John has, unfortunately, failed in his mission. There was a sizable enemy opposition force at the location."

Kirby sighed. "Who was the opposition?"

"We believe the information is now in the hands of a GRU operations officer, a major named Luka Ilyich Rudenko. We code named him Matador several years back."

"The same fellow who killed our officer last night in Zurich?"

"Yes, sir."

His brow furrowed with worry. "Tell me more."

"The asset we sent to Saint Lucia was alone. He found himself facing several of John's security, a large team of local hires working with Matador, and Matador himself. You expressed a need for us to work this problem sub rosa, so I wasn't able to acquire more help for our asset."

Kirby thought a moment, ran a hand through his graying brown hair, then said, "So . . . two copies of that data are out in the world right now?"

"Correct. We don't know how Matador got off the island, or if he is still there. The aircraft he flew in on is still on the tarmac, but it's possible he flew out on a commercial flight."

"He's got papers for that?" Kirby asked.

"He'd have to go through export immigration, but we suspect he has forged documents that show he arrived in Saint Lucia as a tourist, so that won't be a problem for a trained operative like Matador."

"We're checking the airport there?"

She cocked her head. "We *can*, but we haven't yet. I don't have any resources other than that one senior ops officer who just happened to be in Miami when I needed someone to go talk to the asset in the BVIs yesterday."

"This officer. He knows this is sub rosa, correct?"

"*She* knows what she needs to know. She reports to me and no one else. Still . . . for a job like this, she is well out of her league."

Kirby took a sip out of his Yeti, turned, and looked out his window a moment. Finally, he said, "You've done this before."

It was a statement, not a question.

"If you are talking about finding Matador, then yes, I have experience finding, fixing, and finishing threats to the Agency and its personnel. I worked threat security for several years before I—"

"That's not what I mean." The Director turned back to her. "You've worked off book, for Matt Hanley, running denied assets."

Brewer fought an urge to flinch. She had no idea how the new Director knew this, but she could only guess it might have been information the old Director had put together and passed on. Finally, she said, "I did what was asked of me by my department head."

Kirby smiled, then put a consolatory hand up as he walked around the table, coming closer. "Calm down, this isn't a tribunal here. Your ability to play on the dark side is an asset to me, not a hindrance. I don't care what Matt had you doing, I just want to know I can count on you now."

He sat on the edge of the desk; she had to look up to make eye contact.

Brewer said, "You want this badly, don't you?"

"The president wants it. He's come to me. We both see the danger in having CIA poking around all this, just a few days away from the New York summit, so I've come to you. Discreet, quiet, using denied assets. That's the way this has to happen. This is your operation. I'm not folding the DDO into this because, frankly, Mel Brent is risk averse, and we both know it."

The Director was telling the deputy director's special assistant that the deputy director himself was to be kept in the dark on what she was doing. Brewer knew the workings of government well enough to know she shouldn't comment on this.

Instead, she said, "I remain at your service. But help *me* help *you* help the president."

"What resources do you need, keeping in mind no one can know what you're working on?"

"First, give me the ops officer I already have working on it. She's underqualified, but she's up to speed, at least."

"Got it. She's on special assignment to you as long as you need her. What else?"

There was a catch in her breath, and then she said, "Authorize me anything I ask for from collections. All disciplines."

His eyebrows rose. "I don't even know what that means."

She spoke confidently. "HUMINT, SIGINT, OSINT, FININT, TECHINT, GEOINT. Whatever I need."

"Like what?"

"Intel data, facial recog, customs and immigration pulls, bugs and a sur-veillance crew—outsourced, I can handle that with your okay. If you provide me with the authority to ask any department, desk, or station for what I need, then I will find Velesky and whoever has him in Europe, and I will track Matador down, wherever the hell he takes the phone he picked up in Saint Lucia."

This was an unprecedented ask, Brewer knew, especially considering she was asking the Director himself. He'd have to provide her with a letter say-ing she had the keys to the kingdom, and though there would be no paper trail of what she was working on, the Director was, tangentially at least, in-volving himself in her sub rosa operation.

Kirby thought a moment. "Something so broad . . . people are going to be curious."

Brewer nodded. "I have a way around that. The asset we used in Saint Lucia is wanted by the Agency."

Kirby sat back on the desk, momentarily confused. "Go on."

"His name is Courtland Gentry, code name Violator. I assume you've been read in on him."

D/CIA nodded slowly, a bewildered look on his face. "How has it come to pass that you are running the Gray Man on this operation?"

"Expediency. I knew where he was. He's . . . *susceptible* to manipulation, and I capitalized on that." She took a breath, then said, "I can tell everyone I need assistance from that Alex Velesky, the missing banker, is a known as-sociate of Violator. I'll lead the manhunt for Velesky by telling everyone in house I am leading the manhunt for Violator."

"But . . ." Kirby remained confused. "You are saying you want the Agency looking for the man you are relying on to execute the mission?"

"It's the only way for me to get broad access to all intelligence. They won't find him, he's too good for that, but with all resources available to me, I will most definitely find Alexander Velesky."

Kirby whistled. "You're shrewd, aren't you?"

"You want results. This is how I give them to you."

"But . . . Violator. He failed today. Is he the man to use going forward?"

"I don't like him, sir . . . but it is with no hyperbole whatsoever that I tell you he's the best on Earth to do this sort of thing with no comebacks on us."

Kirby thought a moment more, and then Brewer found herself astounded when he asked for no more clarification. "Granted."

She coughed out a reply; a little of the surprise was caught in her voice. "Gr-great."

Kirby assented with a little nod. "You *have* to pull this off, Suzanne. The files contain CIA money transfer information that could compromise us, if not destroy us."

She didn't have to ask for more detail. Clearly there was something in Krupkin's data that could lead to uncovering CIA money flowing through Russia, presumably to support operations in the country.

The Director of the CIA stood, and Suzanne Brewer followed suit.

He said, "This summit in New York . . . if it succeeds, it's going to lead to a resumption of relations and trade between the U.S. and Russia. Between the West at large and Russia."

Brewer nodded. "Russia is getting off easy, aren't they?"

"Absolutely, they are. It's a bitter pill to swallow, but we'll have to go back to fighting them in the shadows. Get me that data, protect this Agency, and protect the negotiations."

"Yes, sir."

A minute later Brewer was heading up the hall to her office. She had ten hours till Violator landed in Zurich, and she wanted to have a target fixed for him by the time he got there.

Thirty minutes later she called Angela Lacy on board the Agency jet, now flying over the Atlantic Ocean. She filled the younger woman in on a number of matters, let her know she now had carte blanche to get the help she needed.

"There is a caveat, however," Brewer said. "First . . . where is Six now?"

"He's asleep in the back of the jet. I'm working up here by the bulkhead."

"Good. You have been granted access to all collection sources, all over the world. You and I have carte blanche from the Agency to see this through."

"That's incredible," Lacy stammered. "I have to ask, how is that possible? You said before we had to keep close hold on—"

"The ruse we have constructed is this: There is an old Agency employee named Courtland Gentry. He went rogue years ago, and now he's a contract killer often referred to as the—"

"As the Gray Man. Yes, of course. What does he have to do with any of this?"

"The Agency has had a kill order on him for a long time. I used to be involved in the search, and I had complete freedom of access from any Agency asset in hunting him down. To aid in our search for Velesky, I've let it be known that he is a known associate of Gentry's, and his capture is integral to us neutralizing this longtime Agency threat."

Lacy took this in. "So you give me code word access to the Court Gentry collection, and I reach out to whoever I need with this code word for access to Velesky."

"That is correct. The code word access for the Gentry hunt is 'Bloody Angel.'"

"Bloody Angel. That will get me into everything I need?"

"Correct again. Your asset, Six. He is *not* read in on Bloody Angel, so you do *not* discuss this with him. Am I absolutely clear?"

"Of course, ma'am. Thank you."

"Good luck, Lacy. This is the most critical operation of your career to date, quite possibly of your career, period. Don't let me down."

TWENTY-THREE

Zoya Zakharova—code name Transit—knelt on the floor of an upstairs hall bathroom in the cold and musty Swiss chalet just north of Wengen, her head positioned over the sink, her bloodshot eyes just reaching the level of the bottom of the bathroom mirror.

She peered into her own eyes a long moment, although she knew what was behind them.

Nothing.

Zoya felt herself imploding. Over hours of staring out the window at a gray afternoon that morphed in front of her to gray twilight and then a black night, she'd watched the clouds come in, then the light flurries that grew slowly into a steady whipping snowfall as her mind surged with urges to drink, to sleep, to cry, to put her fist through a wall.

She did none of this. She just stood guard, doing a job she felt was irrelevant considering the state of the world around her. She was a static sentry protecting a nobody from nothing, as near as she could tell, and she was barely managing to pull this off.

Or maybe she wasn't even managing.

On the edge of the sink in front of her, just inches from her face as she knelt here, was a long thin line of cocaine she'd carefully prepared, and in her right hand she held a rolled five-euro note.

Ten minutes ago her plan had been to only pop into the bathroom and do a bump—a small sniff to get her through the next hour or so, but then Braunbaer had radioed the team that Broussard had just told him the handover had been pushed back till nine p.m. Zoya had been in the cold house since just after seven in the morning, and as soon as she'd learned about the delay, she'd looked at the little vial in her hand that she'd retrieved from her pack and decided to pour the entire contents onto the edge of the sink, telling herself her physical condition was deteriorating by the moment. Exhaustion, alcohol withdrawal, depression, desperation. She was utterly shutting down, and she needed to reboot her system to make it through the handover of the package and then the trip to whatever hotel bar she could find.

Zoya took one last long look into her eyes in the mirror, saw nothing of value there, and then she leaned over.

She placed the five-euro note a centimeter above the end of the line, then began snorting, working her way from left to right. It burned, like the night before; this told her the coke she'd bought off the street in Milan was of low quality, probably cut with something like baby powder.

Or something else. Baby powder, while gross, was among the best-case scenarios, so it was the one she'd decided to believe in.

She continued up the line; she'd vacuumed eighty percent of the powder into her right nostril when her walkie-talkie squawked, startling her, and she lurched up.

She felt the burn enter her sinuses, and it felt as if her nose hairs had been singed, and then she felt a drip of congestion down the back of her throat.

"Braunbaer for Transit."

She snatched the walkie-talkie from where it was clipped near the neckline of her open coat. Clearing her throat quickly, she pressed the talk button.

"Go for Transit," she said, then released the button so she could sniff deeply, a wet snort, pressing her finger against her left nostril to bring the remnants of the drug up into her sinuses on the right.

"Package check," Braunbaer said. "Your turn."

"Got it. Wait one," she replied, and then she brushed the remains of the coke into the sink and stood up quickly, just as the drug lightning-bolted through her nervous system.

"Fuck me," she whispered to herself, riding the wave of heat and energy, and then she clipped the radio back onto her jacket, lifted her Micro Uzi from the toilet seat, and slung it back around her neck.

Ten seconds later she walked up the creaky wooden hallway on newly energetic legs. Ifa, the African asset of Broussard, had been positioned in an overwatch in a room at the far end of the hall with eyes to the north, and Alex Velesky, the "package," remained in a bedroom on the right, halfway between Zoya and Ifa.

She put her right hand on the grip of her weapon as she reached to open Alex's door with her left. Before she made contact with it, however, Ifa appeared at the end of the hall. In French he said, "Hey. Thirsty? Need some water?" He held up a Nalgene bottle.

"Non, merci. Je vais bien," she replied in French. She felt a tremble in her hands, a shiver running down her spine.

The man kept walking up the hall towards her, holding out the bottle.

"For the package, then," he said. "He hasn't had anything to drink since we got here."

"Bon," Zoya replied, and he brought it to her; she kept her eyes averted from his. Even with the dim light in the hall, she was self-conscious about her condition and worried that if she made eye contact with him, he would detect that she'd just ingested a strong psychostimulant. She knew she was probably just paranoid, but even so, when she spoke to Ifa, she looked at the door next to her, not at him.

She took the bottle. "Merci."

"Forty-five minutes," added the African, indicating how long they still had to wait for the bankers to arrive from Geneva at nine p.m.

"Oui."

She moved to open the door, but the African said, "You've had a long day, yeah?"

Shit. She *really* didn't need to get into a conversation right now. She felt herself wanting to be talkative, almost hyper, suddenly, and she knew she had to fight it, because she didn't think she'd be able to hide her condition if she found herself caught in a chat.

In French she said, "Let's just get this done." Quickly she opened the door and stepped in, closing it behind her as Ifa began heading back down the hall to his overwatch position.

Zoya's teeth chattered a little as she looked over the package. Velesky sat up on the bed on the far side of the room, his right wrist handcuffed to the bedpost. His clothes were disheveled, his hair was a mess, and his face wore a two-day-old beard.

She approached, handed him the water bottle, and then took a couple steps back to the middle of the room so he couldn't lunge for her machine pistol, although he seemed like the most passive man she'd been around in quite some time. Once out of range, she clicked the transmit button on her walkie-talkie without removing the device from her jacket's lapel. "Transit for Braunbaer. Package is fine, over."

The reply came quickly. "Good. Get back to overwatch."

"Roger," she said, and she began to turn for the door.

Velesky called out from behind. "Miss. Miss? Please . . . I *need* you to listen to me. Just for a moment."

She kept moving for the exit, but as she did, she replied, "I need you to be quiet."

"Do you know what's happening in the world?" he asked. "The Russians? The war? The criminality?"

She slowed but did not stop, and she made no reply.

"Do you even care?"

She did care, but still she said nothing.

"The information I have," Velesky said. "Not just what's on the phone. There's more. There's additional information I have access to that, when matched with the data on the phone, can bring the Kremlin to its knees. I just need to get it to New York.

"I don't know who you are or why you are doing this to me, but you are American, and I believe you want to do the right thing."

Zoya's American accent was perfect, but she was not American. She tried to continue to the door, but something in her body told her to stop.

It was the coke, she suddenly realized. *It* wanted to talk, though she did not.

And she didn't have the discipline to fight it. Stepping back to him, she spoke softly but quickly, almost maniacally. "Don't make yourself out to be some kind of crusader. You're a corrupt banker who stole some shit from his company. That's *all* you are."

"No! That's *not* who I am. The phone you have? That's not the bank's data. The bank's data I put on the dark web, mailed the address to a man in New York. The phone . . . it's loaded with intelligence about Kremlin money transfers to the West. The data I stole from my bank can tie the transfers to the end users. I have thousands of records that will reveal where the FSB, the SVR, and the GRU are spending their money. This isn't just about seizing the funds, this is about finding out who's getting paid off by Moscow, what operations the GRU and SVR are running abroad. It is fucking crucial I get out of here with the phone so I can reveal the truth."

Zoya froze in place, then blinked hard. *Was this real?*

She shook her head quickly. "You're . . . lying. Lying to get away from all this. The Kremlin launders and hides its funds before it leaves Russia. How would some banker in Switzerland know what the Kremlin is—"

"I'm *not* some banker in Switzerland," Alex said. "I am Ukrainian. I lost members of my family in the war last year, and I was given the data out of Russia from an old business acquaintance who converts rubles into crypto for the siloviki. He is trusted by Daniil Spanov, chief intelligence official for all of Russia, and he connected the dots . . ." Velesky paused a moment. "Two nights ago I was given the information." After a short pause, he said, "Almost as soon I received it, the man who gave it to me was tortured and then murdered. *That* tells you how important this all is."

Zoya sniffed hard. She felt sweat on her brow, a line of perspiration running down the back of her neck. After a long pause, she said, "I'm a hired gun. I can't help you. Maybe the people at Garnier and Moreau can."

Alex scoffed at this. "G&M handles almost as much dirty Russian money as Brucker Söhne, my bank. G&M just wants me and the data so they can steal clients, launder even *more* billions by funneling it into the West in crypto and putting it in shell corporate accounts at their bank." He shook his head. "No." He waved a hand in the air. "All this . . . it's a problem for Russia as long as I have the data. Once G&M gets the data, Russia's problem goes away, and it's the rest of the world who suffers."

"Look," Zoya said, surprised by her sudden loquaciousness even though she knew it was chemically stimulated. "I was brought in to do an easy job. The job got complicated when I saw you get kidnapped last night, and it got more complicated still when I sideswiped your car and got in a gunfight getting us out of there. But now we have you, our clients are on the way to pick you up, and this is all tied in a nice little bow for me. I'm not going to fuck it up by sneaking you and the phone—the phone I don't even have in my possession—out of here for some bullshit sob story about saving the world."

She could see in Velesky's eyes that the man had finally lost faith in her. Softly, he said, "You are just in it for the money."

Zoya had never been in it for the money, but she couldn't argue with him. If she was being truthful about all this, then she was doing a dirty job. Passing up a chance to deal a painful body blow to the Russian government just so some bank in Geneva could get trade secrets from a competitor.

She looked down at the floor, tried to take this in.

"Yes," she said finally. "It's just a job."

Velesky said, "Two nights ago I tried to tell myself the same thing. I tried to convince myself I had no part to play in putting out this world on fire. But . . . but *fuck* my job. And fuck *your* job. The world will remember the people who stood up, who fought back. And the world will remember the people who said, 'I'm just doing my job.'"

Her speedy reply was apologetic but firm. "My job is *all* I'm here to do . . . that's all I'm . . . ready to do."

She began to turn again for the door.

"Please," he implored. "They'll probably kill me when they're done."

She shook her head vigorously. "You're being dramatic. It's a bank, Velesky. Banks don't kill people."

"It's billions of dollars from a despot regime! Who says they won't kill for that? People have been dying for this information for the last twenty-four hours. Would you just hand me over to die? What do you have against me?"

She turned to him and rushed forward. With her coke-addled brain, the movement made her head spin. "It's not about you. It's never about the package. It's always about what the package knows, what the package has, what the package has done, or what the package plans to do. Trust me, nobody involved in this gives a shit about you."

"Including you?"

She looked at him and responded in a fiery tone. "*Especially* me! You're luggage, like I told you. My job was to grab you and babysit you till Garnier and Moreau took possession of you. Whatever you have, I don't care what it is, and I can't wait to get the hell out of here."

Velesky looked at the floor. Softly, he said, "You have no soul."

She answered this in a suddenly introspective tone, contrasting with her hurried soliloquy. "Not really. Not anymore."

Velesky's eyes went dark now. For the first time she saw malevolence in the previously mild-mannered-appearing man.

Zoya felt more sweat run down her neck, tingling her spine at the shoulder blades. Without speaking, she started to turn away for the door again.

As before, Alex called out to her, but this time he said, "You missed a little."

She turned back his way, confused. "I missed *what*?"

Velesky used his free hand to touch the right side of his nose. "A little bit of the cocaine."

Shit. Self-consciously she rubbed her upper lip and nose with the back of her hand.

The Ukrainian smiled at her, an angry grin that expressed his spite. "The nose candy is gone now, but the telltale signs remain. Your cheeks are flushed, your eyes are bloodshot, you're twitchy. Sweat on your forehead in a cold room."

He added, "I bet your heart is beating like you're a gazelle being run down by a lion."

When she did not immediately reply, he said, "I'm a banker. I know cocaine when I see it. Haven't touched that shit since I was twenty-eight, and then only just to party. What are you? Thirty-five? You need blow to make it through your workday upright? And you have a job where you carry a gun?

"You're a fucking mess, lady."

"Fuck you," she said, but softly, as if she didn't really mean it.

"Is that why you're so angry?" Velesky asked. "That damn, unshakable irritability that tags along unwanted with the positive effects of the drug?" He shrugged. "I bet that helps you tune out your morals and push on."

She turned away yet again.

"Oh . . . I see it now. That's why you do it. You *need* it in this line of work. It keeps you like a robot. You don't want to think; you don't want control over your actions. You want to be a wound-up toy soldier, don't you?"

She was out the door; she closed it behind her, did her best to forget everything the package had just said to her.

She'd taken a single step back up the hall towards her overwatch when her walkie-talkie came to life.

It was Braunbaer, the German. "Heads up! Front of the house! We've got company!"

TWENTY-FOUR

Zoya began hurrying back up the hall to her position, aware that her rushed footfalls would probably be audible downstairs.

"One SUV halfway up the driveway." Braunbaer sounded annoyed now. "Transit? What the fuck? Why didn't you call it when they were down on the road out of the tree line?"

The German seemed to be looking out the window downstairs, and from there he wouldn't have been able to see the SUV as early as Zoya would have above him, had she been where she was supposed to be.

"Sorry," she replied into her mic. "I was giving the package some water."

Bello's voice came over the net now. "Are these the guys from the bank? If so, they're thirty-five minutes early."

"I'm checking with Trompette," Braunbaer replied. "Everybody be ready."

Zoya made it back to her upstairs window, then rubbed her eyes hard and peered through a small set of binoculars she'd left on the windowsill. Her shaking hands made looking through the optics difficult, but eventually she was able to focus on the scene in front of her.

She clicked the walkie-talkie on her jacket and spoke in a tempo addled by the drug she'd snorted five minutes earlier. "Seven-passenger SUV, a Toyota Highlander. Parking now, forty meters from the front door, perpendicular to the house." Then, "Three personnel dismounting the vehicle. No weapons visible." After another second, she said, "They are not adopting a security posture or an offensive posture at this time. They're just kind of standing around. Over."

Bello's voice came over the radio. "Sounds like the bankers."

"What's inside the SUV?" Braunbaer asked Zoya. Presumably he was looking at the same scene outside a window near the front door, but he would have known that Zoya would have the better view from above.

Zoya adjusted the binoculars. "Unknown. The chalet's lighting is reflecting off the tinted glass. I can't see anything. We could turn off the porch lights, but we could lose visibility on the dismounts if we do."

"We leave the lights on," Braunbaer said.

Zoya kept scanning the windows of the SUV. She clicked again. "Can't rule out the possibility there are more inside the vehicle, but I don't see any movement at this time."

"All right," the German said after a moment. "Just heard from Trompette; he confirms these *are* the men from the bank. He's in comms with them; I told him we will bring the package outside. Ifa and Transit?"

Ifa responded first. "Roger. We'll bring him down."

Zoya hesitated. She shifted her binos from the opaque windows of the SUV and began looking over the three men. They were in their thirties or forties; they wore suits and ties and long wool coats that were buttoned up to ward off the snowy frigid weather, and they stood close together, waiting by the hood of the running Toyota Highlander.

They appeared serious but nonthreatening.

Nevertheless . . . something felt a little off to her, but the fact that her exhausted brain was spinning with details all swishing around like a tornado, aided by the effects of the psychostimulant, made it impossible to determine just what was wrong.

She told herself it was probably just the paranoia brought on by the coke, but still, she registered a definite feeling of unease.

"Transit?" Braunbaer called, annoyance again evident in his voice.

"I'm on the way," she replied, spinning from the window and charging out of the bedroom to grab Velesky and bring him downstairs with Ifa.

In the hall she found the banker trying to talk the African into forgoing his mission, much the same as Velesky had just tried with her. "You can help me, sir. Help *everyone*. Look, Garnier and Moreau are just as slimy as my bank. The information I have becomes worthless the moment you hand me over to them."

Ifa didn't even seem to be listening; he just shuffled the package along until he got to Zoya, and she joined in, grabbing Velesky by the right arm and walking him towards the staircase with her partner. "Shut up and walk," she ordered.

Velesky did as he was told, his head and shoulders hanging low as the three of them descended the stairs.

In the entry hall of the ski chalet, Zoya saw that the front door was already open. Snow blew in while Bello and Braunbaer stood on the covered porch just outside, using the building's lighting to eye the three men standing near the gray SUV.

Team Broussard all had their weapons out and at the ready, but the three men standing by the running Highlander thirty meters away kept their arms at their sides, their coats were still buttoned up, and there were no guns in sight.

Braunbaer spoke into his phone, presumably to Trompette, as Zoya, Ifa, and Velesky stepped out under the covered porch. "Do these guys speak French or German?" He nodded, hung up the phone, then spoke loud enough to be heard through the persistent hiss of the snowfall. "Good evening."

To Zoya's mild surprise, he'd said it in English.

"Good evening," one of the men replied in a pleasant tone. He was the tallest of the three, about forty but somewhat boyish in the face, and his red hair was already covered in snowflakes that clung to it while it blew in the breeze. He smiled, standing there with the two others, waiting expectantly.

Zoya eyed the man carefully from thirty meters away. The redhead wasn't American; she'd detected some indistinct foreign accent in the short phrase he'd said. The men didn't speak German or French, at least according to what Broussard had apparently told Braunbaer, so she kept evaluating them through the snowfall, somewhat out of professional curiosity but also because the drugs in her system made her even more nervy than usual.

Still, after Alex's story about Russian financial data and murder, she had every reason to be suspicious of whoever would be taking control of the man in her grip and the information on the phone.

Braunbaer said, "Our handler says you check out. We'll bring Velesky down to you. Just keep your hands where we can see them."

"Of course. And the mobile?" the redheaded man asked.

The German retrieved the iPhone from his pocket and handed it off to Ifa.

Zoya took Velesky by his right arm. "Move." Ifa took the banker's left arm and together the three of them moved along, through the wind-whipping snowfall and down the snow-covered drive. Ahead on their left was the Range Rover that Braunbaer, Bello, and Ifa had arrived in, and next to it sat the Ford Econoline van Zoya had stolen in Zurich to recover Velesky.

And then, twenty meters down the driveway, past the two vehicles on the left, the gray Toyota Highlander sat parked across the drive, its lights on and its engine running.

As she closed on the men, she could make out their faces for the first time.

Only the redhead in the middle of the three had spoken, and this made her focus on the other men more closely. Whereas the redhead had a boyish face, the other men were harder, tougher.

Unlike the redhead, the other two appeared especially serious, almost dour, and while the redhead very much looked like he could be Irish, she told herself the two men with the redhead might have been Central European. There were Slavic features evident from twenty meters away that she hadn't detected, even through the binoculars.

She had been told these were bankers. They dressed like bankers, and they acted like bankers might act, oblivious to any danger, but to Zoya, the two men with the redhead didn't *look* like bankers.

This wasn't necessarily bad; she and her own crew weren't bankers, either, they were just intermediaries working for the bank.

But if that *was* true . . . if these three were hired guns just the same as Broussard's people—her cocaine-enhanced unease rose suddenly as she asked herself the question—why are their coats buttoned, and where are their guns?

If they were bankers, they wouldn't have guns. If they were hired assets, they would. But if they were hired assets who were trying to look like bankers . . . then they might hide their guns under buttoned coats, and they might look and act just like this.

This whole scene was wrong.

"Wait," she said, pulling Alex to a stop.

Everyone standing there in the snow looked to Zoya.

"What is it?" Braunbaer called out from behind.

Zoya ignored him, and to the men by the Highlander she said, "You guys are from the bank?"

The man with the red hair cocked his head a little. He clearly hadn't noticed Zoya was female until she spoke. The night, the snow, and the glaring artificial light, as well as her black knit watch cap and her heavy coat, had gone a long way in hiding her features.

With a heavy accent she now thought sounded sort of Irish laced, he said, "We were sent by Garnier and Moreau." He smiled a little. "We're on the job, same as you."

Braunbaer said, "It's okay, Transit. Trompette said these were the clients."

Zoya continued to hold Velesky where he was. Ifa just looked at her with confusion.

"What's the problem?" the redhead asked loudly, snow whipping all around him. Clearly he was growing annoyed by the delay.

Zoya cocked her head. She heard something else in the tall man's voice now. Indistinct, but suspicious. She didn't answer but instead leaned into Velesky's ear and whispered, "If you want to live, you'll do *exactly* as I say."

She continued whispering while Braunbaer called out to the three men by the Highlander, telling them all was fine and to stand by while he sorted it out.

He stormed up to Zoya, Alex, and Ifa, just as Zoya stopped speaking into Velesky's ear. To her he said, "What the hell is wrong with you?"

"I don't like this."

"I don't like standing in the snow," Braunbaer replied angrily. "Give him to me. I'll take him down there myself."

The German took the phone from Ifa and then yanked Velesky on, marching with him down the ankle-deep snow in the driveway, kicking powder out in front of him. He passed the two vehicles parked on the left and arrived at the men at the Highlander. The two silent men took Velesky by the arms firmly while Braunbaer stepped up to the redhead and handed him the phone.

"Thank you," the man said, but his eyes were locked on Zoya.

Zoya looked back at him, standing in front of the hood of the Range

Rover, Ifa still by her side. Bello remained on the front porch ten meters behind them and on the right.

One of the two men holding Alex opened the back door of the SUV now. The interior light did not come on, which Zoya took as a bad sign, but she didn't focus on this for long because she was waiting for something else to happen.

As Braunbaer began walking back through the snowfall towards the chalet, Alex moved as if to get in the SUV. But instead of climbing in, he lifted his left foot up, and then drove it back hard into the shin of the man behind him on his left.

The man cried out in pain and anger as he fell down. "Sukha!"

Sukha meant "bitch" in Russian, and it was a common exclamation of surprise or anger.

"Got you," Zoya said softly to herself, and then she flipped the selector switch on her Micro Uzi from safe to full auto and lifted the weapon, jamming the wire stock of the machine pistol against her shoulder and aiming down the iron sights directly at the redhead in front of the SUV.

No one noticed this because both the man who'd been kicked and the one next to him immediately began punching the Zurich-based banker, slamming him against the side of the SUV, then knocking him down into the snow while the redheaded man, Braunbaer, and the others looked on.

The men beating Velesky only stopped when Zoya shouted at them, surprising everyone for a second time, this time by speaking in her native tongue. "Kto ty, chert voz'mi?" *Who the hell are you?*

Braunbaer stood just meters away from the SUV and raised his hands at Zoya, aware now that one of the assets in his charge was pointing a weapon at the three men sent by the bank.

"What the fuck is going on?" the German croaked.

In English, Zoya said, "That's what I'm trying to figure out!" She switched back to Russian and addressed the redhead. "Hey, Votyak? What's the plan?"

There was no reply from the man; he just cocked his head.

Votyak was Russian slang for someone of the Udmurt ethnicity. Udmurts were a Central European ethnic group who often possessed red hair, uncharacteristic in most other parts of Russia.

Zoya continued addressing him in Russian. "What are you boys? SVR?

GRU?" Alex was forgotten in the snow now; all three men in black wool coats stood over him, looking at the woman and the tiny but potent weapon aimed their way. She directed her next words to the redhead. "I'm thinking GRU. I've never heard of any Votyaks in SVR." Zoya herself had been a member of Sluzhba Vneshney Razvedki, Russian foreign intelligence.

Now the redheaded man spoke again, still in English. "I . . . don't understand."

His fake Irish accent was more pronounced, but Zoya wasn't buying it.

Braunbaer looked at Zoya. "What are you telling them, Transit?"

She spoke confidently, her eye still peering through the tiny ghost ring of her Uzi. "These guys are Russian intelligence officers."

"How do you know that?"

"Velesky's got Kremlin secrets. A gang of Russians show up acting like bankers here for the handover. Then they pretend they aren't even Russians. Not that hard to piece together the fact we've been had."

"How do you know they're Russian?"

"Because *I'm* Russian!" she shouted.

TWENTY-FIVE

Braunbaer had his hand on his rifle now, but he was facing Zoya, his back to the three men by the Highlander. He said, "Our handler vouched for them!"

Zoya shrugged but did not move her eye from her sights. "Then our handler is in on it, isn't he? Either these guys or their masters got to Broussard before we transferred Velesky to the bank. Broussard pushed the bank pickup back to nine so the Russians could get here first."

Bello called out from behind Zoya now. "What if they *are* Russian? I don't care. Broussard is paying us, and he told us to hand Velesky off to these—"

Zoya yelled back at him, her weapon still aimed at the chest of the redhead standing next to Velesky, who had by now rolled into the fetal position. She said, "If the bank is paying us to give them a man and a phone with Russian secrets, we give the man and the phone to the bank, not to fucking Russian spooks."

"But Broussard—"

"They could have a gun to his head right now," Zoya said. "We're not handing Velesky over."

Braunbaer looked to the redheaded man for an explanation. When the man did not speak, the German said, still in English, "Where are you from?"

The redhead sighed. When he spoke, his fake Irish accent was gone.

"We're Russian. But we're working for the bank. *Fucking hell*, man. Tell this bitch to lower her weapon and we'll be on our way."

Braunbaer backed up the drive now, his weapon still pointed down to the snow in front of him. On his right was a low stone wall topped with large concrete planters. He cocked his head at the redheaded man. "Why did you say you couldn't understand her?"

The redhead seemed exasperated now. "Forget this! We aren't here to play games! Get your people in line because we *are* leaving!"

Ifa raised his shotgun up slightly, pointing it even with the smoked windows at the right rear of the Highlander. It was obvious to Zoya the African wasn't sure what was going on, but he knew they hadn't cleared the big SUV of other potential threats.

And then, for the first time since coming outside, Alex Velesky spoke. As he lay in the snow, virtually at the feet of the three Russians, he shouted, "The information I have is damaging to the Kremlin. They've already killed a CIA officer trying to get it. If these men are Russian, then they will kill all of you, and they'll pay your boss off to stay quiet."

Alex lifted his head out of the snow; his right eye was black as he looked up to Braunbaer. "I'm talking about billions of euros. You . . . me? We're insignificant in all this."

Bello shouted from the porch, "Let the Russians take the package and leave."

The German ignored the Italian; he just stared at the men. "We've got to clear this up."

The redhead reached into his coat. "I'm calling Broussard."

The two standing over Alex stiffened up and looked to their leader. To Zoya it appeared they thought he was going for a gun.

Braunbaer shouted, "Everybody stay still!" and he raised his MP7, pointing it now at the three standing at the Highlander.

Zoya made a lightning-quick look behind her to see that Bello's rifle was up and ready, as well, though uncertainty was evident on his face.

The cocaine coursing through her bloodstream made this incredibly stressful situation only more so; her hands shook, her voice cracked when she shouted now at the three men standing around Velesky's crumpled form. "Don't fucking move!"

The redhead stood frozen with his hand just inside his coat, his eyes darting back and forth between Zoya and Braunbaer.

Braunbaer jerked his weapon to the Highlander, then flashed it back to the three men standing nearby. "What do you have in the back of the truck?"

The redhead's boyish but serious face turned to him. "You let us leave with Velesky and the mobile, and you'll never need to find out."

Zoya's teeth chattered. She didn't think the Russian was bluffing; she felt certain they wouldn't have adopted such a casual posture if they didn't know they had significant backup ready.

Braunbaer seemed to be thinking the same thing. "Okay. Everybody stay calm. *I'm* going to get Broussard on the phone, on *my* phone, and we're going to figure this out."

The redhead removed his hand from his coat slowly. It was empty. When Braunbaer saw this, he lowered his weapon.

The Russian said, "We don't have time for that. We're leaving with Velesky and the phone."

The German shook his head and reached for his phone. "Nobody's going anywhere until—"

Now the redhead shouted loud enough for his scream to echo off the trees and back at them. "Davai!"

Zoya knew this word meant many things in Russian, but one of them was *Go!* She reacted first, dropping to her knees an instant before the smoked back window of the Highlander exploded outwards.

She recognized the noise and the cadence of a light machine gun firing in full-automatic mode, and she knew that she and her three associates were in open ground right in front of the weapon's barrel.

Zoya went flat in the snow and squeezed the trigger on her tiny little weapon, and she saw one of the three men in front of the SUV go down. At the same time Ifa twisted to his right and fell, disappearing from her peripheral view after firing a single shell from his shotgun. She felt rounds snapping right over head, and she knew Bello had been standing behind her.

She began rolling to her left through the snow, trying to get between the two vehicles parked there for some semblance of concealment, and while she did this, she fired a couple of rounds into the air over the Highlander. She would have just laid down on the trigger of her machine pistol except for the fact that

Alex was on the ground right beside her targets, and since she was moving, rolling upside down and right side up over and over as she made her way laterally on the driveway, she knew the chance of hitting him was too great if she fired directly at the men.

She wouldn't make hits, but she was determined to make noise, hoping to send the Russians scrambling to cover.

The machine gun kept barking, bursts of disciplined fire now as Zoya found herself between the Range Rover and the Econoline. Here she climbed up to her knees, trying to put the bulk of her body behind the engine block of the van to give her some actual cover from the heavy and persistent fire.

She reloaded a fresh magazine, and as she did so, she looked to her right in time to see Ifa crawling towards her, his shotgun left where he'd dropped it and a trail of blood snaking behind him in the snow.

She knew he'd need some covering fire if he was going to make it to her, so she stood and dumped rounds from her Micro Uzi through the front windows of the Econoline, raking the Highlander twenty yards away with suppressive fire.

She shifted aim to the right, to the area where the three Russians had been standing, but she only saw a man in a wool coat lying facedown and still in the snow, and Velesky frantically crawling on his hands and knees to her right. The low stone wall there rimming the northern side of the driveway was the closest cover, and he was clearly trying to make his way to it.

She had no idea where Braunbaer had gone, and she couldn't hear Bello firing behind her, but just as her Uzi ran dry a second time, she heard a burst off to her right. She turned to see the German up on his knees, on the other side of the low wall and behind a huge and empty concrete planter. His HK MP7 was a more powerful weapon than Zoya's Uzi, and she was glad to see him providing covering fire as Velesky scrambled across the drive towards the wall.

Zoya had one more magazine for the Uzi, but instead of taking time to reload, she let her machine pistol drop; her sling caught it on her chest, and she reached under her coat and pulled her Glock 17 with one fluid motion. Instantly she resumed the covering fire for Ifa, doing her best to occupy the unknown number of adversaries by the truck. She also spun her head left and right, concerned the Russians might attempt to flank her position.

On a quick scan to the right she saw a second blood trail, this one coming off the front porch of the chalet, then down the steps, leading to the low wall on the right of the drive. This told her Bello was injured but possibly still alive, just like Ifa.

But because she wasn't hearing any shooting from him, she feared Bello was out of the fight.

Just then someone downrange began targeting the Econoline that Zoya crouched behind. Bullets shredded through the body of the big vehicle, and she dropped back to her knees, crouching low.

She used this opportunity to reload the Glock, and she handed it off to Ifa when he made it to her. She reloaded her Uzi next, and while she did this, the percussive symphony of gunfire stopped suddenly.

She assumed either everyone was reloading at the same time or all the enemy were down.

She hooked her head under Ifa's arm, stood up with him without exchanging a word, moved down the rear of the Econoline, then turned to the left behind the Range Rover.

They made their way back up behind the engine block there, and while she still didn't have the best cover, she knew it couldn't hurt to have two big vehicles between her and the bad guys instead of only one.

A quick check of her colleague told her Ifa had been shot in the thigh. It bled profusely, gurgling spurts pulsing down his leg, so she pulled a combat application tourniquet out of her backpack and handed it to him. He'd have to put the CAT on himself because Zoya was still focused on searching for enemy through her sights.

As she did so, Braunbaer called her on her radio even though he was less than ten yards from her on her right.

Softly, he said, "What do you see, Transit?"

She raised her head over the hood of the Range Rover, then knelt back down.

"I can only see the front of the Highlander because of the van, but there's one enemy down there. No movement."

"I see the back of the SUV," the German said. "Looks like a body hanging out the rear window, but the tailgate is open, so somebody might have bailed out from back there. Watch for flankers."

Zoya's head shot back to the left, and her weapon spun with it. The coke was making her reactions faster, which was good, but more erratic, which was definitely *not* good. It was a net negative in a gunfight, she realized now.

"What about Bello?" Ifa asked into his walkie-talkie with one hand while he began administering a tourniquet on his leg with the other.

"He's behind me in the snow," Braunbaer said. "He's not moving or responding."

"And Velesky?" Zoya asked.

Braunbaer replied. "He's behind the wall in front of me. He's fine. The Russians might have run off into the trees."

Zoya shook her head, then clicked the transmit button. "If Velesky is telling the truth about the damage his intel could cause, then any Russian assets here still alive won't leave without him."

The German said, "Understood. I'm calling this in to Broussard. Keep covering what you see."

"Roger."

Zoya felt nauseated and assumed it was the addition of cocaine to a scenario that already had her heart beating at maximum capacity. She took a few calming breaths, checked on Ifa, and saw that he had tourniqueted his right leg, twisting the windlass of the CAT tight enough to make him cry out in pain.

Just then, someone shouted in Russian from the direction of the Highlander. "Hey! Lady? You still alive?"

Zoya answered, not worried about giving up her position because behind the cars was really the only place she could have gone during the melee. "I'm here! That you, Votyak?"

"Yeah! It's me!" After a pause, he said, "I've only heard of one Russian woman who operates like you just did. A former SVR asset, on the run from Moscow and working in the private sector." He paused, then said, "Is that you, Sirena?"

Zoya's code name in Russian foreign intelligence had been Sirena Vozdushnoy Trevogi, "Banshee." She didn't know this guy personally, but apparently she had become something of a household name around Russian intel circles, probably because her nation's intel services all wanted her dead.

She didn't answer the question, however. Instead, she just said, "You've lost Velesky. Might as well just get in your ride and get out of here with who-ever you have left."

Zoya aimed her weapon at the rear of the Range Rover, still speculating that other Russians would be attempting to flank while the redhead dis-tracted her. She was ready, however, with a fully loaded Uzi magazine and a partial mag in her back pocket.

The redhead chuckled. "Let's just wait to hear from Monsieur Broussard."

Through the hissing of the snowfall she could hear Braunbaer now, crouched behind the planter on the other side of the drive, talking on the phone.

Ifa grunted with effort as he climbed up onto his left leg, and there he positioned himself, holding the Glock over the hood in the presumed direc-tion of the Russians, twenty meters down the drive.

While everyone waited for the German to talk things over with his boss, the redhead spoke again. "Sirena. When this is all sorted, why don't you come with me? I know some people back home who'd love to see you."

"Yeah," she replied, still peering into the snow falling behind the Range Rover and thinking about her plans in case the gunfire erupted again. "I imagine they'd love nothing more."

"They'd take you dead or alive," the redhead said. "But if you walk slowly to me now with your hands raised, I promise no harm will come to you while you're in my care."

"Hard pass, Votyak."

Ifa put his hand on Zoya's shoulder to get her attention. She turned back around, keeping her weapon pointed at the rear of the truck but following Ifa's eyes. On the other side of the driveway, Braunbaer had stood up behind the wall, still using the planter for cover from the Highlander. He had his phone to his ear, but he was facing Ifa and Zoya.

"Oui," he said in French. "Je vais me conformer." *I will comply.* He put the phone back in his pocket, looked to his left where Bello had crawled wounded over a minute earlier, then turned his attention back to Ifa and Transit. Loud enough to be heard without his radio, he said, "Sudden change of plans."

Ifa kept his pistol over the hood pointed back down towards the Rus-sians, but he spoke up to Braunbaer now. "What has changed?"

"My target," Braunbaer said, and he lifted his MP7 in Ifa and Zoya's di-rection and opened fire.

TWENTY-SIX

Ifa was struck instantly multiple times, his body riddled with 4.6-by-30-millimeter rounds. Zoya had been standing behind the African in relation to Braunbaer, but as soon as the gunfire kicked off, she threw herself flat into the snow and scooted under the Range Rover with a speed heightened by a combination of training, adrenaline, and blow.

Ifa's bloody corpse slammed into the ground a few feet away from where she lay, his dead eyes staring back at her, and more rounds pocked the SUV above her, shattering glass and pounding metal.

She knew she couldn't stay here. She was pinned on two sides: Braunbaer to the north and the Russians to the west. If the Russians had been flanking, then they'd be to the south of her, as well, and it wouldn't take long for them to find her hiding under one of the vehicles.

So she rolled out from the Range Rover on the other side of where she'd been standing and made her way, still clawing through the powdery snow, until she had scurried under the Ford van.

Here she crawled forward again, until her head was between the front wheels of the big vehicle, and she shifted her aim towards Braunbaer. He'd stopped to reload, but there was no respite for Zoya because the Russians had opened fire again, shooting up the Econoline above her, apparently working *with* the German now instead of *against* him.

Zoya knew if she squeezed the Uzi's trigger she would reveal her location to the Russians on her left, and she didn't have a shot at Braunbaer around the planter, so she just waited, cringing at the ripping of metal and the shattering of the last bits of glass above her.

Radiator fluid began draining down on her as the gunfire persisted. The machine gun was in the mix, obvious by its distinctive rate of fire.

But then, for just an instant, she caught sight of Braunbaer. He was behind the planter but had spun around, facing the other direction. He raised his weapon as if there was some threat there behind the low wall, and then he fired a burst, but as he did so he flew backwards and tumbled all the way over the wall, landing on his back on the drive with his feet in the air, propped on the wall.

He'd been shot by the injured Bello, Zoya had no doubt, because she'd seen the blood trails in the snow that told her Bello had climbed over the wall.

And she assumed Bello had then been finished off by Braunbaer's last burst of rounds from his MP7.

Zoya remained frozen, her heart pounding like never before in her life. Braunbaer was dead, Ifa and Bello were likely dead, and she hadn't seen Velesky for the past minute.

She was the last of Broussard's four operators left.

There were still multiple Russians alive, however. She could tell by the gunfire from behind or around the Highlander.

As she lay flat under the Econoline, she looked to her left and saw three sets of feet moving her way: one set from around the front of the Highlander, and two from around the back. She also noted that one of the men at the rear was clearly limping.

She had no idea who was carrying the machine gun, but she also had no doubts all three of them would be armed.

They moved slowly but steadily, and she could tell they were positioning to clear the space where Ifa had fallen behind the Range Rover, knowing that was the last place they'd been fired on from.

Zoya didn't want to start shooting from this vulnerable position under the van, so she waited for all three sets of feet to move past her position, then she rolled to her left and came out from under the west side of the van. She climbed to her feet, then turned and ran for the Highlander, her Uzi high in front of her in case enemy had remained behind at their vehicle. She passed two bodies on her way, and once she got behind the shot-up Highlander, she found another still form and copious amounts of blood, evident on the white snow even in the darkness here.

Zoya knew she needed to get Velesky and then get the fuck out of there. He was off to her left as she faced the chalet behind the Toyota, but she couldn't see him over the wall. She began moving laterally in his direction, but before she exposed herself around the SUV, she came across a wire-stocked AK-47 lying there in the snow, blood all over and around it.

Kneeling down in the dark, she checked the magazine, found it more than half full, then flipped the selector switch from fully automatic to semi-automatic.

She rose up over the hood of the Highlander, saw the redheaded man aiming a handgun around the front of the Range Rover, and shot him once in the back.

He pitched forward into the snow, landing right next to where Ifa had fallen.

Instantly return fire raked the Highlander; she ducked and sprinted across the driveway towards where Velesky had hidden himself behind the wall.

Snow kicked up in front of her as incoming rounds impacted, and she held her AK out behind her and began firing one-handed as she ran in the opposite direction.

Two meters from the low wall, she launched forward, diving headfirst. She flew over the wall and crashed down on the other side, right on top of the banker crouched there.

Velesky screamed in shock, but Zoya just rolled off him, crawled a few meters to her left, and rose with her weapon.

She caught both remaining Russians in the open, moving between the Range Rover and the van, their weapons aimed where she'd gone over the wall, five meters to her right.

Both men saw the movement of her rising directly in front of them, and both began to swing their own gun barrels to combat this threat, but they were caught in a narrow channel between the vehicles, and Zoya just opened fire, sending big 7.62-by-39-millimeter rounds into the men's bodies.

She fired eleven times before her weapon emptied, and then she got low again, crawling all the way to her left to Braunbaer's lifeless body.

She hefted his MP7, the fourth firearm she'd handled in the past three minutes, and scanned the area carefully, kneeling behind the wall but looking over.

The two men between the vehicles were both down, but she shot them each once more with Braunbaer's weapon. The redheaded man was lying on his back now; she could hear a loud gurgling in his throat that told her she'd hit a lung. His weapon was several feet away from his body, and she saw no other threats, so she climbed over the wall and walked over to him.

Still looking through the snowfall for any movement or danger, she stood above the dying man.

The gurgling continued, but through the raspy breaths, the redhead said, "Last chance, Sirena. Come home with me."

"Home? Home for you now is hell." She shot him in the chest.

Alex Velesky stood now, directly behind the woman called Transit, and he saw what she did, watched her shoot the still bodies of both the Russians who'd fallen between the two vehicles and then execute the wounded man.

The Russian woman with the American accent scooped up the Glock 17 pistol lying next to the dead redhead, grabbed an extra magazine from his shoulder holster, and pulled the phone out of his pocket.

She then turned to Alex. "Into the woods."

He said nothing, just followed along next to her until they reached the wood line.

They walked a minute more, and then, without warning, the woman stopped walking, dropped the pistol, and then fell to her knees in the snow.

Alex's shock melted away in an instant as he realized something was wrong. "Hey, are you—"

The woman in the black knit cap began retching, then vomiting; her chest heaved and her body quivered, and she put a hand on the ground to keep from falling over.

Alex knelt over her. "That's good. You're fine. It's just the coke and the adrenaline. Your stomach didn't stand a chance against all that chaos."

She continued vomiting till there was nothing left, and she heaved a few seconds more.

It took her a full minute to stand up and turn away from the sick in the snow.

Zoya Zakharova wiped cold tears from her cheeks and looked around, regaining control of herself. She still had energy, even after the bout of sickness she'd just endured, and she told herself the cold air would probably do her good, as well.

But she didn't know where they were going, and she didn't know what her objective was.

Alex seemed to read the confusion on her face. "Do you believe me now?" Alex asked. "There are nine dead men back there. Nine! Look how many have already been killed for that phone, and we don't even know exactly what it will show us yet."

"Let's go," she said.

"The Range Rover. I don't think it was badly damaged."

Zoya took the man by the arm and began walking back through the trees with him. "We aren't taking the Range Rover. That's Broussard's car, and Broussard's been paid off by the Russians. No sense in driving around with a target on our backs."

"Then . . . what *will* we do?"

"Two, two and a half hours of walking. We'll end up on the outskirts of Wengen. We'll get a vehicle there."

"We'll freeze to death."

She pushed him on. "Not if we keep moving. Let's go."

They walked in silence for a time. Zoya felt the effects of both the drugs and the adrenaline leaving her body, faster than the heat left her body as they endured the elements. She was tired now, drained, and the last thing in the world she wanted to do was talk.

"The men with you," Alex said, disturbing the sound of the crunch of snow under their shoes. "They called you Transit. Is that what I should call you?"

"If we don't talk, then you won't have to call me anything."

"We'll *have* to talk at some point."

Zoya knew he was right. "Don't call me Transit. That's weird."

"Banshee, then?"

Zoya stopped walking a moment. She'd forgotten Velesky was Ukrainian, and hadn't thought about him understanding her conversation with the GRU man.

After a moment, she began walking again, and Alex followed a step behind her. "He said you are former Russian foreign intelligence, but they're after you now?"

Zoya sighed. "Alex, we have a long way to travel together, so let's get one thing clear from the beginning. We're not going to be doing a lot of talking about me." She thought a moment. "Call me Beth."

"Why?"

"Why not?"

Velesky nodded as he trudged along, his breath vaporizing in the frigid wet air. He said, "You are Russian? Really?"

She felt ashamed to admit it, but after a moment she said, "I am."

"Why are you doing this, then? Why are you suddenly helping me?"

She wiped her nose and spit into the snow, ridding her mouth of the remnants of the vomit. Finally, she said, "Tens of millions of us—more, probably—want no part in that war. This world is complicated enough without instigating an armed conflict like that."

"But . . . where are we going, Beth?"

Zoya kept pulling Alex Velesky along. "You said if you got to New York, you could do something with this data."

"Yes."

"Then we're going to New York, aren't we? Now, do me a favor and shut the fuck up."

Alex nodded, but he said nothing more as they trudged through the snow towards the lights of a small mountain village in the cold distance.

TWENTY-SEVEN

The eighteen-year-old Dassault Falcon contracted by the CIA crossed over the Azores at an altitude of thirty-nine thousand feet, heading east above a bed of clouds and under a canopy of stars.

Already seven hours into the flight, Court Gentry was stiff and sore in a luxurious cabin chair in the aircraft's rear, gazing out into the night and thinking about Zoya.

He'd been sleeping, and he'd dreamed about her, and when he woke up, the dream seemed to continue in his semiconscious state.

Shortly after boarding in Saint Lucia, Angela Lacy had brought him the med kit and told him she'd treat him after she spoke with the pilots, but he'd waved her off. He put a compression bandage on the back of his neck and taped it down awkwardly, and then he downed a couple of prescription pain-killers he found in the kit, all while Lacy was up talking to the flight crew about their route to Europe and their plans when they arrived.

By the time they took off he was sound asleep, and he'd remained that way for hours. He needed the rest—he'd been up for nearly two days straight—but now that he'd awakened moments ago, his entire body felt the effects of his car crash; various cuts and bruises on his midsection, arms, and head ached and burned.

Court still wore the T-shirt and pants he'd been dressed in during the raid on Eddison John's home. They were torn and bloody and filthy, but he'd not had time for any shopping between getting yanked out of a car plummeting off a cliff and climbing up the jet stairs of the Falcon, so he was stuck with what he had.

But now that he was wide-awake and hurting, he decided he needed a better understanding of what he'd put his body through in the Caribbean all those hours earlier.

He cleared his mind of Zoya—temporarily, at least—and pulled off his T-shirt slowly and gingerly, the fabric sticking to dried blood on wounds all over his torso. Looking down at his chest, he saw scrapes and purple marks, mostly where the strong palm fronds had battered him, and bruising indicating the position of the seat belt across his chest was evident.

He reached behind and felt his back with his hand, touched a sticky wound at his right kidney, and cringed from discomfort.

His face still a mask of pain, he looked up to see Angela Lacy, the only other passenger on the jet, standing above him with a look of frustration on her face. She could clearly see the pain he was in, but she was unsympathetic.

"I told you I'd treat all your boo-boos after takeoff, but you wouldn't let me."

"I should have listened," Court admitted.

"Have you noticed how you keep saying that to me?"

Court tossed his filthy and torn black T-shirt onto the chair next to him. "Don't rub it in."

"You need more painkillers?"

He shook his head, preoccupied with the sticky wound on his back.

She said, "Hold on. I'll get some ice, then I'll come back to tell you everything I learned while you were snoring."

He cocked his head. "I don't snore." But she'd already moved away and did not hear him.

Angela was back in a minute with three small plastic bags of ice in her hand and the med kit under her arm. She put the ice on the table in front of him and then pulled antibiotic spray out of the kit. He leaned forward, exposing his back.

"You look like you were attacked by a tiger."

"Worse. A Russian assassin with hand grenades."

Lacy said, "Car chases, hand grenades. You and I work in totally different organizations, don't we?"

"You have no idea," Court mumbled, and then he squeezed his eyes shut while she sprayed the antibiotic all over his back and then his chest.

After this came more antibiotics in the form of an ointment, and then she pulled rolls of gauze out of the kit and tore them out of their plastic bags.

Court became lost in thought: still frustrated about all that had gone down in the Caribbean, still thinking about what was in store for him in Switzerland, and depressed about the fact that Brewer had told him she no longer had a line to Zoya. The pain Angela caused by dressing a dozen cuts and scrapes faded from the forefront of his mind and was replaced by worry.

But Lacy worked diligently, and while she did so, she began talking to her brooding patient, refocusing his attention.

"Brewer got me access to European facial recognition data centers."

"I thought you were having to do this all alone?"

After only a brief hesitation, she said, "She found a workaround. She's wrapped me into an ongoing program with access to all intel."

"What program?" Court asked, only mildly curious.

"Need-to-know, Six."

"Right."

Pulling a compression bandage out of the red case, she began wrapping it around his rib cage, covering a layer of gauze that she'd already positioned to keep the antibiotic in place.

While she did this, she said, "Zurich station got a ping on a face."

"Matador? Velesky?"

She shook her head. "No . . . a thirty-eight-year-old GRU officer named Niko Forshev."

"Who's he?" Court asked.

"He's an illegal, living in Zurich, but Z station's known about him for a while. He's not actively surveilled by them, but they keep tabs on him electronically."

"Is he 29155?"

"There's no evidence that he served in the GRU's assassination squad. Anyway, a few hours ago he was photographed at a gas station in Wengen, near the city of Interlaken, along with five other men. They arrived separately in three vehicles, but then they all climbed into one Toyota Highlander and headed off after no more than a minute."

"The other guys?"

"Either they aren't in the database or the images weren't good enough to ID them, I'm not sure which. Forshev has a distinctive look. Tall, red hair. Kind of looks like Conan O'Brien."

"Who?"

Lacy stopped bandaging him and looked him in the eyes. "No TV on your little boat, I guess?"

"No," he said, then returned to the topic of conversation. "These guys that got in the Highlander. Were they carrying any cargo?"

"Everyone in the group had large duffel bags or backpacks."

"How does this tie in to—"

"Within three hours of the CCTV grab, Forshev and eight others were found dead at a private lodge just outside Wengen."

Court whistled. "Nine dead? Holy shit."

"A war zone, at least as far as what the cops are broadcasting. We have Agency officers on the way down from Bern—that's the closest large town. They'll see for themselves, try to ID more of the bodies. So far no one matching the description of Alex Velesky or Igor Krupkin has been identified. Of course, we also don't know if Krupkin's phone is still at the scene."

"So you think the GRU were there to get the data."

"Why not? Six dead in Saint Lucia, nine dead in Wengen. Krupkin's missing, Velesky's missing. It's all got to be connected."

"I agree."

Lacy said, "There were two vehicles at the scene in addition to the Highlander, so there was definitely some sort of force Forshev and his colleagues engaged. Only three bodies in addition to Forshev's group makes me think some of the defenders of the location survived and left."

"I agree," Court said. "We need to land this plane in Bern, not in Zurich."

She cocked her head. "Why not in Interlaken? That's closer to Wengen."

"Because there isn't an airport there."

"Oh," she said, then looked up at him. "You could do what Matador did. Jump out of the plane."

Court looked around. "Any possibility that there's a parachute on board?"

Lacy shrugged, now holding ice on a purple contusion on Court's right shoulder. "Not to my knowledge."

Court chuckled. "Then I like my plan better." Shifting in his cabin chair, he said, "It's an hour to Wengen from Bern; if we land in the next three hours, it will still be four hours before I get to the scene. If Velesky or Krupkin *were* there, then they're long gone now, either taken by the GRU or by some other actor holding them."

"Where would they go?"

"I imagine it's the middle of the night there," Court remarked.

Lacy looked at her watch. "Four forty a.m. in Switzerland."

"I bet they keep moving, getting some distance from the scene. It's what I'd do."

"What do you want from me?"

"Another hit, facial recog, signal traffic, anything, of anybody GRU, *anywhere* around there. Or Krupkin, or Velesky, or any known hard asset from *any* country. They won't go back to Zurich, but you need to set the net wide, covering any big city for a couple hundred miles in all directions. Geneva, Lyon, Munich, Milan . . . someplace like that. If I had that data and a protectee, and then a bunch of my team got slaughtered by a six-man GRU outfit, I'd go to ground in a big city, somewhere I could get really good and lost while I plot my next move."

Lacy seemed to think about what Court was asking of her. She said, "This is work an entire section would do at headquarters. We'd have two dozen collection and analytical types helping us. I've been granted wide access, but Brewer isn't bringing anyone else into the operation. I don't understand why we don't just talk to Zurich station and—"

"That's between you and Brewer. I'm used to working without help and without a net. You'll have to come to terms with it quickly on your own."

After Lacy finished cleaning and bandaging Court's deepest cuts, he took the ice off his shoulder, then picked up his torn and dirty shirt and started to put it back on.

Lifting his left arm over his head was nearly impossible because of the bruised ribs, so Angela helped him.

He said, "You're a pretty good medic."

Once he was dressed, she reclined his chair, then handed him the ice packs, which he placed strategically on his ribs over the compression bandaging.

She said, "I have some abilities. You want another pain pill?"

He shook his head again. "I'll take some anti-inflammatories." She handed him a pack of ibuprofen and stood back up.

"All right, going back to work. I'll run searches at accessed cameras in the cities you mentioned, see if we get lucky."

Court just nodded, swallowed the tablets dry, and looked out the window.

He thought about the people who'd survived the shootout in Wengen, and he wondered what it would be like to be on the run from the GRU in the Swiss winter.

Two hours later, and only forty-five minutes from landing in Bern, Court was upright again, still wearing his dirty clothes but now sipping coffee. The ice had done wonders for the pain in his ribs, and the anti-inflammatories had helped, as well.

Angela sat a couple of seats in front of him on the other side of the little aisle, facing in his direction. She wore a headset and peered at her laptop in front of her, and seconds after he focused his attention on her, her face adopted a look of surprise and excitement.

She yanked her headset off abruptly and rose, then moved back down the aisle to him.

"Milan!" she shouted as she sat down across the aisle.

"What about it?"

"Velesky himself was spotted on facial recog. A street camera caught him slipping into a twenty-four-hour market this morning."

"Alone?"

"Negative. Looks like he was with one male, approximately five foot ten, wearing a knit cap, a down coat, boots, and a backpack."

Court didn't hesitate. "We're going to Milan."

Lacy stood and rushed back up the little aisle towards the cockpit.

He looked out at the dawn, marveling at what he'd just learned. Alex

Velesky, target of an international manhunt with a body count rising by the hour, was traveling with only one other person.

It made no sense. Even if the people who had him—the people either protecting him or holding him—had lost three of their number the previous evening, he couldn't imagine they would have gone all the way to Milan without reinforcing the coverage.

Court wondered again about the guy watching over Velesky by himself, and to him it sounded like some bullshit job he'd been stuck doing more than once in his career.

Velesky and his sole surviving escort were on the loose in Milan, and Court wondered how quickly the Russians or any other bad actor with motivation to get Krupkin's data would descend on the city.

This was a race against time. For Velesky, for the lone asset with him, for Court and Angela, and for the CIA.

He willed the plane to fly faster, and just as he did this, he heard the engine noise increase and the wings tip to the south slightly. Angela had told the pilots about Milan and the urgency of the mission, and he knew they'd get him on the ground there as fast as possible.

Glancing down at an iPad, he pulled up the Italian city on Google Maps, then began reacquainting himself with its roads and features.

TWENTY-EIGHT

Zoya Zakharova woke suddenly; her hand darted out and wrapped around the grip of her pistol, and she listened in the darkness.

There it was again, a strange sound coming from outside her bedroom, somewhere in her little flat.

What's going on?

Her newly alert mind worked quickly to fill in the missing pieces, and she began remembering everything that had happened in a flood of images and emotions.

Bodies in the snow.

The march through the forest, followed by the five a.m. bus ride from Switzerland to Italy, the walk through central Milan to her flat with the Swiss-Ukrainian banker who, allegedly, had a way to damage the Kremlin's operations around the world by disrupting its funnel of money to the West.

When they'd finally arrived here this morning after stopping at a market in Piazza del Duomo for supplies, Alex had commented about how utterly filthy her place was. Every inch of counter or table space was crammed full of dishes, carry-out boxes and bags, foam cups, and 1.5-liter Contari vodka bottles, all of them empty.

Despite Velesky's revulsion, Zoya was in no state to be embarrassed about the condition of her flat; she'd just pointed to the couch and then went into her bedroom, where she'd dropped her pack down next to her bed, re-trieved Igor Krupkin's iPhone from the coat she'd then thrown on the floor, and tucked it into her jeans.

With her boots still on her feet, she unholstered her pistol and put it on the bed and then lay down next to it, where she'd tossed and turned for over two hours, unaccustomed to falling asleep sober.

Zoya had finally nodded off around ten a.m., and though she didn't know what time it was now, she knew she had to investigate the source of the noise before worrying about how much sleep she'd gotten.

She rolled out of bed silently, thinking the noise in the next room was probably Alex but also retaining the presence of mind to know she could safely assume nothing. With the Glock 17 aimed at the door, she began moving forward, soft and steady footfalls across the bedroom all the way.

At the door she lowered to her knees, took the handle with her left hand, and opened it.

She squinted away bright light for a moment, but she fought her eyes back open to fully take in the scene. Curtains were open, lights were on, the television was broadcasting a soccer match on mute.

The little window in the kitchen was open, as well, letting in the frigid cold. In front of it, Alex Velesky stood at the sink, rinsing a plate. He was in his undershirt, still dressed in the corduroy pants and Nikes he'd been wearing since they met.

Zoya looked around the living room in front of her. It was spotless, as was the kitchen to her right. The smell of coffee filled the space, and she looked at the counter and saw that the percolator light was on.

She felt like dog shit, and her mouth tasted like something had crawled in and died, but the prospect of coffee refreshed her suddenly.

Lowering her gun and rubbing her eyes, she headed for the kitchen. Even the cleanliness of her place felt obtrusive to her now.

Alex seemed to sense a presence behind him, and he turned to her as he put the dish in the drying rack. Unlike Zoya, he was obviously wide-awake, intense and energized.

She slid her Glock back into her jeans and made a beeline for the coffee.

"I hope you don't mind," Alex said, reaching for a wet mug to dry. "I like a clean kitchen."

"Knock yourself out," she said as she grabbed the mug out of his hand and poured black coffee into it.

"I've been thinking," Velesky said quickly, and she noticed some trepidation in his voice. "I appreciate everything you did last night, I really do."

"But?" Zoya said it distractedly as she put the urn down.

"But . . . I'm not sure you're in the right place . . . mentally . . . to help me."

Zoya burned her tongue on the coffee but made no reaction. She looked at the Ukrainian for a moment, then said, "I'm fine."

Alex didn't seem to believe her, and she didn't care. He said, "I can go to the police. The FBI, someone like that."

"Do you know who to trust in the West?"

"No . . . but I—"

"You're staying with me. Everything is under control."

Finally, he asked, "Okay, if you've got it under control, what's your plan?"

Her only reply was "We wait for nightfall."

Velesky looked at her. "Do you even know what time it is?"

Zoya used the light through the window to make a guess. "One p.m.?"

"Three thirty."

She put down her coffee and passed by him in the tiny kitchen, opening the refrigerator. She pulled out a jar of Nutella with no lid, grabbed a knife recently cleaned by Alex from the drying rack next to the sink, and dug through the rubbery top layer and into the soft chocolate-hazelnut spread below.

"Three thirty," she said, before eating a big bite off the knife. "Good. Not too long to wait." She put the knife down, reached up, and shut the kitchen window.

Velesky said, "It smelled like rotten garbage in here."

"You know," she said, "I bet it was all the rotten garbage." She went back to her Nutella on a knife and her mug of coffee.

Velesky drank down the dregs of his own mug, then began washing it. He said, "How bad is it?"

Zoya lowered her mug enough to look over it. "How bad is *what*?"

"Your coke habit?"

She sighed, took another sip. "Dude. Don't start."

"You left some powder on the table. I wiped it up." He looked back at the living room. "Along with a lot of other stuff."

"I didn't ask you to clean my house."

"No, you didn't. It's clear you don't care." He looked hard at her now. "The cocaine. Is it going to be a problem?"

"It's *no* problem."

"What about the vodka? Eight empty bottles lying around. More in the garbage."

Putting the chocolate hazelnut spread back in the fridge, she asked, "Did you find any *non*-empty bottles?"

"One," he replied. "I poured it down the drain."

"You're no fun."

Alex put his hand on her arm to turn her to face him. She didn't move, only looked down at his hand and then back up to him.

He let go slowly, chastened. "It . . . doesn't sound like you have much of a plan."

Zoya poured more coffee into her mug. "I might not have been ready for this when it fell into my lap the night before last, but I'm caught up now, I have a plan. Worked it all out this morning." Before he asked, she said, "We're going to Geneva. By train. Tonight."

"*Geneva?* You want to go *back* to Switzerland?"

She ignored him. "We'll arrive just after eleven p.m. Tomorrow morning we'll take the first train to Marseille. When we get there, we'll go talk to someone I know, then head to the airport."

"The airport? I just have my driver's license. I don't have my passport."

Zoya said, "We won't need a passport. From there, we'll go to New York."

Velesky nodded. "How long will it take us to get to New York?"

She drank more coffee, and she felt it finally kicking in. She was a little more alert, a little less rattled by the lack of booze in her bloodstream. "Depends on what plane we get on. We're beggars; we can't be choosers. If the flight lands at JFK, then we should be in the city a day and a half from now. If it lands in Albuquerque, then I guess you and I are driving across the U.S."

Alex seemed mollified knowing the mysterious woman had a plan. "Well," he said, "wherever we go, thank you for saving me last night, and thanks for agreeing to take me to New York."

"Don't get too excited yet. There are a lot of hurdles between here and there."

"I understand. Do you think there's anyone in Milan looking for us?"

She shrugged. "Broussard knows I've been living here, but he'd have no idea where, so the Russians shouldn't be on top of us. Still, transitional spaces, airports, train stations, busy streets . . . We'll be facing exposure in all these locations. The key is to keep your head down and keep moving. Follow my lead and we'll be fine."

He studied her a long moment as she drank her coffee and pretended not to notice. Finally, he said, "Why are you suddenly helping me?"

"I've got my reasons."

"Want to know mine?" he asked.

"No."

She'd answered him flatly, but he told her anyway. "My sister, my nephew, my mom and dad. All killed by the Russians."

Zoya looked down at the floor, holding her mug in both hands in front of her.

"They shouldn't have been there. We knew the Russians were coming, at some point, anyway. Every Ukrainian did. We just didn't know it would be then, even with the escalation. My parents refused to leave, and my sister, seven months pregnant, went down with her husband to convince them otherwise.

"The Russians attacked, and then she was stuck behind the lines, unable to get out. I did everything I could do from Zurich, which turned out to be not much at all."

Zoya bit the inside of her cheek.

Alex continued. "She delivered her baby in the hospital in Mariupol; my parents were right there with her." A tear rolled down the man's face. "They got to hold their grandson, if only once or twice."

He rubbed the tear away. "And then the missiles came. Direct hit on the hospital, intentional, no question. All four of them were buried under rubble. Her husband died on the lines in Donetsk three months later. He wasn't even Ukrainian, he was Dutch, but he stayed to fight."

Zoya's heart sank even lower. She felt personally responsible for their deaths, but she wasn't sure why. After a moment, she said, "After it happened, you just continued to work?"

"No. I fought for weeks to get the bodies out of Ukraine. They arrived here, I had a funeral, I wasn't working at all during that time. My firm was supportive at first, but then the implication became clear: I had to return to the office or leave my position."

"Why did you stay?"

"Because I came to the realization that the only thing in this world I have to market is my ability to hide and launder money for criminals. I've hated every moment of the last year, but I've gone to work and done my job."

Zoya leaned back against the counter, took another sip of coffee, and said, "Until Krupkin showed up."

Alex smiled mirthlessly. "My salvation came in the form of an even bigger crook than me. And a Russian, one who coddled and protected those in power in the Kremlin, one who aided and abetted the murderers of my family." He shook his head, still bewildered by all that had happened. "When Krupkin gave me the phone, my first thought was to toss it in the river. But within moments, I knew what I had to do."

Zoya nodded but said nothing.

Off her silence, he said, "So . . . that's me. What about you?"

"I supported the regime for a long time," she said with a shrug. "I don't anymore. That's it. If I can help you . . . I want to help you."

"What I'm doing now," Alex said, "it's not heroic. I worked with dictators, despots, and criminals for over a decade. It was only when their crimes hit me personally that I rose up to take a stand. I'm not looking for hero status. I'm looking for cold retribution."

Zoya said, "That's as good a motivation as any, I suppose."

He looked her over a long time. "How could you ever work with them? The Russians?"

"I *am* them."

"I mean, in intelligence. Russia didn't just become evil a year ago."

"I believed in what I was doing, more or less." She shrugged. "Sometimes significantly less . . . but . . . but I left before the war, not because of it."

"Why did you leave?"

"Because they were trying to kill me."

He regarded the comment. "That's as good a motivation as any, I guess." She changed the subject. "Who's in New York that you have to see?"

"Ezra Altman. A forensic accountant, the absolute best in the world when it comes to tracing Russian money laundering. He has a database of Western offshore accounts and their owners, maps of money movements into commercial and personal bank accounts. He's been developing it for years. Anyway, I sent him the link to the files I stole. He should receive it tomorrow, I think."

"He's a friend of yours?"

Alex laughed a little. "More like an enemy. An archenemy."

"I don't understand."

"He's been targeting Brucker Söhne, my bank, for years. Me, specifically, since I handled crypto transfers, and the Kremlin was using crypto to get their money out of Russia. He's been a thorn in my side for a long time, but he's never been able to bring us down.

"Still, he's the best at what he does. Dogged, smart, and the files and databases that he's painstakingly compiled about offshore banking and money laundering will be crucial in connecting the dots between the Kremlin and its payees quickly and completely."

"You can't do this without him?"

Alex shook his head adamantly. "There are a couple of other people around the world, but they aren't as fixated on Brucker Söhne as Ezra Altman is. He's obsessed.

"I'm just a piece of the puzzle; Krupkin didn't rope me into this because I was the one who could assemble the puzzle. Ezra Altman, on the other hand, *he* is the puzzle master."

Zoya nodded. "Okay. Let's get this phone to Altman."

Alex nodded. "Thank you."

"Yeah, well, hold your applause. We'll probably both die in the process, but we have to try, don't we?"

"*I* do," Alex said.

"I do, too," Zoya answered somberly, and she headed back to her room.

TWENTY-NINE

At six p.m. Luka Rudenko entered Milan's central train station wearing a dark blue ski jacket over a black cable-knit V-neck sweater, which itself was over a white T-shirt. Over this was a three-quarter-length wool peacoat, and on his head he wore a brown watch cap that covered the bandage on his wounded left ear.

He strode directly up the stairs towards the shops on the first floor.

The majestic station had been in use since the 1930s, and it had been designed to show the power and grandeur of the Mussolini regime. Inside its imposing brick façade, a magnificent concourse led to three grand staircases, and these led to arched train sheds with high glass-domed ceilings. With twenty-four tracks in all, Milano Centrale was the second-largest station in Italy.

He walked through the thick evening crowd climbing on and off trains, rolling luggage along the platforms, or shopping or dining in the dozens of shops and restaurants in the massive communal space, until he took the stairs to the upper level.

Here he arrived at the Mokà café, with tables along a glass wall overlooking the platforms, and he saw a young man sitting with his laptop and a phone on the table in front of him, an espresso in his hand.

Without a word Luka sat down. His tablemate was more than a decade younger than Rudenko; he had short black hair, a dark beard, and slightly Asian features. The man wore a gray down jacket unzipped, and a knit cap was on the table next to him, and when Rudenko sat down, the younger man sat up and looked his way in surprise.

"Sir."

"Luka," Rudenko admonished. "I'm Luka. You're Ulan. Come on, man. You're new, but you're not *that* new."

"Luka. Da, sorry."

Rudenko was a major, the senior man of the detail, and Ulan Bakiyev was a starshina, a first sergeant, and the most junior.

He was Kyrgyzstani, only twenty-eight, and the most technically proficient operator in the ten-man cell that had arrived here in Milan this afternoon, which was exactly why he was seated at a table and looking at a laptop.

"Where are the others?" Luka asked.

"It's just me and Ivan for this whole damn station. He's downstairs in the metro station on the Nikon pulling images for the database, capturing faces the CCTV might miss." He motioned to the laptop on the table in front of him. "I'm up here with this, but I've got a camera, too."

"What access do you have?"

"I'm inside the network here, both within the building and without. Just like Ivan, I'm running faces through the CIPDB."

This was the Combined Intelligence Personality Data Base, a list of millions of images and bios. Everyone any Russian intelligence agency knew about was loaded on here, and with the software, the CIPDB could "soak in" forty faces at a time and perform a one-second check against the database.

Ulan could access all the cameras in the station, so the application was hard at work, ready to send an audio alert to Ulan's earpiece anytime a match was made.

Rudenko looked out over the throngs of passengers. "Weapons?"

Ulan looked over his laptop at his team leader. "Of course."

Rudenko rolled his eyes. "I'm not asking if you are armed. I am asking what you are carrying."

"B&T subgun, under my right arm. Three mags. Same as the other guys."

The Brügger & Thomet APC9K submachine gun was impressively compact, just less than twice the size of a full-sized pistol with the extending stock collapsed.

Luka only carried his Steyr 9-millimeter pistol inside his waistband, with two extra magazines, so he was glad the rest of the team had brought a little more firepower.

He asked a few more questions of Ulan, then pulled out his phone and called Drexler.

"Yes?"

"It's me." Rudenko looked around. "I'm at Milano Centrale. I don't have enough eyes here. Twenty-four tracks, four levels, a metro station, more than one hundred commercial spaces. Even with the technology we have, two men can't cover this."

Drexler replied with an air of confidence. "I might be running your team, but I also have my own assets out there. I have eight people in Centrale right now. Four more in Garibaldi Station, and a half dozen at the airport."

The Russian looked around. "What assets do you mean?"

"Watchers. Most are private investigators I use, or other people who have worked for me. I'm employing eighty in Milan at present, spread among all the transitional hubs."

Luka was pleased to learn this, but it also came with some concerns. He said, "Your people will not act. We will engage with Velesky when the time comes."

Drexler said, "That would be my preference, as well. My people are armed with knives, that's all."

The Russian ended the call and then stood up from the table, looming over his junior teammate.

"You're going to stick around?" Ulan asked, now mostly focused on the laptop in front of him.

"I'll be in my car. I'll head over to Garibaldi Station to check in on the team there. If you find something, alert me, and I'll reach out to Drexler. He has eyes here, he can get surveillance on the target if he climbs on a train."

"Are his people any good?"

"Is Velesky?" Rudenko asked dryly.

Luka shook his head. "Good point. But what about the man with him?"

"Whoever he is, we'll deal with him first."
He turned away and headed for the station's exit.

A little more than five miles to the northwest of Luka and Ulan, Court Gentry's eyes scanned the busy Via Privata Venezia Giulia around him, processing the faces, clothing, and gaits of passersby, as well as the make and model of vehicles that passed. He was busy, nearly frantic, though his face carried the countenance of utter calm.

Well past sunset, the last hues of light in the sky were slipping away by the minute. He sat quietly across from Angela Lacy at a bistro table at a café out in front of the Klima Hotel Milano Fiere. They both had coffees in front of them, and a gas heater next to the table kept them warm.

She wore AirPods and stared at her laptop, her coffee untouched in front of her, but Court sipped his cappuccino. As he did so, he continued surveying the area, trying to find those who didn't fit in, vehicles that might also serve as reconnaissance vans, the reflection of the streetlights in a sniper's scope in an apartment window.

There was a lot to look for, and it was on his shoulders to cover it all, because Angela was totally focused on finding Velesky via camera sweeps around the city.

They'd met here ten minutes ago; he'd arrived on a motorcycle he'd bought earlier in the day, and she'd pulled up in a panel truck, a request made by the man she knew as Six in case he needed a place to stash his bike. She worked calmly at her laptop, but Court felt himself champing at the bit, hoping to get some actionable intel so he could deal with Velesky, find Matador, and retrieve all the missing data.

Neither of them knew if Matador would come here to Milan for certain; it was possible that once he'd made it out of Saint Lucia with the phone, his portion of the mission would be complete. But Court had a feeling that Alexander Velesky, in possession of both the data he'd stolen from his bank and the data given to him by Igor Krupkin, would be sufficient unfinished business for the GRU, and Matador would be deployed to the area.

The Russian assassin would be close by, Court was almost positive.

Krupkin's body had been identified in Lake Zurich earlier in the day;

he'd been dead for some time, so now Court knew that only Velesky, seen on CCTV here this morning, was still in play.

As he sipped down to the bottom of his coffee cup, Angela pulled out her AirPods and turned the laptop around to him, revealing a security-camera-quality image of Alex Velesky, walking into the market here in Milan early this morning. This wasn't the first time Court had seen a picture of his target; he'd looked him up online earlier in the day, finding several articles in obscure financial-fraud-related industry magazines about Brucker Söhne. From what he'd read, Velesky was a significant player in the corruption, an expert on cryptocurrency who worked at a shady Swiss bank to obfuscate billions of dollars of deposits from abroad.

Court hated the son of a bitch for his role in helping Russia, and he thought longingly about that moment when he'd get Velesky on the right side of his gunsights.

Court didn't know why the crypto banker with the high-dollar job was stealing financial intelligence that could hurt America, but the why of it all didn't matter. Court would find him, he'd get back everything he took, and kill him if he had to, along with whoever got in his way.

He began flipping through the still images on Angela's screen that had been taken at the market this morning.

Velesky was in his thirties, smallish but handsome, with light brown hair. He wore dark brown pants and a heavy jacket that appeared to be torn at the right arm, and he appeared even in the grainy stills to be utterly exhausted.

Behind Velesky in the first photo, his face mostly obscured by glasses and the brim of a ball cap, was the other man who had been traveling with him. He was either a bodyguard or a kidnapper, but Court saw no evidence from the series of stills that Velesky was being held against his will.

He flipped to the next image, looking at the man in the rear, and then he flipped again.

Still after still of the pair, and somehow Velesky's face was easy to see while the man in back managed to avoid the camera enough to prevent it from getting any clear shots.

The stranger wore dark pants, a black ski jacket, a black backpack, boots, and the black ball cap that completely hid his hair color. He had tinted eyeglasses, and Court assumed they were costume to obfuscate the facial appearance from getting picked up in computerized recog algorithms.

The unknown subject was definitely male, approximately five foot ten. Although the unknown man wasn't particularly tall, Court noted he had broadish shoulders, evident even under the thick jacket, a muscular chest, and something of an athletic swagger in his walk.

This dude, Court assessed by his good sense of countersurveillance tradecraft, knew what he was doing. And if he was, indeed, the only survivor of the wild shootout the night before in Switzerland, Court had no doubt the man could handle himself, so getting through him to get to Velesky could well be a challenge.

Court turned the laptop back to Lacy after checking the images. In a slightly annoyed tone, he said, "I know what Velesky looks like. I need to know where he is."

Lacy took the laptop and repositioned it in front of her. But before she began working again, she looked up at Court. "You're still mad at me solely because I had the misfortune of being assigned this job by Suzanne Brewer."

"I'm not mad at you. I just don't trust you."

"Even after everything I did to help in Saint Lucia?"

"You'd have to know my history to understand. I've worked shoulder to shoulder with men I thought were brothers, and these same men turned on me. And I know Brewer is looking out for Brewer. If that means some old asset needs to be sacrificed, then so be it."

Lacy looked away a moment. Court wondered if that meant something. Quickly, however, she said, "You aren't that old. We're probably the same age."

"Yeah, well, my mileage is high for my model year."

Lacy looked him over. "I've got to ask. What are you?"

"What do you mean?"

"You *know* what I mean. At first Brewer hinted you were just an ops officer. Then, after meeting you, I assumed you were a NOC." She eyed him up and down now. "But you just called yourself an asset. You're not an operations officer, are you? You're something else."

Court gave a little nod as his eyes searched the area for trouble. "I am something else."

Angela took a couple of shallow breaths. "I've heard rumors about men working as contract killers for Langley. Sub rosa. Deep black. I . . . I always thought that bullshit spy thriller stuff was only in fiction."

"It is," Court said. "Mostly. But there are a few guys like me." He shrugged. His searching eyes suddenly locked on hers. "And we're filed in the nonfiction section."

"That look in your eyes . . . this is where I stop asking questions, right?"

Court chewed the inside of his lip, began scanning the area again. "The dark side is a virus, and I contracted it a long time ago. You seem like a nice person, an honest person. Don't get too close to me, and *definitely* don't get too close to Brewer. We'll just infect you."

She appeared nervous now. "Brewer's already pulled me in deep, though, hasn't she?"

"Most definitely. But hold on to your soul. I'd like to think I have, to some degree, but it would be so damn easy to go full black."

"Like Brewer?"

"Yeah."

"What has she done? What have the two of you done together?"

Court darkened his tone. "*This*, Angela, is where you stop asking questions."

She blinked her brown eyes, gave a tiny nod, and then looked back down to her laptop, while Court's leg bobbed nervously under the table. He needed a target, an outlet for his energy.

He had a man to find. And a man to kill.

THIRTY

Zoya peeked out through the curtains of her living room window at the misty twilight that had fallen over her neighborhood, and she thought about what might be lurking out there with plans to kill her.

Her body felt better than it had earlier, and her headache was gone, but this was only due to the two tiny airplane bottles of gin that she'd found in a handbag.

She'd bought them accidentally weeks before, thinking them to be vodka while stumbling through a market in a drunken state and tossing them in her basket along with frozen pasta.

She didn't like gin; that was the only reason the two bottles had survived untouched for so long, but today things were different. There was no more booze in the house, she'd gone nearly two days without any, and she was desperate to take the edge off and soothe her throbbing headache.

She'd waited for Alex to take a shower, and while he did, she'd poured both bottles into a dirty coffee mug, then found a half-consumed Fanta in her fridge that had lost its fizz a month earlier, and she poured that in the mug, as well.

She drank the concoction down rapidly, with no concern about the taste.

Each bottle was only fifty milliliters, but together that meant she'd shot-gunned nearly 3.4 ounces of alcohol in just a few gulps, and the familiar act of accepting the biting liquor into her throat helped to settle her nerves in seconds.

It occurred to Zoya, and not for the first time, that she was an alcoholic, but at the rate she lived her life, she assumed this to be something she'd die *with* and not *from*, so she didn't worry too much about it.

She pulled her phone back out of her pocket and dialed a number for the fourth time in the past thirty minutes. It rang and rang, as it had done on the three previous occasions, and soon went to voice mail.

She hung up.

Her mobile carried Signal, an end-to-encryption app that obfuscated the phone number and location of both the sender and the recipient of voice calls and texts, video, and audio files.

She wasn't worried about being tracked, but she *was* worried; she was worried that the person she kept calling was dead.

She held the phone down by her side and continued looking out past the window curtains. Downstairs, an organic pizza restaurant attracted a few neighborhood people, but the cold, misty air kept it from doing much business at all.

Zoya had accomplished a lot from her tiny flat this afternoon, preparing for action. She'd called a nearby used-clothing store and talked a beleaguered employee into walking around the shop, picking out several items in Alex's size, and then she'd cajoled him into bringing the two large sacks of clothes to just outside her apartment, where she'd exchanged them for an envelope full of cash, the price of the clothing plus a three-hundred-euro tip.

She had Alex try everything on, and when she confirmed that it all fit, she'd given him one new set of clothes to dress in for this evening, and she packed a second set in a dark gray carry-on bag of hers.

She looked down at the phone again but decided to wait another minute before redialing. If she could get the other party to answer, she just might learn some crucial intel that could help her and Alex make it through the night, but even if she never connected with the other party, she had a feeling she'd unwittingly been given some intelligence from her adversaries earlier.

Something had occurred to her a few hours ago while she and Alex sat in this dark and quiet flat waiting to leave, to go back into the open, to expose themselves again to danger.

It was the redheaded GRU officer Zoya had killed—or, more specifically, something he'd said to her before he died.

He'd made it clear that he was surprised she was a woman, and this meant to Zoya he'd had no idea he'd encounter a woman at the snowbound abandoned ski lodge.

She knew the Russians had gotten to Broussard; Braunbaer had been ordered by the Frenchman to turn his weapon on his colleagues, after all, but for some reason that she could not figure out, Broussard had apparently not told the Russians anything about her. The mysterious Frenchman who'd been passing her contracts did not know her name or much about her background beyond the fact that a mutual acquaintance, a former German intelligence officer, had vouched for her, but Broussard most definitely was aware that Transit, the code name he used for her, was female.

So why the hell wouldn't those Russians know that?

Zoya dialed the number again with a sigh, and as the phone rang, she wondered again if her handler had been murdered and if she'd ever solve the mystery of why he'd both ratted her out and protected what little of her identity he knew.

But this time, instead of continued ringing, she heard a click on the line. After a short moment, Broussard spoke.

He sounded nervous, and his tone held none of the authority it had held in all of their previous conversations.

"What is it?" he demanded.

"It's Transit."

Both of them were silent a moment, until Broussard said, "You might not believe it, I don't expect you to, but I am very glad you're alive."

"They got to you."

Another brief pause, then a long sigh. Finally, Broussard said, "They most definitely did."

"Are you still with them?"

"No. They're gone. For now."

"How did they approach you?"

"Firstly, Drexler called me yesterday afternoon."

"Drexler?"

"Sebastian Drexler . . . he's Swiss, sort of a fixer, usually working for one of the large private banks. He's working for someone else now, I don't know who, but whoever it is, they've given him a team of tier-one assets to run."

"What assets?"

Broussard whispered, as if saying it at normal volume would bring even more danger down upon himself. "The men you met last night were GRU, regular Fifth Directorate operators. But Drexler is commanding an entire field team from 29155."

Fuck, Zoya thought. *GRU hitters.* She'd been hoping it would be a group of henchmen from the Russian mob, but instead she was up against the A-team of Russian killers.

Her breathing deepened, and she racked her brain trying to think if she might have another bottle of liquor somewhere in the flat, because she sure as shit was going to need it.

When she didn't ask Broussard to explain the number he'd just rattled off, he spoke again. "So you know who they are."

"Unfortunately."

"Well, Drexler is in charge of them, for reasons that utterly baffle me. He made his threats, and I found them to be more than credible, so I gave him the location of the transfer of Velesky to the Geneva-based bank."

"And?"

"And when Braunbaer called me, I told him he'd only live through the night if he worked *with* the GRU men, and not against them."

Zoya said, "Braunbaer killed Ifa and Bello."

"And then you killed him? And the GRU men?"

Zoya didn't answer. She'd had help killing the German and the Russians, but she wasn't going to recount the firefight to the man who set her up to die in it.

Instead, she said, "And then what happened?"

Broussard laughed, but dourly. "This morning, after things went bad at the transfer last night, two men from 29155 paid me a personal visit. I was at the park with my kids. They sat on the bench with me, and they let their displeasure be known."

Zoya understood Broussard to be understating the event.

The Frenchman continued. "Please see my predicament. I found myself with little choice. I gave them absolutely everything they asked for." He added, "They are so incredibly motivated to retrieve Mr. Velesky and the data he's carrying. Drexler called me back when they left, just to let me know he's keeping one of the assassins close by me, in case they need to come back a third time."

Zoya had never heard of Sebastian Drexler, but she knew enough about Unit 29155 to know that if they were being controlled by a Westerner, then someone at the very top of the Russian government had sanctioned it.

Zoya filed this away for later, because now she needed to put all her efforts into first getting more intel from Broussard, and then finding a way to scare him even more than the GRU had.

Zoya asked, "What did you tell them about your asset who survived and left with Velesky?"

"I told them you'd told me you were based in Milan, but I didn't know where, and I doubted you'd go back there, anyway."

"My appearance? My gender?"

"I don't know your appearance, do I? But . . . yes . . . Drexler kept talking about you like you were male, and I never once corrected him. I didn't think it would make much difference, but it was my tiny show of defiance. I only referred to you as Transit. He asked if I had pictures of you, and I answered honestly that I did not. He asked if you and Velesky were working alone, and I told them I was sure you were, because you didn't strike me as the type to make friends, and your three colleagues on this operation are now in a morgue in Wengen."

Zoya took a few measured breaths into the phone. "You are *certain* they don't know I am female."

"They *don't* know you're female, they *don't* know you're American, they don't know where you are. All that was clear to me. I might add that if you *were* foolish enough to return to Milan, you might want to get the hell out of there, because with nothing else to go on, they'll surely go there and hunt you."

Zoya had not been foolish to return. Everything she needed was here, and since Broussard didn't know where she lived, she thought her chances of getting here, resupplying, and then leaving after dark were better than anything else she could think of.

She heard Alex turn off the shower. After a slight pause, she brought her shoulders back and pushed some menace into her voice. "Okay, Broussard, now I ask you to be patient while I describe in complete detail what I will do to you if it turns out you are lying to me right now."

"You don't need to—"

"Shut the fuck up."

A pause. Then, *"Oui."*

"Last night, nine men were left dead in the snow in front of that ski lodge. Seven of those men were actively trying to kill me."

Broussard did not speak.

"Only *I* survived, along with my protectee. Nine dead, but not me, and not Alex. What does that tell you?"

"That you're hard to kill. And that you are one hell of a good bodyguard."

"Precisely. If you are lying to me about anything, I promise you I will make it past the next seven men, if only to show up at your door."

"I believe you."

"That's all." She began to hang up, but the Frenchman called out.

"Wait!"

"What?"

"Transit, I have never once, in a career that is longer than I care to admit, turned on my own people. I've been threatened before. I always told myself I was an honorable man, and would rather die than betray those who relied on me."

"Goodbye," Zoya said.

"Hold on. I've . . . but I have children now, and everything is . . . different."

Zoya rolled her eyes. She could tell the Frenchman was getting emotional, but she didn't have time for this.

Broussard added, "Transit, I always liked you."

"Can't imagine how the end of our relationship could have been worse if you *didn't* like me."

"Just . . . just think about yourself. Whatever Velesky has, it can't be worth your life."

"Two things. One, you don't know what he has. And two . . . you don't know what my life is worth."

She hung up the phone, put it in her pocket, and turned around to find

Alex Velesky standing there in the faded black jeans and a cotton button-down and blue blazer she'd bought for him. His hair, following her instructions, had been slicked back with product, whereas before his bangs had hung almost to his eyebrows.

He looked like a businessman, or perhaps a youngish university professor from England taking a semester off to tour Europe.

Without preamble he asked, "Why don't we drive?"

She cocked her head. "We *are* driving. To the station."

"I mean . . . why don't we drive to Geneva? It's what? Five hours? We can split the time behind the wheel."

Zoya shook her head as she reached into the broom closet of the kitchen. She pulled out a black duffel bag and opened it up. Rifling through it, she said, "Driving means passing under streetlight cameras for five hours. It means license plate readers identifying the car and the direction of travel. It also means stopping along the way for gas and bathrooms, which means more cameras."

She found what she was looking for, pulled out a thick manila envelope, and opened it up. From it she withdrew a fat wad of one-hundred-dollar bills. She put them on the counter and pulled out another. Reaching back in, she grabbed another envelope and took out two banded stacks of hundred-euro notes.

Alex thought this must have been twenty thousand U.S. or so, and another twenty thousand in euros.

But she made no mention of the money at all as she continued talking. "There will be cameras at the train station, but not on the trains themselves. It won't be easy getting there, and it will be even harder moving through the station, but if we can pull it off without getting compromised, we'll be better off than taking my car."

Zoya put the cash in a money belt she pulled from the duffel, and then she put the bag back.

Alex nodded; she could see his nerves registering on his face. His skin was pale, his eyes distant, a thousand-yard stare that looked right through the walls of the claustrophobic little flat.

Zoya needed his head right for what was to come. "Look, right downstairs there's a little café. Maybe we go in there and order a bottle of wine. We have time. It will help us both relax, and that will make us better when—"

The Ukrainian looked at her like she was insane. "I want to get my data to New York so I can destroy the Kremlin. I don't want to go to a fucking bar to get drunk."

"I don't want to get drunk, either, I just—"

He waved a hand in the air, obstructing her explanation. Changing the subject, he said, "What did your helper tell you?"

Zoya headed for the kitchen and began opening cupboards she'd already searched multiple times today, looking for some forgotten bottle of booze. "He's a handler, not a helper."

Alex shrugged. "That makes sense, as it doesn't sound like he's been a lot of help."

Zoya gave up her search quickly, realizing it was futile. She'd drunk the last of the booze in her flat, and she knew it. Turning back to him, she said, "He told me Milan will probably be crawling with Russian hit men."

Alex didn't hide his fear. In a voice now suddenly frantic, he asked, "What the fuck are we going to do?"

For the first time Zoya smiled a little. "We're going to walk right through them."

She turned for her bedroom door without another word, the smiling face turning to a mask of intensity as she walked.

THIRTY-ONE

Twenty minutes later, Alex was sitting on the couch, flipping channels on the television, when he heard someone come out of the bedroom. He didn't even look up at first, but when she stepped in front of the TV, his eyes widened.

Velesky had known the woman he called Beth for less than two days, but in all that time she'd always looked extraordinarily masculine to him. From the moment they'd met, he'd acknowledged she had a beautiful face, even unadorned with makeup, but she was broad-shouldered and nearly his height. She'd worn her black knit watch cap even around the flat, and no makeup, and she'd appeared to be nearly flat-chested.

Velesky didn't have the experience to realize she was purposely disguising herself; he thought this was just what she normally looked like and how she dressed.

Now he found himself unable to speak. She was stunning, the epitome of modern femininity, strength, grace, and allure.

Beth wore makeup; her cheekbones were high and her large green eyes were more pronounced than before. A beauty mark on the right side of her chin had appeared from nowhere. Her dark brown hair hung down past her shoulders, her tight rust-colored sweater showed off a surprisingly ample chest, and while she was still broad-shouldered and apparently rather muscular, there were so many other features that vied for his attention that he barely noticed it.

She wore black flats, and this dropped her height significantly from the work boots she'd been wearing. He'd thought she was around five-ten before, but now he saw she was no more than five-seven.

He sat there in silence, gazing transfixed at the changes to her face and body, even to her gait and posture. "You . . . look . . . *different*."

When Beth spoke, despite her soft beauty, her words were delivered with the same high intensity and dominant command she'd used with him before. "Let's get two things out of the way first," she said.

"Wha . . . what?"

"It's a padded bra, and stop fucking looking at it."

Alex Velesky blushed, and his eyes darted back up to Beth's face. He blinked hard.

"Sorry . . . I just wasn't expecting this, is all."

"Were you expecting this?" She handed him a plain silver wedding band. "Congratulations. We just got married." She held up her own ring finger, displaying an engagement ring and wedding band. Obviously unimpressed with her own costume jewelry, she joked, "Fucking cheapskate, I've never forgiven you."

Alex was confused. "I . . . Is this a disguise?"

Her eyes narrowed to slits as she looked at him. "You catch on quick. If the people after you can crack into surveillance cameras, then they probably think you're traveling with a man. They'll be looking for two men trying to get out of town. A husband and wife traveling together won't get the same scrutiny."

Alex nodded. "So we should be fine, right?"

"Disguise is not a sure thing. We're running risks doing this no matter how we dress, but this might give us a slight advantage with any surveillance teams out there. Facial recognition sweeps are harder to beat; we can only do so much, but we'll keep moving and hope for the best."

Alex said, "But what about me? I changed clothes and combed my hair, but I haven't really altered my appearance."

"Follow me."

Together they stepped into the bathroom, and she pulled a small plastic bin out of the cupboard, then opened the lid. From it she pulled a glass bottle and a tiny package.

From the package she removed what appeared to be a perfectly authentic beard and mustache. It was light brown, not too far off from Alex's own hair, but definitely not a match.

He was facing the mirror, but she asked him to turn to her. With spirit gum Beth carefully affixed the beard to his face, then adjusted it for a couple of minutes. All the while Alex stood there in silence.

She pulled out some scissors and trimmed the beard, then touched up the spirit gum under his lip. Finally, she turned Alex around to look in the mirror.

When she took a small step, he said, "The color doesn't match my hair."

Beth saw this for herself, apparently, because she was already reaching for a couple of small bottles of dye from the bin. She mixed them together in the metal lid of one of the bottles, then looked up at Alex's hair for a moment. A third bottle came out of the bin; she added this color to the others, then grabbed a paintbrush and a comb.

In five minutes she'd dyed the beard while Alex wore it; she wiped off a little of the coloring from his cheek below his eye, then turned him back towards the mirror.

He looked it over again, then brought a hand up to it.

"It will dry in a few minutes, but don't touch it as long as you're wearing it."

He nodded and kept staring at himself in the mirror, now utterly fascinated by his own transformation.

Beth had left the bathroom, but when Alex didn't follow, she returned. Though she might have been one of the most beautiful women Alex had ever laid eyes on, she remained as tough-talking as any man he'd ever been around.

She took him by the shoulder and pulled him along roughly. "We're moving, Alex, and we're not fucking stopping till we get on that train."

Thirty minutes later Zoya Zakharova and Alex Velesky entered the grandiose front entrance of Milano Centrale arm in arm, with Zoya carrying a large laminated shopping bag along with her purse, and Alex carrying nothing but a small leather shoulder bag.

This was all one hell of a gamble, Zoya knew. Velesky was a wanted man, sought by God knew how many parties, and at least one of those enemy forces was aware that she lived here in Milan. But she saw the train as the only viable way to get to Geneva. There was no overnight bus, and as she had explained to Alex, taking a car would mean getting their faces recorded on more cameras, and their route could easily be plotted from the images caught along the way. The enemy would be able to assemble in front of them and shoot them down in the road if they wanted to.

The train station had a lot of cameras itself, however, and the route of a train was predetermined, of course, so this method of transportation came with its own dangers. She was banking on the hope that Alex's disguise would hold until they departed, and then on the train, she told herself, she could monitor for any threats and then react to them by getting off at a stop along the way or, if it came down to it, fighting it out in the narrow confines of a coach.

Her decision to go to Geneva via rail decided, now she just had to get herself and her package to the EuroCity 42 on platform four in the next seven minutes.

A bustling crowd moved through the main concourse, and every now and then Zoya saw that she was catching eyes, but she was used to getting a second glance from men when she was dressed as she was tonight. She looked past the men gazing at her body and her face, and instead scanned for someone eyeing her with different intentions.

While she walked, she also kept a tight hold on Alex, feigning a gesture of affection as their arms were wrapped together when she was, in fact, keeping him in line.

And while she did this, she simultaneously looked over everyone in the crowd she could see.

They had made it halfway to the stairs to the platforms when something in front of her triggered an alarm bell in Zoya's mind. Just ahead and moving perpendicular to her way of travel, she spotted a pair of men, both in their twenties; one was bald, the other blond with a man bun. They stood out to her.

Zoya knew what piqued her interest. She saw that they seemed to be scanning as they moved through the throngs of travelers at a pace unique from those around them.

In the counterintelligence realm, it's known as "irregular lines of movement." The men were moving perpendicular to both incoming and outgoing passengers, adjusting their trajectory in unpredictable patterns.

She'd noted that the pair were neither rushed and determined passengers hustling to find and leap aboard their train before it left the station, nor were they idly standing around, people-watching while waiting for their departure.

No, these guys were working, and their job clearly involved finding someone in the masses.

Watchers in the station. She couldn't know if they were here hunting for Alex, but she *did* know she couldn't safely assume otherwise for a single second.

And if she spotted two watchers within moments of entering the station, she certainly expected there were many times that number she'd yet to identify.

Quickly, she made a plan, and then she leaned over to Alex and spoke softly.

GRU First Sergeant Ulan Bakiyev received his third espresso of the evening shortly after seven p.m., and the waiter had just stepped away when he brought it to his lips. He paused before sipping when he heard a familiar audio signal in his earpiece, indicating a match had been found in the database on his laptop. This was the twenty-fourth time this had happened in two hours; diplomats, foreign law enforcement types, anyone the Russians had images of were subject to identification, and this was a busy European train station, so it came as no surprise to hear the beep and, as every time before, he knew better than to get his hopes up as he checked his computer.

On the twenty-three previous times, he'd looked down to see a still image from the video collection of the area cameras in the upper left corner of the screen, and below that an image from the database itself. These were usually passport photos of the person identified, but they could also be file photos held by GRU, FSB, or SVR. The person's name and full details would then scroll down the right-hand side of his monitor.

But this time, he saw something different. On the left was an image of a person taken here from the CCTV, and there was a passport photo of the individual below it, but instead of names and data on the right, he saw red flashing text with a password prompt just below the warning.

Priority One. Code Word Authorization "Scion" Required.

This, Ulan had never seen. With a puzzled look on his face, he reached for the mobile on the table next to the laptop, and he touched a button on it.

Luka Rudenko drove in heavy traffic towards Garibaldi Station to meet with the two men from his unit working there to try to find Velesky in this city of 1.3 million.

As he changed lanes at a crawl in the heavy congestion, his phone rang and he tapped the button on his steering column to answer it. "Yeah?"

"This is Ulan. I've got something here at the central station." Rudenko felt his pulse quicken. He was two kilometers west of Milano Centrale now, in bumper-to-bumper traffic on Viale della Liberazione, and he glanced down at his Mercedes navigation system to figure out how to turn himself around and get back to Centrale as soon as possible.

As he did this he asked, "You have Velesky?"

"No, sir. It looks like a high-priority tasking, though."

Rudenko's hot blood cooled instantly, and he looked back up to the traffic ahead of him, pressing on to Garibaldi. Frustrated, he said, "We're here for Velesky. Let anyone else go, regardless of sanction."

"But . . . this is different. This personality has a lock on their file. Code word access only. This might be something interesting, even if we pass it off to the local office."

Luka didn't give two shits about helping the local SVR station bag some priority target who was not *his* priority target; he only cared about his own career, and that meant killing Velesky, retrieving his phone, and receiving a promotion out of field operations.

But still, he couldn't help but be a little curious about the hold on the file. Distractedly, he asked, "What's the access challenge?"

"Scion."

The blood in Luka Rudenko's body didn't suddenly turn to molten lava, but his interest was, at least, piqued. He shot a glance into his passenger-side mirror and, finding the lane clear, jacked across it to the shoulder of the highway. Here he came to a jolting stop.

Quickly, the GRU team leader said, "That's a level one national target. The Scion challenge's response is . . . Odessa."

He heard Ulan type this into the laptop. Then he heard a soft gasp over the line.

The young operator was apparently taking a moment to read the file, but Rudenko wasn't going to wait. With increasing urgency in his voice, he said, "Did you get an ID?"

"Uhhh . . . yeah. Yeah, I did."

"Well? Who the fuck is it?"

Twenty seconds later, Luka had ended the call with Ulan, and he raced past the traffic at high speed, driving along the shoulder, all while dialing Drexler's mobile.

THIRTY-TWO

Sebastian Drexler rubbed his right knee distractedly as he sat in a suite at the Milano President hotel with his team, who were watching their monitors. His ten surveillance technicians were all hard at work managing a network of some eighty assets out in the field; there was urgency in their task because they knew there was an increased chance their target would move as soon as it was dark.

A cloud of cigarette smoke and coffee cups on every flat surface in the opulent suite revealed both the intensity of the job and the mood of the team. The techs were fueling their bodies with chemicals to stay sharp, ramping up for what they expected to be a very long night.

Drexler was hopeful, but he felt his mood darkening. They'd been up and running since three p.m., and there had yet to be a single sighting of Alexander Velesky.

His mobile phone in his jacket pocket buzzed, and he pulled it out and answered without any excitement at all. "Oui?"

"It's Luka."

Drexler said, "Nothing here yet. You?"

The Russian almost barked out a response. "I'm off the job."

Drexler stood suddenly on his shaky knee. "What do you mean, off the job?" He could hear that the Russian was in a car, and it sounded like he was driving the hell out of it.

After a squeal of tires, Luka said, "It means I have to take care of something that doesn't involve our present relationship. I'm pulling a couple of my guys off, as well, but you can keep the rest."

Sebastian Drexler moved swiftly out of the sunken living room of the suite and onto the balcony for some privacy. With authority in his voice, he said, "Your orders handed to you by your leadership are crystal clear. Spanov himself wants you to—"

"My orders," he interrupted, "were superseded one minute ago when we identified a priority one enemy of the Russian Federation walking through Milano Centrale. I'm going to deal with this, and then I'll go back to helping some Swiss man find a missing Swiss-Ukrainian with banking information."

Drexler was utterly furious. "Who is this supposed high-value target?"

"That's classified. I have to go."

"Wait," he pleaded, but Luka disconnected the call.

Drexler shouted to the ten technicians positioned throughout the dining room, the living room, and even in the kitchen. "Alert everyone in and around Milano Centrale! The Russians are leaving the mission in that location. It's up to us to cover the area."

He waved a finger around towards everyone in the room. "And it's up to all of you to find me Velesky's face in this town!"

Ulan Bakiyev was easily the best technical asset in 29155, and he was also one of the best foot followers on the team. He was the man called on for either of these tasks, even though he'd never been called on to conduct a hit himself.

He'd been an intelligence analyst in the army, and he was gifted and brilliant when it came to anything to do with computers and data, though he was not much of a physical specimen. But when he was asked to join GRU, he was told he was needed in an elite unit, and he'd have to undergo batteries of tests of physical and mental endurance. He spent a year in a pretraining program before going to Ryazan Airborne School, where he was trained as a Spetsnaz operator. Through little more than an iron will he made it through; in fact, he barely survived his training, but he didn't quit. He became a popular teammate in 29155 and was known as one of the hardest workers on the squad.

But he'd yet to kill a man with his own weapon or his own hands.

Right now he walked thirty meters behind Zoya Zakharova, code named Banshee, as she herself walked arm in arm with a bearded male companion. Ulan carried his laptop in a bag hung over a shoulder, and a machine pistol under his arm, hidden below his thick coat.

He had a teammate here at the massive station, but Ivan was several minutes behind him and downstairs in the Metro. Ulan knew it was up to him to track Banshee, and he also knew he could not lose her or Major Rudenko would kick his ass.

Zakharova was more important than Velesky, at least as far as this GRU officer knew, so he suspected his leadership in Moscow would forgive Rudenko and his team for defying their instructions to follow the orders of Sebastian Drexler unconditionally.

Bakiyev knew surveillance tradecraft well enough to keep an eye out for countersurveillance. As he moved he saw no one looking his way in the crowd, and while doing this, he took a quick moment to evaluate the man with his target. He hadn't gotten a look at the unknown subject's face yet, but since the man hadn't yet been picked up in the CCTV scans, Bakiyev discounted him as any sort of a threat.

Banshee turned abruptly to her left in front of him, even seeming to surprise the man who moved along with her. The unknown subject recovered quickly and then followed her over to an automatic ticket kiosk.

Ulan caught a quick glimpse of the man's face through the undulating crowd around them, and he saw that he wore a full beard and eyeglasses.

The Russian pulled up quickly after Banshee did, turned to his left, and walked over to the entrance of a pizzeria. Pretending to look over the menu in the window, he flashed his eyes back to the right and saw Banshee make a selection on the screen on the ticket machine, and then she pulled out cash from her pocket.

While the Russian woman remained focused on completing her purchase, Ulan hurriedly pulled his Nikon out of his pack, turned it on, and covertly pointed it toward her. The male GRU officer glanced back at the entrance to the pizzeria, but he kept the camera down by his hip, and he kept taking shots.

He began moving through the crowd, approaching the pair. He wasn't going to close all the way to them, but he told himself he needed to be the next person up to the kiosk so he could check and see if he could tell where they were heading, and he needed to get the best images possible.

As he neared the pair, he was still shooting pictures but looking off to his right and not at his target.

When he was only ten meters or so away, well ensconced in the masses moving around and positioning himself in the order line at a small café bar with tables spilling out in the concourse, he glanced ahead again and, for the first time, he got a front-on look at the man with Zakharova. He was bearded, perhaps in his midthirties, and well dressed. He saw a wedding ring on the man's hand and immediately assumed the disgraced defector and former SVR operative had gone and gotten herself married while on the run from Moscow.

Ulan looked away yet again; Banshee was pulling her tickets from the kiosk and didn't see him, and now he brought his camera up to his face and began looking over the images on the screen.

He'd taken over sixty stills, but most were obstructed by passersby. Only after he'd scrolled back over a dozen photos did he find what he was looking for.

The unknown subject looking directly towards the camera. Bakiyev was planning on sending the image to Luka just to let him get a visual on Banshee's partner, but before he texted it off, he zoomed in digitally and looked the man over.

He brought the image closer to his face, and he looked it over again.

His Nikon was equipped with a Bluetooth connection to the laptop in his backpack, and he pushed two buttons on the camera and it ran the image on the screen through the database.

There was a delay of no more than one second, and then a green check appeared on the screen, indicating that the man had been located in the database.

Another click, and a name appeared on his camera's monitor.

A small gasp came out of Ulan's mouth for the second time in the past five minutes, and he reached for his phone while Banshee finished removing her tickets from the machine.

Court kept looking down at his watch, the feeling of frustration in his body growing more and more palpable by the minute. Somewhere in this town a man with secrets capable of destroying American intelligence lurked, and he was sitting here at an outdoor café watching some squeaky-clean case officer hunt for him through software on her laptop.

He felt like a man without a mission, and he also knew Velesky could leave town at any time, or worse, reveal everything he had discovered from his bank files to the world.

Just when he was about to stand up and begin pacing the street lot to burn off nervous energy, Lacy held a finger up suddenly, her eyes riveted to her laptop.

Court saw all this, and he sat up straighter. "You got him?"

She shook her head. While she typed something into her computer, she said, "No, not him. But we just got a flag on a GRU operative named Ulan Bakiyev, who we code named Kangaroo. He was spotted on CCTV walking through Milano Centrale train station."

Court was unimpressed. "There are a lot of GRU out skulking around Western Europe these days; that doesn't mean he's following Velesky. He could be—"

Angela hit a button, and then she jolted her head up from the computer, her eyes wide, and Court stopped talking.

"What is it?"

With a new intensity in her voice now, she said, "Bakiyev is a sergeant in 29155."

Court rose from the table now. He knew that the presence of an elite GRU assassin from the same unit as Matador in the same city where the GRU's number one target had been sighted was no coincidence. He said, "The station's twenty minutes away in this traffic. I'll take the bike, you stay here and get me more intel. Look at the station cams in real time—you might see something the algorithm doesn't."

"I know how to do my job."

Court turned for his motorcycle, a man suddenly alive. "So do I. Get me a target so I can end this bullshit tonight."

Luka Rudenko hung up with Ulan Bakiyev, and his heart continued pounding as he threaded his E-Class through the seven p.m. traffic heading east. He was still several minutes away from Milano Centrale, and while he negotiated the near gridlock here, he continued thinking about the opportunity that had just unfolded before him.

His thoughts had been racing at the speed of his heartbeat, but now as he inched along the highway, he said what he'd been thinking out loud.

"Holy shit. Velesky's working with fucking Banshee."

Killing Zoya Zakharova along with Alexander Velesky would be the best thing that could ever happen in his career. He was certain now he'd be promoted to lieutenant colonel instantly.

Serving as a lieutenant colonel in the GRU would get him out of the field, into an office at the Aquarium, the nickname of the headquarters of the organization at Khodinka Airfield.

Russia would be fighting the West for the rest of his life, of this Rudenko had no doubt, and it remained his goal to use this op as a ladder to climb his way to personal safety.

Making lieutenant colonel would go a long way to ensuring he wouldn't die performing a hit in Estonia or get captured on a black-bag job for 29155 in London and spend the rest of his days in His Majesty's Prison Brixton eating baked beans for breakfast. A desk job overseeing field assets could well keep his name off an American kill list and exclude him from operations in rural Africa, where the sweltering heat and disease had almost killed him once already when he was a much younger man.

Rudenko told himself he didn't want anyone else in 29155 acting before he was there, but there was a problem with his plan. He was ten minutes from the station, and he had a feeling he didn't have ten minutes before his target disappeared.

His main target, after all, was no longer the renegade banker with a sudden conscience and no tradecraft. No, his main target now was an exceptionally talented and dangerous asset.

He tapped a button on the steering wheel, and Sebastian Drexler came on the line almost instantly.

The Swiss man spoke in an imploring voice. "Listen to me, please. It is crucial we—"

Rudenko interrupted. "I'm back on your job."

Drexler was obviously taken aback by the quick reversal. "What?"

"As it turns out, *my* HVT is traveling with *your* HVT."

There was a short pause, and then, "You've got to be kidding."

"Her name is Zakharova. Ex-SVR operations. She botched a mission and then killed a colleague, and for the past two years she's been on the run. There have been rumors she was working with the Americans, but nothing was ever proved."

"A woman?"

"Yes. I don't see the guy from the pictures in the market this morning with Velesky, but that might have been her in disguise."

"And Wengen? That was *her*?"

"I wouldn't doubt it for a second. I heard she was one of the best when she left foreign intelligence. Nobody liked her—a royal bitch, apparently— but damn good at her job."

Drexler said, "I'll have my men link up with your men there in the station. My people will get on whatever train they board for coverage, but you have to get your people on to strike Zakharova and Velesky. If he has the phone, then your men *will* retrieve it."

Zoya Zakharova stepped away from the automatic ticket kiosk, intentionally leaving her confirmation in the machine as if she'd forgotten to grab it with her tickets, and then she and Velesky headed towards the platforms.

Behind her and out of her view, First Sergeant Bakiyev moved towards the kiosk.

The train to Geneva was four minutes from departure, but Zoya did not rush, nor did she tell Alex that it was likely they were under surveillance. Instead, they just ambled on through the crowd, following the pace of those around them.

There would be cameras everywhere, and while she had no knowledge that Russian intelligence had broken into Italian security cameras, and even though she thought she'd avoided the two men she'd pegged as surveillance assets, she knew that the less time she and Alex spent in the station, the better it would be for their prospects of survival.

While Rudenko continued talking to Drexler, a call from Bakiyev came through Rudenko's phone, and he put the Swiss man on hold while he answered, simultaneously checking his rearview, making sure no cops were on his tail for speeding.

Satisfied he was still in the clear, he said, "What do you have?"

"They purchased two tickets to Lyon."

Lyon? "Have they boarded the train?"

"They're walking to the platforms now, but the train to Lyon doesn't leave for seventeen minutes."

The Russian's eyes narrowed as he drove, still racing northwest. "Then they won't be on it. It's a ruse, throwing their pursuers off in case they're being watched. They'll jump onto something else and just buy a ticket on board."

"Why do you think—"

"We're talking about Zoya Zakharova. If she had the ability to recover Velesky from me and then shoot her way through a team of armed men, then she's skilled enough not to leave her fucking receipt in a ticket kiosk, and she's also skilled enough not to stand around a highly public and highly surveilled location for seventeen minutes for no good reason. Trust me. Lyon is west, so we now know they're *not* going west."

With complete confidence he added, "It's north. They're going back up towards Switzerland."

"Why?" Bakiyev asked.

"If Banshee is doing it, then she's doing it for a reason. That's all that matters to you and me. Keep on them, and find out what train they're on. Drexler has his own watchers there."

"Yeah, I've seen a couple. They aren't that hard to pick out. Got to figure Banshee's tallied them by now, as well."

"Shit," Rudenko said, and he disconnected from Bakiyev and switched back to Drexler. "Tell all your people at the station to go to the platforms and stand down. Do not look for *anyone*. I want their eyes in their phones, in a book, or on their shoes. No surveillance whatsoever. I have someone tailing Velesky and Zakharova now, and as soon as we know where they're going, I'll call you and you can put your people on their train, but I want no active surveillance, just soft coverage."

"Oui, I will comply."

Rudenko looked at his onboard navigation map, plotting his own course now. He whipped off the road towards the interstate, in the opposite direction of the train station, and floored his Mercedes. "I'll take the E62, as fast as possible, and that will send me to the northwest. I'll get ahead of them and link up with the train en route."

"How do you know they're going—"

"I don't know. I might be wrong," he said, then added, "but I doubt it."

Luka Rudenko hung up and concentrated on his driving. Getting ahead of the train was his best move. This took some guesswork, but he knew there were more routes to the north, west, and east than there were to the south, and he also knew Banshee would be a fool to head east, closer to Russia.

He liked his chances; he just needed young Bakiyev to perform a solid foot-follow to find out what train Banshee chose to get them out of Milan.

Alex and Zoya boarded the 19:10 to Geneva moments before departure, and the six minutes Zoya had just spent walking through the station had felt like a lifetime. Velesky dropped into a window seat and Zoya took the aisle, but she leaned over him to look out, searching the platform to see if the two men she'd noticed earlier had somehow managed to catch them boarding.

She saw people getting on the train, of course, but no obvious hunters. None of the people she examined seemed to be looking around, agitated with the tension of a critical mission.

Eyes were on phones, people were in idle conversation, a couple of men looked asleep on a bench.

The train began to move and she breathed a sigh of relief, but she also knew she had to remain vigilant. Any one of the people she saw board could be a member of the opposition, even if she didn't see the imprint of a weapon or probing eyes scanning sectors. Plus, if the opposition knew which train they had boarded, then they would know where they were going, and there could be enemy waiting for them at every stop along the way to Geneva.

This was going to be a stressful journey, she told herself, and therefore she also told herself she'd wait about five minutes before going with Alex to the restaurant car to buy a couple glasses of wine. Her nerves needed the alcohol like her mind craved it, and she would have to feed the beast, if only a small amount. Alex would bitch about this, there was no question about that, but angering her traveling companion was nowhere near the top of her long list of worries this evening, so she really didn't give a shit what he thought.

In the very last coach of the train, twenty-seven-year-old GRU First Sergeant Ulan Bakiyev sat down in a seat and took a long calming breath. After taking a few seconds more to relax, he tapped a button on his phone, and a call went through his earpiece.

A few seconds later he spoke in English, as there were people around him, and Russian speakers weren't exactly in high fashion in Western Europe these days.

"It's me. I'm on the EuroCity 42, destination Geneva."

Ulan listened for a moment, said, "Okay," and hung up the phone.

His job was complete. Other 29155 operatives, including Rudenko himself, would board at a stop somewhere ahead, and they would do the job.

He leaned his head against the glass and closed his eyes, a small smile crossing his face.

THIRTY-THREE

Court Gentry raced his Italian Aprilia 850 motorcycle past the Cimitero Monumentale in the center of Milan. It was freezing cold despite the knit cap on his head under his helmet and the black down jacket he'd bought that morning before purchasing the bike.

But his focus wasn't on the cold; it was on the train station up ahead and on his right. A call came through his noise-canceling headset as he motored eastward.

He told his phone's automatic voice assistant to accept the call, and then he spoke over the sound of the engine below him. "Yeah?"

As expected, it was Lacy. "We got another facial recog hit. Velesky this time. And he's with a woman. She doesn't come up."

"No sign of the man from earlier?"

"Negative. Just the lady. Velesky's sporting a beard, mustache, and glasses that he didn't have this morning."

"Interesting."

"They boarded a train to Geneva."

"What's in Geneva?"

"Other than the fact it's over the border in Switzerland, nothing that I know of."

"Departure time?"

"Sixty seconds ago."

Shit. The station was less than a half mile away, directly in front of him, but he'd not made it in time. Angela was still outside the hotel to the northwest, so she was in a much better position than he was to intercept the train at the next stop. He said, "Get in your van and start heading north. I'll try to catch up, but it's going to take me a couple of minutes to get turned around and headed back that way."

"We're driving to Geneva?"

"I hope not. I'll freeze to death by then. Find out where its next stop is. We just have to get ahead of the train and get on board."

It took her a minute; Court assumed she was checking her phone as she rushed to get into her vehicle. After a few seconds, however, she said, "First stop is Stresa. Nav system says I won't make it in time."

Court had already opened his throttle on the Aprilia and locked his eyes on an off-ramp that would steer him, eventually, back around to the north. "Your nav system is assuming you'll follow traffic laws. Don't."

He took the off-ramp, then drove down a dark alley, hoping like hell he'd intersect with a road that went north. Court couldn't drive the bike and look at the GPS on his phone, so this was all guesswork. Ideally he would have Lacy giving him directions, but since she was closer to the target, she was already on the move.

He said, "If we miss the first stop, what's the second?"

He heard a vehicle door open and Angela climbing behind the wheel, and breathlessly she said, "Domodossola. It's an hour and a half away."

"And what about after th—"

"Jesus, Six!" she shouted as she fired up the engine. "Give me a minute, I'm trying to fucking drive!"

"Okay, sorry."

Still exasperated, she said, "I can multitask once I'm on the road, but in the meantime just head towards Stresa and chill out."

Court smiled inwardly. Lacy didn't take any bullshit, not even from him, and he respected that. He said, "That's fine." He added, "Considering what happened in Saint Lucia, I guess I shouldn't be one to tell others how to safely operate a motor vehicle, but be careful."

"Right." Angela hung up on him, and Court leaned lower, ducking a little of the cold wind as he rode on.

Luka Rudenko moved through evening traffic slower than he would have liked, and he soon realized that there was no chance whatsoever for him to catch the train to Geneva before it left the station in Stresa to the northwest of Milan. His other teams in the city were all rushing to the northwest, as well, but none of them would make Stresa in time, either.

But Luka's navigation system indicated he could easily meet the train at its stop at Domodossola, and it appeared likely four more of his men, traveling in two cars on the E62 behind him, would make it there, as well.

Waiting an extra half hour to execute the operation was not ideal, this Rudenko knew. But he wanted to be on the train; he wanted to personally take the life of Banshee, to kill Velesky as well, and to take his data; and he wanted to command his troops from the front.

His Swiss handler for this mission wasn't going to like this decision, but Rudenko called him anyway, ready for the inevitable fight to come.

Drexler answered with a proud proclamation. "My team got a hit on Velesky, right as he got on a train to Geneva. I managed to get two men on the train, absolutely covertly."

This worried Rudenko. Masking it, he asked, "Do they have any martial abilities among them?"

"The pair on board now used to be Italian army."

"So . . . no," the Russian said derisively. Drexler's people weren't taking down Banshee; it would remain the job of 29155. "Tell your men to stand down. We'll take care of this."

Drexler said, "That's fine, but you better get to the next stop at Stresa."

"I won't make it in time. I have one asset on the train now, but five of us will join at Domodossola."

The Swiss man was surprised. "Wait . . . if you have a man on the train, *he* should just do it now."

Rudenko continued as if Drexler had not spoken. "The six of us will act as soon as we leave the station at Domodossola."

Luka was thinking about a second gold star on the red-and-gold-striped epaulets of his dress uniform, indicating the rank of lieutenant colonel. He was even thinking—fantasizing perhaps, he acknowledged—about earning the third star of a full colonel. Killing Zakharova and Velesky would earn him the former without question and, depending on just what exactly Velesky had on him, retrieving his data just might well earn him the latter.

He had the opportunity tonight he'd waited a long time for. He could press the trigger two more times in his life, and then he could be safe in the Aquarium.

"We will then pull the emergency handle located at one of the coach doors, and this will alert the driver, who then must stop the train. We will exfiltrate at that time."

"It's because you want to be there yourself, isn't it? You want personal glory and prestige. Killing this woman will put a feather in your cap in Moscow, won't it?"

"Don't be ridiculous. I just want the responsibility any good commander should have. I will be there, in person, to oversee the action."

"I am ordering you to order your man on the train to act now."

"I retain tactical command of the team."

"And I retain command of you! I will call Spanov!"

Rudenko was firm. "Call Spanov, but we're doing this my way."

Rudenko ended the call.

Zoya Zakharova and Alex Velesky sat at a table in the dining car, the fifth coach from the front of the train. In front of him he had a cup of hot tea, and in front of her were two small bottles of Valpolicella and a tiny stemmed plastic cup filled with the red wine. She was sipping, not gulping, but only to appease Alex, who looked at her disapprovingly over his steaming cup.

Finally, Alex said, "So . . . the people who are after us. They used to be your friends?"

She looked him in the eye. "I don't have any friends." She brought her wine to her lips and drank, willing the alcohol to have some effect, because the small amount of ease the gin had given her earlier had already faded away.

Velesky looked outside. She could tell he was having a hard time working with her, so angry was he at the nation of her birth.

She took another drink, then said, "I defected a few years ago. They've been after me ever since. I'm sort of on the run from everyone now, I guess." She shrugged. "Taking jobs here and there. That's what led me to Broussard. And that's what led me to you."

They sat in silence for several minutes, Zoya drinking slowly but steadily, already prepping for the pushback she was going to get from Alex when she gave up on the little cup and began drinking directly from the open bottle. A few times people came into the dining car, either just to pass through towards another car or to buy something to eat, and each time Zoya looked at the window next to her and watched them through the reflection. No one appeared in any way threatening, however, and she continued to divide her concentration equally between keeping herself and her protectee alive and getting buzzed on cheap wine.

Angela Lacy hurried through the small and unassuming station at Stresa, huddled in her down jacket against a cold wind as she climbed up from the stairwell and onto platform 2.

She'd just communicated with Six and learned he wouldn't make it here in time, but if he stayed on the highway with the throttle open, he just might make it to the next stop at Domodossola at nearly the exact same time the EC42 was due to depart.

This meant Lacy would have to sit on the train with the target for a half hour, under the assumption that at least one GRU asset was on board with her, as well.

She'd not seen Ulan Bakiyev get on the train, but he'd been at the station, and she had to assume he was tailing Velesky. If he was any good at his job—and she had every reason to believe all 29155 operatives were quite good at their jobs—then he would be on board, either monitoring Velesky for a follow-on force or else positioning to eliminate Velesky himself.

She was so far removed from her comfort zone at the moment that she felt like she was having some sort of out-of-body experience, but she concentrated on her breathing, calming her nerves slightly.

Looking over the platform around her, she noticed a pair of older men, perhaps in their forties or even early fifties, leaning casually against the railing rimming the stairs from the lower level. They wore backpacks over their shoulders and they were dressed like they worked some blue-collar job. Steel-toed boots, well-worn jeans, rugged heavy coats, and canvas rucks.

She turned away from them and eyed a few other passengers waiting for the train—a pair of older couples who seemed to be traveling together and a college-aged man who looked to Angela like he could possibly be from North Africa—and then she heard a low rising noise from downstairs below the tracks. Talking and footsteps; a large group of individuals neared, a low roar that increased with every second.

Finally the rowdy entourage appeared out of the stairwell. There were easily twenty-five of them in all, and they wore adventure wear and caps, and several had coats on that indicated they were from a Milan-based mountain climbing club.

There were three or four women at most; the rest were men, and the group ranged in age from early twenties into their fifties.

Every single one of the new crowd wore a massive backpack, the exteriors of which were festooned with all manner of gear that didn't fit inside the bags themselves. Crampons, water bottles affixed with carabiners, rope, axes, hiking boots, even aluminum camp stoves.

Angela also determined that either the group had been drinking or else they were just the happiest, goofiest bunch of adults she'd ever come across. Some sang, most laughed, and they clapped one another's backs as they told stories in Italian.

She heard someone in the group say "Alpi Francesi," which she knew to mean French Alps, so this climbing club was apparently heading to Geneva to continue on towards France.

They seemed to be a harmless bunch of oddballs, so she looked again to the tracks coming from the south.

The light of a train appeared flickering in the distance, and Angela Lacy said a little prayer to herself, then did her best to appear relaxed, even as she speculated about what would happen tonight on board the EuroCity 42.

THIRTY-FOUR

Zoya knew they would be arriving at their first stop along the way to Geneva in just a minute or two, and she told herself she'd have to be switched on for that. In the meantime, however, she sipped her wine and then looked at Alex. "You really think this Altman guy will help you?"

He shook his head. "He *absolutely* won't help *me*. But he'll see what I have, and he'll take it and do the rest himself. I need to be face-to-face with him, and I need to explain what it is and where I got it. After that, he'll probably still try to get me arrested by Interpol while I'm there in New York, but I don't care what happens to me after he gets the information."

"You'd hand your life away to make this happen, wouldn't you?"

"Is that so crazy?"

She poured more wine into her mouth from the bottle and swallowed. "Not crazy at all. What are you and I worth, in the grand scheme of things?"

Alex looked at her. "Not much."

"Not much," Zoya echoed. "You never met your nephew, did you?"

Velesky cocked his head. "Why does that even matter? He was family."

She didn't reply.

He seemed to detect something in her, and he said, "You don't have family, do you?"

She shook her head, looked out the window at the black night.

"But you want one. There's something missing in you."

Her eyes remained fixed on the abyss. "There's a lot missing in me." She brought the bottle back to her mouth.

He said, "I know the feeling. I've got no wife, no girlfriend, the only thing I had was my job, my hockey, my—"

Zoya almost spit out her wine. "Hockey?"

"Yeah. Left wing for the Zurich Lions . . . the amateur club, not the professional one, of course. I played growing up in Donetsk, continued at university in Zurich, stayed pretty active in the amateur league around town ever since." He shrugged. "That's all in the past, I guess. Haven't been on the ice in over a year. Since before the . . ."

His voice trailed off, and then he just said, "Since before."

Zoya unscrewed the cap on her second bottle of red, then poured it into her cup slowly. A little smile crossed her face.

"What?" Alex asked, confused.

She shrugged as she emptied the last of the wine into the cup. "I always thought hockey players were tough guys."

He chuckled at this despite his mood. "I was too small to be very physical, but I was fast enough to bother the other team's defense, so I got slammed around a lot." With a little glint in his eye, he said, "I used to say I took enough hits to learn how to deliver one myself."

The train began to slow, and Zoya, who had just lifted the cup to her mouth to drink, put it back down quickly. Looking out the window towards the approaching station at Stresa, she said, "If we make it to New York, and if you don't go to prison, what will you do?"

Alex himself looked out the window, craning his neck back around to see the station. He said, "I haven't spent one second thinking about that, and I guess that's probably for the best.

"What about you?" he asked. "We do this, you just disappear?"

Zoya stared intently at the people under the lights on the platform ahead, then tried her best to look at those outside the lights, because that was where the real threats would lie. "I don't know. I used to worry I wouldn't live to see tomorrow's sunrise. Then I started to not worry as much." Without losing focus on the platform, she said, "Now . . . now it's getting to where I don't care one way or the other."

"That's not good," Alex said, stating the obvious.

"It is what it is."

The train came to a stop. Zoya stood and headed for the door, then stepped down onto the platform. She looked back and forth, trying to get eyes on everyone within view. It was hard work; there were seven cars, fourteen doors, and dozens and dozens of people, but she kept at it. She saw a lone Black woman in a tan coat and a large handbag on the platform several cars behind her, and looking forward, eventually her eyes locked on a pair of men who stood on the other end of the platform.

These two carried packs over their shoulders, and they moved like military men. She couldn't see faces from this distance, couldn't tell if they were amped for action or just a couple of blue-collar workers traveling to Switzerland or northern Italy to a job site. She logged them in her brain, then focused on a single group of somewhere close to two dozen people, all carrying similar backpacks and wearing adventure wear like mountain climbers. They then climbed aboard the second-class coach right in front of the dining car Zoya sat in and began moving through the cars, finding seats in different parts of the train.

It took almost a minute for this group of boisterous passengers to make it up the steps one at a time, and when they were all aboard, Zoya looked again over her shoulder.

The Black woman traveling alone was just lining up behind a couple of others to board at the rear of the train. Zoya discounted her and everyone else in the group as any threat, and she turned forward again, looking once more in front of her.

The two men she'd first noticed at the front of the train looked down the track, and then, when the whistle blew announcing an immediate departure, they climbed aboard the first entrance at the first car.

It wasn't lost on Zoya that this was exactly the tactic she would use if she were hunting for someone who was supposed to be on the train. Pick one end or the other, and then scan until the last second to make sure the target or targets didn't wait till the doors were about to close to deboard.

The pair fit the general mold of the types of men she'd come across already in this operation, and though she couldn't be certain they were here looking for Alex, she knew she had to proceed on that assumption.

Zoya returned to her seat without speaking to Alex, and she took a long swig of her wine.

"Everything okay?" he asked her.

Zoya kept her wine to her lips, and she did not answer.

Angela Lacy climbed the steps at the rear of the train and moved inside, then entered the second-class coach, eighth in line, finding it to be only about one-fifth full of passengers. The train was a push-pull, meaning there was a driver's compartment back here with an angular nose facing south, even though the train itself would be moving north.

The driver's compartment was right behind her as she began making her way through the second-class seats, and looking back over her shoulder, she confirmed it was unoccupied.

She checked the entire eighty-six-place seating area for any sign of either Velesky or the woman he'd boarded with in Milan. Not seeing anyone who matched their description, she took a seat by the window, and then focused her attention out on the platform. Everyone seemed to have boarded, but Angela was more interested in seeing if anyone got off before the doors closed.

Looking as far up the train as she could, she didn't see a single passenger disembark.

Soon an electronic whistle blew and they began pulling away from the station, heading northwest. After a moment to calm a slight but customary bout of nerves, Angela stood, stepped out into the aisle, and began walking the length of the nearly two-hundred-meter-long train. She trusted in her ability to appear nonchalant and unassuming, and she wasn't much worried about appearing suspicious to her targets, but she did know there was a chance there would be others here on board who might be looking for an opportunity to go after the target themselves.

She was unarmed, but that was hardly relevant; she doubted she had what it took to pull a trigger if she had to, so she wasn't going to be mixing it up with Velesky or his companion. Still, she could find herself in the middle of someone else going after Velesky, and recognition of this was enough to give her pause.

She moved up the aisle, beyond the seating area and into the designated luggage area just before the door to the gangway. Suitcases and duffel bags were packed here on racks, and she only looked them over to make sure a person wasn't trying to hide in the jumble of luggage.

Soon she was into the gangway, passing the bathroom on her right as she headed for the door to the next car, while below her the wheels of the Euro-City 42 began revolving faster, increasing the train's speed by the second.

As the train picked up speed, Zoya Zakharova finished her wine in a single gulp, and then she looked Alex Velesky in the eyes.

"I need you to listen to me, but I also need you to stay relaxed."

Alex's eyes widened.

"Things are about to start getting interesting."

"What does *that* mean?"

"It means there are two men on this train who we need to avoid."

"They know I'm on board?"

"It's looking like that's a strong possibility."

"Russians?"

"No idea, but irrelevant."

Alex shot a glance back behind him, and Zoya quickly put her hand on his forearm. "I said relax. We're going to be okay."

"How would you know? You're drunk."

Her eyes narrowed as she glared at him. "I'm not drunk."

"How do you know you're not—"

"Because my tolerance for alcohol is much higher than my tolerance of your nagging, and I haven't even broken your nose . . . *yet*." She leaned closer. "Look, man, this is what I do. You just have to trust me right now."

Four men from the group of mountain climbers she'd seen on the platform entered the restaurant car and headed past them to the counter. Zoya watched them, her senses switched on, but she was unable to detect anything suspicious about the group.

Velesky looked back at them, too, till Zoya squeezed his forearm tight. Softly, she said, "Alex."

He turned back to her. He whispered, "Is it them?"

Zoya shook her head.

He nodded slightly. "What do we do?"

She stood up in the aisle calmly, and then grabbed her backpack from the rack above where she had been sitting. "Follow me."

Ulan Bakiyev had just hung up with Luka Rudenko after letting him know they had left the station at the lake resort town of Stresa and Velesky was still on board, when he saw a Black woman ambling past his left shoulder and then continuing up the aisle, moving towards the front of the train. She glanced his way casually but didn't seem to take any interest in him as she moved by.

He found himself interested in her, not for any reasons pertaining to countersurveillance or tradecraft; he just thought she was hot. He eyed her swaying hips and admired her beautiful face when she looked at the other second-class passengers. She was certainly not giving off any sort of clue that she was anything more than a simple traveler, and he didn't even consider evaluating her as a threat.

Soon enough she passed through the door to the gangway and disappeared from view, and he decided he would wait a few minutes, then go to the restaurant car for a snack. His orders from Rudenko had been to make visual confirmation of the targets, but he had a half-hour until the next stop, his targets weren't going anywhere, and he was in no hurry to put himself within striking distance of Banshee.

THIRTY-FIVE

Zoya Zakharova and Alex Velesky both slipped into the bathroom located in the front gangway of the restaurant car. It was larger than other bathrooms on the train, and really the only one that could accommodate two people without them being pressed together.

She placed her shopping bag and her purse on the sink, and she turned back around to Alex as he locked the door.

He said, "What, we're going to just hide in here?"

"Of course not. They'll check the lavatories."

"So, what's your plan?"

Zoya opened her pack. "I'm going to take my clothes off, and you're going to shut your eyes."

"Wait. *What?* Why don't I just wait outside?"

She shook her head. "I'm not letting you out of my sight. Push yourself against the door so I can change."

Zoya slipped out of her shoes, then took off her coat and stripped out of the sweater she'd worn under it. She unhooked her holster and put it in the sink, then unfastened her belt and kicked out of her pants because she didn't have the room to kneel down to take them off that way.

As she stood there wearing only a black push-up bra, panties, and a flesh-colored money belt around her waist, Alex kept his eyes closed, though she detected a little sweat on his brow.

As she took off her bra, she said, "They identified us in the station somehow, obviously. That took high-level facial recognition, but I don't think it was you who got pegged. I've got you too disguised in those glasses and that beard. That would beat any system I know about."

"Meaning what?"

"Meaning . . . somebody identified *me*. That would be the Russians; I'm not on any Western or Asian biometric database." She paused, then added, "As far as I know."

"So . . . the guys on board, they're looking for *you*?"

"Yeah. But before you just suggest we split up, remember that they're Russians, and that means they're looking for you, too."

Velesky rubbed his face in his hands. "What do we do?"

"They are now expecting you to be traveling with a woman, so we're going to change it up again. You will sit alone near the front of the first car, and I'll sit at the rear of the car where I can watch you."

She pulled a six-inch-wide roll of self-adhesive bandaging out of her bag, and quickly she wrapped it around her chest, binding her breasts tightly to her body.

"What are you doing?" Alex asked, confused by the sounds he was hearing but not willing to open his eyes and risk getting slapped by the woman standing close to him.

"Don't ask."

Zoya stepped into black jeans, replacing the tan ones she'd been wearing, then pulled an oversized gray sweatshirt out and threw it on. It added a little bulk to her frame and helped hide her curves, and when she turned her burgundy down coat inside out to its black lining and put it back on, she'd all but completed her transformation.

A black knit cap went on her head—she'd had a gray beanie on when they'd arrived in Milan—and then she turned to the sink and began cleaning her face with makeup-removing wipes pulled from her purse.

She put uncorrected eyeglasses on, slightly tinted, darkened her hands with a little ashen makeup, and rubbed her cheeks, her chin, and the area above her lip gently. Up close it was completely unnoticeable, but from any distance it would appear she had a five-o'clock shadow.

Finally she pulled out the same masculine-looking hiking boots she'd worn the night before; they took up more than half of her shopping bag, and she slipped them on, and once again she rose to over Velesky's height.

She stowed her flats and her small purse, slid her pistol and its holster back into her waistband, then zipped up her coat and hefted her bag.

Alex slowly opened his eyes when she stopped moving. "What about me?"

"What about you?"

"Should I take off the beard? Change clothes?"

"No. You stay the same."

"So . . . I'm just bait now?"

"I'll stop anyone who makes a move at you."

Alex didn't seem convinced, but he changed the subject. "Where's the data?"

"It's inside the money belt around my waist. If I go down, you get it, understood?"

"If you go down?"

"Yes. If I die, you retrieve the phone from my body, and you get the fuck off this train."

"You really think you're going to have to fight?"

"If these are men from GRU Unit 29155, then yes. They're only sent out when a termination is sanctioned. You and I both are on that sanctions list now. I'm not trying to scare you, I'm just trying to get you to understand you have to do *everything* I say."

"Why . . ." Alex was fighting full-on panic, and Zoya could see it. "Why don't we get off at the next stop?"

"We're better off on the train. They might wait for Geneva before they do anything, since there are civilians on board, but I can't guarantee that. If they *don't* wait, then I like my sight lines on board, my fields of fire. If we climb off the train and the GRU tries to do this in the station, it could be a lot worse than in a train coach, where they can only attack from two compass points."

She took a calming breath herself. "We aren't going to start anything ourselves, but if *they* start something, we can use the terrain on board to our advantage. *This* is where we make our stand."

She cracked open the bathroom door and peeked out, saw that the gangway was clear, and then she and Alex moved into the next car. They continued all the way up to the first car of the train, and here she told him to take a seat close to the front, just a few rows behind the driver's cabin. She stood behind in the small luggage area just inside the automatic gangway doors; the racks were stacked to the ceiling with suitcases and bags and roll-aboards. Two bikes were crammed into the area, as well.

Zoya knew her pursuers would be looking for the shopping bag and purse carried by Velesky's female companion, so she hid her belongings in the luggage racks behind some large suitcases, then pulled a random black roll-aboard from the other luggage stacked there. The owner of the luggage couldn't see her from where the rack was shielded by a smoked-glass wall, and she quickly removed a bright orange tag, making the roll-aboard all but indistinguishable.

This done, she entered the first-class open seating area, but she did not go to where Alex was sitting near the front. Instead, she took the first seat on her right at the rear by the window. There was an empty seat next to her, and across the little aisle, a single seat was also empty at the window on the left.

Velesky sat at the window four rows back from the front bulkhead, in front of which was the door to the driver's compartment.

Once oriented, Zoya carefully looked over everyone in the car that she could see from her position. Then she called Alex, seated twelve meters in front of her. She put a pair of over-the-ear headphones on, further masking her face slightly, and then she curled up as if sleeping against the window.

Alex answered softly. "Yeah?"

"Let's keep this line open. Any time someone steps into this car next to me, I'll let you know. Got it?"

"Got it."

The pair had only been in their seats for a couple of minutes when the door next to her slid open.

Two men entered the car; they weren't the young guys she'd seen at the station in Milan but rather the two older men she'd seen boarding the train in Stresa. Zoya continued feigning sleep, and they paid her little attention, but out of the corner of her mostly closed eye she saw them glance up at the luggage rack above her head as they passed. Seeing a roll-aboard instead of a

shopping bag, and noting the appearance of the sleeping young male traveler, they continued up the car, eyeing each passenger slowly and carefully.

"Stand by," she whispered into her phone. "Two men approaching you
from behind. They don't look Russian to me, but they *do* look like they're
performing surveillance. I don't think they'll act."

"How can you know that?" he whispered back.

"I'm being optimistic."

The men passed Velesky; they looked at each other as they made their
way to just behind the driver's cabin, then took seats at the bulkhead, facing
back in Alex and Zoya's direction.

Zoya didn't think the men were terribly covert. She wondered if they
were Italian; by their looks and dress they appeared so, and she assumed
them to be former military from their postures and hairstyles.

By her positioning Alex in the first car of the train, almost at the front
and facing forward, she'd made it hard for them to get a positive ID without
committing themselves to sit there, because if they turned around and left
the cabin, it would look suspicious.

In her earpiece she heard Alex whisper, "They're sitting down."

"I see them. They're waiting. You sit tight. When we get close to the station, I'll let you know, and you can start walking back the length of the train.
If they pursue you, I'll be right behind them. Understood?"

"Yes."

"Now . . . relax."

"Is that a joke?"

"Of course not," she whispered. "You have to remain calm, no matter
what. There could be others on board, and there will almost *definitely* be
others boarding. But I like our positioning, and I have things under control."

When Alex said nothing, Zoya took that to mean he didn't believe her
any more than she believed herself.

She told herself she *desperately* needed a drink.

Luka Rudenko parked his Mercedes in the lot in front of the Domodossola
railway station at 8:05 p.m., then locked the car and slipped the keys in his
pocket as he hurried for the entrance.

He was exceedingly well-dressed but didn't stand out in this crowd. His spiked blond hair did not stand out, either. Rudenko looked like he could be a rich Swiss banker, a German industrialist, a British computer software mogul, or a Dutch real estate expert, and though he was handsome, well-dressed, and blond, he blended right into the surroundings here in northern Italy.

His only luggage was a leather folio, and inside it he carried an iPad, some clothing, and some documents.

His gun was at his appendix under his sweater inside his waistband, and just behind that, at his three-o'clock position, he wore a Microtech Socom Elite automatic knife. With a press of a button upon the draw, he could fire a four-inch M390 steel drop-point blade out the side, making this a rapidly deployed silent killer, perfect for an assassin like the man known to the West as Matador.

He entered the station, found the right platform for Geneva on the screen, and then moved directly to it, keeping an eye out for anyone else who might be heading in the same direction. He detected no countersurveillance, but when he arrived at the platform, he immediately saw two men and one woman wearing light-blue-on-dark-blue coats with the word "Grenzwacht" on the back. Heckler & Koch P30 9-millimeter pistols hung from their hips, and they wore blue baseball caps on their heads that read "Guardie Di Confine" and level 3A body armor on their chests and backs, rated to stop most handgun rounds.

Shit, Luka thought, Swiss border guards. They weren't supposed to be here.

Switzerland and Italy were both Schengen Agreement states, meaning there were no border controls between the two countries. But for some reason these three cops looked ready to climb onto the train here in northern Italy and take it at least as far as the next stop, in Brig, Switzerland.

This changed everything, as far as Luka was concerned. While he didn't give two shits about killing border cops in the furtherance of the mission that was sure to get him promoted out of field ops, he had to admit this would complicate matters for himself and his team over the next several minutes.

With a frustrated sigh, he reached into his pocket and dialed Sergeant Bakiyev.

. . .

Ulan Bakiyev leaned against the bathroom door to the first coach in the train and looked through the gangway doors into the first-class cabin in front of him.

His phone rang, and he looked down at it.

It was the major. He tapped his earpiece. "Yeah."

"I'm at the station. You should arrive here in five minutes. You've got visual?"

"I think Velesky might be in the first car. He definitely wasn't in any of the others, and I checked all the bathrooms. There's a guy almost up to the front who could be him. I'm in the gangway behind, but if I want to check out that subject in there any more closely, then I'll have to go through the doors and all the way to the driver's compartment and then turn around to look back. It's going to be pretty obvious I'm a tail."

"What about Banshee?"

"No visual. The guy I'm looking at is traveling alone. There are two men four rows in front of him, facing aft. I think they're conducting surveillance, as well."

Dismissively, Rudenko said, "Drexler's boys. He has four on board. Two in the back, two in the front. Don't worry about them, they won't do anything. But Banshee . . . she got on the train?"

"Definitely."

"Then that means she's somewhere in disguise, and she could be watching you right now."

Bakiyev looked back over his shoulder. "What do you want me to do?"

"Keep your eyes on Velesky, but watch out for that woman. Don't do anything stupid."

"Right," the first sergeant replied.

Just then, the gangway door behind him opened, and he looked back to see the attractive Black woman he noticed earlier enter. She wore a purse over her shoulder and her coat was unzipped, revealing an ivory sweater over a nice figure and a gold necklace hanging low. He eyed her up and down as she stepped by him, apparently heading for the lead coach.

He shifted a little to let her pass, a pleasant smile crossed his face, and then she looked into the front coach a moment and stopped.

The woman turned back to him, then in English said, "Sorry, can I get into the bathroom?"

Bakiyev moved out of her way; she smiled and thanked him, then closed and locked the door.

Rudenko said, "What was all that?"

He answered, now speaking in English. "Nothing. It's all under control."

"Not really," Rudenko replied. "Three armed Swiss police are boarding at Domodossola."

"Shit. What are our rules of engagement?"

"Congratulations. You'll finally get your hands wet tonight, Sergeant." He was telling his junior man that he was no longer just there to keep an eye on the targets but would instead be used in the assassination.

After a brief pause, the younger man said, "Understood. I'll find a place to watch him until I hear back."

THIRTY-SIX

Court Gentry nervously eyed the gas gauge of his Aprilia 850, then shot a glance down to his watch. He'd be on fumes by the time he reached the station at Domodossola, and his watch told him he'd be arriving just about the same time the train would be leaving.

He heard a chirp in his left ear, and then a call came through immediately.

"Go," he said as he crouched lower still on his bike, his spine burning in protest from the hard riding.

As expected, it was Lacy, and she whispered into the phone, her voice muffled as if her hand were shielding the microphone. "The GRU guy from Milano Station, Bakiyev . . . he's on board. Watching the first car on the train. I think Velesky is in there, near the front. He is not traveling with the woman now."

"Did you see her anywhere else on board?"

"I did not."

"Okay. Keep your distance from Velesky and Bakiyev."

"Velesky is thirty yards away, but Bakiyev is right outside the bathroom door."

"Where are you?"

"In the bathroom."

Court closed his eyes; he felt so helpless to be so far away, but then he opened them. "Does he suspect you?"

"No. I . . . I don't think so."

"Okay. Leave the bathroom and find a seat. Be ready to react if something happens."

"React? React *how*?"

Court had forgotten Lacy wasn't armed. He said, "I guess scream or something. I wouldn't know how it works for pacifists."

"Very helpful. You'll board at Domodossola?"

"It's going to be close."

"Well, if you miss that stop, the next station won't be till Switzerland, and the train goes through a tunnel, while you'll have to go over the mountains. We'll be in Geneva before you even get to the border."

Court said, "I'll make it onto that train. Call you back when I do." He hung up and concentrated on getting every single bit of energy out of his engine, while simultaneously taking care not to steer his bike off the road in the cold night.

Zoya heard the automatic door slide open from the gangway behind her, then glanced quickly to the left as a man sat down there on the opposite side of the aisle.

He wore a gray jacket and had a scruffy dark beard, and his intelligent, searching eyes remained forward; he hadn't even glanced her way. She kept surreptitious watch on him for a moment, knowing that anyone who entered the cabin could be playing for the other team.

He looked vaguely Asian, not classically Slavic, but the more she looked at him, the more she detected he wasn't just a relaxed passenger waiting for his final destination; he was, rather, active at the moment. His eyes, his posture . . . he wasn't agitated or frantic, but he was professional.

A man at work.

He was one of them.

If he was GRU, then he was Tatar or Uzbek or Bashkir or Kazakh or any of the other Asian ethnic groups present in Russia, but she was sure enough he was a manhunter that she really didn't worry too much about his heritage.

Italians, Russians . . . this guy . . . It seemed like everybody wanted a piece of Velesky tonight.

Alex came over her earpiece now. "Anything?"

She did not answer him, but instead she typed a text message.

One subject seated across aisle from me on left. He might be GRU.

He texted back. So . . . we're surrounded.

Zoya turned towards the window, away from the potential GRU opera-tor, then typed again. He's not about to do anything. Just sitting. Could be waiting for reinforcements.

He replied with Okay, and Zoya put her phone in her pocket, then slid her right hand down to the gun on her hip. The movement was shielded from view, but she also knew she'd have to completely reorient her body to draw and fire, so she just wrapped her hand around the grip and kept looking out into the night as the station approached.

After taking a moment to compose herself, Angela Lacy opened the bath-room door; she saw that Bakiyev was no longer in the gangway. She passed through, then opened the door to the front coach, walked past the nearly full luggage racks, and entered the first-class area.

Bakiyev sat on her left in the first single seat by the window; she didn't look at him as she passed, nor did she look at the other person seated by the window to her right.

Instead, she just walked on; by entering the first coach of the train, she was pretty much committed to staying up here, so she took an empty left-sided single seat about ten rows up from the back. She was directly in front of Bakiyev and therefore unable to see him, but she did have eyes on a man ahead on her right who looked exactly like the bearded Alex Velesky she'd seen in the security camera footage from Milano Centrale.

But if this *was* him, where the hell was the woman who had boarded with him in Milan?

She wanted to look back over her shoulder, but she knew better. If the unknown woman was among the passengers in the front coach she'd moved by on her way to her seat, Angela sure hadn't seen her, but that didn't mean craning her head back around in Bakiyev's direction would be a good plan.

Focusing on what was in front of her, however, she noticed two men facing her direction, their seatbacks on the front bulkhead of the first-class coach, next to the door to the half gangway where the front exit and driver's compartment were. The pair were just sitting there; they didn't seem to be looking either Alex's way or Angela's, but she detected a military vibe to them. Angela's father had been in the Army, and she'd grown up around the military, and working in foreign stations, she was always surrounded by Marine embassy guards. These men looked like former soldiers, and together they appeared to be some sort of hard-edged two-man team.

Whether they were GRU like Bakiyev or something different, she couldn't tell.

Whoever they were, though, they were just ten feet or so away from Alex, so if they were planning on getting the phone from him, Angela knew there wasn't much she'd be able to do to stop them.

She tried to control her breathing, to appear as relaxed as the other passengers around her. She was working without a net, no support from the local station, little support from headquarters, aided only by a mysterious Agency asset who played by a different set of rules than she'd been taught.

She was so out of her element right now, her head was spinning, but she worked hard to keep this from showing to everyone else on the train.

Angela didn't flash another look Velesky's way; she just pulled out her phone and began scrolling Twitter, trying her best to look like any other passenger on board.

As the lighted signboard at Domodossola station announced that the eight-twenty train to Geneva would arrive in four minutes, Luka Rudenko felt a buzzing in his pocket. He pulled out his phone and read a text from Ulan.

Took a seat at rear of Velesky's coach. Have eyes on.

He quickly texted him back. **Banshee?**

No sign.

Rudenko didn't like the sound of this. **She's there.**

No sign, Bakiyev wrote again.

Checking the train's arrival time on the board quickly, Luka typed out a new text. If she's watching over Velesky, she would put herself right where you are. The back of the coach, with a sight line to him.

He waited impatiently for the reply, and when it came, he closed his eyes slowly.

There's someone on my right, three meters away. Can't see face; male, I think.

Goddammit, Rudenko thought. He texted back, She looked male in the footage captured this morning, idiot. That's her!

The pause was longer this time. Finally, Ulan texted, Shit. What do I do?

Luka texted back. Do nothing. Be ready for our arrival. We will act twenty minutes after boarding when we enter the tunnel into Switzerland.

The reply came quickly now. Khorosho. *Okay.*

Luka Rudenko had less than four minutes till the train arrived, but he needed to formulate a plan. Forgoing tradecraft protocols, he walked across the platform to two of his men standing there, and together the three of them made their way past a group of businesspeople to the other two 29155 operators, standing on the raised concrete farther down the tracks. All five of them walked even farther up the platform, two dozen meters from anyone else, and Rudenko began explaining what he wanted out of each of his men.

When he was finished, one of his men, a senior sergeant named Gennadi, said, "What about the cops?"

Rudenko shrugged. "If they're lucky, then they won't even know what happened until we're gone. And if they're *unlucky,* then they will."

The men all nodded their understanding, and Rudenko began crafting a text for Ulan Bakiyev, explaining his role in the upcoming action.

He'd just begun doing this when the train came into view from the south.

The gray train with the red stripes raced by Court Gentry, mocking him with its speed. Court was doing close to seventy, madness on a motorcycle on this wet road, but the train passed him doing every bit of ninety miles an hour, shooting towards its next destination in the town of Domodossola, a mile or so up ahead.

He was about five minutes away from the station, and it appeared the

EuroCity would get there about three minutes before he arrived. On top of this, he'd have to dump the bike and run through the station, and this would take a couple of minutes at least.

He doubted the train would need three or four minutes to disgorge and then take on passengers, so his high hopes of boarding here seemed to be in real jeopardy.

He kept the throttle open, however, hoping for a miracle that he couldn't even make himself believe in.

He hadn't heard from Lacy, but he imagined she'd sent him a text or two about her location because she was close enough to the opposition that she couldn't speak. She would know he'd have no way of reading the texts before he got on board himself, and now that it looked like that was going to be all but impossible, he considered just pulling over to the side of the road, stopping, and texting Lacy that he'd missed the train and to just get herself somewhere safe, because if GRU decided to act on board, then there wasn't a damn thing she could do about it.

The station loomed closer; the train, already hundreds of yards ahead, began to slow, and Court kept the hammer down, willed more speed from the hot combustible engine between his knees, wove left and right through the sparse but increasing traffic as he entered the town.

It was another minute before he could get the lay of the land. The train had stopped at the platform; Court could make out the tail end of the long vehicle, but he didn't focus on his target.

Instead, he looked left and right, trying to find the closest access to the platform itself.

He continued racing along, continued scanning the area, desperate for the solution to this confounding puzzle.

There. He saw something on the near side of the station, two hundred fifty yards away or so, and though it gave him a glimmer of hope, it also filled him with dread.

A footbridge ran over the tracks. The little bridge could be accessed by the road Court was on now, and he could get to it a lot quicker than he could get himself to the platform in the station where the EuroCity sat at rest. He'd only have to jack his front wheel to the right at speed, fire up the bridge halfway, and then dump his bike. From there he could jump from the bridge down to a cargo train parked on the tracks in the dark, and then run towards the platform where the EuroCity was already taking on and disgorging passengers.

There was a lot of danger in this plan, but he saw no alternative.

Fuck it, he told himself. He was getting on that train.

THIRTY-SEVEN

When three Swiss border control officers stepped up to the conductor on the platform in front of the front door of the lead car, Angela Lacy was watching through the window, and she cocked her head in confusion. There were no regular passport checks between Switzerland and Italy, so she couldn't imagine they'd be boarding, but neither could she imagine why Swiss police would be at this northern Italian train station.

As Angela watched through the window on the opposite side of the first-class coach, the conductor blew her whistle.

Instantly, Angela tapped her earpiece.

"Are you on board yet? We're about to leave."

The voice came back over the sound of the revving motorcycle engine. "No. You have to stall them."

"How do I—"

"Figure it out! I need sixty seconds."

Angela quickly stood from her seat and headed for the door, racing to talk to the conductor and the police even though she had no clue what she was going to say.

. . .

As he neared the lighted footbridge over the tracks, Court pulled his gloves off with his teeth and let them fall to the road. The icy wind penetrated his fingers almost instantly. He'd need the grip to get over the bridge railing quickly, but he didn't love the fact that his hands would be less effective in the cold.

Court applied the brake while turning right, slewed his back tire to the left, then skidded onto the bridge, launching towards the center of the span while simultaneously looking to his right, where what he saw gave him something else to worry about.

The cargo train full of boxcars had begun moving in the direction of the station.

Now he realized he'd have to leap off a speeding bike and over a railing, dropping down onto a moving train, before climbing off the train and climbing up to a platform, all in the next few seconds, because he had no idea if Lacy would be able to slow the departure of the EuroCity 42.

He leapt off the bike while it was still moving, letting the vehicle tumble along the footbridge, and at a run he vaulted over the iron railing, spinning around in the air to catch himself on the handrail. The metal was ice cold and slick with a thin sheet of ice; had he been wearing the gloves, he would have surely slipped and fallen some ten feet before slamming onto the roof of the train and, no doubt, rolling off the side, likely to his death.

But his hands held, his feet arrested his fall on the edge of the overpass, and then he quickly dropped again, this time catching his grip around the bottom of the railing.

Looking below him, he immediately saw the thing that scared him most, and it was not the moving train.

It was the wires. These trains were powered by electric overhead lines that ran above the track, with each train having at least one contact point with the wires via a pantograph, a series of metal bars that extended out of the top of one of the coaches to maintain contact at all times with the current running through the overhead wires.

There was a pair of parallel lines running directly over the track, and

Court knew he'd have to drop between them to the cargo carrier or else he'd be instantly electrocuted.

As the train below him moved faster and faster, he shifted his hands on the railing to the right, looking down to try to thread the needle with his body between the high-voltage wires.

On this freight carrier the pantograph was up on the front of the locomotive, so it wasn't an issue, but the wires themselves were terrifying.

Deciding he could put it off no longer, he let go, then dropped through the darkness, between the wires, and ten feet down before his body crumpled on the roof of a shipping container lashed to a flatbed train car.

He rolled backwards a couple of times, almost to the edge of the container, but he grabbed on, stopping himself. Sitting up quickly, he looked ahead, seeing the EuroCity still at the platform.

Into his earpiece he said, "Get me another thirty seconds, Angela."

He didn't wait for a reply. Instead, he rose to his feet and began running forward on the moving train, ready to climb down and land next to the tracks shortly before passing the station.

Angela Lacy had heard Six's plea but ignored it, because now she stood with the three police officers and the conductor on the platform by the front right-side door, her hands on her sides. She spoke in French and continued complaining that her umbrella had been stolen shortly after she boarded in Stresa and went to the restroom, and demanded, for the third time now in less than a minute, that the train be held here at the station until the police conducted a thorough search.

She could see in the eyes of the Italian female conductor, as well as those of the Swiss cops, that they thought she was bonkers, but they were polite enough. The female officer explained that she and the other two were just boarding to check for illegal immigrants attempting to migrate into Switzerland, but she promised she'd ask around about it and keep an eye open as she went down through the coaches.

The Italian conductor was less patient, and she told the woman, for the second time in the past forty-five seconds, that they had to leave the station, and eventually she all but shoved Angela back in through the front door.

Angela went back to her seat, praying she had done enough to get Court on board, and the border guards climbed up the steps after her.

Court ran through the train yard as fast as he could, ripping his motorcycle helmet off and flinging it away. He had a Glock pistol on his hip with one extra magazine, but he didn't even have a backpack on, which he decided would look suspicious for a traveler on a transnational train ride.

Still, he told himself he'd pull this off, if and only if he got to the rear door of the train before it started to move.

He heard the conductor's second whistle when he was fifty feet from the platform, and he managed to pick up his pace even more, then roll up to the concrete and race for the door.

There was no one left on the platform when he pushed the button, and the rear door on the last coach on the train thankfully opened with a hiss.

Court boarded, completely winded but doing his best to hide it to those here in the second-class cabin.

The train began to move three seconds after the door closed behind him.

As the train began rolling to the north, Angela Lacy watched as the female conductor began heading back down the length of the car. The three police officers lagged behind, stepping up to the first person in the first row behind the driver's compartment. They spoke to him briefly, and the man pulled out an Italian passport and flashed it.

The cops didn't open it or even take it, they just nodded and moved on.

Angela reached into her purse and removed her passport, readying it for them as the border guards here began checking the documents of the two men she suspected as being Velesky's followers.

There was no incident during the quick exchange, but Angela had tried and failed to either hear what language they were speaking or see what color the men's passports were, so she'd not been able to identify them.

The border control officers moved down to a couple of other passengers, and then one made his way to Velesky, who seemed stiff and uncertain in his actions. Angela noted that he fumbled in his jacket for a long moment looking for his wallet, then looked back over his shoulder a couple of times. She wondered if he knew Bakiyev was on board, if he knew the two men facing him at the bulkhead were watching him, or if these were just the quirky mannerisms of a man on the run being forced to interact with the police.

The female cop dealing with him waited patiently while Velesky searched his pockets, but he eventually retrieved what he was looking for, and the instant the officer recognized the Swiss driver's license, she just thanked him in French and moved on without even taking a closer look.

These were incredibly perfunctory checks. They were clearly profiling, looking for illegal immigrants, these days coming from Ukraine or Syria or some other war-torn nation. Switzerland was a Schengen nation, she knew, but apparently the Swiss had reinstated these immigration checks for the purpose of keeping undocumented foreigners out.

The female police officer continued down the aisle to the next cluster of passengers, with the other officers already moving ahead to check someone on the opposite side.

Lacy kept her eyes on Velesky a moment more, and she saw the man look back again, then straight at the two men seated in front of him and facing back in his direction. She felt certain Velesky *did* know there were people on board who were watching him, possibly even waiting for an opportunity to do him harm, and she wondered if there was any chance in hell Six was going to get here in time to do his job before the Russians beat him to it.

While a bearded Swiss cop checked Zoya's passport, she lost sight of Bakiyev because the female police officer was in the aisle between them checking his documents. She took her forged U.S. passport under the name Zoe Zimmerman back from the bored-looking cop, and then her eyes returned to the two men who faced Velesky all the way at the front of the coach.

From this distance she could see little more than their heads and upper torsos, and she could tell that one of the men was holding his phone to his ear. After a moment he put the phone down, then leaned closer to his partner.

As the three Swiss cops left the first coach and began heading out to the gangway leading to the second coach, she kept her eyes on the pair, and she detected a sudden difference in their demeanor. Whereas before they'd been relatively still, now they were shifting and moving, their heads looking around.

They were readying themselves for something, and to Zoya, this was very bad news.

To her immense relief, Angela heard Six's voice in her headset. He sounded utterly winded. "Damn good job, Lacy."

She smiled and answered softly. "Hi, honey. Did you catch your train?"

"By the skin of my teeth. Going to do a quick change of clothes and be up to your car. Everything the same as it was last time we talked?"

"Well . . . more or less. Check your texts."

He pulled out his phone and looked at it. Angela had sent him a single text, so he opened it. Lead coach, he's about ten rows ahead on my right near the front. Two unsubs ahead of him, facing his direction. No sign of the woman. Bakiyev behind me.

"Okay," he said, his mic broadcasting to Angela as he slipped his phone back in the pocket of his jeans. "Be there in about five minutes. We'll keep this line open. When I tell you to, I want you to get up and start walking back this way."

In a cheery voice twinged with a southern accent she hadn't put on display for Court before, she said, "Oh, honey, that sounds wonderful. I can't wait." She then added, "Sending you another text right now."

Court entered the seventh coach, took his coat off, crammed it into the luggage stored on the community racks, and kept walking quickly up the aisle through another two-by-two-seat second-class compartment.

He passed the gangway of the seventh coach, then entered the sixth. Here the luggage racks were stuffed to the gills with large and colorful mountain climbing backpacks. He saw ice axes and crampons and carabiners and colorful rope hanging on the hooks and straps of each bag, and even big boots hung off some of them, and he knew this was his opportunity for a quick change out of the motorcycle outfit that might have been seen by someone on the platform and communicated to the train. The cabin beyond the racks was mostly full of boisterous people sitting two-by-two, and no one was paying any attention to him back here and out of the way. Quickly he hefted a pack along with a pair of large men's boots, then turned around and went back into the gangway between the sixth and seventh coaches, entering the bathroom. Here he frantically opened the bag and began pulling out clothing, hoping like hell it fit him.

A text came through and he checked it. **Three Swiss border police on board. Moving front to back.**

Court hadn't expected any sort of immigration control heading into Switzerland, but he was pleased by this news. The last thing he wanted was for Russian assassins to start shooting on a train full of passengers, and the police might be enough of a reason for them to wait till Velesky deboarded before they pulled their weapons.

Then again, he told himself, depending on their orders, they might blow this entire train to hell to stop Velesky and his information from getting away from them.

He continued changing clothes. He pulled steel-gray fleece-lined ski pants out and slipped them on over his jeans, then pulled out a thick, heavily padded vest. He wasn't sure why the article of clothing was built the way it was—it didn't seem either terribly comfortable or terribly warm—but he put it on to add some bulk to his frame and some padding on his torso if he found himself in a fight. Over this he pulled on a green raincoat, and this he zipped all the way up. He fished around and retrieved an insulated black ski mask, yanked it down over the top of his head like a cap, and then left the pack and the rest of the gear there in the bathroom.

The entire change process took nearly four minutes, but when he emerged, he was fully dressed and looked nothing like the man who'd boarded the train.

Court went back into the sixth coach, walking past a few members of the mountain climbing club as nonchalantly as possible, and then he headed through the gangway between the sixth and fifth cars.

Zoya continued watching the two men facing Alex; they had spent the last few minutes becoming increasingly agitated, with quicker movements and more conversation between them, and the Russian operative at the opposite end of the train coach took this to mean they were readying themselves for some sort of action.

She was on an open line with Alex, so she just very softly called his name. "Yeah?"

She whispered now; she didn't want Bakiyev to even know she was talking, much less what she was saying. "I need you to stand up and then I want you to casually walk back here, past me, and catch up with the three border control officers. Stay in the same car they're in, wherever they go, but try not to make it obvious."

"Why? What's happen—"

"Do it now."

A slight hesitation, and then "Okay."

Zoya watched Velesky stand, a little more urgently than she would have liked, but he recovered, climbed out of his seat, and began walking back in her direction.

Her eyes flashed over to Bakiyev on her left, and she saw his mouth moving; he was speaking so softly she couldn't hear a sound, but this gave her the impression he was talking to others on board about Velesky's movements and *not* communicating with the pair at the opposite end of the train car, who had gotten up and started walking down the aisle.

Are there even more *Russian killers on this damn train?* Zoya wondered.

THIRTY-EIGHT

Ten minutes after leaving Domodossola, Luka Rudenko and his four men entered the nearly empty restaurant car from the rear. A female conductor had just entered from the opposite gangway, and she chatted with the woman behind the snack counter. Luka and the others grabbed plastic menus out of a rack and sat down at two tables near the door in the back. Soon the conductor began making her way through the car.

There were only a half-dozen other passengers in the coach, so the ticket checks didn't take long. She stepped up to the Russians' tables, and the men dutifully passed over their tickets. When the conductor moved on to another table across from them, Luka and two of his operators stood and headed up the length of the train, leaving the other two men behind to provide rear security.

Soon Luka entered the gangway to the fourth coach from the front. As the three men reached the glass door to take them into the second-class section in front of them, Luka's phone beeped in his ear and he tapped the earbud to answer it, sitting down in an open seat on his left just inside the door past the luggage rack. As he did this, both his colleagues sat on the other side of the aisle.

Before Luka could speak, he heard Ulan in an urgent whisper. "Target's up. He's leaving the cabin, heading your way. Drexler's men are following."

"Where's he going?"

"Don't know, but he looks nervous. Drexler's guys took a call and then started amping up. I think they'd been ordered to grab him. Maybe the target saw it on their faces and is trying to bolt." Even more softly, he said, "Target's passing me now." There was a brief pause, then, "Three cops left the coach five minutes ago; he might be trying to stick closer to them."

"Banshee?"

"Somebody's still on my right." And then, "Wait . . ."

The pause lasted five seconds. Bakiyev whispered, "It's her. She's leaving, too."

Rudenko had been hoping to use a knife on both Banshee and Velesky, well after the police moved on towards the rear of the train but before the train entered the tunnel. But now that plan had gone up in smoke before his eyes. If Velesky was going to stay close to the police, it would make things difficult for Luka.

He'd been at this long enough to know this was going to be a fucking mess if he acted on the train at all.

That said, there were four more stops before Geneva, and two of them, Montreaux and Lausanne, were relatively large stations. Geneva was the biggest station on the route, of course, but Velesky and Banshee could possibly slip off at any stop and melt into a crowd before he could get to them.

He made his decision, and then, to Bakiyev, he said, "We're still doing this on board, but we might have to do this loud. Wait thirty seconds to see if anyone else is trailing, then get up and start moving back this way. Catch up with Velesky, and watch out for Banshee."

"Fuck," Bakiyev muttered, but Luka knew the man would do what was asked of him.

He turned to his two colleagues. "We wait right here. Velesky's coming this way."

Court Gentry entered the restaurant car and, as the door shut behind him, he heard Angela whispering through his earpiece.

"Velesky just exited the lead coach, heading back in your direction. The two other men left behind him."

"Still no visual on the woman?"

"No. Velesky was definitely alone."

"What about Bakiyev?"

"Hang on." Court pictured Lacy turning all the way around to check on the GRU assassin, and he hoped she hadn't been at Langley so long she'd forgotten how to be covert about it. After a second, she said, "He's still here at the back of the coach, but there's another man dressed in black leaving out the gangway."

This told Court that Alex, the two men with military bearings who'd been surveilling him, and at least one other person had all left the front car at the same time.

But for some reason the GRU officer had kept his seat.

While he thought about what this meant, Lacy asked, "Do I follow them?"

Court didn't answer, because he'd just figured it out. Either the three men tailing Velesky now were planning on taking the man down between one of the cars, or else there were more GRU on the train blocking his way, positioned to do the job.

"Do I follow him?" she repeated.

"Yeah. Keep your distance, though, and be ready to find cover if this all starts going to hell."

Lacy whispered into her earpiece. "Please don't start shooting people."

"I'm not starting *anything* on a train full of civs. But we can't bet on the Russians to be so discriminate."

"Shit," she muttered.

Zoya followed the two men, who themselves followed Alex through the gangway to the second car; she checked her six more than once in case the man she'd pegged as a potential GRU operative in the lead car decided to follow.

This was incredibly stressful; a train would be an unbelievably claustrophobic place to fight, plus the inclusion of dozens and dozens of passengers. The glass and a half of red wine she'd consumed a half hour earlier had no lingering effect on her anxiety level at all, and she caught herself hoping that nobody acted against her protectee at least until they reached the restaurant car so she could down another drink.

Entering the second car now, she saw that the police had already left. There were just a few passengers here, and the checks clearly had been relatively pro forma. She whispered to Alex, telling him to keep moving along up the aisle, even though his two followers were just meters behind him. Zoya hadn't been noticed by either of the men ahead of her; they weren't closing on their prey, and there was nothing in their hands, but she caught them exchanging quick glances with each other from time to time as they walked, and it made her worry they were going to try to just tackle Alex and muscle him to the ground.

They wouldn't do it in front of the cops, and the cops surely couldn't be much farther down the train, so whatever was about to go down was about to go down soon, probably in the empty gangway ahead.

They wouldn't make it as far as the restaurant car, she told herself, then muttered, "So much for that drink."

She looked back over her shoulder. Bakiyev was not in sight, which was good, but the attractive Black woman she'd seen in the front car appeared out of the gangway behind her, a purse over her shoulder, her tan coat unzipped, and her ivory cashmere sweater exposed.

Zoya didn't size this woman up as a threat, but she also wasn't here to help her. If the woman had sat tight, she would have probably stayed out of danger, but now she was about to stumble into trouble, and there was nothing Zoya could do for her, or for any of the other passengers in the car.

Alex spoke softly, his voice coming through her earpiece. "These guys are right behind me."

"I know. You're fine, just get to the next car and the police will be there. Run through the gangway."

"What if I don't make it to—"

Still at a whisper, she said, "I'll stall these fuckers. You just keep going till you see the police."

Alex passed the luggage racks, opened the gangway door between the second and third cars, and then rushed quickly to the next door, surprising his attackers. Just as they started to break into a run themselves outside the gangway door, Zoya put a hand on each of their shoulders.

They stopped, spun around, and saw a boyish-looking woman standing there in a black outfit with a black beanie on her head.

"Che cosa vuoi?" *What do you want?* one of them asked, speaking Italian in a native accent, with agitation in his voice as if disturbed by the sudden interruption.

In a strong British accent, Zoya replied, "Beg your pardon. You gents wouldn't happen to know if they've a dining car on this train?"

The men turned away without responding, their intensity only momentarily interrupted, and Zoya looked past them to see that Alex had made it through the gangway to the third car.

Court began walking up the aisle of the restaurant car, but he'd only moved a few feet before his eyes locked on a pair of men at the other end of the long space. They stood at the snack counter; one man dunked his tea bag into his paper cup, and the other had a full beer in front of him. They were together, this was obvious to Court, but they weren't speaking to each other at the moment.

They wore big coats, just like many others on the train even though they were protected from the cold, and Court was unable to see any print of a weapon underneath their outer garments, though he wouldn't be able to see the right side of their bodies until he passed them, some twenty yards away.

But even from here, to Court's practiced eye, they looked Russian.

And they looked like spooks.

And they looked like they were on the clock.

Neither man paid any attention to Court, which pleased him greatly, but he knew if things started going loud with Velesky farther up the train, then he'd have to tear his way through these two to get to his target.

He bought his ticket from the female conductor, waited for the woman to begin leaving through the door behind him, and then looked around, devising his course of action. He'd bypass these Russians here if he could, get himself as close to Velesky as soon as possible, and take it from there.

Just then, two Swiss border control officers, one male and one female, entered from the fourth coach, and they chatted amiably with the woman behind the counter. They were in no rush, and it was abundantly clear that nothing had happened farther up the train to excite or alarm them.

This was good news, but Court knew better than to relax. If Bakiyev and the two other guys with him were on this train, and if these two men in the restaurant car were, in fact, GRU as well, then they were definitely planning on making a move on Velesky at some point.

Soon the cops checked the passports of the men at the counter. Court was too far away to be sure what nationality the passports belonged to, but they were dark purple in color, and he knew this could mean they were Serbian. If so, it was only more evidence these guys could be Russian, as Serbia had kept relations with Russia throughout the war.

Finally the border control officers began making their way through the tables in his direction. He thought about getting past them, then moving farther up the train to find Velesky, careful to keep an eye out for this mysterious woman who'd boarded with him in Milan, as well.

He'd grab the banker, fight off Ulan Bakiyev and any other GRU assassins he could find, and then pull the emergency lever by one of the gangway doors. Once the train stopped, he would escape with Velesky into the darkness, and Angela could just leave with the other passengers.

This wasn't much of a plan, Court acknowledged, but such was the nature of in extremis work.

Once again, the cops began heading his way, but they stopped at a young couple from the group of mountain climbers who were drinking beer at a table across from him to check their documents. He tapped his foot in anxious frustration as he watched the cops move casually up the restaurant car.

Hurry the fuck up, he said to himself.

THIRTY-NINE

Zoya followed Alex and the two Italian men through the third car and entered the fourth coach, and now she was able to see the situation.

The police were not in sight; apparently they'd moved on to the restaurant car beyond, but a dozen or so people dressed in adventure wear sat amid another dozen passengers.

All these people had apparently just waved their passports to the cops, who couldn't have possibly looked them over with any seriousness before moving on to the next car. From the stacks of huge backpacks in the luggage area, she got the impression many of these passengers were from some sort of mountain climbing club, and she wondered if they came this way often enough that the police just recognized them and moved on.

Alex wasn't running, but he moved quickly up the aisle, and the Italians seemed well aware that he was fleeing them, so they fast-walked after him. The mountain climbers were all speaking Italian, and they seemed as if they were too wrapped up in their own conversations to even notice the drama unfolding in their midst.

As Zoya herself sped up to remain in striking distance of Alex's pursuers, she saw Alex stop suddenly, directly in the center of the coach.

The Italians and Zoya stopped, as well.

Looking beyond Alex, she saw three men sitting in the last row before the door to the gangway, and she wondered if this was why Alex had come to a halt.

As one, the three men stood, and Velesky spoke into his mic. "Oh, no."

"What is it?" she asked, still standing there, five steps from Alex on the other side of his two followers.

Alex turned around suddenly and started moving back towards the Italians, who put their arms out to stop him.

Zoya realized they were just going to go for Velesky right here, in a coach more than one-third full of passengers.

Alex tried to push through the two men, but they knocked him to the ground in the aisle and fell down with him, and in so doing gave Zoya a sight line on the three men who had just stood from their seats and entered the aisle.

A man with a brown cap over his head stood in front.

Zoya and the first man in the aisle stared at each other, while at Zoya's feet Alex screamed from under the two big Italians.

"It's him!"

Just then, the man in the green cap smiled and spoke in Russian. "Banshee, I presume?"

Zoya recognized him now; he was the kidnapper she'd hit with her van two nights earlier.

She raised an empty hand and held it out in front of her, imploringly. Surrounded by twenty-five or thirty innocents, she shook her head slowly. In English she said, "Please. I'm begging you. Not here."

But she saw his intent in his eyes before he spoke. "As good a place as any," he said with a little smile.

Shit.

Then the man began dropping to his knees.

Zoya knew this move; he was getting out of the way of the guns behind him, and she began her draw stroke before his knees hit the aisle.

Behind him, both of the men there held squat machine pistols, and they raised them to their shoulders as Zoya's own pistol came out from under her coat.

Zoya dove right as she drew, pulled her trigger first, and the passengers all around in the coach screamed in surprise.

. . .

Court sat at a table in the restaurant car and smiled as he took his passport back from the female officer who'd just glanced at it, when a muted but unmistakable bang came from the next car up the train. The two police officers turned to the sound and began reaching for their pistols, though they seemed unsure as to what they'd just heard.

Court, on the other hand, knew exactly what he'd heard. It was a gunshot, but before even he could react, a fully automatic weapon began thumping off at virtually the same moment.

He knew Angela was in that direction, probably walking down an aisle as he'd instructed her to do, so he rose and began pushing past the cops, but the male officer grabbed him by the arm to stop him from heading in the direction of the noise.

A second submachine gun began firing, adding to the cacophony coming from farther up the train.

Court shook away from the cop and kept running forward, but the two men in coats ahead at the snack bar scrambled up onto and then over the counter, tumbling behind it for cover next to the attendant there.

Court watched the men and knew they were well trained to act with such speed, and he assumed they would now be crouched low and drawing weapons.

He dove behind a table and yanked his Glock from his hip.

He shouted "Get down!" in French to the cops behind him, but they continued standing out in the aisle towards the back of the car, still unsure what was going on. The female officer said something into the radio on her shoulder, but otherwise they did not react to what was happening.

As the Russians remained hidden, a new burst of fully automatic fire began tearing through the restaurant car from the front of the train.

Finally the cops knelt and drew weapons, and the few other passengers in the car began screaming and crawling over one another towards the rear exit of the coach in a desperate bid for safety.

There was a lull of a couple of seconds, and Court began rising back up, but almost instantly the sound of gunshots, shattered glass, and ripping metal returned, sending everyone down again.

Court turned back in the direction of the two border guards, now crouched two tables behind him. In French he said, "Russian agents! I don't know how many! The guys behind the counter are with them." He began running, aiming in on the restaurant counter, looking for either of the two GRU men who'd sought shelter there.

The driver of the train heard the gunfire somewhere far behind him, and after ducking low instinctively for an instant, he reached up to pull the brakes and halt the train so the passengers could safely evacuate. But just as his hand grabbed the brake lever, he stopped himself.

Looking out the windscreen into the night, he realized they had just entered the Simplon Tunnel. If he slammed on the brakes now at this speed it would still take many hundreds of meters to stop, and then minutes to reverse back out of the tunnel. In the meantime, terrified travelers would pour out of the train into the narrow shaft, and he'd run the risk of hitting them as he reversed.

The Simplon railway tunnel had been carved through twenty kilometers of rock in the early 1900s and was the longest railway tunnel in the world until the 1980s. Three thousand miners worked to expand the channel about seven meters a day, building the massive underground structure in only seven years.

One hundred six people had died during its construction.

And now, the driver realized, a new tragedy was unfolding.

He had no good options. He could race the train forward for twenty kilometers and then stop at the station in Brig, Switzerland, just on the other side, or he could spend three or four minutes executing an emergency stop and reverse now.

More gunfire crackled behind him.

Maybe the border guards can get control of the situation, he told himself.

He decided to continue on at top speed; this would shorten his time in the tunnel to no more than eight or nine minutes, and he reached for his radio to call in the attack, but he stopped himself.

The fucking tunnel. No radio transmission would get through for the next eight minutes.

The train accelerated to over one hundred miles per hour as bullets ripped into the driver's cabin. He knelt down lower but stayed at the helm, because the locomotive was built with a dead man's switch, a handle he had to put his hands on every forty-five seconds to indicate there was a driver still at the controls. He couldn't hit the deck entirely; he had to keep his hands up near the dash, or else the train would stop automatically.

He wondered if he himself would be a dead man in moments, and then the train would stop in the middle of a dark and tight tunnel with no way out for the passengers.

Zoya knelt between a pair of seats in the center of the fourth car, and she did her best to assess her dire predicament.

Alex was being held down just meters away from her, but in open view of the Russians just inside the door leading to the restaurant car. She knew she'd hit one of the three, knocking him backwards as he fired his weapon, sending 9-millimeter bullets in a sweeping arc as he fell. But the other gunmen had dived behind the seats, and they were now intermingled with the flood of passengers frantically hiding themselves as they wailed and cried.

She thought she was in a difficult situation, with four or five enemy in the same narrow train car, but her situation suddenly got worse when she heard a shout from the opposite end of the car, behind her and over her right shoulder. She didn't rise to look, but she understood the Russian, undoubtedly spoken by the Central Asian–looking man she'd seen in the first car earlier.

"Gde ona?" *Where is she?*

Fuck, Zoya thought.

She didn't know how to get to Alex, and this worried her, but she also knew she was the one with Krupkin's phone, and she had to get it to New York. Alex was less important to her than damaging Russia's chance at resuming open trade with the West, and now *she* was the key to making that happen.

She rose and aimed for the three men in front of her, but all remained under cover.

Just as she turned to check for the shooter on the other side of her, she felt the overpressure of a round whizzing by a foot or so from her right ear, and she dove across the aisle to the other side, crashed into the seats, and tumbled down onto two passengers huddled together there.

She looked down at her body in terror, but she'd not been shot.

Still, she'd given away her location, so it was time to forgo stealth in favor of a hell of a lot of noise.

She reached over the seatback concealing her and fired a few rounds up the length of the train, then went flat on top of the passengers there, crushing them with her weight while return fire came her way.

She waited for it to stop, and thought that it sounded as if the man firing from the gangway leading to the third car had expended an entire magazine, and she also figured this would have kept the armed men on the other side of the car in cover, because those rounds fired at Zoya would have raced up the length of the train.

With one man reloading and the rest ducking down, she saw an opportunity and she leapt to her feet, dove over her seatback, then did it again at the next row, passing people who were screaming or crying; she assumed people were injured here, as well, but she didn't look. Her only objective was to get some space between her and the three men she'd first engaged, and she wanted to get closer to the lone Russian operator, eliminate him, and thereby open a corridor towards the front of the train.

Moving a third row back, she fired multiple times down the length of the car towards the three, over where Alex was still being held in the aisle, but after this she knew she'd pressed her luck long enough, so she fell back down in the seats just as subgun fire erupted from both directions.

Foam and fabric and metal blew into the air above her; she lay on her back holding her weapon to her chest, waiting for the onslaught to subside to get back into the fight.

FORTY

As the sound of gunfire rose and fell in the next car, Court continued ignoring the cops behind him, both of whom knelt behind a table, aiming in on the coach ahead, as if attackers might burst through the door at any moment.

The gunfire from the next coach was relentless; occasionally glass or metal would shatter or clang back here when a round made it through the gangway.

To the police, Court responded in French. "Don't shoot me, I'm the only chance you have."

And with that he began moving farther up the aisle towards the counter and the men concealed behind it.

The American went flat on the ground and began crawling on his chest even closer, hoping the cops would draw a little fire and buy him time to close.

Suddenly he heard movement behind him. The female police officer was in the aisle, moving forward quickly, her pistol in front of her.

This was the wrong play, Court knew. She was exposing more of her body to the enemy, and just as he was about to shout at her, she began shooting at the counter.

From the doorway to the coach with the gunfire, Court saw a man run into the restaurant car. He wore his big alpine pack on his back and he looked terrified, obviously fleeing the shooting there, but Court tried to wave him down to cover, knowing he was no safer up here with the two Russians on the other side of the counter.

Automatic gunfire suddenly erupted close; Court was too low to see what was happening, but soon the mountain climber caught a burst of gunfire in his chest and fell back in the center of the aisle, just next to the doorway that led to the area behind the counter.

The Swiss border guards opened fire, shooting over Court's head towards the men behind the counter, but almost instantly the female officer pitched back, shot in the arm. She fell onto her back in the aisle, and the male officer grabbed her uninjured arm and began pulling her to concealment behind a table.

Court went to the door next to the dead climber and opened it, swung in with his Glock, and immediately encountered one of the GRU men. The Russian's weapon was still trained on the cops as he prepared to fire, and he wasn't ready for an armed man popping up on his left.

Court shot him through the side of his face; his head snapped back, and the other GRU man swung Court's way and opened fire from low behind the counter.

Court spun back out the door, unable to return fire because of the female cashier crouched there behind his enemy, so he retreated and barely avoided catching a blast from the man behind the counter, even while still listening to the gun battle going on in the next coach.

He needed to get in there and help Angela, but first he had to deal with the GRU man still here in the restaurant car. He spun away from the doorway, then leapt up onto the counter, swinging his legs over.

The surviving Russian was in the process of rising with his MP9, and the two men slammed into each other, Court in midair, the Russian sweeping his weapon in his direction.

Court knocked the man's gun arm away before landing awkwardly behind the counter, and then the Russian kicked a heavy boot up and caught Court's wrist.

The Glock fell to the floor and bounced out the door, into the aisle next to the dead mountaineer.

Unarmed now, Court executed a kick to the man's rifle, knocking it up and away, and a long burst of rounds tore through the thin ceiling of the restaurant car.

Court dove for the man; they collided against the back of the counter, knocking bottles and coffeepots and food items in every direction. The American had taken hold of the Russian's weapon, but it was held around the GRU officer's neck by a canvas sling, so he couldn't pull it away from him.

Each man held the gun and kept one hand free, and they swung at each other. Court tried a knee to the man's groin but pounded his thigh instead.

"Sukha!" *Bitch*, the man shouted as he struggled, but Court wasn't any less caustic.

"Fuck you!"

Amid more slamming of bodies against counters, the sixtyish woman on the floor finally clambered over the front counter and tumbled down into the aisle, then ran back in the direction of the police.

Another burst of automatic gunfire ripped through the restaurant car from the car in front of them; Court heard the zings close by and the shredding of metal and the shouts of people, but he was unable to see what was going on because he and the other combatant had both fallen to their knees. A bottle of red wine and a plastic container of mayonnaise had broken in the melee; Court felt glass slice into his leg, and he reacted to it, instinctively shifting his body and using the hand that wasn't holding the Russian's weapon to grab at the glass embedded in his shin just below the knee.

This gave his opponent a chance to slide around on his own knees, using the mayo for lubrication on the floor and no doubt catching some of the broken glass in the process, but Court realized the man's idea was a good one.

The Russian muscled behind Court and got him in a vicious choke hold with his left arm while still pulling on his gun with his right. Court knew he'd be unconscious in seconds, so as he held the front end of the subgun with his right hand and tried to get his left behind him to use the small shard of glass he'd yanked out of his leg as some sort of impotent weapon, he looked around at his surroundings, desperate for anything else he could employ to get him out of this rapidly deteriorating situation.

Right in front of his eyes, he saw something. He was facing out into the coach at the open door to the snack counter, and the dead mountaineer still propped up by his pack was in front of him in the aisle. Upside down and attached to each side of the big black bag on the man's back was an ice axe, with an aluminum shaft and a sharp serrated steel pick counterbalanced by a stubby hammer on the other end.

The axes were each affixed with two Velcro straps, one at the top and one at the bottom, and the tools were attached downwards facing, with the pick ends at the bottom, about six inches off the floor where the dead man rested in a sitting position.

Court had used similar axes to climb and to self-arrest—to stop himself from falling down an icy decline—but he'd never had cause to use one offensively. But now was not the time to evaluate the efficacy of the potential weapon in front of him; it was time to act, because he could tell he'd be unconscious from loss of blood to his brain in a matter of seconds.

He dropped the blood-and-mayonnaise-covered shard of glass from his left hand, keeping his right hand up by his right shoulder where it gripped the forward rail of the squat weapon with all its might, with both he and the Russian yanking back and forth, but the Russian having control of the important parts of the gun: the trigger and the handgrip. With his left hand Court reached out for the axe in front of him, groaning with the incredible effort to push away from the choke hold. He just got a fingertip on the top Velcro fastener, and he ripped it open, causing the aluminum shaft to immediately drop and hit the floor at the dead man's hip.

The axe was facing upwards now at an angle, and it seemed like it was in reach, but just as Court extended his left arm and hand again to get a finger on it and slip it out of the bottom Velcro strap, he was yanked back violently, sliding across the mayo on the floor. His incredibly strong opponent must have seen what he was doing and pulled him out of reach of the potential weapon.

"Sukha," the man grunted out again, his voice full of effort and exhaustion and determination.

Court reached again for the axe, but his fingers were easily ten inches away from it now. Struggling to scoot forward again, the man behind him held firm. In English now, the Russian said, "I break your neck!"

The American felt his hold on the gun weaken now as the oxygen left his brain; he knew he was down to about three seconds before he lost consciousness, but even in his panicking and oxygen-depleted brain, an idea came to him. He gripped the MP9 to the right of his head even more tightly, yanked it forward an inch or two, and then slammed his head hard to the right, smacking the side of the weapon with it.

Then he did it again, harder this time.

The man behind him laughed a little through labored breathing, then spoke into Court's left ear. "What is *that*, bitch? Stupid, dead American."

Court banged his head a third time against the gun, but this time he pushed up a little on the fore-end with his hand clutching it there, raising the weapon a half inch or so just as his head made contact.

The right side of Court's skull slammed into the magazine release button on the B&T subgun, and this caused the weapon's magazine to drop free, just in front of Court's shoulder. His left hand shot over to the right and caught the end of it, and then, in one swift motion, he launched his left arm out again, used the nine-and-a-half-inch thirty-round magazine to extend his reach, and he hooked it under the pick in front of him.

His eyelids began to close but he fought them back open and shoved the magazine up, snagging the pick and flinging the ice axe into the air.

He dropped the mag, grabbed the aluminum shaft of the axe, and spun it around, then slammed it straight back over his head.

The stainless-steel spike embedded in the top of the Russian's skull. Quickly the man lost his hold on the subgun; Court pulled it out of his grasp completely, then turned and struggled to his feet, slipping on mayo twice in the process but managing to avoid slicing himself again on the glass all around.

The Russian just knelt there, lowered onto his haunches slowly, blood draining from the top of his head down into his eyes, flowing like a creek over his beard and lips, dripping onto the floor.

He wasn't dead; his eyes were blinking still, but Court assumed he'd damaged the man's brain to where motor functions were no longer easy or even possible.

As he stood fully, Court wrenched the pick out of the man's head and struck him again, blood splattering everything behind the snack counter.

The Russian fell onto his back, his eyes wide open now in death.

Court was exhausted from the struggle, but the blood was now flowing unrestricted into his brain again, and then a new salvo of gunfire from the fourth coach revived him further.

He dropped the bloody axe, pulled the MP9's sling off the man's neck, and reloaded it with the magazine he'd used to grab the ice axe. Checking the see-through polymer mag, he saw about half the ammo remaining, but he didn't take the time to go through the man's coat to see if he had another magazine.

No, time had been of the essence a full minute ago when this kicked off, and now it was nonexistent. He had to do something to help Angela and to secure Velesky from the Russians.

Court shot out of the restaurant car and ducked low next to the bathroom door in the gangway on his way to the fourth car of the train, because two-way gunfire had kicked off again there, and bullets tore through the soft aluminum frame of the bulkhead, threatening him here even though he was concealed from the action.

He had no idea how many adversaries he was facing ahead or even where they were, but they would have heard him fighting back in the restaurant car, and the Russians would be unable to raise the two men he'd killed, so he knew they'd be aware of his presence back here.

Court carefully peeked around the turn in the gangway and looked through the shattered glass doors into the train car ahead, and instantly someone fired his way, missing wide to the right, but even though he didn't know if he'd been the intended target, he knew that entering from this direction would be suicide.

This was what was known as a fatal funnel of fire. Like any doorway, when an adversary knows that you'll be coming through it, it's damn easy for them to concentrate their fire on the area.

Court went flat on the floor again, then crawled back around the turn where the bathroom door was.

He'd seen gun smoke and bodies, wounded and huddled passengers, but he saw no way to get into and through the next car without likely killing a lot of innocents. Thinking quickly, Court ran back to the car behind, scooped up the ice axe he'd used to kill the GRU man, and then released its mate from the dead mountaineer's pack.

Leaving everything else, he quickly secured the submachine gun on his back, tightening the sling, then moved across the aisle of the restaurant car to the police officers.

He stepped past the two border control officers, looking down at the injured woman while he did so. To the other cop he said, "Use your belt as a tourniquet. You get it tight enough and high enough on her arm, she'll be fine."

The man just nodded, fully involved in aiding his partner.

Court stood on the seat by the table and lifted his right foot. The window here had three holes in it from the Russians' gunfire, so when he thrust his leg forward, the rest of the glass gave easily, shattering and falling outside the speeding train.

Instantly, roaring noise and blistering cold invaded the coach.

Looking outside, Court couldn't tell if the tunnel walls were three feet away from the train or thirty, but he reached out to his right and slammed his left axe hard into the metal just above the window frame. Hooking it there on the frame, he rocked outside the train, reached up with his right hand, and, with a violent swing, pierced the aluminum wall of the vehicle with the hot-forged-steel point of the ice axe.

The noise and wind were unreal; he had a feeling they were traveling in excess of one hundred miles per hour now, and the fact that they were in a narrow tunnel wasn't lost on him at all. He kept his body as close to the train as possible as he pulled himself higher up its side; he retrieved his left axe from its hold and heaved himself up with his right arm, his boots scraping for purchase on the cold aluminum, and slammed his left axe into the top of the train.

He began moving forward, fighting unreal wind resistance, pitch-black darkness, and the uncomfortable knowledge that he was inside a tunnel with concrete walls he couldn't even see. Standing would likely mean decapitation, but he wasn't sure if kneeling would, as well, so he stayed as flat on his belly as he could, striking the roof with the steel axe, pulling himself forward a foot and a half or so, and then repeating the process with the other axe.

He went across the roof of the restaurant car, hoping like hell the sporadic shooting going on in the coach ahead didn't send rounds up through the ceiling and into his torso, but preferring his chances here, risking this over barreling into the fatal funnel waiting for him if he entered the fourth coach from the gangway to the restaurant car.

His plan was to drop into one of the first three cars of the train and then attack from the opposite vector, hopefully catching the shooters by surprise. He saw this as the better option, but he also knew that the time it would take him to get a car length or two ahead might be more time than he had. At any moment the Russians could get Velesky and his data, and they could move to another car and bunker themselves until they came out of the tunnel.

He remembered his earpiece, useless now in his left pants pocket, and cursed aloud for not putting it back in before climbing outside the train, but he reasoned it probably wouldn't have stayed in his ear with the wind whipping across him.

He just kept moving as fast as he could, using the strength in his arms and back to yank himself onwards, pulling as hard as he would if he were climbing a vertical surface due to the intense air resistance pushing him back. A desperate man with nothing more than will, a submachine gun with a half-magazine load of 9-millimeter hollow points, a dumb plan, and a prayer.

FORTY-ONE

Thirty-one-year-old Wachmeister Joel Sutter had served in the Swiss Border Guard Corps Command for six years, but this was the first time he'd ever pulled his service weapon with the intention of using it. He'd been finishing his business in the gangway bathroom two coaches back when the shooting began, and he quickly buckled his belt, pulled his Walther pistol from it, and began moving low and carefully down the train, desperate to catch up with his two colleagues.

His progress was impeded, over and over, as people tried to push past him, desperate to get to the front coach, presumably to be farther from the gunfire but probably also, Sutter assumed, to implore the driver to stop the train so they could get off.

The Wachmeister knew they were in the tunnel, however, and there would be no way the driver would intentionally stop.

He made it to the third car, recognized from the sound that the shooting was coming from the fourth, and then pushed past more frantic passengers, two of whom held their arms where they'd been hit by wayward gunfire.

Finally he reached the gangway between the third and fourth cars. Carefully he peered forward; there was a lull in the shooting, and then he ducked in, his pistol waving in front of him.

Seeing no one, he stepped past the bathroom and aimed up the aisle, then began walking forward. In the fourth car, he saw three men in the aisle, all on top of one another; there was movement but he couldn't tell if all of them were alive or if any of them were injured.

He'd only just begun moving into the coach, his heart pounding in terror but his mind dead set on saving innocent lives, when a man rose over a seatback at the far end of the car, a submachine gun in his hands. He fired a quick burst Sutter's way, and then the Wachmeister himself fired multiple rounds.

The shooter across the coach ducked back down and Sutter advanced forward, moving towards the threat, keeping one eye on the three men impeding his way up the aisle.

On his right, a woman dressed in black rose over the seatback, her arms high in surrender, and then she kicked over the seat and dropped into the one behind her. She did this again while the officer scanned the rest of the coach, dismissing her as any threat.

GRU First Sergeant Ulan Bakiyev had ducked into the restroom in the gangway between the third and fourth cars to load the last magazine into his B&T submachine gun. As he stepped out, he looked back into the fourth car and immediately saw a big man in the blue uniform of a Swiss border guard, maybe a quarter of the way down the coach. The man was facing away, aiming a pistol at the other exit, and Bakiyev calmly raised his weapon at the officer's back.

Before he fired, however, he saw Banshee climb over a seatback just beyond the officer and on his right. Bakiyev slewed his aim towards the movement and opened fire just as the woman fell back down between the seats.

Angela Lacy crouched with other terrified passengers in the fourth coach, low between the seats. She held her hand to her left ear, pushing her earbud in place. "Six? Six?"

There was no response.

People had fallen on top of her multiple times in the past minute, mostly staying out of the aisle and instead climbing over seats to move away from gunfire, but she herself had not risen from her position here on the floor.

After a fresh salvo of shooting, she saw a woman wearing a black coat and a black knit cap come into view, diving over a seatback and falling down to the floor directly across from her. The woman's hands were empty, and as the seats above her took direct fire from the direction of the front of the train, the woman in black just calmly lay there, her knees to her chest so they didn't stick out into the aisle.

Angela realized this woman was the person she'd taken for a man in the front car of the train minutes earlier.

The woman sat up as soon as the shooting stopped, and the two of them locked eyes for a moment. Now Angela saw something she didn't expect to see. It wasn't panic, and it wasn't the abject terror she herself was feeling.

The woman's face was one of calm resolve. Her eyes shifted away to her left, Angela's right, as if she saw someone or something coming up the aisle from the front of the train. She knelt down lower; Angela did the same instinctively, and then she heard a fresh exchange of gunfire, from both her right and her left.

Squeezing her eyes shut for a moment, she then opened them to look up and see a male Swiss police officer, bloodied from the left knee down, stagger into view in the aisle between her position and the woman in black, the officer's pistol raised in front of him, smoke wisping from the black barrel.

Sweat dripped from the bearded man's face, already contorted with pain, panic, and determination, as he squeezed off a single round at some target Angela couldn't see because she was flat behind the seats. She watched the officer's eyes widen even more; he aimed in on a new target, but before he could press the trigger, a fully automatic burst of gunfire erupted from Angela's right, the officer lurched forward, and then he staggered back and slipped from her view.

The weapon in his hand tumbled from his fingers and bounced in the aisle four feet from where Angela lay.

She focused on the pistol as she cowered behind the seat during another lull in the shooting. Riveted in position, unable to move for a moment, she heard a sickening gurgling on her right. The fallen officer was taking his last breaths, simultaneously bleeding out and drowning in his own blood. She had no way to pull him to her; she could only see his boots in the aisle, and obviously shooters were positioned on both sides of the coach and would be able to see her if she crawled out to render aid.

But the weapon remained untouched, just out of her grasp. All she had to do was crawl a foot, reach out into the aisle quickly, and retrieve it.

Angela told herself she'd have to do it as a last-ditch measure to keep herself and others in the car alive. She rose to her knees and first looked at the weapon, but then her eyes locked on the woman in black crouched across the aisle from her.

The woman looked right back to her, and she spoke now in an American accent. "Don't even think about it, bitch." Then she launched herself into the aisle, grabbed the weapon, and rotated the muzzle to her right, pointing the gun down the aisle in the direction the most recent gunfire had come from.

Angela went flat on the ground again as the woman in the black knit cap squeezed round after round while lying on her side, and then she stopped firing, pulled herself up to her feet, and began running forward, in the direction she had been shooting, while now firing down the train car in the opposite direction. Whoever the woman was, Angela could tell she knew how to handle both a weapon and a high-stress, life-or-death encounter.

Angela heard return fire coming from down the train; she stayed low, paralyzed in fear, wondering if Six was dead and also wondering if the only person on the train who seemed to be fighting back was a friend or a foe.

Luka Rudenko was well aware the men he'd left in the restaurant car had been engaging enemy back there, but he presumed they were shooting it out with the Swiss border guards. This didn't overly concern him; his Unit 29155 killers would handle a couple of cops.

The firing had died down behind him; he assumed his teammates would be joining him soon, which would be good, because one of his men up here lay dead, slumped in a seat against the bulkhead, a bullet entrance wound in his left jaw and an exit wound out his right temple, his brains splattered across the smoked-glass partition to the luggage area behind him.

Banshee had tagged him with her very first shot, and this had caused both Luka and Boris, his other GRU assassin up here with him, to seek cover immediately.

At present Luka wasn't concerned about the health of the two men in the restaurant car, and he wasn't threatened by some hapless Swiss cops back there, assuming his men would have dropped them with ease.

But he *was* concerned about Banshee. She had made it farther up the coach in the direction of Bakiyev, and while Bakiyev had returned her fire, Luka had been sent to cover by Banshee's shots in his direction, so he hadn't seen any more to that exchange.

He was hoping she lay dead or wounded between a row of seats, but he had no confirmation, and he wasn't ready to go looking for her.

He spoke into his earpiece. "Ulan? Do you read me?"

Ulan Bakiyev's voice came through. "I'm hit. In the hip. Not bad. I can operate, but I've retreated to the third car to treat it."

This told Luka that no one had eyes on Banshee now. He quickly popped his head back over the seatback in front of him and took in the situation. He saw a couple of dead passengers in their seats, and he saw Velesky still held in place in the aisle by the hunkered-down Italians, but everyone else—Banshee included, apparently—was still concealed behind the seats.

"I can't see her," Luka said to Bakiyev, "but she was heading your way."

"Roger. I'm good. Covering forward."

Luka called again to the two men he'd left in the restaurant car, but still they didn't answer. Suddenly concerned about getting caught from behind, he called across the aisle to Boris, the only other 29155 man alive up here. "Keep your eyes on our backs. The boys aren't responding."

Boris did as instructed, swiveling his Brügger & Thomet towards the gangway, just visible to him where he lay between the two right-side second-class seats. Aiming with his weapon to his shoulder that itself was pressed into the floor, he said, "Covering behind."

Luka peeked out again, and he saw no sign of Zakharova, so he shouted in English to Drexler's two men, still lying on top of Velesky, "Bring him to us! I'll cover you!"

The men had been all but still, but they did as instructed, glad to finally know which way they could run since the gunfire had been coming from both directions. After climbing to their feet, the two men pulled a noncompliant Velesky by the arms down the aisle towards the back end of the coach.

They took no more than a few steps before a gunshot cracked and one of the Italians stumbled forward, shot in the back.

Luka hadn't seen the muzzle flash, but a faint wisp of smoke most of the way down the coach on the left gave him his target's general coordinates.

Boris spun around now, and both men rose and began firing on the area where Banshee had fired from.

A three-round burst of Boris's bullets went wide, however, and they shot down the aisle, through the next gangway, then the next, slamming into bulkheads and coming out on the other side.

Two of the rounds lost momentum, but the last one made it all the way to the driver's compartment, embedding itself in the cabin lighting control panel behind the engineer's right shoulder.

Instantly the overhead lights on the train flickered, then went out.

Their multiple bursts of fire had depleted Luka's and Boris's magazines quickly, and soon both men were back down and reloading the last of their ammo in pitch-black darkness, while people moaned and screamed and pleaded and shouted throughout the coach, their cries barely audible over the roar coming in from the shattered windows.

Luka Rudenko released the slide on his pistol, chambering a round from his last magazine. He was enshrouded in the near darkness, with no light coming in from all the shattered or intact windows due to the fact that they were still streaking through the Simplon Tunnel.

He couldn't see Zakharova now, he couldn't even see a quarter of the way up the coach, so he rose and began moving forward, with Boris on his right, just behind, with the squat barrel of his submachine gun in front of Luka's right shoulder.

Luka reached Velesky and the surviving Italian, both huddled between seats on his right. He didn't acknowledge as he stepped past them; he just kept his focus on the impenetrable darkness ahead.

Luka shouted now, his booming voice more than overtaking the howl of the wind. "Ulan! We'll press, you cover. She's six rows from you on the right!"

The reply came instantly. "She's not getting past me. Press her."

When the lights went out, Zoya pushed herself flat against a dead passenger, a heavyset male, using his ample body for some semblance of cover. She saw the darkness as an opportunity, however, so soon she climbed back up to her knees, readied the dead cop's pistol in her hands, and began to rise.

Just then she heard one of the GRU officers at the rear of the coach shout out to the man in the gangway at the front. "Ulan! We'll press, you cover. She's six rows from you on the right!"

She didn't think they could see her, so she dove across the aisle.

There was no one between these two seats, so she was able to scoot around and face back towards the aisle, her leg muscles screaming at her for returning to a low crouch, and she thought about her options.

She was in a three-on-one fight in, essentially, a two-dimensional space. She was in a defensive position with little ammo and no maneuverability, and she was surrounded.

Fresh gunfire ripped from up the train, breaking window glass and poking more screaming holes in the coach's sides and roof.

Zoya's tactical brain had no trouble formulating and delivering the bad news.

She was fucked.

FORTY-TWO

Court knew this was taking too long. He figured he was barely two-thirds down the fourth car in the train, and at this pace, he wouldn't get to the other side of all the fighting and into the fight himself before all the fighting was over.

He wouldn't mind missing a claustrophobic shootout in the dark if not for the fact that he wanted to help Lacy and he needed to get Velesky's data.

But he kept trudging forward, slamming the axes down into the roof and pulling, then repeating the motion with the opposite arm.

He'd made it only another five feet when fresh blistering two-way gunfire kicked off directly below him, and then he heard the ripping of metal on his right. With each subsequent pop of gunfire, the tearing metal noise got closer, and he knew someone was shooting the ceiling of the coach; whether they heard him up here or were just firing wildly, he had no idea.

As more rounds missed his face by just a foot, he realized he had no choice, he had to get off this roof, and there was no way off this roof quickly other than swinging off the side and through a window, directly into the middle of the firefight below.

Slamming his left axe down into the edge of the roof by the left side, he let go of his right axe and pulled his B&T off his back, holding the little weapon one-handed.

Another blast from a handgun poked a hole not a foot from his right knee. He couldn't see it in the darkness, but he heard it over the raging wind, and he kicked his body off the top of the train, one hand holding the aluminum shank of the axe as he readied his feet to lead the way through the window and directly into the fray.

Zoya withstood the long and frantic spray of bullets coming from up the train car, mostly because it was inaccurate fire, rounds fired into the ceiling obviously to keep her head down while the two men coming from the other direction neared her position in silence.

When the shooting stopped, she shifted her body to lean into the aisle, ready to dump rounds up the train towards the gangway where the most recent fire had come from, and she rose, but just as she did, she heard a crash of breaking glass to the right of her left shoulder.

A form, darker than the air around it, swung in through the window; she felt the feet of a flying human striking her in the left arm and torso, and this knocked her sideways into the right-side double seats.

The man—it had to be a man—crashed down, not quite on top of her but instead landing on her lower legs, and she swung her pistol around in his direction.

Gunfire flashed from the middle of the aisle down the gangway; she didn't know if she or the man who'd flown in from the window was the intended target, but almost instantly the man lying in the aisle in front of her began returning fire with a weapon of his own.

She couldn't identify him through the blinding muzzle flashes of his gun, but she did identify him from his weapon. It sounded like the B&Ts the GRU men had been using.

But why was this Russian shooting down the train, where the other GRU men had been approaching from?

She retained her pistol in her hand even after the kick she received and the awkward fall she took, so she raised it at the man firing, but then she took her finger off the trigger.

If he was firing in the direction of the Russians down the coach, then he was keeping their heads down.

Taking this to be a case of blue on blue—the GRU men shooting at one another in the fog of war and the near pitch-black conditions—she decided to take advantage of this slim opportunity to escape.

She climbed to her feet, leapt over the seatback, then the next, then the next.

She heard blows and men grunting behind her; a hand-to-hand fight had somehow begun where she'd just been crouched, so she darted into the aisle and then ran for the gangway, the Walther out in front of her.

She'd made it into the area between the two cars, just past the bathroom, and when she swung in to clear it with her weapon in the darkness, a man fell out and on top of her. This time her gun *did* fly from her hands; she tripped on the top of the three steps down to the coach doors and then landed hard on the steps, her back to the door.

This man fell onto her; he tried to get his hands around her throat but she knocked them away, then speared him with her fingertips in his Adam's apple.

He jolted back but then grabbed her again, and the pair began rolling in the gangway, fighting for their lives.

Court Gentry had come through the window twenty seconds earlier, smashed into some asshole in the middle of the aisle and knocked him flat, and then Court himself landed on his back, hitting a seat arm on the way down to the floor. Gunfire came from down the train coach almost instantly, so he shifted his aim from the figure between the seats at his feet and fired five times at muzzle flashes, hoping to suppress whoever the fuck was shooting at him, and then he'd done a back roll to between the seats, ending up crushed against a man crouching in his seat with his head between his knees and sobbing.

The gunfire stopped suddenly, and he saw movement in the dark across the aisle; the person he'd just slammed into was climbing over seats towards the front of the train to get away, and he rose with his subgun at his shoulder but was immediately waylaid by a fast-moving figure from his right.

His gun left his hands as he fell again into the aisle. He desperately groped through the dark to control the hands of the man who'd tumbled down with him, lest he be stabbed or shot by them, but he failed in this and instead caught a punch to his head, high above his temple.

This told him the man had at least one hand not operating a weapon, so Court lunged for the man again, and this time wrapped him up. Making his way to his knees, he realized there was another threat in the aisle behind him when a flashlight's beam illuminated him at a distance of three feet for a split second, and then the operator of the light raised it high in the air and struck down at Court with it.

Court parried this blow and threw a punch of his own, landing it on the attacker's left biceps and knocking his swinging arm away; he knew no man would swing a flashlight at someone if he had a gun to use, so Court stood up in the aisle and traded blow after blow with the enemy.

A sudden stinging sensation on his right arm at the base of the deltoid told him he'd just been slashed with a knife.

Frantically he kicked out and struck his attacker, and the flashlight fell to the ground. The figure with the blade moved closer while Court rushed back, and then he fell over a man lying there who was very much still alive.

He and this man grappled; he found this attacker to be just as strong and capable as the man he'd fought with in the restaurant car.

The difference this time, however, was that Court had two adversaries, and he did not have access to an axe to lobotomize the sons of bitches, so the fight went on.

Angela Lacy was three rows ahead of the group of men battling one another in the aisle, but there'd been no shooting for several seconds, so she decided she'd use this moment to try to get out of here. She climbed to her feet, stayed low in the darkness, and felt her way down the aisle. Twice she'd stifled a scream: once stepping on a body in the center of the aisle, and a second time when someone bumped hard into her, pushing her out of the way as he ran on in the same direction she was going—towards the restaurant car.

The darkness in front of her made balance difficult, and she used the seatbacks to continue on; behind her she heard men struggling in hand-to-hand combat as more terrified passengers filled the aisles both in front of and behind her.

The noise of the wind rushing through the broken windows was intense near the gangway because the glass all around had been shot out and the ceiling perforated. Angela could feel the holes in the ceiling by the cold air blowing down on her, but she made it into the gangway, then through it, and then into the restaurant car.

Here she stumbled into a dead body, climbed over it, and then continued down the aisle until she tripped over a leg extending out from a table. Landing on the ground, she put her hand on a pistol, and she lifted it up.

It was so dark she could barely make out the weapon in her hand, but she thought it might have been police issue, meaning it had been dropped by an injured border control officer, who'd then been dragged into another coach.

Crawling up to her knees, she raised the gun in front of her. There had been no gunfire for over half a minute, but she couldn't see a damn thing and had no idea what dangers lurked in front of her.

Softly, into her mic, she said, "Six? Six?"

Still there was no reply.

A voice called out in the darkness in English. "Help. Help, please."

Angela crawled up the aisle to a female border control officer who had been wounded in the arm. Next to her was the body of a male officer; his eyes were open and rolled back, and blood covered his mouth and throat.

Angela put the pistol next to the injured woman and began putting pressure on her bloody arm.

FORTY-THREE

Court understood there were two men who intended him harm within five feet of him, but the roar of the train's movement through the tunnel coming from the broken windows made it nearly as impossible to hear where they were as the darkness made it impossible to see them.

This was an utter clusterfuck, he knew without a doubt, but somewhere down on the ground was his subgun, and it still had a few rounds in it.

He dropped down onto a chair arm and then flung himself back onto the ground, reaching frantically, finally grasping the sling of the weapon where it lay under a seat; he started to yank it to him, but a man grabbed him from behind and heaved him up to his knees.

Court kicked a leg out, however, and his foot found the stock of the MP9. And then he felt the blade of a knife against his throat, and he froze.

Luka Rudenko would have shot the man dead when he came through the window forty-five seconds earlier if he'd had any ammunition left in his pistol, but his gun had run dry trading lead with Zakharova.

Instead, he'd had Boris, also with an empty gun, attack the man barehanded so he could close in to stab him to death.

He didn't know where the fuck Ulan had gone; he wasn't responding on comms, and Luka worried that Banshee had escaped somewhere up the length of the train and had killed his man, as someone had apparently done to the two in the restaurant car.

Luka had a flashlight and his stiletto, but when he'd slammed the light down on the man and then swung with his blade, the target had punched away the lethal strike and then fallen out of reach over Boris.

Luka had managed to cut the man, but not gravely, and he could tell this operator was one hell of a good hand-to-hand fighter. Luka assumed he was here helping Velesky, but this definitely was *not* Banshee.

He shouted to Boris in Russian. "Got him at knifepoint! Hold his arms."

"Got them!"

Boris wrestled the man's arms tighter behind his back in the confines of the aisle.

Luka leaned closer to the unknown man. In English he said, "Where is Banshee?"

The answer, to his surprise, came in Russian. "Matador, I presume?"

Luka Rudenko stood up slowly, and he didn't try to hide the shock on his face, because it was too dark to make it out. He took a step back, forced away the surprise eventually, and answered calmly, "I haven't heard that name for a long time." He chuckled a little in the dark, then pulled out his phone and used the light from it to shine on the prisoner. Looking him over, he saw a man with cuts on his face and neck, and a bloody gash through the coat on his right arm. The man was down on one knee; the other leg jutted out away from his body and under a seat on the left side of the train.

He had a smell to him, and it took Luka scanning his body up and down to see that his legs were covered in both blood and what looked and smelled like . . . mayonnaise.

Luka said, "The only people who call me Matador work for the CIA. That means, friend, that you are CIA."

To Rudenko's astonishment, the man being held from behind and facing off against a long stiletto a couple of feet away smiled, squinting into the glare of the light. After a moment, he said, "Buddy . . . you . . . fucking . . . wish."

Rudenko cocked his head. *This guy's crazy,* he said to himself. As the man began dragging his extended leg back from under the seat, Luka laughed a little, then said, "You won't be the first CIA officer I've killed this week."

"You're damn right, I won't."

At first Rudenko had a bemused expression on his face, but quickly he again adopted a little smile. "Bravery in the face of defeat. A trait I respect. Goodbye, American."

He moved forward again to slash this bastard's throat so he could get back to the important work of finding and killing Banshee and Velesky before they got out of the tunnel and the engineer stopped the train.

Court had seen the figure moving towards him; he knew the knife would be drawn across his throat in an instant if he didn't do something, but he actually *was* doing something.

He'd spent the previous few seconds surreptitiously kicking off his left tennis shoe with help from the seat base on his left; then he used his socked foot to locate the grip of his MP9 lying there out of view under the seat.

As the man began moving forward, he dragged his foot back to him quickly, bringing the weapon closer by squeezing his toes around the trigger guard.

The MP9 is a small light submachine gun, and Court oriented the weapon up the aisle in front of him by leveraging the stock against the inside of his knee, then pushing his foot to the left a little. The big toe of his left foot found the trigger, and just as Matador brought his knife hand back to whip it forward and slash Court's throat, Court clenched his toes.

A single shot cracked in the darkness, the sudden flash blinding, and Matador screamed out as Court felt the thud of the weapon's stock against his knee.

Court skidded his feet under him on the aisle, rose a little, and threw his body forward now with all his might, flipping the man who had been kneeling behind him and holding him tight, sending him over his body, bouncing him against seats before he then fell into the aisle.

Court dropped back to his lacerated knees and grabbed the submachine gun off the floor.

As the man right in front of him now tried to scramble back to his feet, Court shoved the short-barreled weapon under the man's chin and pressed the trigger again, this time with the customary appendage for firing a gun, and after the flash and the bark of the weapon, Court could hear the Russian's brains splatter on the roof of the coach even over the roaring sound of wind through the broken windows.

Court then peered into the blackness in front of him, desperate to see Matador, but he saw nothing at all.

He considered firing more rounds up the train car, certain that the surviving Russian was making for the gangway, but he knew there were still innocents alive on board, so he held his fire. Instead, he stood, turned, and continued up the coach, assuming Velesky had darted off closer to the front of the long train because he hadn't run into him back in the restaurant car a few minutes earlier when the shooting began.

Angela Lacy held her phone in her mouth, using it as a flashlight while she used her hands to treat the injured woman's gunshot wound. She'd found paper napkins on the table and packed the bloody mess, pressing hard to stanch what flow remained from the ragged hole.

As she was focused on this, she'd heard a single gunshot from the next car, the first in perhaps thirty seconds, and seconds after this, she heard a noise in front of her in the restaurant coach, someone moving in her direction, but awkwardly, as if stumbling.

The gun she'd found in the aisle moments earlier was next to her, but she didn't reach for it, assuming whoever was coming her way to be another injured passenger in need of her help.

When the person was almost on top of her in the aisle, she tilted her head back to use the flashlight to see them, her hands still busy putting pressure on the arm of the wounded officer.

Then she stopped moving, frozen still, as a wave of panic enveloped her.

The man standing in front of her was Matador. His green cap was off and now his blond hair was on display, as was a bandage on his ear and a mask of agony on his face. He limped as he moved, and while he didn't seem to be carrying a weapon, she felt instantly intimidated to the point of panic.

In English, the man shouted, "Get out of my way!" and his voice was so intimidating that it broke her free from her paralysis. She scooted into the seat at a table next to her, moving to the side while he stepped by, using the light in Lacy's mouth to guide him.

In seconds he'd hobbled through the gangway out of the restaurant car towards the back, and Lacy saw a trail of blood left on the aisle where he'd passed.

Something was apparently wrong with his foot or leg.

She knew she should have picked up the pistol and gone after him, but she was too terrified to do so. Instead, she went back to bandaging the woman's damaged arm, and only when she finished did she pick up the pistol and then sit up in one of the seats.

Zoya Zakharova had spent most of a minute in hand-to-hand combat on the floor in the gangway between the third and fourth cars. She tasted blood in her mouth and felt her muscles weakening from exhaustion, but she lunged forward in the dark again and caught her opponent low, just over his knees, knocking him back into the closed door.

She didn't have the physical strength of the man she was in combat with, not even close. But she was fast and efficient with her movements, and her adversary was clearly dealing with a gunshot wound, because she'd slipped in blood on the floor once, and the two times they'd separated from their scrum, he'd been unable to quickly get back to his feet, giving Zoya the opportunity to knock him back to the floor again.

Now the GRU officer was down on the steps, on his back against the door, the windows of which had been shot out. He seemed as drained as Zoya felt, in his case probably more due to blood loss than exertion.

Still, he threw punches at her, and she did her best to block them in near total darkness, while sending her own fists, elbows, and knees out, trying to do some damage herself.

Suddenly, the sound of shoes crunching glass came from behind, as someone ran into the gangway from the fourth coach. Zoya's heart sank, expecting it to be an armed Matador ready to end her and save his colleague. The GRU officer leaning against the door had both of Zoya's arms held, and she didn't have the strength to break free or to get her legs swung around so she could try to kick him, and she certainly didn't have the strength to battle yet another well-trained fighter, so she saw no way out of this that didn't end with her dying right here on the floor.

But from behind, the crunching footfalls stopped, and she heard a man speak.

"Beth?"

It was Alex. It was too dark to see him even if she'd been able to turn around and look, and she assumed he couldn't see her, either, but he would know two people were fighting just feet away from where he stood.

She shouted to him. "Pull the door release!"

The GRU officer on the floor with his back to the door yanked one of Zoya's hands forward, pulling her closer, but she used it to her advantage. She head-butted him in the nose, stunning him a little, and then she yanked herself free while he regained his senses.

Quickly she rose to her knees, and as she did so, Alex came up on her left, then pulled the red emergency door latch down from the wall.

Just then, the pitch-black gangway was flooded with a sudden wash of dim light, giving detail to the scene.

They'd just shot out of the Simplon Tunnel and back into moonlight.

The door behind the GRU man did not open immediately; instead, Zoya launched to her feet and threw her shoulder into it while grabbing onto a handrail on the wall. She pushed up and to her left.

The door flew open behind the Russian; he grasped Zoya by her coat and hung on, the impossible wail of wind behind him.

Zoya began to fall forward as the man began to fall backwards out of the train.

Just as she was about to be yanked out along with her enemy, she felt arms wrap around her waist from behind. It was Alex, and he pulled her back with all his might, breaking her free from the GRU man's grasp.

The Russian rolled head over heels out of the train, his frantic scream lost in the wind and engine noise just one second later.

Zoya and Alex fell together to the blood-soaked gangway floor, she on top of him, and then she turned around and rose back to her feet on wobbling and wearied legs. She reached back down in the dim light to help Alex to his feet.

And then she heard crunching racing footsteps on her right.

She turned and raised her arms to protect herself, but as soon as she did, a body impacted her at full force, knocking her wildly back to the ground.

She grunted with the impact, and then the man climbed off her and rose into a combat crouch. She pushed off against the wall of the gangway by the door to retake her feet, and she herself put her fists out.

Alex lay on the slick bloody floor where he'd fallen, just six feet from the open door showing a dim moonlit view of a snow-covered railway yard.

Zoya assumed this was Matador in front of her; the moonlight filtering in wasn't good enough to identify facial features, but he'd attacked her, so she wasn't going to ask for an ID before she went to work on kicking his ass. She threw a punch that he ducked low and to the right of, and then he fired out a jab as he kept moving around her, glancing it off her head above her right ear.

Zoya's left fist connected with the right temple of the man; he stumbled a little, then dropped to a knee just two feet from the open door. As the train began to slow, wind still swirling through the open door and broken windows all around them, she took a half step back and reared back her right hand to rain down a right cross to the kneeling man's jaw.

Just then the train began rushing alongside lights on high poles in the train yard.

The light in the gangway that had gone from nonexistent fifteen seconds ago to just very dim once they got out of the tunnel now rose to a level where Zoya could make out the face of the man five feet in front of her.

She started her swing just as her attacker looked up at her, his arms coming up to defend himself.

And then she froze midpunch.

The man on his knee in front of her did the same.

Alex Velesky squatted low across the gangway from Beth and the man trying to beat her to death. He was six feet away still, looking at the pair between him and the open door when the gangway was flooded with the glow from the artificial lighting outside.

But whereas before there had been nothing but a furious frenzy of violent action and motion from the woman he knew as Beth, now she was still as a statue, a look registering on her face that he could not identify.

Alex didn't recognize the man, but the man's intentions were clear. He was blood covered from combat and he'd already rained down punches on Beth, so Alex knew he had to do something.

He grabbed on to the railing by the stairs next to him on his side of the gangway and pulled his beaten body to a standing position as he looked on at the pair, both of whom remained frozen as they stared at each other, their fists up by their faces.

Zoya couldn't believe her eyes, so much so that she squeezed them shut and then prized them back open, confirming that the image was still there.

"Court?" The word came out in a husky whisper.

Even through all the disorientation of the flashing lights, the whipping icy gusts through the open door and shot-out windows, the shaky balance brought on by the slowing of the train, even through the haze of catching several blows to the head in the past minute—through all of this she could clearly see that he was as surprised to see her as she was to see him.

He spoke now in the low light, his voice revealing the astonishment she'd seen in his eyes.

"What . . . the . . . fuck?"

Alex Velesky appeared on Court's right, low and fast out of the darkness. Court turned to the movement just as Zoya watched Alex throw his body through the air, impacting Court on the right side of his torso.

And then Court was gone.

Velesky fell flat on his face in the gangway by the steps as Zoya watched Court fly sideways, outside the train, and disappear into the night.

Zoya screamed.

FORTY-FOUR

Alex Velesky climbed back up to his feet now, invigorated by what he'd just done. He could tell Beth was beaten, stunned, perhaps badly injured or at least just exhausted from the multiple altercations of the last few minutes. He told himself it was up to him to get them out of this from here on. Looking to Zoya, he said, "I'm going to go find the cops!"

He turned and raised his hands and headed into the coach, back the way he'd come from, and Zoya leaned back against the wall behind her, slid down to the cold floor of the train, and stared into the cold black night outside the doorway.

The train yard passed by at nearly sixty miles per hour.

Angela Lacy had been using the light of her phone to pick her way forward through the fourth coach on the train, stepping over bodies along the way, moving past passengers huddling alone between the seats, their heads covered.

She had the Walther pistol out in front of her; she told herself she could fire the gun if it came down to it, but she still wasn't sure she had what it took to take a life.

There was commotion in the gangway ahead of her; she shined her light through the doors and then, at a distance of fifty feet, she saw Six facing away from her, standing by the open door, his arms up high as if he were in a fist-fight.

And then she saw someone charge from his blind side and knock him out into the night as the train sped on.

She heard a woman scream, and she screamed herself.

Frozen in shock, she kept the light ahead of her and soon saw a man running towards her, up the aisle from the gangway, and she raised the pistol. Just before she shouted at the man, ordering him to stop, she realized she was looking at her target, Alex Velesky.

He'd been the one to knock Six out the door, and the thought occurred to her that she should just shoot him now, but she made no move to do so.

"Police? Police?" Velesky asked, his arms extended over his head as he raced up to her; clearly he could see nothing past the glare of the flashlight.

"Freeze," she said, feigning authority and danger as best she could while simultaneously in a state of near shock.

Velesky slowed, stopped less than ten feet away. "Police?" He said it as a question again.

Lacy recovered a little from the disbelief that Six was gone, and she mustered more power into her voice. "Give me the phone, Velesky."

"What?" Alex cocked his head.

"I will fucking shoot if you don't give me—"

"You are American? You are CIA?"

"Give me the phone," she said again.

"You are CIA." The Swiss-Ukrainian man said it with assurance now. "You need to help me."

"Just . . . just give me the damn phone."

"We are on the same side. Put your gun down. The phone will reveal Russia's crimes in the West."

"Where is it?"

"Get me off this train and I'll give it to you."

"Give it to me now."

"I don't have it. You kill me and you won't ever see it."

Angela didn't think she could kill anyone—this was all bluster spurred on by panic and desperation—but she kept the gun up.

Someone approached behind Alex; Angela raised both the pistol and the light at the new movement.

It was the woman in black. Her face was bloodied and badly bruised, her coat torn in multiple places.

She appeared to be unarmed.

"Drop it," the woman in black said. As before, she sounded American, but this time her voice was halting, weaker.

Angela's hand shook, but she held the pistol and her phone out in front of her.

"Put . . . put your hands on your head."

The woman continued moving forward, and now her voice regained some of its authority. "Only one of us is ready to kill right now. If you think it's you, then pull that trigger. If you don't think it's you, drop the gun, we walk away, and you live."

Angela Lacy held the gun firm at first, but then it started quivering in front of her. The phone light's beam shook, as well.

"You aren't going to shoot me." The woman in black said this with confidence, but her eyes were wild and wet, glistening with tears.

"I need the phone," Lacy said.

Velesky said, "She's CIA. Give her the phone. We'll never make it now; we have to give it to the Americans to have any chance at—"

The woman moved up next to Velesky, tightly pressed together in the aisle, and she looked over the top of the beam of white light in her face. She said, "No. If she's CIA, and if she's been sent on a capture/kill mission to get this information back, then that means somebody in America wants to cover this up."

Lacy tried to sound resolute. "Do you have it?" she said to the woman. "Hand it over."

"Do you even know what's on that phone?"

"Yes. Financial transfers between the West and Russia, and between Russia and the West."

The woman in black shook her head, but before she spoke, Velesky said, "What are you talking about? I got the intelligence from Igor Krupkin; he has nothing to do with Western money moving *into* Russia. He's not a banker. He wouldn't know the first thing about that.

"This is money Daniil Spanov moved through Brucker Söhne to pay off informants and agents and collaborators around the world. That's *all* that I have."

Angela stood there; the confusion showed on her face, she was certain, but the other woman said, "The information Alex took is only dangerous to those working for Russia *in* the West. And if your superiors are willing to kill their way across Europe to get their hands on it . . . then you might need to ask yourself some serious questions about your superiors."

Angela's gun wavered; she didn't know what the fuck was going on. Six was dead, the target had just told her the mission she'd been on for days was utter bullshit, and she also knew that somewhere on this train there were likely more Russian killers.

"Look," Angela said, "Just give me—"

A loud whining noise came from outside the train, and almost instantly Angela began tumbling forward. The gun and the light fell from her hands as she dropped and hit the side of a seat on the way down. The engineer of the train that had been slowing for the past minute had applied full brakes suddenly, and the resulting forces sent her flat on her face. The jarring of the train slowing continued, and all Lacy could do was grab a seat leg and hold on, looking up ahead of her and catching glimpses of Alex and the unknown woman running towards the front of the train in the flashlight's hazy beam.

And the woman had Angela's gun in her hand.

Fifteen minutes later, Zoya Zakharova and Alex Velesky trudged along a road towards the town of Brig. Police cars, fire trucks, and ambulances had been racing past them for several minutes, and they'd just ignored them, continuing at a steady pace.

Alex had been understandably amped up after all the death and destruction on the train, and he'd not stopped talking, but Beth had said next to nothing.

Her eyes were fixed ahead; in addition to her bruised face, she looked tired and frayed, and Alex said, "Why aren't you talking?"

It wasn't the first time he'd asked this in the last fifteen minutes, but this was the first time he got a response.

Beth slowed, stopped, and turned to him. He saw that her eyes were wet and red. "You don't want to know what's wrong."

"Of course I do."

She seemed to think over a reply for a moment, and then she said, "The man, the man you knocked out of the train. He wasn't with the Russians."

Alex was confused; he shook his head. "I . . . I saw him attacking you. Just like all the other ones. I wasn't able to get the others away from you . . . I was held down. But as soon as I could get up, I ran to see what I could do, and I . . ."

"And you *what*?"

"I . . . I guess I saved your life."

She shook her head. "He wasn't going to hurt me."

"He hit you in the face, Beth!"

Beth stopped talking, began walking, and Alex trailed behind before catching up.

Just before he was about to ask her, once again, what her damn problem was, she said, "I know him." After a few more steps, she corrected herself. "I knew him."

"He would have thrown *you* out that door."

She began crying, but she marched on, even faster now towards the town ahead.

Velesky ran his hands through his hair. He was utterly flummoxed at first, but then he had a moment of clarity. "He was someone to you? A lover?"

"He was someone," she said.

"I'm . . . so sorry. I couldn't have known that. You guys were fighting each other, so of course I assumed—"

She rubbed tears from her eyes. "He . . . he could have survived. There was a lot of snow on the ground. If he hit at the right angle, landed in a drift maybe . . . then . . . there might have been a hill, there might have been—"

Velesky didn't think for a second the man could have survived, but he didn't say anything about it. She stopped walking, and she saw the look on his face.

"You don't know him! You don't know what he's lived through!"

Truly, Velesky did not know the man he'd shoulder-checked out of the train, but even though the train had been slowing down, they were certainly still traveling at least one hundred kilometers per hour, so as far as he was concerned, the man's prospects of survival were nil.

After a moment, he said, "He was working with the Russians."

She pointed angrily in his face. "Not in a million years would he have been working for Moscow."

"But he—"

Beth turned away. "Let's just get to New York, and let's not talk about this again."

"I'm sorry, but—"

"You're talking about it again, Alex."

Velesky stopped talking and continued walking, picking at the cuts and bruises on his face, aware he was freezing but still too amped up by everything to care about himself.

He'd just killed a man, and now he'd just been told he'd killed the wrong man. "What . . . are we going to do now?"

"We're going to steal a car and we're going to drive to France. When we get there we're going to stop, and I am going to go into a market and buy a bottle of vodka. You are going to take the wheel, and you are going to keep your fucking mouth shut about it. Do you understand?"

"We . . . we are still going to Marseille? To New York?"

"Yes, we're still going."

Alex nodded.

Beth turned away and began walking again, as Alex trailed behind.

FORTY-FIVE

Angela Lacy stood in the postmidnight cold, her coat zipped up to her throat and her arms tight across her chest. Still, she shivered as she stood there on the train tracks, nearly a half mile from where the EuroCity 42 sat at rest, surrounded by ambulances and other first-responder vehicles and encircled by a pair of helicopters, only five hundred yards or so past the train station at Brig.

She'd gotten a ride in a local police car that had stopped to help the people who'd fled the train, many with bloody injuries. The police had taken the woman aboard when she told them a man had been flung from the speeding vehicle and might be lying injured along the tracks. They then raced up a road through the railyard until they made it to within a few hundred yards to the entrance to the Simplon Tunnel, and then they parked.

Angela was told to wait in the squad car while the two cops took flash-lights and went trudging through the snow along the tracks, searching for the reported victim, and Angela complied at first. She sat there, still trying to lower her adrenaline with breathing and clear her head of the horrific minutes of the past hour, and only partially successful in doing so.

She thought of calling Brewer as soon as she was alone, but she decided to wait, if only for a few minutes.

She wasn't in the mood for Brewer.

Eventually Angela saw one of the distant flashlights frantically waving in the air, and then, less than five minutes later, a second police car and an ambulance arrived.

She climbed out of the vehicle now and began walking through the snow. It was shin deep on the flats, with much deeper drifts in gullies alongside the rails, so she stayed up on the tracks.

She was terrified about what she would find when she made it to the other cops in front of her, but she kept moving, doing her best to ignore the cold, hoping against hope that her fears were not about to be realized.

As she neared, she stopped and stood alone. The cops were obviously standing next to something important just feet from the rail line, but she couldn't see what it was.

A light whipped over the scene, and Angela caught her breath when she saw that the people were surrounding a body, and the body was not moving.

Other first responders had arrived across a bridge over the Rhone River, just to the north; a helicopter flying over the train was called over, and it swept its wider, brighter beam over the entire scene.

Angela looked on.

She watched as the body was dragged up the hill through the glistening snow and to the tracks. The person was dead, that much was clear, as there was no attempt at providing care whatsoever and the head was allowed to hang and bounce along with the awkward movements.

Once the body was laid to rest on the train tracks, not fifty feet from where Angela stood, the white spotlight from the circling helicopter shone bright over it, revealing the scene perfectly. Angela peered forward a moment, got a full and lengthy look at the dead man's face, then reached up with a hand half-frozen from the cold and wiped fresh and warm tears from her eyes.

As the spotlight held its position over the action, a body bag was awkwardly placed around the corpse by a group of medics who'd just arrived from the bridge, and then it was zipped tight.

Angela turned away, reached into her coat, and retrieved her phone.

She dialed a number and held the phone to her ear as she began walking back in the direction of the distant EuroCity.

It took several seconds of lumbering over the gravel and snow, but eventually she heard an answer on the other end of the line. "Brewer."

"Lacy," she replied, her voice cracking a little as she spoke. "Iden three, three, Golf, India, Victor, seven, one."

Brewer's voice was clipped and urgent. "Confirmed. What's going on?"

"Violator . . . he's . . . gone."

A loud sigh was followed with "Goddammit!" Then "Where the hell did he go?"

"No . . . He's dead, ma'am. On the train to Geneva. Maybe a dozen innocents killed here, as well. Several opposition dead. It's a fucking nightmare." She added, "The target has escaped."

Brewer apparently hadn't heard anything else after Angela's first sentence. "Violator? You are saying Violator is KIA? Are you certain? *How* can you be certain?"

"I just watched them drag his body up a hill like he was a dead deer, and then they zipped him up in a body bag." Frostily, as a product of the stress, she said, "That good enough for you, ma'am?"

Brewer remained astonished. "*Matador?* Matador did this?"

"No." Angela saw a row of four buses coming up the road from the bridge, and then they passed her, continuing on towards the train in the distance. She imagined that passengers with their luggage were already lining up to board. All had obviously been hastily but efficiently arranged by the Swiss authorities in the late night. "It was Velesky himself," she said. "He knocked him off the train. We must have been doing sixty, seventy miles per hour."

"My God." After a moment, she said, "Let me think." It was clear to Lacy that Brewer had no backup plan that involved this at all. "This is a complication. I'll have to bring in a new asset. I certainly didn't plan on Violator dying *before* the mission was accomplished."

Lacy cocked her head and stopped walking. She took a slow breath before saying, "You were going to have him killed after?"

Brewer sniffed. "That's not what I meant."

Angela thought that was *exactly* what she meant. She lifted her chin and began marching up the tracks again. "Something else. I spoke with Velesky after this happened."

"Wait. You . . . *spoke* to him?"

"I did."

After a pause, Brewer's tone changed from shock to annoyance. "Then why is he not in your possession?"

"It's complicated."

"I'm bright, Lacy. Try me."

Angela sighed. "I *did* mention a dozen dead innocents, right?"

"You did."

"It was chaos. I got control of him for a moment, at gunpoint, and then the woman escorting him arrived. When the engineer slammed on the brakes, we all went flying, and when I made it back to my feet, they were gone."

Brewer immediately shifted. "What did the target say to you?"

Lacy bit her lip, knowing this was the point of no return. Forcing herself to remain stalwart, she said, "Frankly, ma'am, in my brief conversation with him, he said that everything you've been telling Violator and me over the past three days is a lie."

"*What's* a lie?"

"He says the data in his possession is about Kremlin transfers *into* a specific Swiss bank. Nothing *at all* going the other way, into Russia. He says Krupkin wouldn't know the first thing about Agency financial transfers to agents in Russia, because he's a money manager, investing and parking billions abroad."

Brewer didn't sound convinced. "Why would our intelligence be so off base?"

Angela Lacy knew she was venturing into dangerous territory now, but she didn't give a shit. After a beat, she said, "According to Velesky and the woman with him, the only people with something to lose from him getting his data compiled and revealed would be those Russia is paying off around the globe." She added, "Velesky genuinely seemed to think the Agency should be helping him, not targeting him."

"That's absolutely insane," Brewer said.

"I believed him to be credible."

"Desperate people can be convincing, even when they're lying." When Lacy said nothing, Brewer said, "Look . . . I'm getting my information from a more-than-reliable source, and I'm giving you that information unaltered."

"Who is the source?"

"You know better than to ask."

"I *thought* I knew better than to get into a gunfight on a train. I'm not sure *what* I know now."

Angela walked along the tracks; it would be another ten minutes at this speed till she made it to the train, and the cold was getting to her as her adrenaline dropped by the minute. Still, she felt a seething anger inside her that warmed her blood.

As she continued west, Brewer said, "Come home. This op is completely blown. I'll reset and talk to you in a couple of days, at most."

Lacy replied, "I was better suited for this when I believed in what I was doing. Now I have a strong suspicion I was just involved in an operation that was corrupt at every level."

Brewer breathed into the phone a moment. "You'd better think carefully before you say anything else right now. If the intel was wrong, it was wrong before it got to me. I'm telling you what I've been told."

Angela said, "The man we were all after turns out to have data implicating Westerners for working illegally with Russia, hardly a national security threat to us. Pardon me for not buying anything you are selling right now."

"You're . . . off base," Brewer said, but slowly. "I . . . I believe the information I have to be true."

"You said that before, ma'am, but the first time you said it, you seemed a whole lot surer of yourself."

Angela hung up on her superior. A police car heading in the direction of the train pulled up on her right and shined a light on her. Seconds later she climbed inside, accepting a ride to the row of buses pulling up to the train in the distance. She shuddered as she thought about what had happened, and she shuddered again, wondering if this was all over, or if it had only just begun.

FORTY-SIX

The small medical facility in Ville-la-Grand, a suburb of Geneva, was just a simple clinic; it had no surgical suite, no ICU, not even proper hospital beds.

What it *did* have, however, was a nurse practitioner who worked primary care at a local hospital, and she was available to come out in the middle of the night because she was also employed by an off-the-books network of providers, offering medical treatment to anyone, for cash.

No insurance, no records, no questions.

The woman was in her fifties; she met a carload of Russian men at one thirty in the morning in the tiny lot in front of the clinic after waking up to a ringing phone a half hour earlier, and when a man was helped out of the back of the car, she rushed to unlock the clinic's door and to quickly turn off the alarm.

Ten minutes later, Luka Rudenko lay on a gurney, his left boot having been cut off with a saw and his blood-soaked sock removed with shears, and the nurse practitioner looked over her patient's foot carefully, washing off the blood with a bottle of antiseptic while she tried to come up with a prudent course of action.

Luka had been given OxyContin immediately upon his arrival, but it hadn't killed the pain; it had only blunted it to the degree that he could brood about other things.

His four remaining GRU men, the ones who hadn't made it to the train to Geneva before all hell broke loose, were all here with him, but Drexler was not. In his one brief phone conversation in the car on the way here, the Swiss man told him his team of technicians were still in Milan, breaking down equipment and getting it to the airport, but he himself was boarding a private plane, though he did not say where he was headed.

Rudenko looked down at his foot, not for the first time, but for the first time since his boot was off, and saw for certain that his little toe was gone. With the mind of a pragmatic expert, he assumed what remained of his toe was now wedged into a ragged bullet hole in an aluminum bulkhead of the train. The bullet that hit him had also traveled down under the skin on the right side of his foot, and the agony he felt from this would have caused him to grit his teeth or even cry out from time to time if not for the fact that his men were here with him.

The nurse practitioner didn't seem to know where to start. Eventually she looked up at him. In English she said, "I suppose there is no chance you would consider hospitalization?"

Before Luka could answer, Vitaly, a captain and his senior deputy, said, "Would we have come to your shitty little clinic if we were considering a hospital?"

The woman did not answer; she just returned to her evaluation.

Luka's phone rang. Kirill, a senior sergeant, grabbed it off a tray and handed it to his superior officer.

Luka answered in English, because he assumed he knew who was calling. "Yeah."

"It's Drexler."

"Why do I get the impression you aren't calling to ask about my well-being?"

"That's *exactly* why I'm calling. I need to know if you are well enough to travel."

Luka looked down at his mangled foot. The nurse used a #15 surgical blade, a curved pointed steel shank, to slit open healthy skin next to the wound, opening it up further to clean out debris from the bullet before suturing the entire wound shut.

Luka bit the inside of his mouth but said, "Of course I am."

"Then you are going to New York."

"When?"

"Now. I'm confident your people can get you the papers you need for travel to the U.S."

Luka only took a moment before saying, "I can get the Geneva station to deliver me a new Finnish passport within the hour. Finns don't need visas to go to the U.S. for stays less than thirty days."

"Good. Fly commercial. As soon as possible. Into JFK."

Luka made a face, ignoring the pain in his foot. "What's in New York?"

Drexler sniffed. "New York is Alex Velesky's ultimate destination. I don't know how long it will take him to get there, but you need to be there first."

"It's a big place. How do I find him?"

"*You* don't. *I* will." Then he added, "Not alone. I will recruit like-minded parties, and we will have Velesky fixed as soon as he gets there."

The nurse injected Luka's foot two more times, then looked up at him. "Ten minutes for the local anesthetic to kick in, and then I will begin the suturing process."

"I don't have ten minutes. Do it now."

"But . . . monsieur, the pain will be—"

"Do it."

The woman heaved a deep sigh; she seemed to show the pain on her face that she felt Luka would soon begin to feel himself, but she picked up her suture kit and disinfected the hooked needle and a pair of forceps.

Rudenko turned his attention back to his phone call. "I'll head out this morning. I'll see you there?"

"Initially, no. I'm on my way to the States now, but I have a stop-off to make before I get to New York."

The needle went into the top of Rudenko's foot, and he cursed the man who had somehow managed to shoot him with his hands held behind his back. Then, fighting a grimace, he said, "An American was there, on the train. I took him for a CIA officer, but he said he wasn't. Dark hair, thirties. He was . . . I *think* he was the man in Saint Lucia the other day." Rudenko added, "He's like nothing I've ever encountered."

There was silence on the line a long time. And then, "I've encountered someone *exactly* like that. He's *not* CIA."

"Who does he work for?"

"Private sector." Drexler sniffed. "He might be working with your Zakharova. I don't know."

"You know his name?"

"I know what people call him. Believe me, I curse it every day. He was the man who blessed me with my limp."

The suturing process was pure agony; Luka's face reddened but he made no outward reaction to the indescribable pain. "If it's the same man, he blessed me with my limp, too. What do they call him?"

"Congratulations, Rudenko," Drexler said. "You, like me, have come face-to-face with the Gray Man and lived to tell. I should think we are members of an incredibly small guild."

Luka's Oxy-addled eyes widened. "The Gray Man."

The needle dug deep into wounded meat, crossed under the opening in Rudenko's foot, and poked out the other side. But Luka barely noticed now. "I beat him in Saint Lucia. He beat me in Italy."

Drexler said, "If he's working for Velesky, then you need to bring some help with you to New York so you can be certain you beat him there."

"I have four men. We'll all go."

"You will have additional assets in New York. I'll call Spanov myself and get your crew sorted before you arrive."

Another prick of the needle; Luka gritted his teeth but did not make a sound. He hung up the phone on Drexler and looked down at the woman at the end of the table.

"I need to be able to walk out of here."

"I have crutches. I can—"

"I'm not using crutches."

She looked at him like he was an idiot, but she was in the process of stabbing a needle in his foot at the moment, so Luka wasn't overly aggressive about it. "I don't have to run a marathon, I just have to be able to get around."

The woman nodded while she continued suturing. "I'll wrap your wound with triple the dressing, and I'll get you an orthopedic boot. Every step will hurt, but your foot won't move when you walk, so the pain should be manageable." She looked up at him now. "As long as you are taking the painkillers."

"Deal," Luka said, and then he switched to Russian to tell his men what Drexler had told him.

FORTY-SEVEN

Suzanne Brewer had spent the night in her office and she looked like it, but when the urgent call came ordering her to meet with the Director at eight a.m. on Monday morning, she raced to a mirror and did her best to fan out her wrinkled clothes and tamp down her hair.

Within moments she marched down the seventh-floor hallway, and a minute after this she was led into Jay Kirby's office and ushered to a chair in front of his desk.

The Director did not acknowledge her at first. His feet were up on a small bookshelf behind his desk, and his eyes gazed out a window at northern Virginia.

She just waited patiently. This was a power play, she saw. He knew everything had gone wrong, again, and he knew that she knew that he knew. He was going to make her sweat a moment, and she conceded it was something she might do to an underling herself to add a layer of pressure upon the already tense moment.

Finally, without looking away from the window, he said, "I heard such incredible things about you from my predecessor, Suzanne, and yet you continue to underperform for me."

Her reply was delivered calmly, defensively. "I am hamstrung in this endeavor with operational restrictions."

Now he lowered his feet from the shelf and spun around. "What restrictions? You asked for the keys to the kingdom and you got them."

"You gave me access to intelligence product. You didn't give me teams of Ground Branch, you didn't give me station access overseas, you didn't give me crews of techs or surveillance experts or approval for military aircraft."

He cocked his head. "What . . . you wanted the Air Force to strafe Europe to kill Velesky?"

She frowned. "I am talking about cargo flights to move equipment into the operational theater. We didn't get the equipment or the personnel to operate it; I only assumed we wouldn't have been given access to military aircraft to transport it."

Kirby nodded his head, conceding the point. "There is a level of discretion required on this op, discretion I might add that was *not* on display when your asset began shooting up a train full of passengers in a failed attempt to access and detain the target."

"My asset, as far as I know, did not injure any civilians. As I told you before, GRU officers along with some unknown subjects engaged police and Velesky's compatriot. My asset then engaged the GRU men."

Kirby waved a hand in the air. "I get it. I'm sitting here at a fucking desk trying to armchair-quarterback this thing. Your man, the allegedly superhuman Gray Man, wouldn't have died without facing serious opposition, and I shouldn't downplay the threats."

Brewer nodded, then said, "I heard from my officer on the scene. She spoke with the target briefly before he was liberated from her by his partner."

Kirby leaned forward, especially intent now. "What did he say?"

"He said that the intelligence we are getting is bad. He said the data Krupkin exfiltrated from Russia is one-way financial traffic. The Kremlin to Brucker Söhne Holdings in Zurich. Full stop. And Velesky said that what he stole from his bank was all account data related to the Russian transactions. Nothing in there whatsoever about any outgoing money movements from anyone in the West, much less the CIA."

Kirby sat back in his chair; she couldn't read his face. He paused a long moment, then looked like he was going to speak, and then he paused even longer.

Brewer waited him out, and finally the Director of the CIA said, "You are right, you don't have the assets you need, especially now as we reach the most critical stage of this operation. The summit starts today up in New York; I'm hearing it will last two days before the signing of the accord." He shrugged. "That's all Western nations need to green-light the reopening of trade.

"Nothing, I mean *nothing*, needs to come up to derail these accords, and that's not me talking; that is by order of the president of the United States."

Brewer thought it strange he had not addressed what she'd just told him about the intelligence product he'd provided her.

Then he said, "There is a man I want you to meet. He will arrive in D.C. later today."

She cocked her head. "What man?"

"Lunch. Two p.m. Bistrot du Coin in Dupont Circle. I made the reservation myself."

"You will be there, sir?"

Kirby shook his head. "Just go talk to him. Alone."

Brewer nodded. "The reservation is under what name?"

"Suzanne Brewer."

"And that's all you're going to tell me?"

Kirby nodded. "He's here to help. Use him."

"Use . . . *who*? Your source for all this?"

"*A* source."

"Fine," she said. It seemed a very cloak-and-dagger thing for the D/CIA to be so cagey about an identity, even to the point of making a lunch reservation for a deputy, but nothing in the last three days had seemed very typical to Brewer.

She stood to leave, but Kirby held a hand out to stop her, and she dutifully lowered back into her chair.

"The asset. Violator. This . . . Gray Man," he said.

"What about him?"

"Are we doing the covert-star-on-the-wall thing?" The CIA Memorial Wall in the entrance to their McLean, Virginia, headquarters is a white Alabama marble slab, upon which a star is chiseled every time an asset dies in the field. For officers who die in denied operations, only the star is shown; no name or details are given in the Book of Honor that is positioned under glass jutting perpendicularly out of the wall below the flag-bracketed memorial.

"You are asking if we will be memorializing Court Gentry?" She said it in a scoffing tone. "How about no? I was going to target him with every re-source we used to target Velesky just as soon as Velesky was dealt with." She gave a little smile. "My objectives are being fulfilled out of order, but I'm sure they will all be fulfilled just the same."

She added, "But again, nothing about this Velesky information makes sense."

Kirby looked back out the window. "It will make more sense after lunch, Suzanne. I'll keep a window open in my schedule this afternoon, because I have a sinking suspicion you'll be back."

He sounded dour suddenly, and Brewer didn't know how to take it, but she left his office, ready to head across the Potomac to D.C. this afternoon for lunch with a stranger.

FORTY-EIGHT

Eleven hours after Zoya and Alex leapt out of a shattered train and into the snowy woods east of Geneva, the two of them climbed out of a yellow four-door hatchback with Swiss plates in the town of Le Rove, France.

Alex had been behind the wheel, and as he stood, he felt the aches and pains of his various ordeals, only accentuated by sitting for the last several hours.

They were both exhausted, and both of them had gotten the shit kicked out of them eleven hours earlier, with Zoya both showing and feeling the effects more significantly than Alex. She had a black eye she'd done nothing to hide, a serious scrape up the right side of her nose, and a busted lower lip that was both swollen and scabbed. There were abrasions on her neck that looked like purple finger marks, clearly where someone had tried to strangle her. She walked with a limp; Alex thought it looked like she might have picked up a back injury, but she'd brushed off Alex's questions about her condition, just as she'd brushed off literally everything he'd said to her today.

In addition to the wounds Alex noted on the woman, there was one other thing diminishing her capacity at present.

As near as Alex could tell, she was drunk.

They'd gone into a market at eight in the morning, she'd bought a 750-milliliter bottle of cheap vodka, and she'd drunk swigs of it straight while

Alex drank coffee and drove the little four-door Kia Picanto through the French Alps.

He'd not dared to ask her to stop drinking, or to even moderate her consumption a little bit. Ever since she'd accused him of killing her friend, she'd been so cold to him he halfway wondered if he was in physical danger from the incredibly capable and even scary woman, so he'd mostly held his tongue.

This is all so fucking insane, Alex thought.

Velesky himself had a very sore back and neck where he'd been pummeled by the two Italians in the aisle of the train car, and his knees, ribs, and chest were bruised from clambering over people, seatbacks, luggage, and the like in his mad scramble to get away from gunfire.

Here in Le Rove, they walked down the street between two long rows of middle-class zero-lot homes, and Beth eventually stepped up to a porch and knocked on the door. It was one p.m., the sun was shining though the temperature hovered just a few degrees above freezing, and Alex joined her and waited with her in the sunshine and the cold, still without saying a word.

It took two more knocks before the door was opened by a woman in her forties. She'd clearly been sleeping, which Alex thought was strange seeing how it was past noon, but he didn't ruminate on it long, because before the woman could speak, Beth pushed the door open farther, then shoved her way in past the woman, forcefully but not exactly violently.

The woman took a moment, but then she reacted. It was clear she knew Beth; Alex registered this in her face, and he registered the fear this knowledge caused the woman, as well. She just stared at Beth as if frozen there in the entry hall.

"Bonjour, Tonja," Beth said in what sounded to Alex to be a perfect French accent.

"Bonjour," the woman replied timidly, her voice holding an accent the Swiss-Ukrainian banker could not immediately identify.

Beth switched to Russian now; Alex heard the slur in her voice that came from the bottle of vodka she'd held in her lap all morning. "Are you alone?"

"Yes."

"Good. We told you this day would come."

The woman's eyes flicked Alex's way for the first time.

Then she nodded. "You did. I am ready . . . but . . . I did not know there would be . . . others."

"Me and one male. You can make that happen, Tonja." It was said as a demand, the slightly slurred speech doing nothing to mitigate the authority in Beth's voice.

The woman looked conflicted, scared, but she nodded her head. "Where?"

"The United States."

Tonja nodded immediately. "There's a 777 leaving for Boston . . ." The woman looked down at her watch. "Four hours from now."

Beth nodded. "We're on it."

Tonja nodded herself, then looked back to Alex. "I will need to go in to work to prepare something for your . . . your guest."

Beth's eyes narrowed, chilling Alex even though they weren't pointed at him. "Tonja . . . I need you to come through for me on this."

The other woman glanced back at Beth, then down at the floor. "This is where you begin to make threats."

"I don't have to threaten you if you tell me I don't have to threaten you. But if you . . ." Alex saw Beth fight to keep her balance for a moment; she put a hand out on a narrow table in the entry hall, then shook her head a little to recover. "But if you have any ideas about a double cross, just know that—"

"Why on earth would I try to double-cross the SVR? That's a death sentence, and I know it." The woman continued, "I'll get you to the U.S. This evening. I promise. Just don't hurt me."

Alex realized the woman thought Beth was with Russia's foreign intelligence service, and Beth was doing nothing to assuage these thoughts.

Zoya Zakharova nodded at the woman, took her hand off the table because she felt like she had her equilibrium back, and then turned to Alex and gave a nod.

She knew how to manipulate when she had to, but it appeared to her right now that she wasn't going to have to work very hard.

Either Zoya herself or someone else in the SVR had threatened this woman to serve her nation. Zoya couldn't specifically remember if she'd personally promised payback to Tonja for noncompliance; they'd met once before, but she knew she'd threatened many civilians in the past to help her achieve her objectives.

She didn't have the mental bandwidth to lament what this woman was going through right now. Tonja had made a deal with Russian foreign intelligence, and even though Zoya was no longer a member, she still occasionally carried the cachet that the SVR brought when it came to cajoling assets around the world.

Tonja nodded slowly. "I'll get uniforms, badges. You'll jump-seat like regular employees. Don't worry about the pilots talking to you about your jobs. They won't. You're just hub labor, they'll leave you alone."

Zoya nodded. "You need a picture of us?"

The woman took out her iPhone and snapped Alex in front of a blank white wall, then took one of Zoya. "I'll text you the address at the airport. An employee parking lot. I'll have everything there, and you can change."

Zoya said, "The rest of your life depends on what you do today. Just nod if you understand that, and there will be no need for further action or discussion on the subject."

Tonja readily nodded.

Zoya looked at Alex. "We'll stay here. Get comfortable." Glancing back at Tonja, she said, "I'll be watching out the windows to make sure Tonja holds up her end of the bargain."

"I told you." The woman sounded annoyed now. "I will do what you ask."

"Good. Also . . . I need to borrow some makeup."

Tonja eyed Zoya's battered face. "Oui. You *really* do, but I don't know if I have enough."

At four p.m. they met Tonja in a DHL employee parking lot just outside Marseille Provence Airport. Under the fluorescent lights they saw her approaching, and once satisfied she had come alone, Zoya took her hand off the pistol under her coat, stepped out between a pair of cars, and took a bag full of clothing from the woman.

Alex stepped between a pair of white vans and put on the uniform of a hub worker at DHL; a badge with his picture on it and an assumed name already hung from the breast pocket.

Zoya did the same, unconcerned about undressing in thirty-eight-degree weather in front of a man and woman, and soon the pair of them looked like regular employees. Tonja, in contrast, wore civilian clothing, but she had a lanyard around her neck with a pass that allowed her and the other two access to the airport itself.

Zoya had cleverly applied makeup to hide the cuts and bruises on her face, but she still walked like she was in pain, and still Alex refrained from talking to her about it.

An hour later the Russian freelance intelligence asset and the Swiss-Ukrainian banker on the run from the Russians sat in jump seats of the Boeing 777 as a pair of pilots, one from the UK and the other from Morocco, began taxiing towards the runway.

They were both exhausted, but Alex recognized that his companion remained deeply stricken by what had happened on the train. There was no alcohol on the aircraft, of course, so Alex hoped she'd spend the next ten hours or so away from the booze and that would somehow wean her off her addiction.

It was a lot to hope for; he wondered if his own fatigue was clouding his thoughts and keeping reality at bay, but as the aircraft took off, he looked over at the woman with the faraway eyes and told himself that both of them needed to somehow keep their shit together for a few more days.

FORTY-NINE

Forty-six-year-old Petro Mozgovoy climbed out of the subway and into a frigid and gray Manhattan afternoon at 59th and Fifth, and he took in his surroundings. It was one p.m., pedestrian traffic was heavy but manageable, and though it was cold and the streets were lined with gray slush, the snow had held off, at least for now.

Mozgovoy didn't mind the snow; it reminded him of home.

Summertime here in New York could be miserable, he'd learned shortly after his arrival the previous June, and he much preferred the climate and environs of his homeland.

Petro Mozgovoy had been born in Donetsk, eastern Ukraine, to Russian parents who had moved there in the seventies when it was part of the USSR. They then moved just over the border into Russia after the split of the Union, but the family retained close ties to fellow Russian Ukrainians.

His father had been a grain farmer, but Petro wanted to see the world, so he joined the navy at eighteen. A hardworking young man, he was noticed quickly by his superiors and promoted to signals intelligence technician on a frigate in the Black Sea Fleet.

But he felt destined for something more.

At age twenty-five he sought out a job with the GRU. He failed his entrance exam but nevertheless impressed the agency with his tenacity. He was hired as an agent for the service, a foreigner because of his Ukrainian roots, and he was immediately deployed into the eastern portions of Ukraine, at first to foment pro-Russian sentiment and collect intelligence about Ukrainian border defenses.

When the war began in Donbas in 2014, his desire to liberate his people from Kiev's choke hold exceeded his desire to work for Russia, so he joined the Vostok Battalion, a separatist militia made up of men and boys from the region.

Eight years of combat later, trenches and ditches, shit food and shit conditions, and a couple of injuries that healed well enough, the broad Russian invasion of Ukraine began. Within a month Petro was approached by the Donetsk People's Republic Security Service Battalion, the intelligence arm of the separatists in Ukraine. In an office building in Horlivka within artillery range of the Ukrainian army, Petro was asked if he'd like to play a bigger role in the struggle against Western fascism.

He agreed without knowing what, exactly, he was agreeing to, and then he was immediately whisked to Russia, where he received a four-month intensive course along with a group of over two hundred people from all over Donbas. He and the other Ukrainian separatists learned tradecraft, communications, hand-to-hand combat, improvised bombmaking, rudimentary foreign language, and other skills, and then they were given Ukrainian passports smuggled out of diplomatic offices in Kiev by a pro-Russian behind the lines.

Mozgovoy already spoke some English, having learned in the navy, and he worked well under stress, as evidenced by the fact that he was a much-respected noncommissioned officer in his combat unit. He expected to be infiltrated into Kiev or Lviv or somewhere in the west of the war-torn nation, but instead he was told he would be a secret agent for the Donetsk People's Republic Security Service Battalion, and he'd be traveling to New York City to run a cell of operatives.

At the time the Russians told him they'd have no more communication with him, that he would get his orders from the DPR SSB and not Moscow, and for this he was glad.

Moscow was mucking up their war, they were likely mucking up the intelligence battle just as badly, and he had every confidence in the world that the DPR would use him to deal critical blows to the United States, one of the vanguard nations when it came to supplying Kiev with weapons.

He would degrade America's ability to arm the fascist government in Kiev, and he would come home a hero.

The GRU had provided one caveat to this, however. They equipped him with a challenge/response code phrase and said if he was ever given the first part of the phrase, then that meant Russia itself needed him, and to drop everything and heed the call.

And then he was assured this would never happen. Russia wanted to keep its dirty hands cleaner than whatever the Ukrainian separatists had in store overseas.

A day later, Petro Mozgovoy flew to New York fully planning on conducting sabotage, targeted killings, and the like.

Now, seven months later, he had yet to conduct a single act against the United States, but he was hardly disheartened. He was in training for something on the horizon, and he had kept himself and his team honed to a razor's edge waiting for the day the call would come.

He had a weapons cache with rifles purchased by straw-man buyers, ammo bought online, and various illegal weapons delivered to him by mystery men who arrived every few months, spoke Ukrainian, but said nothing about themselves or their plans.

But even with the weaponry he had access to, he was not armed with a gun as he walked through Manhattan this afternoon; it would be foolhardy of him to carry in New York, but he had been well trained in hand-to-hand combat, and he wore a small boot knife with a two-inch blade, legal here in the city.

He bought a coffee at Starbucks, drank it while looking out the window, then strolled east until he stopped in an antiques store as it opened. Here he stayed near the front of the shop, again gazing out at the street from time to time.

He strolled a little over a mile in distance, and it took him well over an hour, but this had been by design. He was running a surveillance detection route, and he took this as seriously as he took everything else he did in his service of the DPR.

Finally he went back down into the subway, shook off the chill to some degree, climbed aboard the 6 train at Grand Central, and took it down to Canal. Another twenty minutes' walk had put him on the corner of Broad and Exchange, just south of Wall Street, and here he stepped into Blue Bottle Coffee on Broad Street.

At this time of the afternoon there were just a few people sitting around with laptops, and Petro ordered an espresso and took it to a table in the corner with a view to the street.

He didn't need the caffeine—he had adrenaline to burn—but still he sipped the hot coffee, waiting for his meeting.

Less than a minute later the door opened again, and another man entered. Petro Mozgovoy didn't make eye contact; he just continued looking outside at the streets while the man stepped up to the counter. Once the man had his beverage, he sat next to Petro, but the two men did not look at each other as they both put earpieces in their ears and pretended to dial numbers on their phones. Anyone watching them from behind the counter or while walking by would assume they were both on their phones and not talking to each other.

Still, the man whispered when he spoke. "What is it?" He was American, in his thirties, and he made no attempt to hide his displeasure in being summoned to today's meeting.

Petro spoke English. "You were supposed to drop off forty thousand dollars three days ago, but I never heard a word."

"I know."

"It's your job to see that I have what I need."

"No, it's my job to execute the wishes of my client who—"

Mozgovoy interrupted. "Who wants me to have what I—"

"Who," the man interrupted right back, "is having some short-term issues transferring funds. I'm just the middleman here, and you know that."

Petro took another sip of his espresso. "What is the problem?"

The man sipped his own coffee and continued talking softly. "The funnel of cash has been compromised."

"What does that mean?"

"It means none of the money we can give you is safe. If you touch it, if we touch it, then we can possibly be identified as working in the interests of Russia. Do you want to end up like your countrymen who got thrown in jail back in November?"

The Ukrainian separatist took this in. The previous fall, another cell of SSB agents was caught at a port in Queens photographing military shipping. All six men were arrested and charged with espionage.

After a moment, Petro said, "What about you?"

"What *about* me?"

"How long will they continue to be your clients if they can't pay you?"

"We don't get paid through GRU accounts. My firm wouldn't touch suspect money like that, even before the compromise."

Petro turned to him now. "Then, however you are being paid, use that money to finance my operation."

"No," the man said flatly. "Look. Just wait. Anyway, whatever it is you were about to do, you're probably not going to have to do it."

"What does that mean?"

"This summit starting today? When the accords are signed, the war will end, as least as far as the West is concerned." He added, "I don't know your mission. I don't know anything about you or the people you represent. I'm just the guy at my firm who doles out the money as per our client's wishes."

He sipped his coffee. "That being said, I watch the news. Everybody is ready to end the conflict, to resume relations. The Europeans want dependable energy, and Russia wants billions of dollars; America wants to say they brokered peace and to ease tension with Moscow and to stop giving billions in weapons to Ukraine." He turned to Petro. "Don't know where that leaves you, but my guess is, in a few days you'll be told to go back home and grow wheat by whoever it is you report to."

Petro felt a wave of panic wash over him. He wondered if the mission he'd been sent here to complete, the one he'd been told he was just days away from executing, would ever happen.

If the stand-down order came, all his time away from his fighting unit in the thick of war would have been wasted. He would have been living in Brooklyn, five thousand miles away from danger, drinking espressos and waiting out the conflict at home, while his friends died, while his family was under constant bombardment.

No. The DPR SSB *had* to use him here in America, otherwise he would consider himself a failure, a coward, a traitor.

"I'll call Donetsk. They'll call Moscow, and Moscow will order you to give me my money."

Now the American chuckled, still looking out the window in front of him. "No. The person you are insinuating your people would call? His problems are bigger than you. Go back, wait for word that this whole damn thing is over."

The American stood and left the coffee shop without another word, dropping his half-full cup in a garbage can on the way out.

Five minutes later, Petro Mozgovoy walked down a sidewalk lined with traders, lawyers, and bankers towards the Wall Street subway station, hands in the pockets of his jeans, his head down against the cold that hadn't bothered him at all when he came this way earlier but now annoyed him to no end, just like the people around him.

The Americans had prolonged this war, more than the Europeans, more than Ukraine itself, which by now would be unified if Russia and the DPR had been left alone to handle matters. He hated the nation he walked through right now, hated every person who lived here, and he told himself he'd be damned if he wasn't going to go forward with actions against this damn country.

He'd just gotten to Wall Street Station, had just begun walking down the stairs, when he received a text from a number he didn't recognize.

The single line of characters was in Cyrillic, Russian, and translated they read,

The best time to plant a tree is twenty years ago.

Instantly Mozgovoy stopped, turned, and ran back up the steps, hearing the curses of several commuters while doing so.

Once back at street level, with a shaky thumb he tapped out a response.

The second best time is now.

It was the challenge response, a fail-safe way for him to receive information from the GRU in emergencies, though he was all but assured he'd never have to use it.

At once, both hopelessness and hope coursed through his brain. Was he being recalled? It seemed likely, considering what the stupid American had just told him.

But there was also a thread of hope in the text he'd received. Moscow wouldn't be the ones recalling him to Donetsk. He didn't work for them. If they were reaching out instead of Donetsk, then maybe, just maybe, it would be for some urgent operational need.

A new text popped up.

Tomorrow morning. Eight AM. The Pond. Central Park. Alone. Eighth bench from northern end. Challenge: "I can't wait for baseball season." Response: "Spring training will be here before you know it."

Petro acknowledged receipt, and then he stood there, forgetting now about the cold wind that whipped down Wall Street. He looked at his phone for several minutes, but nothing else popped up.

That was it. A meeting tomorrow in Central Park.

Moscow surely to God would not send a man just to tell him to close down his operation here and head home.

Something was coming, this he knew, and it was coming from the GRU, not the SSB.

He also knew that, whatever it was, he and his team would be ready.

FIFTY

Suzanne Brewer walked out of a chilly and cloudy afternoon and through the doors of Bistrot du Coin, a French restaurant on Connecticut Avenue just an eight-minute drive northwest of the White House. The often raucous atmosphere was subdued at two p.m.; most of the lunch crowd had just departed, but there were several tables of patrons throughout the restaurant.

She gave her name to the hostess and was informed her guest had already arrived, so Suzanne followed her upstairs to a quiet area with only one man sitting at a table in the back. He had flowing brown hair and a pleasant smile, and he wore a bright blue patterned sports coat and a silk shirt, open at the collar, with French cuffs and gold links. His reading glasses hung around his neck on a gold chain.

He instantly looked European to Suzanne, wealthy, perhaps someone involved in politics or the arts.

His bright white veneers shined in the overhead lighting.

He stood and extended a hand, and Brewer noticed he required help from a cane to do so. "Miss Brewer, lovely to meet you."

She thought him to be French from his accent, and she wondered if he'd picked this restaurant for a taste of home or if Kirby had chosen it, knowing something about the man.

She shook the man's hand; it was strong and he kept friendly eye contact. She found his cheeriness to be manipulative, especially knowing something about the matter they were here to discuss, so she did not smile back.

Brewer was all business. "You know my name. I do not know yours."

Apologetically he bowed. "With apologies, my name is Sebastian Drexler."

"You're . . . French?"

"Swiss. Proudly so."

The two sat down; Brewer ordered an iced tea, and Drexler had arrived early enough to already be nursing a glass of champagne. As soon as the server left the table, Brewer said, "I confess I know nothing about you or even the nature of our meeting today, other than in the most general sense."

"I believe Director Kirby told you this is related to the situation involving Alexander Velesky."

"I do know that much, yes. But . . . tell me about yourself?"

He shrugged. "Me? I'm nothing in all this. I most assuredly don't have the pull to speak with the Director of America's CIA. I'm just a middleman, and the interests of the people I represent are the same as the interests of your government."

"What people do you represent?"

"Let's just say, recovering the material Alexander Velesky took from both Russia and his bank would be beneficial to both parties: your nation and my employer."

He did not answer the question, and this was not lost on Brewer, but she let it go. "And you could provide some information about that?"

Drexler smiled, nodded while sipping champagne, then said, "I know where Velesky is."

Brewer cocked her head. "Where?"

"Manhattan." He held a hand up. "Or . . . if he's not there already, he will be very soon."

"This pertains somehow to the summit that began today?"

Drexler nodded; the server brought Brewer's iced tea, and he waited for the server to leave before saying, "Everything pertains to the summit. The entire Western world is hoping . . . praying . . . that a good result comes from the talks. America wants détente with Russia, my continent wants détente as well, peace even, but we also want gas. Oil. Trade. A reduction in financial sanctions against Russian businessmen."

"And the information Velesky has can jeopardize this?"

Now the Swiss man nodded gravely. "Very much so."

"You seem to know what he has. I've heard conflicting information about his intelligence product."

Drexler shrugged. "I don't have to know exactly what he has. But, generally speaking, he has material that could put Russia in a bad light, right now, when we need public opinion to improve for the sake of going forward."

"I'm sorry," Brewer asked. "What is it you"—she caught herself—"your employers are looking for from me?"

"We need the Agency's help to recover the information taken, here in the United States. Many of the assets under my control were . . . eliminated last night at the Italian-Swiss border."

Holy fucking shit, Brewer thought. This man was working for the GRU, and Jay Kirby had sent her to work with him.

She gave nothing away—she was too practiced and too cool for that—but carefully she asked, "What assets do you have now?"

"Here in the U.S.? Limited, but not nonexistent. I am here on a mission of damage control. My employer has spoken with your Director, and your Director has matched the two of us up to eliminate the compromise." Drexler added, "I'm told your president is demanding this, and may I say he is quite wise to do so."

Brewer pressed again. "Who do you work for, Mr. Drexler?"

Drexler did not answer immediately, and Brewer said, "I can ask Jay as soon as I return to HQ, or you can tell me now. Either way, I don't proceed without knowing more."

Drexler nodded at this. "I am working with influential members of the Russian government."

Brewer blinked hard now. It was all on the table.

The Swiss man continued. "Obviously, this is a unique situation. But both parties, yours and mine, need the accords to be signed this week, and Velesky has stolen data that would make matters difficult."

It passed through her mind again. *Kirby is working with the Russians, and he wants me to do the same.*

She fought off the wave of disbelief. "Specifically," she asked, "what assets do you have in country?"

"Russian assets. That's all I know."

She did not think he was being truthful. There was something slimy and insincere about Sebastian Drexler. She felt certain he was working directly, in the United States of America, with Russian foreign intelligence or Russian military intelligence. Either way, in most circumstances the CIA would not be legally allowed to operate inside the United States, and there existed no circumstance *at all* where Russian intelligence would be allowed to operate here.

This was insane.

Drexler seemed to read her mind. "We pool our resources. You help me find Velesky in the city. Then you go away, and you leave the rest to me and my people."

"What the fuck is on that phone?" Brewer asked, her voice almost hoarse.

Drexler finished his champagne, then raised his hands as an apology. "Ours is not to reason why, Ms. Brewer. I look forward to working with you." He picked lint off the cuff of his jacket and said, "There is a little complication I'm not sure if you are aware of."

Every word out of this man's mouth had been a complication, Suzanne thought. But she just said, "Namely?"

"Namely . . . the Gray Man."

Brewer's eyebrows almost touched. "What about him?"

"He's been involved in this, in an adversarial role. He has been spotted at various locations involving the data that was exfiltrated from Russia. I just want you to be aware of his participation in this, as I know your Agency has been looking for him for some time."

Brewer's eyes narrowed now. "He was killed on that train last night. His body has been positively identified."

Drexler sat up straighter. For the first time he was the one on the receiving end of information. "I see." He wiped his mouth with his napkin. "In that case, you and I should have no trouble going forward."

He stood, surprising the senior CIA officer. "Return to your office, speak with the Director again. We've met. You know what I need, and you know what your masters want from you, just as I know what my masters want from me."

With a parting smile and a little bow, he said, "I will see you in the Big Apple. Tonight, hopefully."

Without another word, and with the help of his cane, he headed to the stairs, and then he began descending, while Suzanne Brewer just looked on.

Brewer was turning into a regular in the Director's office. The secretary waved her in immediately without a word when she stepped through the outer door, and she found Kirby seated at his desk, looking her way as she came through the inner door.

There was no wait here, either.

"Can I get you some coffee?" he asked, but the special assistant to the deputy director for operations did not answer.

Instead, she sat down. "So." She made no pretense whatsoever that she was not blown away by her lunch meeting. "A shady Swiss . . . fixer, I guess you call it, is your cutout to Daniil Spanov, head of all Russian intelligence."

Kirby was clearly ready for the line of questioning that was to come. "Back-channel relations are often the most prudent."

She nodded slowly. "And . . . Velesky is in New York."

"On his way, we think."

Another nod. Brewer was making Kirby spell this out for her, lest he try to wiggle out of anything later. "We're working with the GRU now."

"In this delicate and very crucial matter . . . correct."

"On the streets of New York City."

"In this delicate and very crucial matter . . . correct."

Brewer said, "Just like we were working with them in Switzerland."

Kirby shook his head. "No. We hadn't linked up at that point. If we had, you would have known about it. Zurich station was sent to intercept Velesky, unaware GRU was closing in on him, as well. It was an unfortunate green-on-green casualty."

Brewer knew that "green-on-green casualty" was military-speak for a friendly fire incident. Just to make Kirby say it, she asked, "Are you saying Russian military intelligence is our ally?"

"Right now, they are."

Brewer took a few breaths. On the entire drive back to McLean from D.C.

she'd been planning what she would say, but now she was just freestyling. "Matador killed our officer in Zurich. Will he be there in New York?"

"He was apparently there in Zurich *and* in Milan. If this moves to New York, then I can only assume he will be there."

"He murdered a case officer in Zurich," she repeated.

Kirby frowned. "Look. I don't like it, but this is the situation we find ourselves in. Matador's gotten closer to Velesky than the asset you sent, and by the way, as you said, the asset you sent is dead."

"But Matador is an enemy of the Agency."

Kirby leaned forward onto his elbows. "So was Violator . . . and you had no problem pulling him in."

Brewer could not disagree with this logic. Still, she just shook her head in disbelief. "You'll have to excuse my bafflement, sir. It's a lot to take in that we are working with Russian assassins on the streets of the United States."

The man shrugged. "The enemy of my enemy."

"So I go to New York. Work with this shady Swiss bastard. Find Altman. Wait for Velesky to show up, and then I leave so the Russians can do the act?"

"All before the accords are signed."

"What's on that phone? What does Velesky have on us? And don't tell me we are doing this to protect sources, methods, and assets, because, sir, that is bullshit. There are financial transactions from Russia into the West that we don't want anyone in the West knowing about before the signing of the accords."

Kirby nodded, gravely again. "The Russians have been waging a back-channel campaign for some time. Using the wealth the Kremlin commands to . . . *influence* opinion in the West."

"And?" Brewer demanded.

"And the campaign has involved powerful people in the United States. People who can ensure that the trade pact is signed, as long as they are not exposed as being compromised by Moscow."

Brewer hesitated, and Kirby said, "I am following the president's orders, Suzanne. Just like you will."

After several seconds, Brewer shook her head. "No. This isn't about the president, is it? This is you. This is you trying to cover up something in the Krupkin file that *you* don't want to get out."

Kirby scoffed loudly. "Now you're being ridiculous. Don't try to Sherlock

Holmes your orders. Just execute them. Go to New York. Link up with Drexler. Find a target for his assets." He smiled a little. "Before the summit at the UN wraps up."

"What if this all gets out *after* the accords are signed and the resolution is passed? If the information is so damning, wouldn't that just nullify whatever had been ratified?"

"It is our hope that the information never comes out. But if it *is* revealed after the resumption of trade, we'd have to see if Europe and America have the balls to shut down commerce with Russia again." He shrugged. "It will be a little hard to put that horse back in the barn."

Brewer stood. "I don't believe you. I believe you have a personal stake in all this, and that's why I was pulled into it. You know I've worked dirty jobs in the past, you know I don't have a problem with . . . *questionable* motives, questionable outcomes. You brought me in because you expect me to do for you what I did for Matt Hanley."

Brewer continued, "You knew what the Russians had, didn't you? You knew what this kind of a leak would do."

"Yes," Kirby replied. He leaned forward. "Have I misjudged you, or are you a woman who has her price?"

"My *price*? Is that a bribe?"

Kirby said nothing at first, and then he cleared his throat, thought for a moment. "When this is over, your work will be appreciated by the Director of the CIA."

She nodded slowly now, and took her time in answering, as if something were coming together in her head. Finally, she said, "You're damn right, it will be. I can keep my head down and my mouth shut . . . if it's in my own interests to do so."

"And this is where you ask me to tell you why it is in your interests to do so."

"Exactly."

"So," Kirby said. "Now it's not a bribe from me . . . it's extortion on your part." He laughed. "You name your price."

"It's not extortion," she countered. "I'll come back here once Velesky is dead and all the dirt on you and those like you is in my hands. And then you will find me to be just a valuable employee asking for a promotion."

Brewer had something on Kirby now, and Kirby knew it. "Primaries are coming; it's going to be tight, so I don't want to show discord around the Agency right now. The president is holding on to Congress by a fingernail; he wouldn't stand for any disruption. He also wouldn't stand for me replacing the deputy director for operations at a time like this."

"But?"

"But . . . Suzanne, the primaries will be over soon. You do your job in New York, and you will be sitting at Mel Brent's desk within a couple of months."

Brewer stood up straighter. "I would be honored, sir."

"Now . . . get to New York and tie this shit off."

Brewer smiled a little. "Say it, Jay. Tell me what you want."

"Help the Russians kill everybody they need to kill."

Brewer nodded, the smile remained, and she turned for the door.

FIFTY-ONE

Gamba Court is a quiet cul-de-sac in Vienna, Virginia, just nine houses of moderate size with small front lawns and tree-covered backyards. The little residential cove is a half-hour drive from Washington, D.C., in good traffic, and only twenty minutes to the CIA Headquarters building in McLean, Virginia.

At just before two a.m., a woman slept alone on the second floor of a 1,600-foot split-level at the end of the cul-de-sac, but then she rolled over, and her eyes opened slowly.

CIA officer Angela Lacy called this time of the night "the one-thirties"; it seemed she almost always woke somewhere between one thirty and two in the morning, and she lay here, sometimes for a half hour, sometimes more, and she stressed about work, about life, about problems.

Today seemed no different at first, but after less than a minute contemplating the complications in her life, she realized something was off.

It took her another full minute more before she discerned what it was.

The air around her felt different. Not a breeze, but a freshness, a slight coolness, as if it wasn't coming from the recirculating heater.

There was a draft somewhere in the house.

Lacy sat up, looked out her window over the cul-de-sac, and saw nothing amiss. The neighbor's dogs weren't barking, and there were certainly no noises inside her home that alerted her to trouble, just the purring of the HVAC system trying to keep the warmth up to sixty-eight degrees.

A futile effort if a window or door had been opened, she realized.

With a pounding heart, she rose and headed for the door, then took the stairs down to the first floor. Here she went to her sliding glass back door and made to open it to look out at her backyard, but she was still a few feet away when she realized the door was already open.

Cold air drifted in, blowing the curtains slightly.

Lacy didn't scream or run or panic; her heart continued to pound, but then she simply nodded to herself, cleared her throat, and spoke to the dark room behind her. "Were you planning on coming upstairs to wake me up?"

A man's voice came from behind, from the direction of the kitchen. She found herself startled, although she had been expecting this to happen. "I couldn't find a firearm near your bed, so I figured if you woke up and felt the draft, then you'd scramble to whatever you have to defend yourself."

Chills went down her spine, but she slowly closed and locked the door, feigning calm. "You've done this sort of thing before. Broken into people's homes in the dead of night."

"More often than you'd care to know."

"I *do* have a weapon," Lacy said. "The Agency makes me own a SIG pistol, though I've literally shot it the minimum number of times to keep my qualifications up. I keep it locked up in my closet behind the coats."

"Next time someone breaks in, you might think about grabbing it."

"Next time someone breaks in," she said, turning away from the door now, "it probably won't be you, so I will."

After a short pause, the man said, "You don't seem too surprised by my visit, and I find *that* surprising."

The man she knew as Six sat on her kitchen counter across the room. He wore jeans and a thick black sweater. A gray coat and a black knit cap lay on the counter next to him.

She moved forward a few feet, across the living room in the low light. "I saw you fall out of that train. I sent the police to look for you. They found one body in the snow after the tunnel, and I got a good look at it. It wasn't you."

"Well, *that's* a relief."

"Who was it?"

With a shrug, he said, "Beats me. I didn't toss him out. I was hardly the only lethal threat on that train."

"Tell me about it," she said, and then she moved to a couch, waved Six closer. "I knew you survived, but I don't understand how."

Now Six slid off the kitchen counter, stood, and crossed the floor, where he sat down on a chair across from her. She saw that he was moving gingerly, as if dealing with some pain. He said, "You ever hear of something called an alpine airbag vest?"

"No."

Six shrugged. "Neither had I. I needed a quick change after I boarded the train, so I stole one of the mountain climbers' clothes. I put a big dumb vest on under a coat for a little padding, and when I got knocked out the door, a computer with a gyro and an accelerometer inside the vest detected that I was flying through the air, so it deployed airbags around my torso and the back of my neck. Saved my life, no doubt about it, although a four-foot accumulation of snow in a gully along the train track helped out."

Lacy laughed, despite the tension in the pit of her stomach. "You are the luckiest man alive."

"The luckiest man alive wouldn't get T-boned out of a train by a one-hundred-thirty-pound banker."

Lacy conceded the point with a nod, then said, "A lot of people who stayed on that train didn't end up so lucky. Twelve dead civilians, seventeen injured."

Six just said, "I didn't shoot anyone who didn't have it coming."

She changed the subject. "I saw Matador. He was injured."

Six nodded. "I know. I injured him."

Lacy made a little face now. "I wouldn't be congratulating myself *too* much, you only shot him in the foot."

"Yeah, but I shot him with *my* foot, so I get at least a little pat on the back for that, don't I?"

"How the hell does one—"

"Pulled the trigger with my big toe." Six looked out the window over her shoulder. "Second time I've done it."

She scoffed now. "You're fucking with me, aren't you?"

He looked back to her. "First time with the left foot."

She just shook her head; she didn't believe him.

He let it go and asked, "How did you know I'd come here?"

"Firstly, my home is in my name. I figured you'd have no problem looking up property records. And secondly, we have unfinished business. Am I wrong?"

"You're not wrong, at all. Look, something is completely off about the mission we were sent on. Our op was dirty, Angela. Brewer was playing us."

Lacy did not respond to this, so Six said, "The woman with Velesky, the one you said didn't come up on facial recognition scans."

"What about her?"

"She's . . . she's a friend."

Lacy cocked her head. "And she's helping Velesky?"

"If she's helping him, he must be someone who deserves to be helped."

"Who is she?"

"A Russian national, former SVR, but she—"

Lacy was astonished. "You're kidding me. You're friends with an SVR operative who is working against Agency interests and you think she's doing the right thing?"

"*Former* SVR, and she *is* doing the right thing. The reason her face didn't come up in your sweeps is . . . she was in the same program I was in. For the Agency, I mean. This was after her defection. It was sub rosa, and Brewer ran it for Matt Hanley."

"We ran a former Russian foreign intelligence officer off book?"

"Our faces and biometric data were washed from all records. I think mine might have been put back in the database—the Agency is looking for me again, but she's clean."

"I've never heard of anything like this."

"She is one of the good ones. She's rough around the edges; I could see her engaging in some kinds of criminality to make a living, but there is absolutely no way in hell she would be working in the interests of the Russians."

With complete self-assuredness, Six said, "If she's on Velesky's side, then I am, too."

"But . . . the woman I talked to. She sounded American."

"She's good like that." He looked off. "She's good at a lot of things."

Lacy nodded, after a time. "I believe you. Not because I trust that woman, but because I talked to *him*."

Court leaned forward, put his elbows on his knees. He was clearly astounded by this. "To . . . *Velesky*? When?"

"On the train. Right after the shootout."

"Holy shit."

Lacy shrugged. "Then the woman showed up, got him away from me." Lacy shrugged. "That problem I have with pulling triggers."

Court went back to Velesky. "What did he say?"

"He said everything he has involves Russian money going *into* the West. Paying for agents, influence, black ops . . . *everything* Moscow is doing dirty in the West went through Velesky's bank, and he's got bank records to match up with Krupkin's stolen Russian data."

"Jesus Christ," Court just said softly, and then, "I have some ideas as to where Velesky has gone."

She cocked her head. "Where?"

"After I got away in Switzerland, I made it to France and patched myself up. Then I reached out to Melnyk; he was the guy that I was working for when you dropped in on me in the BVIs."

"The one helping you sink the mega yachts?"

"Yeah. I told him what I was into, that the Russians were flooding the zone with front-line GRU assassins to get this financial intel back, and I asked him where a guy like Velesky would take it."

"Do you trust this Melnyk?"

Court sniffed. "Not to water my plants, but if it comes to shady finance and fucking over the Russians . . . yeah, I trust him."

"Where did he say Velesky would go?"

"There's a man in Brussels, he's running the EU's efforts to track Russian money. There's a woman in London, doing the same thing for the Brits, but she's mostly looking into British banking's underhanded dealings with Russia. And then there's a guy in New York. He's been working with U.S. federal prosecutors for years, and he's put together the best algorithmic software based on offshore banking records that have been leaked out over the past decade."

"What is algorithmic software?" Lacy asked.

"I don't have a clue, but it sounds cool. I was hoping you knew."

"Must be some sort of data mining stuff. Anyway, go on."

Court continued. "This guy is also laser focused on Velesky's bank. Melnyk said if he had to guess, then he would guess Velesky was headed to New York."

Lacy sat back and crossed her legs, put her arms up on the back of the sofa. "Want to take a guess as to who else is headed to New York?"

Six's eyes narrowed, and then they widened. "You're kidding me."

"Brewer. I reached out to her yesterday afternoon as soon as I got home, following up on my expected debrief after Geneva, but her exec assistant told me she'd just jumped on a train for Manhattan."

"Oh my God," Court mumbled. "The CIA is in New York to kill Velesky before he hands off the data."

"What's the man's name there?" Lacy asked.

"Ezra Altman."

Lacy nodded. "Of course. He has a private forensic accounting firm, originally hired by the DOJ, but Washington has cut ties with them in the past few months."

"Why?"

"Obviously because Washington wants this trade agreement with Moscow to go through, and Altman digging up dirt on Russian crimes right now would be bad for the agreement's prospects."

"That figures."

"How high do you think this goes?" she asked.

"There's presumably millions of dollars getting into the West. It's going somewhere, it's tainting someone. I don't think we can rule anything out."

"Six, if the CIA is involved, we have to assume other federal agencies are, as well, or at least members of them."

Court nodded. "DOJ, Homeland Security. Fuck, why just federal? The NYPD could have Russian agents pulling its strings."

Angela Lacy rubbed her face in her hands. "Who do we even trust?"

"We trust the people we didn't trust forty-eight hours ago. We trust Alex Velesky and . . . and Anthem."

"Who is Anthem?"

"The Russian woman's code name."

Angela noticed something in the way Six spoke. "What is it about her? She's important to you?"

"Yeah. I mean . . . I think so. Used to be, anyway."

"Sounds a little vague."

"I hadn't seen her in a year, and then when I *did* see her, I punched her in the side of the head."

Lacy shrugged. "Personally, I thought she was a bitch, and she didn't seem to have a very high opinion of me, either."

"Just wait till she finds out you work for Suzanne Brewer." Six sighed now and said, "I'm going to New York. I'm going to find Velesky and get the data back, and I'm going to find Matador and kill him, because I guarantee if I can find out where Velesky is, the Russians can, too."

He thought a moment. "But if Brewer is there, in New York, then she's going to be looking for me. I never checked in after Geneva, because I knew the mission was bullshit."

"I don't think Brewer will be looking for you," Lacy said.

"Why not?"

"Because I told Brewer you were dead."

Court sat up, utterly astonished. "You're kidding."

She shook her head. "I thought it might buy you some time."

"Not sure if you know how things work at Langley. Your boss can lie to you, but you can't lie to your boss."

"I found it cathartic." When Court said nothing, she added, "I'm pretty sure she was going to have you killed when this was all over, just like you said." She shrugged. "Even though it's *not* all over, I thought I could at least get you out of her sights for a while."

"Why would you risk your career to help me?"

"Our conversation about making a difference." She shrugged. "I might not be part of the solution, but I sure as hell don't want to be part of the problem." She thought a moment. "Brewer isn't high enough on the food chain to affect policy. She's doing the bidding of someone else. Why? Money?"

Six said, "She's not in it for the money. It's about power and prestige to her."

"I don't give two shits about prestige," Angela said. "Power, on the other hand, if used in the right way, is a good thing."

"If used in the right way," Six repeated. "The 'if' in that statement is doing some heavy lifting, wouldn't you agree?"

Lacy shrugged. "Power is out there. It's going to be in *someone's* hands. I think I have a good moral center." She smiled at him a little. "I haven't gone to the dark side, not yet, anyway."

"Yet," Court said, and then he stood. "Well, you're all I've got."

"What a ringing endorsement."

"Hopefully I'm wrong, again, and you are the best, most honorable, most capable executive to ever work at the CIA."

Angela stood, as well. "Let's just shoot for 'not Brewer.'"

"Not Brewer . . . I can work with that."

"I'm coming with you," Lacy said. "She put me on paid leave for the week. I figure she doesn't want me running around HQ until she figures out what to do with me."

"I'd be worried about what she decides to do with you once shit kicks off in the U.S."

"I've been thinking the same thing. I'll come with you to New York. Hell, I like my chances better there."

"Bring your pistol," Court instructed.

Lacy shook her head. "*You* can bring my pistol."

"That's kind of what I meant."

Six extended a hand, and she took it. He said, "Please be one of the good ones, Lacy."

"Right back at you, Six."

FIFTY-TWO

Shortly before eight a.m., Ukrainian separatist and GRU-trained intelligence asset Petro Mozgovoy finished his ninety-minute SDR around Brooklyn and Manhattan, and he crossed 59th Street in front of the Plaza hotel, heading for the southeast corner of Central Park.

He'd told none of his team about today's meeting, as per instructions received from GRU. Instead, he'd spent the entire previous afternoon and night ruminating about what he would learn and what he would be asked to do, and this morning he'd bundled up against the cold and stepped out into the gray early dawn, walked to a bus stop, took a bus to a subway stop, then walked through Midtown before heading subterranean and taking the train to Columbus Circle. Here he strolled with the morning commuters east to the Plaza, and soon he found himself walking on a footpath through the park.

The bench he'd been directed to by the Russians sat across the footpath from the Pond at Central Park, just fifty meters from the Gapstow Bridge, and Mozgovoy found it empty when he arrived. He sat down, looked out at the frozen pond, and glanced left and right to eye the area for any surveillance. His knowledge of countersurveillance, first taught to him in Russia, had been well augmented by his handler here in the city, a sixty-eight-year-old former GRU illegal who now owned a dry cleaner in Soho. The old man met weekly with the Ukrainian cell at a property they owned in Manhattan, and he trained them beyond what they'd learned in their crash course a year earlier.

Petro completed his first scan; he saw no one paying attention to him, but he also didn't see the man who had sat down next to him till he spoke up, startling the Ukrainian separatist.

In English, the man said, "I can't wait for baseball season."

Petro turned to him and saw a man slightly younger than himself, with blond hair and a small bandage on his left ear. He wore a black cardigan under a dark green North Face coat that looked brand-new and probably cost a few hundred, and he had high-end-looking brown leather gloves on his hands.

Petro himself was dressed as a laborer: jeans, a sweatshirt, an off-white down jacket, and a thick wool cap on his balding head.

He nodded at the man and then replied in a thick accent, "Spring training will be here before you know it."

Looking down now, Petro realized the man wore a brown leather boot on his right foot, and a black orthopedic walking boot on his left.

"What did you do to your foot?"

"I didn't do anything to it." He left it there, and so did Petro.

The Ukrainian said, "Okay. I don't know who you are, and I don't know why we are meeting."

"You know who ordered you here."

The blond meant GRU, and Petro nodded. "Who are you?" he asked.

"Luka."

"I mean . . . who *are* you?"

Luka turned to the man now. "I'm from the Aquarium."

The man from the DPR Security Service Battalion knew the nickname for the GRU's headquarters, so he reacted with a little surprise in his posture.

"Calm down," Luka admonished.

The man looked back out to the frozen pond. "Rank?"

"Major."

Mozgovoy raised his eyebrows, then turned back in the man's direction.

Luka spoke softly. "If you fucking salute me right now, I'm going to beat you to death."

"I wasn't going to salute. I'm just enthusiastic, sir. And worried. We've

been working on something . . . orders from Donetsk. We are ready to implement it. We're just waiting for the go-ahead. If you have come here to bring
me home, then I—"

The man interrupted. "Would they send a Russian major to the USA to
bring a Ukrainian agent home?"

Petro conceded the point with a little shake of his head, and the man
called Luka continued talking. "We are going to locate a man in the city, and
we are going to eliminate him and retrieve something, either from his person or from whatever location we find him in."

Petro looked back out to the pond now.

"One man?"

"My guess is that by the time we find him, we will have to silence others.
The mission goals of this operation are currently in flux."

Petro looked out over the water. "But . . . as I said. We have been training
for . . . for something else."

"Well, that's between you and your service. *My* service needs this from
you, and you *will* comply."

The Ukrainian was somewhat crestfallen. Yes, this was operational work
being handed to him, but it wasn't the big play he and his team had been
planning on. Still, he said, "I and my cell will do your job, of course. But if
you have any information about the larger operation we plan on conducting,
I would be eager to—"

"What's the status of your cell?" Luka asked, again interrupting, as if
Petro weren't even speaking.

Petro recovered. "Ten of us, myself included. All from Security Service
Battalion. Most of us with combat military backgrounds."

Luka said, "I have four more with me. Me and my men need to keep a
lower profile; we don't know what the Americans know about us."

Petro nodded. "Send us out. Wherever. No one is looking at us here. We're
invisible." He thought a moment. "This man. Does he have protection?"

"Very much so."

"Who is our opposition?"

Luka did not hesitate. "NYPD. Homeland Security. Perhaps other American federal agencies."

"Shit." What Petro had thought was just a small side matter seconds earlier, a distraction from his real work, was now turning into something bigger. With a little defiance in his voice, he said, "We're not cannon fodder."

"Neither am I. If the shooting starts, I'll be right there shooting along with you. My men, as well. Our low profile will end when the target has been located."

"Good. We are honored to help the cause in whatever way we—"

Luka turned to the man for the first time. "I don't want to hear about a cause. I don't want to hear about anything. I tell you what to do, and you do it. You need no other motivation beyond my voice. Do we understand one another?"

"Da . . . I mean, yes. Of course."

"How long will it take to assemble your cell for a meeting?"

Petro looked back to the water. Shrugged. "Several hours. You can meet them tonight."

"Eight o'clock. Text me the address."

Luka stood and began limping away on his walking boot without saying another word.

"Majors," Petro said to himself. He'd been in one military or another for virtually all his adult life, and he'd never been an officer.

He sat quietly on the bench for five minutes, though it killed him to do so. Then he stood and headed back to the subway, opening up the Signal app on his phone and sending out texts to his people as he walked.

FIFTY-THREE

The offices of Altman Globus Accountancy LLP were on the thirtieth floor of a seventy-two-story skyscraper on Third Avenue and East 52nd Street, and as the light faded from the gray sky outside just after four p.m., the lights on floor thirty shone bright.

Traffic was heavy on eastbound East 52nd Street, but just across from the building sat an Irish pub with a green façade and a dark wood paneling interior.

Zoya Zakharova sat at a raised cocktail table by the window, and though she wasn't exactly dressed to the nines, she looked good in a figure-flattering black sweater, light-colored jeans, and brown boots.

Makeup covered the contusions that remained around her eyes and nose, impossible to discern from only a few feet away, but the gray-purple bruising and red scratches could be seen by anyone looking at her more closely.

"I don't like it," Zoya said to the man seated on the other side of the table. Alex Velesky wore a new suit and tie he'd bought that afternoon, and he'd shaved for the first time in days just an hour later at the Kimberly Hotel on East 50th. Zoya had outfitted him with eyeglasses, dyed his hair from a light brown to a dark brown with streaks of blond, and put lifts in his shoes.

They had arrived in New York the previous evening, and as soon as Zoya had checked into the hotel under the name Zoe Zimmerman, she'd left Alex, telling him she needed to run out for a few items.

She'd seen it in Alex's eyes; he thought she was going to get drunk.

He was only partially correct; she did stop at a wine bar on Fifth Avenue for two glasses of Sancerre, ordered together and consumed in rapid succession. She'd then gone down to Penn Station, the busiest transportation facility in the Western Hemisphere, where, at a quarter till midnight, she met a fifty-something-year-old man outside a bodega adjacent to the station and followed him back inside.

The man appeared Thai, and though he spoke very little, his accent confirmed this. Zoya passed a woman behind the counter who looked like she could have been his daughter. The younger woman didn't look up at Zoya, her eyes locked onto the floor behind the counter as if these had been her instructions from her father.

In a back room the Thai man had everything she'd ordered on the dark web earlier in the day laid out on a cheap plastic table for her review.

A black Smith and Wesson Shield subcompact 9-millimeter pistol, a Smith and Wesson 442 five-shot revolver in .38 Special, extra loaded magazines for the semiauto, and two speed loaders for the wheel gun. There were rudimentary holsters with each weapon, as well.

Next to the gun was a folding knife with a four-inch blade.

The guns and the knife were what the man here in New York had available at short notice; they weren't necessarily her first choices for her mission at hand. She couldn't remember the last time she'd fired a revolver, and the nine-round capacity of the Shield pistol seemed paltry considering that most handguns she carried could spit out thirteen to sixteen rounds before requiring a reload.

Still, these were damn good weapons, and though they both looked used and worn, after checking them over for a few seconds, she decided they would work, even if they didn't particularly excite her.

Next to the guns, however, was something that *did* excite her. A single plastic baggie, three inches square and an inch thick, holding a fine white powder. She looked at the Thai man, and he gave a little nod, and then Zoya opened the knife, carefully popped open the little zip-lock, and used the tip of the blade to take a small portion of white powder.

This she brought to her nose and sniffed.

Zoya winced. The coke had been "stepped on," meaning cut, mixed with another material, but the quality was high enough for someone who wanted the drug and didn't have a lot of options.

"I'll take it all," she said as she reclosed the bag carefully.

"Five thousand." Zoya found herself pleasantly surprised that the man hadn't arbitrarily decided to go up on the agreed-upon price, and she took a folded stack of hundred-dollar bills out of her pocket.

The man spent longer counting the money and testing each bill to make certain it wasn't counterfeit than Zoya had inspecting the gear itself, but soon she was back out on the cold dark street, passing homeless people near Penn Station, heading back towards their suite at the Kimberly with her equipment.

On the way back to the hotel, after texting Velesky's newly purchased burner phone with her own burner that all was well, she stopped off in Connolly's, an Irish pub on East 47th Street. It was nearly two a.m.; the bartender had already given last call, but her alluring smile and her feigned soft, sweet voice cajoled him into making an exception.

She drank a double Tito's on ice; the bartender's eyes widened as she downed the liquor in just a few gulps, and soon she was back on the street, trudging on through the cold night.

And now, most of a day later, she had made herself more presentable, though inside she knew she remained an unmitigated disaster.

Looking across the little table, she saw that Alex looked much better than she felt. Her bruises and scrapes from the train to Geneva were somewhat improved after thirty-six hours, but her mood was as dour and depressed as she'd ever felt in her life. She had a drink in front of her; she wanted to guzzle it, but she just held it in her hands. A security blanket, there for warmth when she needed it, which, she knew, would be seconds after Alex left her sight.

Velesky said, "I have to do it this way. I can't just call up Ezra Altman on the phone and say, 'Hi, I'm Alex, that guy you've been trying to throw in prison for five years, want to go out and grab a pizza?'" He took a sip of his Diet Coke. "No. He wouldn't know it was really me, he wouldn't talk over an open phone line, and he wouldn't trust me.

"By now he would have received the letter I sent him with the address to the material I took from Brucker Söhne, so he knows my pseudonym. I walk in there, tell his people my name is Pavel Chyrkov, and then, hopefully, he'll escort me right into his office."

"And *then* what?"

"We will talk, I'll tell him why I've had such a change of heart, and when I tell him about the Krupkin files, he'll understand why Krupkin had such a change of heart himself. At that point, I believe, he will give me the time I need to show him everything.

"From there, hopefully, he can do his magic, connect some dots, and figure out where the money went after it left my bank."

"Your plan relies on a lot of hope."

Alex shrugged now. "There is no hope in any other plan I can think of. Anyway, you still have Krupkin's phone, so even if I get arrested, you can try to get it to Altman."

Zoya fidgeted, looked down at her vodka. "Still . . . I'm worried about letting you go in there alone."

Alex looked down at her drink, as well. "And I'm worried about leaving you here alone in a bar."

She looked out the window. "I've got eyes on the entrance from here. Not a hell of a lot I can do if the feds pull up in a dozen sedans, but at least I'll know what happened to you."

Alex chuckled. "Don't get drunk, and don't start killing American cops on my behalf."

Zoya said nothing, even though she was certain she would be able to comply with only one of Alex's two requests.

Finally, the Ukrainian sighed. "Okay . . . I'm off. If his security doesn't tackle me and take my burner away, I'll text you updates."

Zoya nodded, then looked into Alex's eyes. "You are very brave."

Alex's eyes shifted down and off to the side, as if he were looking at the floor next to the table. "Krupkin was right. This isn't about being a hero. It's about salvaging a little bit of my soul."

He slid off the barstool and headed for the door. Zoya brought her drink to her mouth and gulped while she looked out the window, watching her partner in this affair appear out in front of the bar, then pick his way through gridlocked cars, crossing the street. Soon he opened the door to the lobby of the skyscraper that loomed in the darkness outside.

Five minutes later she was on her second Belvedere on ice. The Polish rye vodka was smoother than what she was used to, but she wasn't complaining. She normally only demanded a buzz from her alcohol; taste and drinkability were far secondary and tertiary in her requirements, but she had no problem drinking the good shit when it was available.

Her phone buzzed on the table; she looked at it and saw that it was Alex. **Inside lobby. Waiting to see what they do. Lots of security around. Moment of truth, I guess.**

She responded, **See if you can get him to come over here and talk, away from his office. He might be more easily persuaded without his goons.**

Alex texted back, **These aren't goons. They are uniformed Homeland Security officers. Don't know if that's good or bad.**

Zoya took another drink. She didn't think the presence of uniformed American government officers was particularly good, considering the fact that the woman on the train seemed to be CIA, and she seemed to have interest in either taking control of the Krupkin files or else making them go away. Altman, she reasoned, might be better off with rent-a-cops than he would with American federal agents.

Zoya held her eyes on the entrance across the street most of the time, but even with a drink in her hand, she kept her personal security responsibilities near the forefront of her mind. She gazed around her environs once in a while. People toasting one another, happy-hour drinking, a basketball game on the TV that dozens were riveted to.

No threats.

The door opened and she looked to see a group of businessmen enter, shaking off the cold as they pulled out of their wool coats, and then they hung them on racks and headed straight for the bar for a drink.

She couldn't see all their faces, but she saw enough of them to discount them as any sort of a danger for her.

When the waitress came by, Zoya ordered another Belvedere. She gulped the remainder of her vodka now, the depression inside her almost but not quite bubbling over; only her determination to finish this mission was driving her now.

After that . . . *if* she completed this operation, what next?

She didn't know if she would survive the mission, or even if she could survive *after* the mission.

And she wasn't sure she even cared.

She shot eyes over to the bar and saw a few businessmen looking her way. She retained the self-confidence, even in her current state, to know she'd be "good enough" for some half-sauced Wall Street asshole to make a play at.

One of the men in the group had moved away from the rest. He faced the bar, but not where the mirror reflected his face; she tried to discern something about him, but she didn't get far before a man in his thirties, handsome with ample gray at his temples, confidently walked over.

Zoya took her next round of Belvedere from the passing waitress and immediately took a swig.

"Are you meeting someone?" the man asked.

"Yes," she replied; her put-on American accent was certain and clear.

"Well." He slid onto the barstool across from her. "How about we have a drink while we wait? Husband? Boyfriend?"

"Girlfriend," Zoya replied, her eyes cold. "Look, dude, you aren't just out of your league here, you're not even on my menu."

The man slid off the barstool, looked over to his friends—everyone except the man facing the bar was watching intently—and then muttered, "Whatever. Your loss."

Zoya didn't bother with a comeback. She returned her attention to the street and the building across it, and the man went back to lick his wounds and to tell his friends, she imagined, about the lesbian bitch by the window.

It was a few more minutes of surveillance; she was two-thirds of the way through her drink when she felt movement to her left as she looked out the window to her right.

She turned at the source of the disturbance, but not before another man in a suit and tie had sat across from her. She didn't even look at the man's face. She just sighed and muttered, "It's not going to end any differently with you than it did with your buddy."

The figure did not move.

Gazing down at the new would-be suitor's hands, she saw that he held a cup of coffee between them. This seemed a weird beverage for a young businessman at four thirty in the afternoon. With a tired sigh, she looked up at him.

And then her heart grabbed tight in her chest; she caught a quick gasp before it came out. Instantly she felt a flood of tears fighting to form in her eyes.

Her mouth quivered a little as she sat there, transfixed as if a spell had been cast upon her.

Her words came out hoarse, like she had not spoken in months. "Is . . . it . . . you?"

Court Gentry gave her a nervous smile, his hands quivering a little where they cradled the coffee.

FIFTY-FOUR

His charcoal suit, his burgundy tie, and his blue dress shirt fit him perfectly; he wore tortoiseshell glasses and had the beginnings of a beard and mustache, more facial hair than he'd had during that brief frantic moment when she saw him on the train to Geneva two nights earlier.

Before that, she hadn't laid eyes on him in a year, and she had no pictures of him, so his presence in front of her, a slight smile on his face, was almost more than her mind could process. She didn't know what was going on, and she also didn't know if she'd be able to keep her shit together.

"It's me." He looked down at his coffee, slid it across the table, and exchanged it with Zoya's vodka. "How 'bout we trade?" He pulled her drink up to his mouth and took a sip.

His eyebrows rose and he made a face.

Zoya wasn't paying attention. She was still trying to compute the situation through a brain only slightly altered by drink but well waylaid by both fatigue and utter surprise. Finally, she said, "You . . . you fell out of that train at high speed."

"I wouldn't say I *fell*."

Still utterly spellbound, Zoya said, "It had to have been doing seventy miles an hour."

"My hip, my right knee, and my right ass cheek tell me your calculations check out."

She cocked her head. "The snow?"

"I hit a snowbank, whipped around like a whirligig through a gully, and I would have died, snow or not, except for the fact I was wearing an alpine airbag."

"A *what*?"

"I'd never heard of it, either. I looked them up, after the fact. It protected my chest, abdomen, spine, hips, and even my neck, though the rest of me is pretty beat up."

"And you just happened to be wearing it?"

"I wanted to look like those mountaineers on the train. Took it from one of their bags. I thought it was just a big goofy vest."

Zoya marveled; cocking her head, she said, "How are you so fucking lucky?"

He shrugged a little. "The *really* lucky people on that train didn't get shoulder-checked out the door at top speed."

"And the really unlucky people are in a morgue in Geneva."

"True," he said. "Along with those who richly deserve it."

He sipped more of the vodka, then held up the glass. "This works for pain, right?"

"Depends on the type of pain you're suffering from." Zoya held on to the table now; she was almost overcome with conflicting, swirling, and confusing emotions. He looked so perfect, so composed, so put together, and so in control.

She didn't feel any of these things about herself.

Finally, she said, "What are you doing here?"

"The man you're protecting. I was sent after him and his data. But now I—"

And with that, her head cleared instantly. "Then you've been sent on a bad op."

"Yeah . . . I pieced that together." He shrugged. "Eventually."

Zoya took her hands off the table's edge and grabbed the coffee. Sipping it, she found it black and bitter, and she winced. The vodka had been so damn smooth. "Who sent you after Alex?"

"Suzanne Brewer."

She put the coffee down and looked away from him for the first time, back out the window at the street. "And you looked so fucking intelligent in that suit for a minute."

Court conceded with a shrug. "I knew I was being played by her, to some degree, anyway. But I saw a chance to help the Agency and to target a GRU asset involved. Thought that would get me back in the seventh floor's good graces."

"How can you possibly remain so optimistic after everything that's been done to you?"

"It's more of a dream than it is optimism. But yeah, maybe it's just a pipe dream." He regarded her a moment, and then he said, "How did you get involved?"

"I was sent after Velesky on a private job. Just find some asshole banker on the run and deliver him to a competing bank to get what he knows out of him. I grabbed him, and then the GRU showed up. Velesky told me what he had, and I realized I had to help him." After another sip of coffee, she said, "It's been all downhill ever since."

Court explained his own journey now. "Suzanne sent me and an operations officer out of Langley to the Caribbean to retrieve a phone full of data out of Russia. The pretense was that it had compromising intel of CIA monies going east."

"Did you get it back?"

"No. A GRU guy got to it first."

"Who?"

"The Agency calls him Matador."

Zoya raised her eyebrows. "Rudenko. I've heard of him. I knew the Agency was after him." She shook her head. "I don't know what he looks like."

She sipped the bad coffee again. It wouldn't sober her up, but it helped pass the time before she reached over and pulled her drink out of Court's hand in a minute or two. "Brewer sent you to Milan to try to get Velesky?"

"Yeah. I was still hunting Matador, too. Ran into him, actually."

"Where?"

"He was on the train. You might have seen him. Blond hair, chiseled face. A bit of a grump."

"Yeah," she said. "He shot at me."

"Well," Court went on, "I wounded him. Don't know how bad, but doubt he's out of action. If the GRU knows about Altman, then he's probably here now, though I've spent the past two hours looking for Russians with an eye on Altman's building. Couldn't find anybody." He smiled. "Except you."

Zoya asked, "How did you know about New York?"

"The case officer and I figured out we'd been had, either by Brewer or whoever is pulling Brewer's strings. Then we—"

"The woman on the train? African American? Thirties? Pretty?"

"Angela Lacy. She's good. Honest."

Zoya put the coffee down. "Says the guy working with Suzanne Brewer."

Court smiled. "I am an incredible judge of character."

Zoya scoffed at this, even though she knew Court was kidding. She then looked at him closely. "She's weak, Court. Had me at gunpoint on the train. Could have recovered the data from me and pulled Alex home with her. But I saw it in her eyes; she didn't have what it takes to take a life."

"She's complicated. A pacifist."

Zoya was unimpressed. "Well, she's in the wrong line of work."

"She's not in *our* line of work, Zoya. She's a midlevel exec on the fast track at Langley. The dirtiest shit she's probably ever dealt with is getting D.C. police to fix parking tickets for friendly foreign intel services."

"Then why did Brewer put her in the middle of this?"

"Initially, it was to get me on board. She couldn't send Ground Branch for a chat with me because I'd start shooting. But Lacy handled herself well in Saint Lucia, and she handled herself well in Zurich. After that, Brewer stood her down."

"But . . . she's *here*?"

"I asked her to come to New York to help me out."

"And she just said yes? Doesn't sound like she'll be on the fast track for long, does it?"

Court smiled a little. "She might be one of the good ones, Z."

"Again, your judgment calls regarding character have, historically speaking, left a lot to be desired." Before he responded, she said, "I'm talking about Brewer, and I'm talking about me."

Court cocked his head. "Brewer, I get. But why you?"

She looked away, out the window into the rain, but said nothing.

. . .

Court caught himself staring at Zoya as she looked at the rain. Her eyes glistened bright, like puddles reflecting electric lights in the street outside.

And then she began to cry.

He thought of all those nights on his boat, looking up at the stars, wishing more than anything he'd ever wished for in his life that he could look into her eyes again.

But now that he was here, that this was real, it felt off somehow. Like she wasn't the same person he remembered. She seemed fragile, unsure, conflicted.

Now she said, "You disappeared on me."

Court sipped the vodka, put it back down on the table, but kept his hands on the icy wet glass. "Again, your buddy pushed me out of a train."

She shook her head. "No. I mean last year. In Germany. Everything seemed so perfect." She shrugged. "Well, perfect enough for people like us. And then you were just . . . gone."

Court felt the pain in his heart that came from letting down someone he cared about. He hadn't felt it much in life, but he recognized it for what it was immediately.

"It wasn't by choice, Zoya. I swear to you. Hanley told me there was a new target on my back. The Agency was going to come at me for everything that happened. He told me to run, said the Agency would be on my ass like never before, but this time he wasn't going to be on the seventh floor covering for me."

Court shook his head. "Hanley and Brewer were bad enough, but Brewer *without* Hanley is downright terrifying."

A single tear ran down Zoya's right cheek.

Defensively, he added, "Taking you with me would have just exposed you to more danger."

She sniffed out an angry laugh. "So you left me alone, where ever since I have been so perfectly safe. How honorable."

Court could see the bruises under Zoya's makeup; he was pretty sure the blow he'd thrown at her had just glanced off the side of her head. He'd not seen much of anything she'd gone through on the train to Geneva, but he'd sure as hell *heard* the battle she was engaged in.

No, leaving her alone had not made her safer, and now he wondered if he was just making excuses for himself as to why he ran away from her.

He thought of some explanation, but the only thing that came out was "I'm sorry."

She took a few breaths, then scooted the coffee away from her, reached across the table, and took back the half glass of iced vodka. She drank the rest of it down, motioned to the waitress for another, then placed the glass on the table.

"It's okay," she said.

Court did not have a good working radar for detecting the inner feelings of others when it came to emotions, but he was pretty sure it was *not* okay.

FIFTY-FIVE

"I missed you. Every single day." Court said it without thinking, then wished he could have taken it back immediately, because he knew he was exposing his heart to the potential for more pain.

Fresh tears filled her eyes. He didn't know what they meant, and he had given up on thinking of things to say, because every word out of his mouth seemed to upset her.

He'd thought of this moment for so long, wanted it so badly, and now everything seemed to be going so incredibly wrong.

Zoya said, "You're always trying to do what you *think* I need. And you're wrong a lot. Why can't you just listen to me?"

Court had no words.

They sat in silence for twenty seconds; she wiped tears away and they reformed. Their staring contest was only broken when the waitress came and put the fresh glass down. She saw the beautiful crying woman, perhaps she even saw the bruising through the makeup, and the waitress gave Court a long, intense "eat shit" look, which he didn't really need at the moment, before walking away.

Zoya blinked tears from her eyes, then said, "I am embarrassed . . . but . . . but . . ."

"What?"

"I could really use a hug."

Court all but leapt to his feet, stepped around the little table, and embraced her tightly, him standing, her sitting on her barstool.

"I missed you," she whispered into his ear, and he clenched his eyes shut, feeling a wave of emotions he was smart enough to know he couldn't control or fight. There was confusion—this wasn't the Zoya he knew—but there was also affection, there was also love. Pure love, as if she were the only one out of eight billion people on Earth that he could ever have such a strong connection to.

After a moment, he pulled his head back, she looked up at him, and it felt right, so he moved to her lips. They kissed, and he reveled in the moment, his mind awash with the sensation of this contact that he'd been thinking about with every fiber of his being, never knowing for sure if he'd ever see her again.

She sniffed loudly; the tears were still there, and she broke away from him to wipe her face a moment.

"It's so stupid," she said.

"What is?"

She sniffed again, barely in control. "I'm pretty sure I'm supposed to be furious, and I might be if I sat and thought about it, but I just needed that a lot."

"I did, too."

Court sat back down and considered calling the waitress over for a drink of his own, but then he thought better of it. He didn't need her scorn, and if there were others around after Velesky, he needed to keep his shit together, because as much as he loved the woman in front of him, from an operational standpoint, she looked to be a shambles.

Once again, he said what he was thinking. "Are you okay?"

Zoya rubbed her eyes as she looked out at the street. "I'm not really great right now. You ever been like that?"

"Most of my life." Court smiled a little. "You're going to be fine."

She didn't look like she believed him, but her eyes seemed to clear, and she turned back his way. "Velesky is talking to Altman right now."

"I figured as much. I saw him leave here and go in, so I thought you might be in here running countersurveillance."

She brought her fresh drink to her mouth. "Yeah, *that's* what I'm doing."

Court smiled. "Let me help. I've been scanning this room in the mirror behind you since I sat down, and the only threat I've identified is the pack of wild douchebags at the bar who want to take you home with them."

She rolled her eyes. "That's literally the only thing on planet Earth I'm *not* worried about right now."

"Well, maybe I *can* do something to help you with the other stuff. Let's pool our resources. Work together. Let's get Velesky's intel out into the world."

Zoya didn't react at first; she wiped a lingering tear, and she consumed more of her vodka. Court purposefully did not look at her while she did it. She was abusing alcohol, not for the first time, but he didn't want to appear judgmental, because that seemed like the last thing she needed right now.

Finally, her head seemed to clear a little. "Tell me how you knew to come to New York."

"I found out Ezra Altman was probably Velesky's final destination with the intel he took, and Lacy found out Brewer herself came to town yesterday. My guess is she's looking for him and knew he was on his way here."

"If the CIA is involved, why didn't they just call up the FBI? They aren't supposed to be operating like this in the U.S. They could have had Bureau agents jump out of vans and tackle Alex the second he got near that building."

"Good question," Court answered. "Maybe Brewer is playing this close hold. She's running a shadow op. No other departments involved. I just don't know who we can trust."

"She's *got* to be working with someone. She's not a field operative. Who?"

Court admitted he had no idea, but then Zoya said, "She wouldn't be colluding with the GRU, would she?"

"That seems a stretch, even for Brewer," Court replied with genuine surprise.

Zoya shrugged. "I wouldn't put it past her."

Court still thought this was ridiculous on Zoya's part, and probably the liquor talking. He said, "Well, if Matador shows up, you can ask him if he's working with her."

"If he shows up, how about I just shoot him?" Zoya asked.

"That might be best." Then Court cocked his head. "You have a gun?"

"Two, actually." She smiled a little. "I have a two-inch Smith you can borrow."

Court nodded at this. "Beats throwing rocks, I guess. Actually, I've got Lacy's SIG."

Zoya gave Court a disapproving look. "Yeah, she won't be needing it."

She then wiped the remaining tears from her eyes, picked her phone up off the table, and turned it over. Court could see several text messages.

"Shit," she mumbled.

"What?"

"Alex . . . He's been trying to reach me."

"He okay?"

Just then the door to the bar opened; Zoya looked past Court and then showed obvious relief. Court turned to see Alex Velesky enter, alone; he headed right for their table but slowed when he saw Court. He continued forward, a questioning look on his face as his eyes flashed over to Zoya.

Court was the Gray Man, and this meant no one ever sized him up as a potent force, a threat, but somehow this Swiss banker detected danger.

Or else, Court reasoned, the man might have just been a scaredy-cat who was afraid of everyone.

To dispel this as quickly as possible, he extended a hand. "Hi, Alex."

Velesky shook his hand. He was amped up; he had something he wanted to tell Zoya, Court was certain, but first he was trying to figure out what this stranger was all about.

Court tried to help. "We met briefly, in Switzerland."

Velesky cocked his head. "Oh . . . we did?"

"Yeah. You might remember. You knocked my ass out of a moving train."

The poor man's eyes widened; he lurched back a little in utter shock.

Court followed with, "It's okay. I guess I had it coming."

Zoya giggled now, the first time Court had heard that beautiful noise in over a year. She said, "Alex, meet . . ." She seemed to struggle for a name, then said, "Charlie. He's going to help us. Trust me, we want him on our side." She turned to Court. "Charlie, Alex knows me as Beth."

Court looked at Zoya, mouthed *Charlie?* questioningly, but then looked back to Alex. "Pull up a barstool."

Velesky did so reluctantly. When they were all seated close to one another, the Ukrainian said, "How . . . how are you alive?"

"Everybody keeps asking me that. You've got a pretty good shoulder charge. Soccer? Rugby?"

Velesky was still dumbfounded that he was talking to the man he thought he'd killed. But he shook his head. "Hockey."

"Hockey," Court said. "Makes sense." Court changed the subject. "I was sent to hunt you down. I know Beth, and when I saw her on the train and realized she was *helping* you, I knew in that moment that I was probably playing on the wrong team." He added, "I also found out some information on my own. That's what led me here, to Ezra Altman."

This was a lot to take in, Court understood, and Alex was accordingly slow to process it.

Zoya tried to help. "We're going to watch over you. It will just be us, for now. We can't trust the U.S. government."

"Why?" Alex asked.

Court said, "Someone high up is demanding that you and your data be destroyed. We don't know exactly *how* high this goes, who's involved . . . honestly, there's a bunch of shit we don't know. But Beth and I *do* know we can trust each other, and we will keep you safe."

Velesky nodded; he seemed to be with the program now. "That's basically what Altman just told me."

Zoya cocked her head. "What's that?"

"I told the guard at the lobby the pseudonym I gave Altman, then waited for fifteen minutes. I thought they'd lead me up to his office, but instead he came down."

"What did he say?" Court said.

"He took me aside, shook my hand, and stuck a note in it. He said it's the number for a burner phone he keeps in a safe in his bedroom. He doesn't trust the government security men around him, thinks they've stopped watching for threats against him and have started spying on him."

"Shit," Court said, rubbing his face with his hands.

"Yeah, and he thinks his office and house are bugged. He told me we could text tonight after he goes to bed, but we absolutely could *not* meet." He looked at Zoya. "I didn't have the Krupkin data on me when I met him, so I don't know how we're going to get it to him now."

Zoya said, "There was too great a chance you could have been captured; I couldn't give you Krupkin's phone." She then asked, "Do you think he will work with you?"

"He's very interested in what I have, so yes, we don't have to worry about him turning me away. We *do*, however, have to worry about all the guys with guns surrounding him."

Court said, "If we can communicate with him clandestinely through his burner, then I can find a way to get him the data."

Alex replied, "He gave me the address to his home, as well."

He handed the note over to Court, who took it and typed it into a Signal text for Lacy. After he hit send, he handed the paper to Zoya.

Court said, "If Altman can't trust the people protecting him, and if GRU and CIA are after him, then we don't have a hell of a lot of time."

"Neither does he," Zoya said.

Court rose. "I'm going to go outside and make a phone call."

Suspiciously, Zoya said, "A call to who?"

"Someone who can get the news out, once we actually have some news. You guys have a place to stay?"

Zoya nodded. "Yeah, we rented a suite on East Fiftieth and Third."

"We'll go there," Court said. "Recon Altman's neighborhood remotely on the laptop for a couple of hours while Angela gets us a safe house in that area and some equipment we'll need. We'll work up a plan to get the phone to Altman tonight."

"Wait," Alex asked. "Who is Angela?"

"A friend," Court replied. "Someone else on our side."

Zoya crunched a piece of ice from her drink and eyed Court critically. "Allegedly."

FIFTY-SIX

At five p.m. the newsroom of the *Washington Post* was a hive of activity.

The summit at the UN Headquarters building in New York had begun this morning; word on Capitol Hill was that the following day around noon the foreign ministers would sign the accords. The Russians would then be subjected to a pro forma, sternly worded lecture from the United Nations Security Council, and then, immediately after the dressing-down, a UN resolution would be signed encouraging nations to resume trade with Russia as long as Moscow adhered to some semblance of a cease-fire.

Immediately trade would begin booming again. Gas, oil, and grain would flow; Western commercial interests inside Russia would reopen; banking and finance sanctions would be eased.

It would be the perfect ending for many, but not the perfect ending for all.

Russia would remain in control of tens of thousands of square miles of Ukrainian territory, having killed tens of thousands of people, many civilians, in the war. Ukraine, being Ukraine, would not accept the accords and would continue its attempt to push into Russian and separatist-held regions, but Western nations would agree to stop supplying Ukraine with weaponry.

In the name of lasting peace.

Everyone knew, whether they were admitting it publicly or not, that Russia would be the net winner of this agreement, with the West benefiting, as well, in terms of trade and relations with Russia.

Ukraine, on the other hand, would be the loser, but the West could say the Realpolitik of the moment meant this was the best outcome for all, Kiev included, because the situation had become so perilous.

Needless to say, the *Washington Post* was all over this story, attacking it from various angles with reporters here in Washington, at the United Nations building in New York, and in Ukraine itself.

Senior national security reporter Catherine King had been mining her sources here in D.C. for days, trying to determine Russia's next move once emboldened by the trade pact and the peace agreement. According to military and intelligence leaders—speaking on background, of course—the signing of the New York accords would embolden Russia and allow it to declare victory domestically and retool, rearm, and reequip militarily. Many highly placed officials asserted the signing of the accords would lead to inevitable attacks on Lithuania and other border nations before long.

King was a reporter; she didn't get to express her opinion in her work, but personally she was flummoxed by the shortsightedness of the West. She'd be here late tonight, working on her piece up until, she was certain, her ten p.m. deadline.

As she transcribed her notes from an interview she'd conducted today with the director of a Near East think tank in their offices in Adams Morgan, her phone rang on her desk. Snatching it up distractedly, she said, "Catherine King" while grabbing a pen and a notepad, a second-nature habit of hers after thirty years as a journalist.

An unfamiliar male voice spoke up. "Miss King. You might remember me, we met a couple years ago. In D.C."

King had met thousands of people in D.C., and she didn't have time for a long back-and-forth. "Maybe I will remember you if you give me your name."

"Well . . . that's the thing. I'd rather not."

King didn't even look up from her notes as she spoke. "Look, friend, I meet you secret-squirrel types all the time. I'm sure you feel you're special, maybe you are. But I can't recall every single contact I've made in the intelligence realm by the sound of a voice."

"That's fair." There was a pause, and then, "I'm the guy you went to Israel to learn about."

Catherine King dropped her pen and looked up from her notes now. She said nothing for several seconds.

"Ringing any bells?"

Now the woman replied softly, "How do I know it's you?"

"You zapped me in the neck with a stun gun once. Did you ever tell anyone else about that?"

"Of course not."

"Me, either. It's embarrassing, frankly."

King recovered quickly. "It's nice to hear from you. So glad you are still among us."

"For now, anyway." The senior national security investigative reporter had met the former Agency operative when he'd been in D.C. trying to find out why the CIA was trying to kill him. She'd been a great help in his success in this endeavor, both in shepherding him through his predicament and in finding answers from his past, and he and Catherine had parted ways with strong mutual respect.

"How can I help you?" she asked. The individual known as the Gray Man had her full and undivided attention now.

"Would you be able to come to New York?"

King cocked her head. "For what reason?"

"A meeting with me. A meeting that will make for one hell of a story."

The pause was brief. "As big as last time?"

"So much more important than last time." He laughed into the phone and said, "This time you'd get to print it."

King raised her eyebrows. The CIA had appealed to her to not report what she'd learned from this man years earlier, but now the same asset who'd provided her with one of the biggest stories of her life was promising he could top it. If so, she instantly told herself, she'd print what she learned, the Agency be damned.

She said, "I'd love to speak with you, but I am reporting on the meeting at the UN, remotely at the moment, and have an article due—"

"This is directly related to that. I will introduce you to someone when you get here who will give you crucial information that you couldn't get any other way."

"Who?"

He did not answer. "In person. It has to be."

"Okay. Give me three hours to finish my article, and then I'll take the ten p.m. express train. It arrives at Penn Station at one fifty-five. I can meet you tomorrow morning."

"That will be fine."

"Where?"

"I'll give you a number." He read off a phone number, which she wrote down, and indicated she should use Signal to contact him. "Call me at seven a.m. tomorrow and I'll tell you where to go."

King nodded, then said, "Can you give me any more context as to what is going on?"

The man replied, "See you tomorrow. You won't be disappointed."

"I believe you."

"And, one more thing. Don't tell anyone you are coming. This goes high, we don't know how high yet, but I'm not trusting anyone."

"Except me?"

"You did right by me before. I hope they haven't gotten to you since."

With a commanding voice she said, "*Nobody* gets to me."

"Good."

It was all such subterfuge, Catherine said to herself as she hung up, but this man was the real deal, and she'd go to New York to see what he had to tell her.

At six forty-five p.m., Petro Mozgovoy unlocked the front door of a three-story clapboard-façade bungalow on Windsor Avenue in East Rutherford, New Jersey.

The property deed was in the name of a trust that meant nothing to anyone, and the home, while usually unoccupied, was kept neat and arranged by a monthly maid service that was paid in cash. Utilities were paid in cash, as well, at a grocery store up the street, and when anyone *did* stay at the residence, they kept the blinds drawn.

Neighbors assumed the small property to be an Airbnb managed rather unsuccessfully, but no one paid much attention to the house, since no one there ever caused any trouble and it looked like most every other building on the street.

· Mozgovoy took off his coat and hung it in a closet, then walked around the entire house, the old hardwood floor creaking with each step.

In each room he waved a handheld device with an antenna slowly as he walked around, checking the property for bugs. It was a frequency detector; it electronically scanned the area for hidden wireless microphones and cameras. He didn't think there was any chance the FBI would be aware of his safe house, but having fought in a brutal war for nine years, he knew better than to leave anything to chance when it came to his enemy.

An hour after he arrived, he had the stereo playing through the home's built-in ceiling speakers. Electronic dance music contrasted wildly with the staid décor of the place, but the noise would further serve to inhibit any other types of surveillance. Laser listening devices could be positioned up to four hundred meters away; as long as they had a line of sight on a window of the home, a surveillance expert could record conversations inside, but the thumping bass and tinny high tones of the music would confound the lasers and obfuscate any voices inside.

He barely heard the doorbell through the music, but he'd been listening for it, so when it chimed, he went downstairs to the entry hall and looked through the glass.

Two men in heavy coats stood there in the dark because Petro hadn't turned on the porch light. But he recognized them and unlocked the two dead bolts on the front door, and then he let them in, relocking the door behind them immediately.

The pair were grizzled-looking men with square jaws and distant, mistrustful eyes, and it would be clear to anyone who saw them that they were related. The Bondarenko brothers came from the Donbas town of Toretsk; they had fought on the front lines in the war against Ukraine for nearly a decade, and they, like Petro, were Ukrainian separatists with Russian ancestral roots. Taras was thirty-nine, Evgen thirty-six, and they'd been pulled into the separatist intelligence service at the beginning of Russia's wide invasion of Ukraine, same as Petro himself.

Petro found the Bondarenko brothers to be capable fighters, but he also appreciated their cover jobs. They ran a small Brooklyn hardware store, and this meant they had easy access to all manner of equipment the cell needed to prepare for its missions.

Shortly after the Bondarenkos went into the kitchen to pour themselves some tea, there was a knock at the door. Petro checked the stoop, then opened the door to let two more men in. The Ostopenko duo were not brothers but rather a twenty-year-old named Pasha and his thirty-six-year-old uncle, Arsen. Arsen Ostopenko had served as a senior sergeant in the war since its opening days, and though he did not speak much English and had never been out of eastern Ukraine prior to his trip to New York, he possessed sufficient intelligence and more than enough cruelty to do whatever Petro Mozgovoy demanded.

He worked in a boxing gym in Manhattan's Little Ukraine on the Lower East Side, and he was tough as nails. His nephew Pasha had studied English for a couple of years in school, but equally important for the mission, he was a welterweight boxer and an aspiring MMA fighter. He, like his uncle Taras, was from Luhansk, and Mozgovoy knew he was lucky to have them on his team.

Olek Kuzmenko arrived alone. He was just twenty-two, but he spoke fluent English with very little accent, and he knew New York City like the back of his hand, having grown up in Bensonhurst before returning to Donbas at seventeen to join the fight. The intelligence services had picked him out of his front-line infantry unit because of his language skills, and Petro relied on Olek to impersonate a WASPy American around other Ukrainians during surveillance missions, when paying bills in cash for the cell, and when doing other jobs where a Russian-sounding accent might cause problems.

Antoin Zhuk arrived just after Kuzmenko. He was thirty-one, from a tiny village in Luhansk Oblast, but he'd lived in Pittsburgh for a few years, working as a car mechanic for his expatriate uncle. He, unlike the rest of the team, had not been trained by the Russians but rather by Petro himself, along with the former GRU man who ran a laundromat in Manhattan and advised the cell on behalf of Moscow.

Barabash came next. Mozgovoy only knew him by one name. A former enforcer for the Ukrainian mob, he'd lived in the USA for two years, working in a bakery in Queens. He'd gone back home to fight at the beginning of the Russian invasion over a year earlier, but he'd never seen combat. The Security Service Battalion snatched him out of a recruitment line after someone had recognized him, and he was told he was needed for a dangerous mission back in the nation he had just left.

Barabash was heavyset but strong, and his sunken eyes and Cro-Magnon forehead telegraphed menace long before he used his mouth or his fists to do the same. Unlike bright-eyed and cheery Antoin Zhuk, Barabash was not used for surveillance work, as he stood out in any crowd.

Yeva Nesterenko arrived as a light snow began to fall outside; he brushed it off his coat as he entered, then took off his glasses and wiped the fog off them.

Yeva was twenty-six, both the smallest and the best-educated on the team, having graduated from the University of Luhansk with a degree in English. He'd been recruited by the SSB after the war started; they'd plucked him, as they had Barabash, out of a recruitment line and quickly identified his intelligence and language skills. He'd excelled in tradecraft training in Russia, and what he lacked in strength and combat capabilities, he more than made up for with his clever brain and unceasing energy.

Yeva was, essentially, Mozgovoy's second-in-command. Arsen Ostopenko had been the same rank as Petro in the military, and he was a decade older than Yeva Nesterenko, but Petro relied on Yeva for counsel, not Arsen.

The last member of the ad hoc unit to arrive was the lone woman, but that was by design. Twenty-nine-year-old Kristina Golubova had been watching the comings and goings in the neighborhood all afternoon, since Mozgovoy had put her in a third-floor walk-up across the street, and she served as countersurveillance every time the team met.

Kristina had trained as a citizen soldier in the Ukrainian territorial defense in Kramatorsk, Donbas, before the conflict in Ukraine began, but then her husband, a Ukrainian army captain, pledged allegiance to the separatists, and she followed suit.

She served in noncombat roles in the Donbas People's Militia, while her infantry officer husband quickly rose to the rank of major.

When the Russians entered Ukraine proper, they'd ordered her husband's unit south to the front lines to the east of Kherson. On the fifty-first day of the war, he was blown to bits when the armored personnel carrier he'd been traveling in was hit by a Javelin missile given to the Ukrainians by America.

Kristina had not yet retrieved his body parts and put him in the ground when she'd gone to the Donetsk People's Republic Security Service Battalion and demanded to be sent behind enemy lines to assassinate those responsible.

Her request eventually passed across the desk of a GRU officer, and he called her in for a meeting; he told her if she really wanted to strike a blow to honor her dead husband, he would train her in Russia, then send her on a trip to the United States, so that America itself could begin to share in the burden of this war.

By seven forty-five, all ten members of the SSB cell were assembled in the white clapboard house in East Rutherford, drinking tea or coffee, sitting around and waiting on a meeting that Petro had yet to brief them on.

Fifteen minutes later, Petro Mozgovoy got a text telling him Luka was outside. Puzzled that he hadn't just come to the door and knocked, Petro went outside himself and stood on the porch, looking around at the snowfall on the one-lane street.

All was quiet for several seconds, and then men vaulted over the railings on both sides of the porch and pushed Mozgovoy back inside, then more men rushed in behind them, weapons on their shoulders.

All ten Ukrainians in the house were caught by surprise.

Four men entered in all; they carried submachine guns, and they corralled everyone into the living room in a matter of seconds.

Petro thought this must have been the FBI, though the attackers were dressed in civilian clothes and wore ski masks on their faces.

And then the front door opened again, and Petro saw Luka.

He just stared at the GRU officer. What was going on? Had he been duped? Was this Russian speaker in fact an agent of America?

Luka wasn't carrying a subgun like the others, but as he limped in with the walking boot on his left foot, his North Face coat shifted open a little, and a quick flash of the black grip of a pistol was evident jutting out of his waistband at the appendix.

The boot made loud footfalls on the creaky hardwood floor, until Luka stood still in the center of the room. He slowly regarded the ten sitting on the sofa and standing at the walls, and then he focused on Petro Mozgovoy, standing not far from the front window. In Russian he said, "Please tell me we trained you better than this at the Aquarium."

Petro felt a slow wash of relief at first. Luka *was* GRU; he had just charged in here to teach the Ukrainian cell some sort of lesson. But his relief didn't last. He was angry at being made a fool of in front of his cell, and he felt the shame of it all, so he spoke with defiance. "I wasn't trained at the Aquarium. I was trained at a makeshift school in an old factory in Kursk."

"Nevertheless, you need to work on your tradecraft, don't you?"

Still with defiance, Petro said, "We have cameras, motion detectors, alarms. Normally, I wouldn't unlock the door and stand there, but you texted me that you were outside."

With a motion of Luka's hand, the four ski-masked men lowered their weapons, then secured them in their coats, hanging them from single-point slings under their arms.

One of Luka's men stepped up to Mozgovoy and extended a hand. "No hard feelings, tovarich. We're just making a point."

Petro shook the man's hand reluctantly. "What was the point?"

Luka answered for his underling. "That we are here doing a serious job, up against serious adversaries, and even though you aren't actual GRU intelligence officers, we are going to hold you to that high standard."

"Of course," Petro said, and he could feel the tension in the room from his cell members decrease.

But only until Luka spoke again. "Two nights ago, I lost five men, and another asset assigned to me, going after the same asset we are seeking here in New York."

Kristina Golubova spoke up now. "Geneva?" When everyone turned to look at her sitting on the sofa, she said, "It was on the news. Russian nationals killed in Geneva, along with civilians. Said nothing about . . . about what they were doing there."

Luka nodded. "These men here with me? They are no better trained than the five men I lost. Our adversary is a very dangerous foe."

Petro said, "I believe you. But . . . I and my people, the mission we've trained for . . . it could end America's involvement in the war."

Luka sighed. "I know nothing about the mission you've trained for, nor do I care. But the mission I am sending you on"—he waved at his own men—"along with the five of us, if it fails, it will prolong the war, damage Russia, and, by consequence, the DPR. Forget about what you were planning on doing. Concentrate on the mission at hand."

Petro nodded slowly, looking around at his cell, then back at the Russians. "The dining room, it is where we have our meetings. More spacious."

"Fine," Luka said, and then, "Can we change the music? I hate techno."

"We play it to subvert laser listening devices."

With an annoyed tone, Luka said, "I know why you are playing music. But pick something else. Soft rock, played loud, works just as well."

Five minutes later, the ten cell members sat at an oblong wooden table for twelve, while the four masked GRU officers stood around the home, looking out windows with their guns ready. Luka paced the dining room slowly, circling the Ukrainians, while yacht rock boomed throughout the house.

To begin his meeting, he said, "A man named Ezra Altman lives in a brownstone on West Eighty-First Street along with his wife and two children, teenaged boys. Altman's home has a full-time security force of four. Two out front, two inside. Police make regular patrols, as well."

"Altman is the target?" Petro asked.

Luka shook his head. "He is the bait. A man will make contact with him. When he does, we will go after that man. He is believed to be carrying information that could be troublesome for my nation, and your nation, as well."

"What about his office? Where does he work?"

"He works in Midtown Manhattan, but his office is protected by Homeland Security officers." Luka hesitated, then said, "We will conduct operations at his home, because we do not assess that our target will risk contact with American federal agents.

"I have secured a location across the street from Altman's property, and we will begin conducting surveillance. When the target arrives, we will eliminate him and retrieve his product."

Luka added, "His target is not alone. There are two individuals helping him, and these two individuals killed many or maybe all of my five men the other night." He stopped pacing and looked around at the table full of Ukrainians. "They will kill you, as well, unless you do everything I say."

Petro asked, "When do we begin surveillance?"

"Right now. You and four of your cell will accompany us to our safe house, and then in eight hours, you will be relieved by the rest of your team. Eight-hour shifts will continue until the operation is complete."

Luka pulled an iPad out of his pack and brought up a picture of Velesky. He slid it onto the table. "Here is your target. Study his face, because this mission must not fail." He looked around a moment. "And don't let me catch you with your guard down again." He sighed, looking the team over carefully before addressing Mozgovoy. "Pick half of your team and let's go."

FIFTY-SEVEN

While Alex Velesky rested in one of the two bedrooms in the suite at the Kimberly Hotel, Court Gentry and Zoya Zakharova sat in the small living room conducting online research on the neighborhood around West 81st Street, where Ezra Altman lived with his family.

They didn't dare go in person—not yet, anyway—because they were worried Brewer or the Russians might already be monitoring security cameras in place there looking for Velesky, but they used Google Maps to survey neighboring streets. They evaluated access vectors to the property, surveyed the rooftops of the nearby buildings, and looked over the shops and bars and restaurants, checking camera angles.

The conversation between them remained on their work; for the most part, Court got the idea that Zoya was better when she had something to do. When he'd found her there in the bar that afternoon, she'd been alone with her thoughts, and whatever it was that was getting to her right now must have been internal, because alone with her thoughts seemed to be the most dangerous place for her.

Court decided that the two of them had a lot more to discuss besides this operation, but it would be better to wait until *after* the op to do so.

For now, he needed her sharp and focused.

He received a Signal message just after ten p.m., and then he woke up Velesky, and the three of them packed up and went downstairs, and Zoya had the valet bring her vehicle around. She'd rented a gray Toyota Sienna minivan, and with it they drove to the Upper West Side, to West 87th Street, halfway between Columbus Avenue and Amsterdam Avenue. Here they found street parking, then went to a five-story brownstone apartment building and took the steps off the sidewalk not up but down to a small basement apartment with a tiny front door completely invisible from the street.

Court knocked, and Angela Lacy opened the door.

The CIA officer had rented the furnished space earlier this evening after getting Altman's address from the man she knew as Six, and as soon as she had the keys, she'd spent the next few hours running around in Ubers, buying things they would need for the work they had in store.

As Zoya, Alex, and Court entered the small space, Court made quick introductions.

"Angela, this is . . . Beth."

The two shook hands but said nothing, and Court felt a pang of anxiety when he saw the expressions on the women's faces. There was mistrust from both sides, this much was clear, and only Court's assurances had put these two people together, when they clearly did not want anything to do with each other.

Court then said, "And, Angela, I'm Charlie." When she looked at him quizzically, he added, "Just roll with it."

He then introduced Velesky to Lacy. The CIA officer said, "I hope the material you have is as valuable as you say it is."

Alex nodded. "It is. Or it *will* be, if I can share it with Ezra Altman."

"That's why we're here," Court said, and he looked to Lacy. "Did you get everything I asked for?"

With an annoyed look, she said, "Yeah, eventually. I wish you'd sent me your shopping list all at once instead of over a three-hour period. I've been all over the place trying to get everything you asked for."

"Our plan came together in pieces."

"What *is* the plan?" Alex asked.

The four of them sat on cheap fake leather sofas in the living room of the little rental, and Court pulled up Google Maps on an iPad. Finding Altman's home on West 81st Street, he scooted the image to the right. "Okay, we are taking it as fact that someone will be watching every doorbell camera, every traffic light camera, every commercial CCTV device around Altman's home, looking for Alex to show up."

Everyone else in the room agreed.

"This is a neighborhood of row houses. All these buildings on the south side of West Eighty-Second are connected, as are all the buildings on the north side of Eighty-First where Altman lives. There's an alley between the two rows, and every single door back there is going to have a security camera with motion detector lights, so we can't use that to access the rear of Altman's building." He touched a point on the satellite image. "But right here, about five buildings down from Amsterdam Avenue, the roof of the building on Eighty-Second is one story higher and only about fifteen feet away from the roof of the building on Eighty-First on the other side of the alley."

Zoya took over now. "So, Charlie and I access the rooftop of this apartment building on the corner of Eighty-Second and Amsterdam via the fire escape, and we make our way over to the five-story building. Charlie jumps across the alley, and I throw him one of the two ropes Angela bought tonight."

Alex looked at Court with bewilderment. "You can jump fifteen feet?"

"When I have to, I can. And since it's five stories down to a concrete alleyway, I really *do* have to."

Zoya continued. "Once he secures his line to something on the roof there, he goes across the roofs of the brownstones on Eighty-First towards Altman's house while I secure the other end of the rope on the roof on Eighty-Second."

Court said, "Alex, you tell Altman to go out to his fourth-floor balcony. I'll drop down from the roof and give him Krupkin's phone, then retrace my steps, using the rope to get back to Eighty-Second Street. Beth and I move back to Amsterdam, climb down the fire escape we used before, and then head back here."

Angela Lacy hadn't spoken, but now she said, "What about cameras on Amsterdam? How do we know Brewer or the Russians aren't just running facial sweep algorithms on the entire neighborhood?"

"Beth and I will be well disguised."

She nodded. "Well, *that* explains a lot of the stuff you made me go buy."

Alex said, "So, I just have to text Altman that a man will appear on his back balcony sometime in the middle of the night and give him the data." He ran a hand through his hair. "My part is easy."

Court said, "So is yours, Angela. I need you to just stay back here and monitor our comms."

She looked at him a moment, then said, "I'll be watching through all the same cameras Brewer will be accessing."

Court was confused. "What? You can get into the cams around here? How so?"

"I've got an all-access pass to intelligence collection."

"But . . . you aren't on the op to find Velesky any longer."

Lacy hesitated, looking to Alex and Zoya. Back to Court, she said, "Can you and I speak in private?"

Court turned to Velesky. "Take five. Go in one of the bedrooms."

Alex did as instructed. As soon as the door shut, Lacy looked at Zoya, but Court said, "Anything you want to say to me, you can say in front of her."

"Actually . . . no, I can't."

"Why not?"

"Because this is classified, and whatever the hell she is, she's *not* Agency."

"I just love it when people talk about me as if I'm not sitting right in front of them," Zoya growled.

"Look," Court appealed. "We need to all be on the same page here."

"But she's not Agency!" Lacy repeated.

"Wait," Zoya said with confusion. "You think *he's* Agency?"

Angela was herself momentarily confused. Then she said, "I was tasked to work with him by Brewer, and of course I assumed he was another ops officer. Whatever he is, I know he works with the Agency, at least as an—"

Zoya turned to Court. "She doesn't even know who you are, does she?"

Court sighed inwardly. "We're getting lost in the weeds here." He looked back to Lacy and spoke emphatically. "If you can tell me, then you can tell her."

Lacy was exasperated. "Not sure if you have the social skills to pick up on this or not, Six, but your dear Russian comrade and I do not like one another."

Court closed his eyes. Interpersonal relationships were always so complicated to him, and he felt like he'd gotten no better at navigating them as he'd grown older. "You don't have to like her, but I'm asking you to trust her."

"Trust a Russian. What could go wrong?"

Zoya just looked on. Court was surprised she wasn't standing up for herself here, but he attributed it to her mental state.

Lacy didn't look happy about it, but she did seem to recognize they were wasting time. After looking at Zoya a moment more, she returned her attention to Court. "Okay. Brewer contacted me the other day, just after Saint Lucia, and she told me we now had access to anything we wanted, intelligence collection wise."

"But . . ." Court was confused. "That was when you were hunting Alex."

Lacy shook her head. "We were never officially hunting Alex himself. Brewer needed entrée to everything without anyone knowing what we were doing, so she tied searching for Alex into another ongoing manhunt. A Special Access Program, something so high-level, so widespread, that it gave us the keys to the kingdom, and that kingdom included any domestic surveillance we required. I checked my access this afternoon while you were watching Altman's office. I'm still in. It means I can get into Homeland Security computers, and then monitor the same cameras Brewer has access to."

Zoya's mouth opened a little and hung there, and then she said, "Oh shit. I think I see where this is going."

Court, however, did not. "Who was the stated target of this operation?"

Lacy sighed. Clearly she hated talking in front of a former Russian agent. Finally, she said, "A program called Bloody Angel. It's targeting an ex-Agency asset named Courtland Gentry. There's been a kill order out for him forever, and it's one of just a very few existing manhunts so wide-reaching that—"

She stopped talking when Zoya blurted out a loud laugh.

Court gave Zoya an angry eye, but she just put her hand over her face and continued laughing.

"What?" Lacy asked, genuinely perplexed. The brooding Russian woman was suddenly almost in hysterics.

"Beth," Court said, "do you mind giving us a minute?"

The brunette shook her head adamantly. "There is no fucking way I'm leaving this room right now."

"What's going on?" Lacy asked, becoming annoyed that she was in the dark.

Zoya said, "Tell her."

Court groaned a little, but he turned back to Lacy.

"Tell me *what*?"

"Brewer was hunting for Alex . . . by hunting for the guy she had hunting for Alex."

"*What?*"

"I'm Court Gentry."

Lacy folded her arms; she wasn't buying any of this shit. Zoya, on the other hand, laughed again as she looked at Court. "How many times have I told you Brewer tried to kill you? And still, you keep working with her."

Lacy's face changed from incredulity, to bafflement, to realization.

After a time, she said, "You . . . you are the Gray Man?"

"Give the girl a prize!" Zoya said.

But Lacy wasn't listening. Looking at the table in front of her a moment, she said, "It all makes sense now. Holy shit." She was having trouble processing this new information, but Court just sat silently.

Finally, she looked up at him. "They said you killed your Ground Branch team, went solo."

Court said, "It was a little more complicated than that."

"But you *did* kill Agency employees?"

"Only the ones who tried to kill me."

She turned away from him. "Jesus Christ. Why on earth would they—"

"An off-book program I was put on . . . it went south. Somebody had to take the fall. It was a bullshit job from the start, but I didn't know, I just did what I was told." He sat back in his chair. "I don't just do what I'm told anymore."

Lacy asked, "Then why are you palling around with Brewer?"

"Does it look like we're palling around? I was on the run from the Agency, and she found me. And then, when they needed a deniable asset in the Caribbean who could act immediately, I suddenly proved to be useful again." Court thought about what he'd said for a second. "Well . . . she thought I'd be useful, at least."

Zoya was clearly enjoying Court's discomfort, but Lacy didn't notice.

"They say you're the guy who did the thing in L.A. The thing in Paris. That crazy shit in Kiev. That thing in Hong—"

Court interrupted. "They probably say I put the crack in the Liberty Bell, too. Don't believe everything you hear."

But it was clear Lacy did believe everything she'd been told about the Gray Man. Her jaw clenched tight a moment, and her eyes narrowed. "I can't believe Brewer sent me down to climb onto the Gray Man's boat without telling me who I was up against."

After another quick bark of laughter, Zoya said, "That's Brewer for you. She had a gun pointed at Court's head once, would have killed him if I hadn't shot her."

Lacy shook her head to clear the bafflement. "You *shot* Brewer?"

"Yeah, I would have killed her, but then this dummy shot me."

Court rubbed his face in his hands. "Guys, we really need to focus on—"

"This shit is so crazy," Lacy said. "All of you guys."

Alex Velesky opened the door of the bedroom. "Hey, it's time for me to text Altman. Are we going to do this or not?"

Court turned to Lacy. "Get those camera feeds up. We're going to need all the help we can get."

She stared at him still, but finally she nodded a little.

When Zoya stood up, she leaned over Lacy. With a smile, she said, "I figured it out for myself a couple of years ago. Didn't have to have it spelled out for me like you did."

Lacy just looked at her like she was nuts, but she didn't respond.

FIFTY-EIGHT

In a large loft apartment in a former warehouse on West 58th Street, Suzanne Brewer and Sebastian Drexler stood in the middle of ten people, each sitting at a workstation with multiple laptops open in front of them.

Drexler and his people had converted the posh rental unit into a makeshift tactical operations center over the past several hours, and now, to Suzanne, it appeared to be not dissimilar to remote CIA TOCs she'd worked at around the world.

Brewer was the only Agency representative in the room, but Drexler's people, she could tell, were first-rate surveillance technicians. Even so, she knew they couldn't have gotten one-quarter the access they had without her help. She'd logged in to a secure Homeland Security digital clearinghouse for local camera access and set a five-block radius around the Upper West Side residence of Ezra Altman, and this information was split among the workstations, while built-in software read and identified faces visible on the cams.

While Drexler and his group were busy monitoring, Brewer had been working the phones, and in so doing, she'd made contact with a member of Altman's office's Homeland Security team. Using her Agency bona fides, the man confirmed that Altman had left work at six forty-five p.m. and was driven directly home by his close protection unit, and another team of four men would watch him and his family throughout the night.

The security officer said that, on order of the deputy director of Homeland Security, Altman's offices were bugged, and his phone was regularly snuck away from him at work and checked for the presence of clandestine communications apps. Further, one person on each security detail was tasked with keeping an eye on him to note anyone he met with either while at work or away from it.

Brewer was aware she was breaking laws, but it was nice to know she wasn't the only one doing so. Either Kirby had gotten Homeland Security involved in all this, or else someone high in Homeland Security had their own reasons for keeping Krupkin's data undiscovered.

Either way, as far as Brewer was concerned, her eyes remained on the prize. Two of her bosses—both former Deputy Director for Operations Hanley and current Director of the CIA Kirby—had seemed dead set on using her for denied operations, and this told her the only way to advance up the career ladder was to finagle her way into the DDO spot, where she would have more leverage and the ability to send others out into the gray to do the dirty work.

But she would only ascend if Velesky and his information disappeared.

To this aim, Brewer tried to anticipate her target's next move.

If Velesky made contact with Altman, everyone agreed, it would be in person, or else it would be through his surrogate, Zoya Zakharova. She just had to find out about this contact, and then she just had to get Drexler to send his Russian bastards in to kill everyone involved.

Just as she poured herself a cup of coffee in the kitchen, Drexler stepped up to her. "I just spoke with the leader of my assets."

"You mean the Russians."

"One of the Russians, yes. They are moving into position now to begin the surveillance phase. They will have people ready to hit Velesky in the street before he has a chance to make contact with Altman, assuming that is his plan."

"Good. If nothing happens tonight, and Velesky comes to Altman's office tomorrow, I'll be notified by Altman's security detail."

"We can't get into his office," Drexler said.

Brewer shrugged a little. "It certainly would not be ideal, but if we absolutely had to, I think I could find a way."

Brewer left Drexler in the kitchen as she headed back to watch over the surveillance technicians. She stepped up to a young man whom she knew to have a German accent and who looked like he might have been of Turkish descent.

"What cameras are you watching?" she asked.

"Right now I'm looking at live cameras at Altman's office on East Fifty-Second."

"But . . . he went home hours ago."

"Correct. I'm just moving around the system in his office as a test run, just in case Velesky doesn't show up at the house tonight and we need to check in real time at his office tomorrow."

"Good," Brewer said, and she began to walk to the next workstation to check on that person's duties, but instead, something occurred to her.

"If you're in his office servers, does that give you the ability to look at camera recordings?"

"Yes, of course. Want me to check something?"

"I want you to check everything. Altman's security said all his meetings today were with known clients, and he didn't go out for lunch. There's probably nothing, but maybe just double-check that for me."

He nodded, then looked up to Drexler, who had overheard the last of the conversation.

The Swiss man said, "You heard the woman, Franz."

"Ja, Herr Drexler."

On the south side of West 81st Street, Luka Rudenko stood in a completely blacked-out third-floor bedroom and looked out the window across the street. Altman's home was five houses down on the left, but the brownstones on this street were narrow, four and five stories tall, so Luka could see Altman's front stoop from where he stood.

Two of his GRU men were here, along with five of his DPR separatists, including their leader, Petro Mozgovoy. The rest were back at the house in East Rutherford, resting until their shifts began at five a.m.

"There's a police precinct on Eighty-Second," Luka said. "Whatever we have to do, we have to do it quietly."

"I understand," Petro said.

"My people here in the city are up on the cameras in the neighborhood. We just need to be armed and ready to take Velesky the second he arrives."

At one fifty a.m., Court Gentry stood in the middle of the basement apartment on West 87th Street, doing everything he could not to breathe through his nose.

Alex and Angela were in the living room with him, and they, too, were having difficulty breathing regularly now, because Court smelled like rotting garbage.

Zoya had spent the last forty-five minutes working on the clothing Lacy had purchased that evening at a Goodwill in Chelsea, making it dirty by first taking the items out into the back alleyway, then wiping them around on the inside walls of a dumpster. She then took used wet coffee grounds from the kitchen and rubbed them on the knee and elbow areas of the clothing.

Court now wore dirty black jeans, a black long-sleeved T-shirt, a torn but thick rust-colored wool cardigan under a light zip-up nylon jacket, and a filthy gray watch cap, none of which fit him well, but all of which would help maintain his cover as he approached Ezra Altman's home, as well as keep him all but invisible in the darkness.

He had an earbud in his ear under his hair and cap; Lacy's SIG Sauer P226 in a holster at his three-o'clock position; and a flashlight, a multitool, and Zoya's four-inch folding knife all on his person. The money belt with Krupkin's iPhone was still in Zoya's possession, but he'd need to cinch that under his clothes around his waist before they left.

He also had four Advil in his bloodstream, taking away a measure of the pain he was still suffering from after getting knocked out of the train two nights earlier.

He was ready to go now, but Zoya was still in the bathroom, apparently working on her own disguise.

Court stepped into the bedroom, then knocked on the bathroom door. "It's time."

"Yeah, just one more minute."

Court stood there in the bedroom, but Velesky came through the door to the living room, then motioned for him to follow him back out.

Angela sat at a little dinette table; she wore her headphones and was completely fixated on her computer, and it didn't seem as though she was listening.

"What's up?" Court asked Alex.

The Ukrainian moved closer to Court, a little wince on his face as if the smell of garbage was still giving him trouble. Softly, he said, "I get the impression it's been a long time since you and Beth have seen each other."

"So?"

"So . . . I just wanted to let you know something."

Court wasn't about to discuss his love life with a guy who, up until a week earlier, had been funneling funds into the West for Russian intelligence. He started to walk back into the bedroom, but Alex took him by the arm, halting his progress.

Court looked at him with annoyance, but before he could speak, Alex said, "I don't know if you know about . . . her . . ." His voice trailed off.

"Her *what*?" He spoke louder than Alex clearly wanted him to; he brought a finger to his mouth and looked back over his shoulder at the closed bedroom door.

"Her . . . problem."

"What do you mean?"

He looked at Angela, then back to Court. "I'm not talking about the alcohol. I'm talking about the coke."

Court's eyebrows furrowed, but he said nothing.

Alex continued. "Didn't think you knew. I caught her doing cocaine a few days ago; she was amped up another time, probably did it again then. I don't think she smuggled any into the U.S., but last night when she went out to get the guns . . . I don't know, she had the opportunity, anyway." He added, "And she has the cash. She traveled here with at least twenty thousand U.S. dollars."

Shit, Court thought. He tried not to show any of the concern he now felt, and instead he just said, "It's fine. I'll take care of it."

"And as for the drinking," Alex went on, "it's bad. Watched her do a full bottle of vodka on the drive from Switzerland to France. When she doesn't get alcohol for twelve hours or so, she's an absolute mess."

This was, quite possibly, the last thing Court needed to hear right now, both for operational reasons and because he loved Zoya, and it pained him enough already to see how fragile she was. Knowing she was using a drug classified by federal and state law enforcement as a narcotic stimulant just to make it through the day only added to his fears about her well-being.

He was still thinking of something to say when Zoya appeared out of the bedroom dressed like a homeless person herself. Filthy, ragged jeans Lacy had bought at Goodwill; a threadbare and grimy sweater under a track top that itself was under a heavy and soiled canvas coat with rips in it. On her head she wore a cheap yarn cap that covered the sides of her face and could be tied below the chin, and her skin had been made splotchy and dirty looking with makeup.

There were two fifty-foot strands of coiled rope, one hooked around each side of her neck and shoulders under everything, adding size to her frame, as well.

But Court barely noticed her clothes and her size because he was too busy evaluating her eyes and her mannerisms. Her pupils were slightly dilated, he could tell, and she wiggled her nose a little as if it itched, but she didn't bring a hand up to wipe it.

He was relatively certain she'd just snorted cocaine in the bathroom.

Jesus Christ.

Zoya handed Court the phone inside the money belt. As he slipped it on, Lacy looked up from her laptop for the first time and took off her headphones.

"You look lovely." It was said to Zoya, sarcastically but not humorously. "As soon as you two leave, I'm opening the windows. I don't care that it's freezing out there."

Velesky looked to the others and said, "I told Altman I'd text him when you were on the roof. He has the sensor on his fourth-floor home office balcony door already turned off, and will sneak out there to meet you."

Lacy stood now, looked at Court, and their eyes met. "I'll be watching cameras here, and we can stay on a conference call the entire time. I'll let you know if I see anything."

Court thought a moment. "I'll initiate the call when we get down on Eighty-Second."

Lacy nodded. "Good luck."

"Thanks."

Zoya and Court left the apartment and began walking up the street towards Amsterdam Avenue, adjusting their gait to make themselves appear worn down by the effects of age and living on the streets.

Court was good at gait changing; knowing computerized gait pattern analysis was an important component in identifying targets in the field.

But as with all aspects of altering one's appearance, Zoya was better at it than he. As they walked, she instantly adopted the gait of someone with a bad back and an injury to the right hip, and she walked a little faster and more erratically than Court did.

Court rushed to catch up, and when he did, he wondered if she was really in character or if the blow she'd just done was also changing her usual mannerisms.

He wanted to talk to her about it, but she spoke first, all but whispering even though there was no one around.

"She's attractive."

Court's eyebrows furrowed as he walked. "*Who* is?"

She scoffed, then adopted her impersonation of his voice. "*Who* is?"

Court was confused at first, but then he pieced it together. "You're talking about Lacy."

"You two seem to have a little chemistry."

Court shook his head as he walked, his own gait stiff looking, not as dramatic as hers but certainly different from normal. He said, "She thinks I'm a serial killer."

"And yet she wishes you luck."

"It's not like that, Z."

"I didn't say it was like anything."

"I know what you're insinuating."

"You two would make a cute couple."

Court rolled his eyes. They were still fifty yards from the lights of Amsterdam Avenue, shuffling along the sidewalk in the low light of quiet and residential West 87th. He took a couple of breaths, thinking over his next move, then said, "You're doing blow?"

She remained silent long enough for Court to know that any defense she used would come out looking a lot like offense.

"Alex told you?"

"He did, but I would have figured it out by now, anyway. You did a bump in the bathroom, didn't you?"

"Don't get on a fucking high horse, dude. In certain situations, it helps. You'd put *anything* in your body if it gave you an edge against your adversary."

He just said, "I pretty much stick to coffee."

"Whatever."

He hesitated, then said, "I need to know I can count on you tonight."

"It would be a mistake for you to doubt my abilities or my commitment."

"It's your judgment, frankly."

"I did what I had to do to stay sharp for the mission. I'm not stupid. I know this isn't a sustainable situation. We get done with this job, we get Krupkin's and Velesky's intel out into the world to hurt Russia, and we stop this bullshit summit from succeeding, and *then* I'll get to work on fixing me.

"Until then," she added, "how about we drop this, just so you don't piss off the lady who's in charge of tying off one end of the rope that's going to keep you from falling five floors to your death?"

Annoyed but defeated, Court said, "I just worry about you."

Zoya was silent for a long moment, and then she said, "I fell apart when you left. I was in a bad place. Then the war started, and I fell apart even more."

"You didn't have a damn thing to do with that war."

"I was a Russian intelligence operative up until two years ago. I'd say I'm one of them, wouldn't you?"

"No. I wouldn't."

They both remained silent as they passed an old man in a heavy coat and thick hat walking his toy poodle, and then, when he was well behind them, Zoya said, "I'll be fine. You just worry about what you have to do tonight, what we both might have to do in the next few hours."

Court knew he had to let this go. "Okay. You can always talk to me."

"I know," she said, but it sounded to him like she was just trying to shut the conversation down.

FIFTY-NINE

A few minutes later, Court and Zoya left the lights of Amsterdam Avenue and receded into the relative darkness of West 82nd Street. They'd kept their phony gaits up the entire way, and they'd kept quiet, as even at two a.m. there were enough cars and enough people on the street that they didn't want to risk breaking cover.

Or that was what Court tried to tell himself, anyway. He also thought it possible Zoya's silence was due to the fact that she was still upset with him for calling her out about the drugs.

Either way, the silent treatment served their operational purposes at the moment.

Two doors down from the corner, they crossed to the south side of the street and stepped up to a five-story apartment building. A narrow alleyway ran down the side, and a fire escape climbed up the wall.

Court brought Lacy up on his earpiece now. "Okay, we're at the fire escape. Any updates?"

"All clear on all cams" came the professional reply from the CIA senior operations officer.

Court acknowledged, and then he and Zoya took a moment to look around, making sure there was no one in sight and double-checking for any cameras here in the darkness. Determining themselves to be in the clear, he put his hand on Zoya's shoulder.

"How do you feel?"

"Judged," she replied.

Court sighed. "I'm not judging you. I just need to know you're ready for this."

"You have no idea what I've pulled off in the past four days."

This was, indeed, true. Court didn't know what Zoya had experienced getting Velesky out of Switzerland, and then out of Europe, but he knew she'd been through hell. He told himself she'd be fine tonight, despite her current state, and he needed to worry about his own performance.

"Okay," he said. "Well . . . let's do this."

Court stood directly under the drop-down ladder and bent down a little, and Zoya faced him, then put her arms on his shoulders and a tennis shoe on his angled thigh.

Court said, "Three, two, one," and then he hoisted her into the air by her hips, and she pushed off with her leg on his thigh, leaping up and catching the lowest rung of the drop-down ladder.

She immediately began climbing up, using only her arms to do so until her feet could swing up and catch a rail, and Court looked around at the street, again making sure they hadn't been noticed by anyone.

Zoya might have been coked-up, depressed, hardly in her peak physical condition, but she was one hell of a good climber, far superior to Court himself, and after just a few seconds she unhooked the drop-down ladder and lowered it to where Court could access it. He climbed up, and then they pulled the iron ladder back up and rehooked it as before.

It was a simple matter to walk up the five flights of the fire escape to the roof, but the pair needed to do this with as little sound as possible. There was still significant traffic on nearby Amsterdam Avenue, but both Zoya and Court knew how sound traveled, and close-in sounds, while softer than more distant, louder noises, registered in the human brain differently. It would just take one person living in one of the apartments in this five-story building to wake up with the sense that someone was outside their window to ruin this entire operation.

But they kept ascending, and after a couple of minutes they found their way to the top landing. One more ladder led them to the flat roof, and here they knelt next to an HVAC system, looking over the lay of the land.

Court tapped his earpiece. "Lacy? We're still good?"

Angela Lacy reported in immediately. "Nothing showing up on Eighty-First Street. The alley between your row of buildings and Altman's row of buildings seems to be clear, as well, but it's dark, and I'm still scanning it."

"Good," Court said, and now he and Zoya rose and began moving east across the rooftops.

Some adjacent buildings were one story higher or lower than their neighbor, so they had to climb up or drop down to make way, each time landing with nearly silent footfalls. They both wore black tennis shoes, but Zoya softly complained to Court that Lacy had gotten her shoes that were a half size too small, and her feet were hurting.

They reached the five-story building at two fifteen a.m., and they stayed low as they moved to the southern side of the roof. Here, Court lay flat and crawled towards the edge to look into the dark alleyway below.

He looked across the fifteen feet between himself and the rooftop across the alleyway, one floor below where he now lay. Evaluating his intended landing zone, he double-tapped his earpiece to mute his voice, and then he leaned closer to Zoya. Whispering, he said, "No way I can leap fifteen feet, drop an entire flight, and land on a concrete roof without making some noise." Court thought it over. "I need to jump with the rope tied to me."

"Why?"

"The whole process of throwing the rope over after I land will make noise, too. One unidentified sound can be ignored. Not two."

"You're adding weight and drag if you leap over there with one end of a half-inch line tied around your waist."

"I can do it," Court said.

Zoya rolled onto her side and looked at him. "You need to remove all excess weight. The jacket, the sweater, hell, I wouldn't even take the pistol. Just the knife."

"The pistol isn't that heavy, Z."

"Two pounds, loaded. Two pounds might make a difference."

"Thirteen rounds might make a difference, too."

"You're not going to shoot Homeland Security officers. You're not going to shoot Altman."

"I'm keeping the gun."

Zoya rolled her eyes. "Whatever, just make the jump."

Court smiled. "You almost sounded like you cared there for a minute."

"I care about getting that phone to Altman."

Court began to rise to take off his jacket, but Zoya sat up and grabbed him by the arm. "I care about you, obviously."

They smiled at each other in the darkness, but only for an instant, and then their game faces switched on.

As Court took his bulky clothing off to reduce the weight he'd have to deal with while airborne over the alley, Zoya tapped her earpiece. "Alex. You read?"

"I read you."

"Tell Altman that Charlie will be crossing over in a few seconds. Should be to him in five minutes."

"Okay."

Court was now dressed in a black long-sleeved T-shirt and black jeans; he was cold already, but he rose to his knees and took an end of one of the fifty-foot lines from Zoya. He tied it around his waist securely while she placed the remainder of the coil near the edge of the roof, then tied the other end loosely around a protruding kitchen vent so it wouldn't fall down into the alleyway when he jumped.

And then Court stood, and he looked at Zoya. "Here goes nothing."

"You've got this," she said.

Court turned and walked through the cold darkness across the roof, all the way back to the north side. Then he turned around. He had seventy feet of runway before his leap, more than enough to get him over the space. He knew the world record long jump was nearly thirty feet, and though he was no Olympian, he was in a higher position than the roof across the alley, so he wasn't worried about the distance.

He was, however, worried about his landing. He'd need to do it safely and quietly, and considering the high speed at which he'd be traveling and the low light he had to contend with, he knew this would be a challenge.

He took a long, slow breath, rolled his shoulders a couple of times to relax, and surveyed the area in front of him, readying himself to act.

Suzanne Brewer stood in the industrial-style loft apartment on West 58th Street, now looking over the shoulder of a French employee of Sebastian Drexler who was monitoring doorbell camera feeds on the houses all around Altman's property.

She had her eyes on the two-man Homeland Security guard force parked in front of the brownstone. The men were obviously awake; the light of a cigarette glowed and moved in their marked car, but neither of the guards seemed exceptionally vigilant. There was no other movement on the street, however, so Brewer stood back up, heading to go see what the next workstation over was looking at.

Just then the German technician whom she'd tasked with looking at the day's digital files from Altman's office called out to her. "Ma'am?"

She stepped over quickly. "What've you got?"

"I've been searching recordings of Altman's office feeds today, and I might have found something interesting."

Brewer knelt down, her knees cracking in her slacks as she did so.

The tech said, "Altman met with four different people throughout the day; none of them were Velesky or Zakharova, but around four forty-five p.m. I got video of him leaving his office. He was back twelve minutes later."

"Bathroom break out in the public men's room on his floor?"

"That's what I assumed, but I checked the cams in the hall, too. He got on the elevator. His security guys had wandered off to a break room, doesn't even look like they saw him slip out."

"Interesting."

"I picked him back up in the ground-floor lobby after a minute or so. Here, he talks with this guy."

He ran the video on his center monitor, and Brewer peered closely at the screen. Ezra Altman was a slightly heavyset man, in his fifties, clean-shaven, in a white dress shirt and open collar. He wore a yarmulke on his head, and he stepped up to a man in a dark blue suit whose back was to the camera. "I . . . can't see his face," Brewer said.

"Me, either," admitted the German tech. "He seems to be about Velesky's age, but he looks a good bit taller to me."

Brewer kept watching. Altman seemed to be speaking exceptionally closely and urgently with the man, and the CIA officer started to feel bile rising up in her stomach. "Shit," she muttered.

After less than a minute and a half, the meeting off to the side of the lobby ended, Altman turned and headed back for the bank of elevators, and the man he'd been speaking with turned away and headed for the front door of the skyscraper.

There was a lobby security camera positioned in the ceiling over the door, and before she could even ask him to, the German froze the frame when the unknown man was just twenty feet away.

"Enlarge it."

The tech did so, then recentered on the man's face and cleaned up the resolution.

Brewer squinted for a few seconds, then rose back up quickly. Shouting to the entire apartment, she said, "Velesky's already made contact with Altman! Over eight hours ago. Altman could have the data right now, could be sitting there at his house processing it, getting it ready to send to the *New York Times*."

Drexler had been standing across the room, but he pulled his phone from his tweed coat and pressed a button, then brought it to his ear. After a slight pause, he said, "Luka. They need to go in. Now."

Court Gentry barreled across the roof of the row house facing 82nd Street, his speed increasing with each step. He raced past Zoya, who held the coiled rope attached to him in her hands, ready to toss it over the side as he leapt so that it wouldn't cause too much drag while unspooling on the rooftop.

He planted his right foot just inches away from the ledge of the roof, then launched off it, swinging his hands and legs in the air, flailing as he rocketed over the alleyway, gravity taking hold, dropping him down as his momentum generated by the run and the leap sent him forward.

He sailed through the night sky over bare trees, over the narrow alley full of dumpsters and chained bicycles and kids' toys and storage containers; he crossed over the edge of his landing rooftop with three feet to spare, and then he loosened his legs, his arms, and his torso, collapsing himself as his feet hit in front of him. He rolled and rolled, slowing his momentum as his body spun along the concrete.

Finally he came to rest on his back, staring at the sky. He reached up and found that his earpiece had fallen out, and he felt around for it in the dark for twenty seconds before finding it halfway back towards the northern edge of the roof.

His knees and elbows were skinned, and his already bruised hip throbbed with agony, but he was still in one piece, and he didn't feel like he'd made much noise at all.

Putting the earpiece back in, he whispered, "All good, I think."

Luka Rudenko stood on the third floor of his surveillance location, looking out the window and up the street at Altman's home. He listened through his earpiece to Sebastian Drexler, then said, "Wait. You want us to hit the house? *Now?* Velesky isn't there."

"It doesn't matter. They met already, this afternoon. Altman might have the information in hand, and he might be working on it now."

"What if he *doesn't* have it? Velesky will disappear if we kill Altman, and he'll just find someone else who can help him process the data."

"We're not going to kill Altman if he doesn't have the data, but we need to get in there in case he does."

Luka thought a moment. "We can take out the guards with our suppressed weapons, and we'll retrieve all sensitive material. Computers, drives, phones, whatever."

Drexler said, "Send some Ukrainians, too; there might be a lot of equipment to take."

"And if we find nothing?"

"If we find nothing, you kidnap Altman and his family, and that will give us the leverage we need for Altman to help us trick Velesky into meeting with him again."

Luka continued looking out the window. Finally, he said, "Understood."

"How long till you get over there?"

"Give me five minutes."

Court had completed his leap and his landing a minute earlier, but already the scrapes and bruises that hadn't yet healed from the train over two days ago had now begun fighting for real estate on his body with a myriad of fresh contusions. He stood in the center of the roof untying the line around him, then walked back to the fire escape on the edge by the alley and tied the rope off on an iron beam in the concrete.

This done, Zoya pulled her end of the rope as tight as she could and tied it more securely to the steel support leg of a large HVAC system.

Seconds later Court was moving east across the rooftops, carefully dropping down into a posh patio area that appeared understandably unused during the winter months, then climbing up to access the next building, a plain surface just a few feet higher than its neighbor.

Finally arriving on the roof of Altman's building, he lowered to a crouch and headed back towards the edge of the brownstone that faced the little alley, then he dropped to his knees before looking over the side.

The balcony was directly below him.

In his earpiece he whispered. "In position."

Lacy responded, "Alex is texting Altman now."

Court went prone and lay on the cold concrete, waiting for the forensic accountant to show.

SIXTY

Luka Rudenko moved into the kitchen of the brownstone on the south side of West 81st Street with two of his GRU officers and Petro Mozgovoy and explained to his men and the commander of the DPR team his intention to move on Altman's property.

Mozgovoy took in the information, then said, "The NYPD's Twentieth Precinct is only seventy meters away. There will be fifty cops there, even in the middle of the night."

Rudenko said, "Me and my men have suppressed pistols. The three of us will lead the way. Send four of your men to help us." He held a finger up. "Me and my men will do all the shooting."

Petro looked down at Rudenko's injured foot. "*You're* going over there?"

"An officer leads from the front," he said, shutting down this discussion. He pulled his suppressor out of his jacket and drew an HK VP9 9-millimeter pistol, then began screwing the long can on the weapon's threaded barrel. As his two men did the same, he said, "We will eliminate the security team in the car out front; they should have a key to the front door of the house. Once we get in, we overpower the guards and have them turn off the alarm. Then we shoot them."

He added, "Remember, he has a wife and two teenaged boys. They must not be harmed. If the drive isn't in the house, then we will need hostages to force Altman to get it for us."

Petro said, "I'll gather the men, let them know their job is to collect all the computer equipment and phones."

Luka said, "This cannot go loud, so your men will not take guns."

Petro shook his head. "I'm not sending them over there without guns!"

"You will do what I order you to do! The three of us will handle anything. Take knives. No guns, unless you want the Twentieth Precinct taking us all down one minute later."

Petro sighed angrily, then left the room, heading for the stairs. Vasily, one of the GRU men, looked to Luka now. "Boss . . . me and Mischa can handle it. You don't have to go."

Luka knew Vasily was thinking about the injury to Luka's foot, but he waved the comment away. "I'm one hundred percent."

He wasn't; his foot hurt like hell, and his mobility would be affected by the walking boot. But there was no way he was going to let his men do this job without him.

Court waited on the roof for about a minute before he heard the quiet sliding of a door below him. A few seconds after this a figure appeared, standing between some deck chairs set up on the little concrete balcony. The figure seemed to look around in the darkness, so Court whistled very softly.

The man spun around and looked up. Court scooted his body around to the side, lowered himself down with his hands, and put his feet on the arms of one of the deck chairs. From here he stepped onto the cushion and then carefully down to the surface of the balcony, a freshly skinned knee under his jeans protesting the movement with a fiery sting that was almost as annoying as the severely bruised hip he'd picked up in Switzerland.

Standing in front of Altman, he put his hand gently on the man's shoulder and brought him away from the sliding glass doors, away from the stone railing, and into the southwestern corner of the little balcony. This would make it impossible for anyone in the alley to see them, and equally impossible for anyone from either Altman's family or the security officers to see him through the glass door.

As he did this, the middle-aged man said, "Stay very quiet."

No shit, Court thought, but he just nodded, reached under his shirt, and pulled the phone out of the money belt. Softly, he said, "Did Velesky give you the code?"

"Yes. Dymtrus."

Court nodded. "It's been explained to you that you can't trust anyone right now?"

"If this is indeed a record of all Russian intelligence services money moving into the West, then I know exactly how much danger I'm in. I've been tracking and cataloging suspicious movements of money from Brucker Söhne for years, but I never knew who put the money in the Swiss bank.

"Ever since Krupkin got out of Russia with his phone, my own security has been watching me carefully. That means this goes up high in the Justice Department."

Court nodded. "U.S. intelligence agencies are involved, as well."

Altman sighed, then cocked his head a little. "How do I know I can even trust you?"

"You don't need to trust me. I'm just the courier here. I'll be on my way."

Altman nodded. "I have a laptop in my office here set up with my database so I can get right to work on this. Combining this information with what Velesky posted on the dark web and my own database of offshore accounts, I should be able to connect some dots."

Angela Lacy sipped her coffee at the dinette in the basement apartment on 87th. Alex Velesky sat next to her as they continued looking over video feeds from the streets and alleys just six blocks south of their position on her computer monitor.

There were seventy cameras she'd managed to tap into, made easy with her access to secure Homeland Security websites by invoking the Bloody Angel Special Access Program, and each thumbnail on the monitor was represented on the laptop. It was impossible to make anything out on these tiny images, but the software was set up to enlarge a feed to full screen if it detected the movement of a human.

A man walked his dog on the eastern end of 81st Street, but when he turned onto Columbus, the feed that had broadcast his movements returned to one of the seventy thumbnails arrayed on the screen.

Lacy put her coffee down, but as soon as she did this, she froze.

Another camera feed enlarged to full screen, and instantly both she and Alex leaned in closer.

A pair of men wearing dark clothing moved across West 81st, heading west, proceeding quickly though not running. There was something about their haste that made both Angela and Alex stare in rapt silence.

A new feed replaced the first one, this from a doorbell camera right across the street from Altman's four-story brownstone, and it did so because the two men had left the coverage of the first camera and moved into its view. They continued west, closing on the rear of the Homeland Security car, and then, as one, the men drew pistols from under their coats.

Angela instantly tapped her earpiece. "Shooters on Eighty-First Street!"

Alex pointed to another part of the screen, where another man trailed behind them. He seemed to be walking with a limp, and he carried a suppressed pistol, same as the other men.

"I think Matador might be with them," she said, knowing that the Russian's foot was injured.

Four more figures came into view behind the limping man, moving in the darkness of the middle of the road, away from the streetlights.

"Shit!" she shouted. "Seven men. I count three suppressed handguns."

Court had already said goodbye to Altman and was positioning himself on the deck chair to grab the roof ledge when he heard the transmission from Lacy. He dropped back down, reached out, and grabbed the older man by the arm as he was in the process of opening his sliding glass door, and then he heard the soft muffled *pops* of suppressed pistols on the other side of the building.

Lacy's voice came over the net. "Shit! They just shot the guards out front!"

Altman clearly didn't recognize the noises for what they were; he just looked at Court questioningly.

Lacy's voice came back over the line. "They're . . . they're rifling through the bodies in the car; three are up at the front door. Are you reading me, Six?"

"Christ," Court said aloud, tapping his earpiece. "Copy. Keep reporting."

"What is it?" Altman asked.

But before Court could answer, Zoya's voice came through his ear. "Coming to you, Six. ETA is three to four mikes."

Court didn't acknowledge, he just held on to Altman's arm. "Your family is here?"

The older man cocked his head. "Yes. Everybody is here. Why?"

Court spoke into his mic. "Beth, I need you to meet Altman on the balcony."

The reply was instant. "En route."

"What's going on?" asked Altman, his voice a little louder and a lot more frantic than before.

This was a rare occurrence where Court found himself at a moment of decision but with no clear path to take. He couldn't shoot it out with the Russians here. He didn't have a silencer on his weapon, and the sound of gunfire in such a heavily populated area would bring everyone out, including the entire night shift at the 20th Precinct.

He considered just firing a few rounds into the brick wall of the building on the other side of the alley to bring the cavalry out in the form of the NYPD, but he decided against this. If this place started crawling with cops, there was no way Altman was going to get away clean with Krupkin's phone and reveal the data on it. The CIA would get involved, as well as any other important parties tainted by the intelligence smuggled out of Russia.

No, they had to handle this quietly.

Court knew he couldn't let Altman himself go into the house. He needed this man alive, regardless of what happened to his family, so he pushed Altman up against the wall roughly, got in his face, and spoke softly but with an imploring tone in his voice. "You need to trust us right now. Stay right here, do *not* make a sound, and we will take care of it."

"Take care of *what*?" Altman was still unaware the Russians were in the building, though Court heard more faint pops from inside through the glass door. "Is something wrong? My kids, my—"

Court got even closer to Altman's face. "Whatever happens, whatever you hear, stay here with the phone until my friend comes for you. If you go in the house, you will risk everything, including your family's lives."

The home alarm sounded; it wasn't loud outside but it was unmistakable. This, however, Altman clearly heard. "Who's in there?"

"I'll handle it," Court said.

A fresh panic on Altman's face, evident even in the dark, told Court there was a fifty percent chance he was going to ignore his instructions and storm into the house if Court left him here. There remained no good options, but the fact that he couldn't even fire his pistol made one of those options no option at all. He considered hoisting the bigger and heavier man up onto the roof and just retreating with him, but Court knew he couldn't sit by while this man's family was taken or killed.

With a finger in Altman's face, Court said, "Don't . . . fucking . . . move."

To Court's relief, the panicked man gave a little nod. "Please, sir. My family."

"What floors are they on?"

"All the bedrooms are on the second floor."

Shit, Court thought but didn't say. The Russians were a lot closer to Altman's family than he was.

Quietly he slid open the door, entered, and found himself in a well-appointed study. All the lights were off save for a banker's lamp on Altman's desk next to his laptop, and he pulled the chain on this as he passed by on his way to the hallway, completely blackening out the room in the process.

Softly, into his mic, he said, "Beth . . . Altman has the phone. Get him, and get the fuck out of here."

"What about you?" He could tell by the exertion in her voice that she was climbing the rope over to the rooftop four houses away.

Court said, "I'm going for his family. We have to keep this quiet, whatever happens."

Court unfolded the four-inch blade of the folding knife and moved to the doorway to the fourth-floor hall.

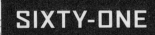

SIXTY-ONE

Luka Rudenko stood at the alarm panel by the front door, the suppressor of his HK under the jaw of the only Homeland Security officer still alive.

The man was young, maybe twenty-five, and his shaved head and ruddy face were covered with sweat and blood after Vasily had busted the officer's mouth while relieving him of his weapons.

His partner was on his back on the hardwood floor in the entry hall, his rifle on the ground next to him and a pair of bullet holes in his chest.

Luka had shot him even after Mischa had him at gunpoint, because he knew they only needed one of the men to turn off the alarm, which now blared throughout the home.

The GRU major looked into the terrified man's eyes. "You need to deactivate the alarm, or I'll blow your head off."

The man looked conflicted, but when Luka pressed the hot suppressor harder against his chin, he reached up and tapped in a four-digit code.

The siren stopped instantly. Luka knew the alarm service gave a forty-five-second grace period before calling and a much longer wait before dispatching the police, and he also knew he'd gotten the system shut off after only thirty seconds or so.

Once the beeping stopped, he said, "Thank you," and then he took an awkward step back with his booted left foot and shot the man between the eyes.

His two men had already gone upstairs to hunt for the Altmans, followed by the four Ukrainian separatists, so Rudenko walked the ground floor of the narrow but deep brownstone, clearing the area with his pistol.

In under a minute, a pair of bleary-eyed and dark-haired teens who appeared to be brothers, both wearing boxers and T-shirts, were brought down by a Ukrainian and told to sit on the stairs right in front of the two dead Federal Protective Service officers of the Department of Homeland Security. The boys did as instructed; Luka took the weapons of both of the dead officers and disassembled them, and the kids sat there, disoriented by the activity in the house.

Thirty seconds later Mischa brought down Sarah Altman, a woman in her midfifties with red hair and a slight build. She broke away from him, running down the stairs when she saw her boys, and she hugged them both before noticing the bodies on the floor in front of the stairs.

She looked up at Luka, obviously determining him to be the man in charge.

"What have you done with my husband?"

Luka eyed Mischa, who answered in Russian. "Vasily's still sweeping, no sign of Altman yet."

"Get the others loading up the computers."

"On it."

He looked back to the woman and switched to English. "Where is he?"

She shook her head in surprise. "I . . . You have him . . . don't you?"

Rudenko's eyebrows furrowed as he moved to the center of the entry hall, affording himself a view all the way up the spiral staircase, where a skylight gave a little illumination to the space.

Court remained in the fourth-floor office, his knife in his hand and his body shielded from view by the open door. A man had shined a flashlight into the room as he'd passed by on the landing moments ago, but then the footsteps and the light's beam continued on toward another part of the floor.

A second flashlight's beam moved around the spiral staircase now, as if someone else was heading up to the top floor.

Court was certain the Russians had already captured the family, and there was little he could do without a silencer on his pistol, so he'd spent the last minute hoping some asshole with a can screwed onto the barrel of his gun came up here and got within knife range.

But so far, he hadn't seen any weapons, only lights.

He heard a faint noise behind him, near the balcony, and he instinctively drew his pistol and pointed it before he realized it was Zoya coming through the glass doors. He angrily reholstered, then turned his attention back to the landing and the staircase.

Zoya stepped over to him after crossing the floor in complete silence, and she leaned close. Outside the office, the flashlights' beams seemed to be closing, and he could hear people speaking Russian. Court whispered, "Where the fuck is Altman?"

"Zip-tied him to a chair on the balcony."

"I told you to—"

"Shh," she said. Two men began speaking outside the door. One was still on the stairs, the other on the landing, closer.

Court heard Russian, but Zoya cocked her head. "Guy on the stairs is Ukrainian."

"What?"

She was certain. "Speaking Russian. But Ukrainian. Other guy is from Saint Petersburg."

A light appeared close now; the footfalls of a man came up the landing from the opposite direction of the stairs, and seconds later someone stepped into the room.

Court saw the tip of a suppressor's barrel around the side of the door, so he moved in front of Zoya and then grabbed the man's gun-hand wrist with his left hand, while Court's right hand jabbed out with the knife in it, stabbing the Russian on the left side between the ribs.

To Court's surprise, however, the man yanked hard to the right, knocking him off-balance. Both men fell to the floor, Court still controlling the man's gun hand, the knife still buried in the man's chest.

The Russian shouted out now. "Help! Help!"

Zoya drew her 9-millimeter and aimed it at the doorway, while backing up into the room to get closer to the two men rolling on the floor.

Just then a flashlight's beam appeared in the doorway, and instead of firing at it she raced forward, flicking the safety up on her pistol so it wouldn't accidentally fire.

A figure appeared from the left side of the doorframe behind the light; Zoya tackled him while striking him in the side of his head with her steel-and-polymer 9-millimeter, and the two of them fell out onto the landing. As they tumbled, in the spinning flashlight's beam she saw that the man held a knife in his left hand.

After she slammed onto the landing alongside him, he stabbed out at her, but she avoided the blade by sitting up and leaning over to the right, and then she came up behind the thrust and slammed the pistol against the man's nose while wrapping her left arm around the arm with the knife.

The man—Zoya thought this was the Ukrainian she'd heard speaking on the stairs—got a hand around the barrel of Zoya's Smith and Wesson pistol, and he, too, shouted out for help from his comrades below.

Court couldn't believe this motherfucker. The Russian was mortally wounded, a knife hilt-deep into his lung, but he wasn't giving up. Still holding the gun, the man fired, but Court had the weapon controlled and pointed away from him, but also away from Zoya on the landing and Altman on the balcony.

The round went into the ceiling, and the man fired again, this time striking the western wall of the brick-and-stone house.

Court used both hands now on the gun arm, but while he did this, he climbed back up onto his cut-and-bruised knees, then shoved his thigh hard against the hilt of the knife in the man's chest.

The Russian reacted to the pain, loosening his grip, and Court ripped the silenced HK pistol away from him, then spun it around on his finger and pointed it against the man's temple.

He fired once, and blood and bone splattered across the oriental rug on the office floor.

Behind him, he heard both Zoya and another man yelling, so he rose to his feet and ran through the dark towards the landing, adjusting the pistol to a two-handed grip as he advanced.

The Ukrainian fighting Zoya on the landing was big and burly; in the soft moonglow from the skylight above she saw a big forehead and deep-set eyes, and she quickly realized this man knew how to fight. He was stronger than her, as well, so when he tossed his knife away and put both hands on the pistol, she knew she was seconds away from getting it ripped out of her hands. She also heard more footsteps moving up the stairs, past the third-floor landing.

Zoya knew she was running out of time.

Her gun was wrenched from her clutches, and the now-seated man turned it around, pointing it at her chest, at a range of just three feet.

"Sukha," he said. *Bitch*. And he pulled the trigger.

The gun did not fire because she'd engaged the safety, and as soon as the man realized this, he lifted his thumb up to snap it down.

Zoya lunged forward for the gun; she didn't think she'd get it away from him before he shot her dead, but just then a suppressed shot came from above her. The man's head snapped back and he dropped onto the hardwood landing.

Zoya clawed her Smith and Wesson Shield away from the dead man and leapt to her feet, retreating to the office, passing Court as he crouched low, a suppressed pistol in his hands.

Court then began firing over and over at the source of flashlight beams at the top of the stairs.

Zoya heard a body fall, and others scramble away, and soon she was back on the landing behind Court. She watched while he leaned over the balcony, looking for a target through his new pistol's sights, but instead he received a salvo of return fire from two different suppressed weapons below. Rounds shattered the skylight above his head, and Court was forced to lurch back and out of the line of fire.

Zoya took him by his shoulder and pulled him back into the office.

He said, "I've got to go for his family!"

"You don't have a chance! We'll get them back. Lacy can track them wherever they go!"

Court took only an instant to think about it, and then he nodded, admitting she was right. He covered the landing while she went back to the balcony, and while he stood there in the office, he tapped his earpiece to contact Lacy. He needed her tracking any vehicles that left the area, and he needed Alex to haul ass to 82nd Street to pick them up in Zoya's minivan.

On the first floor, Luka Rudenko pointed his weapon up the open center of the circular staircase, hoping like hell to see any more movement. A man had appeared on the fourth floor seconds earlier, almost invisible other than a slight silhouette below the skylight, but Rudenko saw him aiming a weapon down in his direction, so he'd opened fire.

This was not Ezra Altman, that was obvious, and Rudenko had an idea about who he might have been.

Mischa had been racing up to support the others when he, too, exchanged gunfire with the subject on the fourth floor.

After a few seconds, Luka called out. "Mischa? You good?"

"I'm good."

"Can you make it to me?"

"Yeah, if you cover above."

"Move."

Mischa came running down the stairs from the second-story landing, finally making it to Rudenko on the ground floor.

He said, "Vasily's not reporting in. I saw one of the DPR guys on the stairs, wounded, but he's not going to make it."

Luka looked around. Two Ukrainians had made it down here; he assumed the other two, along with his man Vasily, were all upstairs dead.

Luka said, "Shit. That's not Altman, and that's not a security guard up there. What did you see?"

"Nothing. No noise other than our pistols."

"Fuck." Luka looked to the three hostages, now well away from the stairwell and huddled together next to the coatrack by the front door.

After a moment he called Mozgovoy, and the DPR asset answered on the first ring. "Yeah?"

"Immediate evacuation. Get two vehicles over here now."

"What happened?"

"We've lost three men between us," he said, and then he hung up.

This hastily planned operation had been mostly a bust. He'd not gotten Altman or Krupkin's phone, but there was an upside. First, it was unlikely the police had been alerted, nor would they be unless some neighbor happened to check their security camera and see the shooting out front.

And second, Luka now had Altman's family, and he knew Sebastian Drexler would reach out to the forensic accountant and impress upon him how important it was that he do exactly what he was told from here on out.

He opened the front door slowly, then looked out into the street. It wasn't far to their surveillance location; he could hobble over there on his bad foot, but he didn't want to do it while moving hostages.

Zoya Zakharova snipped off Altman's restraints while Court grabbed Altman's cell phone and MacBook Air, pocketing the former and cramming the latter behind him into his waistband. He took the rope Zoya brought with her and began tying it around the man's waist.

Altman remained in a state of shock. "Where's Sarah? Where are the boys?"

Court didn't stop working on his knot as he spoke. "Listen very carefully. You need to be very quiet while we do this."

"Do what?"

"I'm going to lower you down to the alley."

The man stood as soon as Zoya finished cutting off his last restraint. Court looked at her and said, "Go."

She nodded, then grabbed the concrete railing and kicked over. She moved over to a metal drainpipe and began climbing down.

"Where's my family?"

"Ezra, I promise you. We're going to get them back."

The man was on the verge of hysteria now, and Court wasn't sure how he was going to get this man down four stories, but he knew he had to figure it out fast.

"The Russians have them?"

He was getting louder, and this was worrying Court, as well. He whispered in the man's face. "They are already gone, but we know how to find them, and we're going to have a team handle it." He did not, in fact, know if they'd left the building or not, but he had no way to get to them even if they had not.

And he had no team with him that could handle anything like a hostage rescue.

Still, he knew he had to appear confident, even in the face of all this uncertainty, to keep Altman as calm as possible.

He said, "There are more Russians around, so you have to be quiet. I'm going to lower you down the side of the wall now, and you're going to help me by keeping one hand and one foot on this drainpipe at all times."

Altman was crying now, but eventually he nodded. Court tapped his earpiece. "Beth, I'm sending him down."

"Copy," she replied immediately.

The process took over three minutes, but eventually Court, Altman, and Zoya were in the alleyway, and they bypassed Altman's home to find another way back to the street.

Once they were on West 82nd, Alex Velesky pulled up in Zoya's rented Toyota Sienna, and everyone packed in.

As soon as the door to the minivan shut and they began moving west, Altman shouted as loud as he could, "Shit!"

SIXTY-TWO

Suzanne Brewer looked over a technician's shoulder at the doorbell camera image of the gray Toyota Sienna as it turned onto 82nd Street, and she watched it stop just five doors down from the NYPD police precinct.

She didn't have an angle to see who got into the minivan, but she was able to watch it head up to Amsterdam Avenue, where it turned right, heading north.

A red light camera recorded the tag number before she lost the minivan, but when she ran the tag she learned it had been rented in Boston less than two days earlier. She had the resources to find out who rented it, but not at three a.m., so she told herself she'd identify the driver in the morning.

Drexler had stepped out onto the balcony of the loft apartment to call his Russians, using his cane to help him along, and he'd been out there for the past several minutes. Brewer didn't know what she was going to learn from him when he returned, but she feared the worst.

She'd seen the Homeland Security men murdered on the street from a nearby camera, and the team of Russians were in the home for more than ten minutes before they came out. She saw the hostages get picked up by a van, and more men leave the house carrying three bodies, which were tossed into the same van before it slowly drove away.

She'd lost sight of the Russians when the Sienna arrived on the next block, but she knew Drexler would return with both a status report and a body count in a few minutes.

Just then, the Swiss man limped back off the balcony and sat down next to Brewer, holding his cane across his lap. His mood was unmistakably grim. "We've lost three. Altman was not recovered, nor was the data, but we did capture his wife and two children."

Brewer closed her eyes. *Kidnapping now? Christ.* "What a fuckup," she muttered.

"I will reach out to Altman, via email and phone, and arrange a trade."

The CIA officer looked off into space a moment, then turned back to Drexler. Cocking her head a little, she said, "You've done this before, haven't you?"

Drexler smiled, but it was a tired smile. "I have done what has been required of me by my employers."

"I'll take that as a yes."

"It *is* a yes. I've been told that you are able to paint outside the lines when necessary yourself."

Brewer did not respond to this. Instead, she said, "What's our next move?"

"My field team will move the Altmans to a safe house nearby. They will be well protected there."

Drexler put his hands on his knees and began rubbing his left one as he talked. "I do have one concern, however."

"I have more than one," Brewer responded. "But, by all means, let's talk about you. What's *your* one concern?"

"No one on my team here saw anyone enter that home all evening other than the Altmans and their four-man security force. The man in charge of my field team, he just told me—"

Brewer interjected. "Let's just call him what we call him at CIA. Matador."

Drexler raised his eyebrows, as if he were in a chess match and his opponent had just made a clever move. "Fine, *Matador* told me the four security men all died without firing a shot, and neither he nor I believe for an instant Altman killed our three assets himself."

Brewer understood. "Someone else was in the house. It had to have been Zakharova."

He shook his head. "Matador says he clearly saw a male shooter. He thinks it might have been the same man he encountered on the train, and also last week in the Caribbean."

Brewer shook her head. "No . . . impossible. That man died in Switzerland. It's been confirmed."

"Confirmed by . . ." Drexler asked questioningly. "By you?"

"Not personally by me, no. But I—"

She stopped talking suddenly. Drexler cocked his head. "What is it?"

"Oh my God."

"What is it?" he asked again.

Suzanne Brewer didn't answer him. The muscles in her neck tensed, and her face reddened.

She reached for her phone.

Ten minutes earlier, Alex Velesky parked the minivan in front of a diner on Columbus and West 87th Street, and then he, along with his three passengers, began walking through the night up the street.

Court stayed at the rear of the party, checking behind them as they walked to the east. He didn't hear any sirens close by, which was good news, but since he had no idea whether they were being watched on security cameras, he wasn't terribly confident about their predicament at the moment.

Still, they entered the basement apartment; Lacy was there at the dinette, her computer still open and scanning the area on the Homeland Security secure website.

Altman was almost catatonic now. He wore black pajama bottoms and a white T-shirt, with a heavy cardigan over it that he'd put on to meet the mysterious man on his balcony, and he said nothing as Zoya led him over to a sofa and helped him sit down.

Velesky sat right next to him, ready to talk about Krupkin's files, but immediately he realized he had to give the man a few minutes to collect himself.

Zoya knelt down in front of Ezra now. "Sir, we are tracking the Russians, and as soon as we know where they're going, *we're* going to get your family back."

Ezra said nothing, so Zoya stood and headed for the kitchen. She poured a Solo cup of Cabernet from the box of wine she'd brought over from the suite she'd shared with Alex the night before, and brought it back to him.

Altman drank it slowly, but he did drink, so Zoya went back to the kitchen and poured a cup of red for herself.

Meanwhile, Court sat down next to Lacy at the dinette. "You have them, still?"

She was distracted talking to him because her eyes were locked on her laptop. "For now, I do. I keep having to expand coverage zones, working very fast, here."

"Where are they?"

"They're definitely going west. Looks like they're almost at the George Washington Bridge; they could be heading over to New Jersey."

"Shit," Court said. "Newark Airport is over there. Teterboro, too. No commercial flights at three a.m., but they might have a private plane. Can you check on that?"

"Not if you want me to keep tracking them. You keep forgetting that I'm just one person, Six."

"Right," Court said, frustrated by the fact that he couldn't just take over the computer while she checked to see if there were any departing private flights.

Just then, Angela Lacy's phone began vibrating on the table next to her laptop. Both Court and Lacy were surprised by this considering the time, and together they looked at the screen to see who was calling.

"Oh, for fuck's sake," Court muttered softly.

Lacy looked up at Six. "What do I do?"

Zoya stepped out of the kitchen next to the dinette, her Solo cup of wine in her hand. "Who?"

Court looked up at her. "Brewer."

"Shit. She knows," Zoya said. "We've got to get out of here."

Court nodded, but then his attention went back to Lacy as Zoya chugged her wine and headed off to tell Alex and Ezra they would be leaving immediately.

Lacy asked, "Do I answer?"

Court rubbed his hands through his hair. "Would you normally answer at three a.m.?"

"No. Well . . . I mean, if I was operational, of course I would."

"Well, you aren't. Not for her, anyway. Don't answer."

"She'll call me back in the morning, and then I'll—"

Court said, "That's a problem for later. We have other problems now. Just keep tracking the van while the rest of us get ready to scoot."

Angela Lacy watched Six hurry over to talk to Alex and Ezra, and then she looked back to her computer. The van with the hostages had just made it onto the George Washington Bridge; she began pulling up camera networks to the west, shutting down networks in Manhattan while doing so.

But she hadn't gotten very far at all when all the camera views disappeared, replaced by a blue screen with a single message on a pop-up in the center of the monitor.

Access Restricted. Credentials Invalid.

Her heart skipped a beat, and she grabbed Six by the wrist as he passed by on the way to the bedroom. "Actually, it might be a problem for now. She's locked me out of Bloody Angel. I can't get on the Homeland Security site."

"So you can't track the van?"

She looked into his eyes. "Six . . . I can't do *anything*."

"Fuck." Softly, he said, "We've lost Altman's family."

Lacy continued. "It's even worse than that. Think about it. If Brewer thinks I'm working against her, then she's probably already figured that I lied about identifying your body."

Zoya passed by within earshot and saw Lacy still sitting at her computer. Angrily she said, "Let's go, Lacy."

"Excuse me?"

"You heard me. We've got to move."

Lacy rose slowly, staring Zoya down.

Just what we need, Court thought.

Lacy pointed an angry finger at Zoya's face now. "I don't take orders from fucking Russian spooks."

Court pushed between them quickly. "We're all on the same mission here. We've lost visibility on the enemy, and for all we know, Brewer could have a team on the way here now. Let's *please* work together."

Zoya and Angela faced off another second, but then Zoya turned and looked to Court. "You know what this means, right?"

"What *what* means?"

"This means Brewer is working with the Russians. *And* the Ukrainians."

"Ukrainians?" Lacy asked, and as quickly as the conflagration between her and Zoya had begun, it ended.

Zoya didn't answer her; instead, she pulled her phone out. "I'm calling an Uber. We can't take the minivan. We leave everything we can't stick into a couple of backpacks."

"What Ukrainians?" the CIA officer asked again.

Zoya turned away, but Court answered. "Beth said she heard one of the men in Altman's place speaking with a Ukrainian accent."

"Like . . ." Lacy was confused. "A separatist?"

Altman overheard them, and he spoke in a voice that surprised everyone else in the room with its calm, so different from his panicked state before. "Late last year, November maybe, a cell of Donetsk People's Republic sleepers was arrested by the FBI here in the city. They'd been caught photographing shipping leaving out of Red Hook. Military equipment going to Europe to be brought into Ukraine."

Lacy said, "Yeah, I remember that. It was a domestic thing; the Agency didn't have much to do with it, so I don't know if other cells were suspected."

Altman walked up to her. "They're out there. Big Ukrainian population here, and they aren't all aligned with Kiev."

Court marveled at what he was learning. "And now the Agency is working with Russian military intelligence *and* Ukrainian spies . . . in fucking Manhattan."

Zoya lowered her phone now and turned back to Court. "It's not the whole Agency. It's Brewer, and it's whoever Brewer thinks can give her something she wants."

Court nodded, because he knew Zoya was right. "Only two people above her. The DDO, Mel Brent, and the D/CIA, Jay Kirby."

Lacy said, "Brent is the head of operations, but he's never met an operation he likes. He's a typical suit."

"Kirby's a suit," Court said.

Lacy shook her head. "A politician. Not a bureaucrat. Something this nuts . . . the Russians . . . it's *got* to be Kirby."

Zoya looked down at her phone again. "SUV here in four minutes."

"Where are we going?" Court asked.

Zoya answered authoritatively. "Back to the Kimberly Hotel so Altman can get to work."

And Lacy said, "And after, I guess we're going to New Jersey."

In the loft apartment near Columbus Circle, Suzanne Brewer double-checked her computer, making certain Angela Lacy's access to all secure government portals had been removed.

This done, Brewer leaned over her desk and put her head in her hands.

What she had envisioned as a quick and relatively clean job in New York—a few hours' surveillance today and tonight followed by catching the first shuttle back to D.C. in the morning while the assets did their part—had now turned into a protracted manhunt, a kidnapping, and multiple murders of federal officers.

She didn't know what she was going to do, but she knew this job was now as much about self-preservation as it was career enhancement. She had to succeed now. Not for Kirby's reputation but for her own.

Drexler sat down next to her. "Let's put our situation in perspective. I am not sure what motivates you now, Suzanne. Jay Kirby's carrots, or Jay Kirby's sticks. But as for me, I am very motivated by Daniil Spanov's sticks."

"He'll kill you if you don't do this for him?"

"If this mission fails and any of those GRU or SSB men are left standing, then they will be sent after me before I leave the U.S. If I should manage to make it back home, then there will be more there waiting for me."

Brewer cocked her head. "SSB?"

"Ah, yes, you didn't know. Well, there is no reason not to fold you into the entire operation now. The GRU has activated a cell of agents from the DPR's Special Security Battalion, here in the city. They are aiding us. Ten operatives"—he shrugged—"minus the two who died tonight."

"A sleeper cell? In America? We're working with them?"

Drexler breathed out a tired sigh. "Desperate times, Suzanne. Desperate times."

SIXTY-THREE

Although it was past three thirty in the morning, the two women and three men in the living room of the two-bedroom suite at the Kimberly Hotel on East 50th Street were all wide-awake, adrenaline and stress keeping their blood circulating.

Alex Velesky sat on a sofa with Ezra Altman, pleading with him to get started working through the data on Igor Krupkin's phone. Altman, for his part, said little; he'd been crying intermittently, running his fingers through his hair, fraught with worry over the fate of his family.

As soon as they made it into the room, Zoya assured Altman, over and over, that his family would not be harmed as long as he was free, and no one was going to ask him to publicize the data until Sarah and the boys were safe and sound.

When Ezra suggested bringing in the FBI, Angela Lacy stepped over to him and told him it was quite possible the head of the Central Intelligence Agency was involved in a conspiracy to protect Russian assets in the West, and there was every reason to believe other agencies and departments had corrupt officials with a vital need to destroy the information that now resided on an iPhone on the coffee table in front of him.

It didn't seem as though Altman believed her, and it also didn't seem like Velesky's pleas were going a long way in getting him off the sofa and onto his computer. Still, Lacy picked up the phone, walked over to the little writing desk by the wall, and put it down next to Altman's laptop, along with the cabling required to connect them, getting everything ready in hopes Ezra would recover from his grief and his suspicions enough that he could begin to do his magic.

Court Gentry had been busy re-dressing the knife wound to his arm that he'd picked up the other day in Switzerland; it had torn open during his leap across the alley between the apartment buildings, his fight with the Russian, or his climb down the four-story drainpipe—he wasn't sure which, and it hardly mattered.

He stood there with no shirt on behind the bar in the suite, wrapping gauze and compression bandages Angela had bought earlier in the day around the wound. His chest and back were covered with contusions, as well, and he was exhausted beyond belief. But as he finished dressing his arm, listening to everyone appealing to Altman, he decided he needed to take a different tack than the others to make things happen.

He crossed the room, stood over the middle-aged forensic accountant, and said, "I am the one who will get your family back. I will have help, yes, but it doesn't happen without me. Do you understand that?"

Altman had been all but ignoring Velesky while he talked, but now he looked up at the man covered from the waist up in nothing but welts, scrapes, and bandages. After a moment, he said, "What do you want from me?"

"I want you to find out where your family is."

"How . . . how can I do that? The kidnappers haven't called me. When they do, I will—"

"They will call you once they have your family somewhere secure. And if you don't give them what they want, they will kill them."

Altman nodded. "I know."

Velesky looked up at Court like he was crazy now, as if this was the last thing in the world he needed to say to get Altman over to the computer and working on the data.

But then Court said, "The problem is, Ezra, if you *do* give them what they want, they will also kill them." He paused. "Their only chance at all is for us to find them before you hand anything over to anyone. Not to the kidnappers, not to the press.

"Does that make sense to you?"

Altman nodded a little. "But how do I—"

Court pointed to the table with the phone and the laptop. "Money leaves a trail. Whoever is holding your family is being paid through Brucker Söhne. We know there are Ukrainian DPR assets here; we expect they've been here for some time, and I strongly suspect they are being paid by the Russians. You just have to find money flowing into New York, see where it goes there: a bank account, a credit card payment, whatever. Something that ties people or places here in the city to Russian intelligence. You do that, and we have a shot at getting your family back."

Ezra sat up straighter. After a few seconds, he said, "I can try."

"Good," Court said, and then he helped the man to his feet and physically walked him over to the writing desk.

As he sat down, Lacy, Alex, and Zoya stepped up, as well. Zoya passed Court a green Goodwill T-shirt out of a bag, and he put it on gingerly.

As he fired up his computer, Ezra muttered, "I knew this would happen someday. I just thought if it did, my family would be better protected."

"This time tomorrow," Lacy said, "this will be over. We just have to have faith."

Altman said, "If the accords are signed today, recovering my family is the only thing I can hope for. Even revealing Russian agents around the world won't stop the world from reestablishing trade ties if the news doesn't get out before the accords are signed.

"I mean . . . yeah, it will do some damage to Russia, but nothing they wouldn't be able to survive." His computer screen came up, and he plugged the phone cable into the side of his laptop. After doing this, he said, "My family is more important to me, of course, but we have to get this done before noon."

He added, "I thought I hated Russians before . . ." His voice trailed off.

Court flashed a look at Zoya, who looked down at the floor. He said, "You just haven't met the right Russians."

Zoya's eyes looked back up at him, and a soft, tired smile grew on her lips. Instantly all the aches and pains in Court's body melted away, if only for a brief moment.

Altman was unaware any of this was going on. "You're right. I *do* know good Russians, lots of them, but they live under a brutal dictatorship, so many of them have to go along to get along. But the people I target: the oligarchs, the siloviki"—he looked to Velesky—"the foreign enablers . . . those people I'm not particularly fond of."

Altman typed the password into the phone, then added, "There was one asshole in particular at Brucker Söhne able to move the Russian money in crypto, from system to system, until I lost any sight of it."

Velesky raised a hand. "Guilty as charged."

"Well . . ." Altman said, "I'll give you this. You're going a long way to redeem yourself by bringing me this phone."

Court said, "Do you have everything you need?"

Altman shrugged. "Not really, no. With what I have on my laptop, I might be able to find information about things that will help you find my family, account data and banking info, but only *I'll* be able to interpret the data in this state. Trust me, it would be too arcane for the average person to understand. I can't create a blueprint for the complete money trail without user interface software, and that's on my server in my office.

"*That's* what we need to burn the Russian operation down."

Court said, "Well, at some point we'll go to your office, but first let's secure your family."

Data loaded on Altman's screen from the phone, and he began looking it over. After just a few seconds, he said, "This is all the information about those who sent the money. These accounts, these aren't real financial institutions. They're money-laundering enterprises, based in Russia, funneling cash, but these are known Kremlin accounts."

Velesky nodded. "Krupkin was right. Now, pull up my data on the dark web."

Altman typed in the twenty-three-digit code on CyberGhost, a virtual private network, and soon a new set of data appeared in a new window. It looked like utter nonsense to Court, so he didn't focus on it.

But Altman did. "Transfers out of the accounts, into what are probably blind trusts, mostly. No way to know the identity of the recipient of the money . . . unless you happen to have built the biggest and best cross-referencing database of account information in the world."

"And you've done that?"

Altman nodded distractedly; he moved blocks of data around on the screen while he talked. "I've got the database here on the laptop. Again, it's impenetrable to anyone except for me." He added, "I just can't believe, of all people, that Igor Krupkin turned into the Kremlin's whistleblower."

Alex said, "His son died fighting in Ukraine. He blames the State."

Zoya said, "His misfortune is our fortune."

"I met Krupkin once," Ezra said, still distracted by his work. "Ironically, it was at the Cambridge International Symposium on Economic Crime. I was presenting a paper, and he asked some pointed questions from the audience. After my talk he tried to engage me in conversation. I flat-out told him he was a crook and walked away. That night the most beautiful woman I've ever seen in my life bumped into me on the elevator up to my room and threw herself at me."

Court raised his eyebrows. "What did you do?"

"I'm as regular as any guy out there, but the one thing in this world more alluring to me than a beautiful woman is the desire to stay out of a Russian labor camp. I literally ran to my room, locked my door, and called my wife."

Zoya and Court both laughed. Zoya said, "The SVR didn't know what to do with you after that."

"Guess not. Ever since, they've done a lot of dragging my name around online, trying to accuse me of this or that, but that all stopped a couple months ago when they started talking about the summit in New York."

Velesky said, "What is it that makes you so incorruptible?"

His computer screen filled with new information, still nothing Court could make heads or tails out of, so he didn't try. While Altman began typing on the laptop, he said, "My grandparents were wealthy German Jews who lost everything during the war. They survived, made it to Sweden, but they had millions in fine art stolen from them, and it all went to Switzerland, where helpful 'neutral' banks were all too happy to take it in and sell it off.

"I was raised knowing the difference between right and wrong, and with a strong sense of justice. It's just more important to me than anything else."

Finally, he looked up from his laptop and around at the people watching him. "I don't know what you are thinking, but this is going to take some time. Hours. There's no point in watching over my shoulder."

Zoya said, "You want some coffee?"

"Of course I do."

Court turned to Alex. "Why don't you make it? Zoya and I are going to have to be sharp as soon as we have a target. We're going to try to get a little sleep."

Alex went without protest. It was clear he needed coffee as much as Altman did. He said, "Only if I can stop calling you Charlie and start calling you Six like everyone else is."

Director of the CIA Jay Kirby answered his phone at ten minutes after four in the morning, climbing out of bed and leaving his bedroom so as not to disturb his sleeping wife.

He saw that the call was from Suzanne Brewer, and he prayed for good news.

"Suzanne?"

There were a few hot breaths on the phone, and then Brewer said, "Ukrainian separatist spies, Jay? Really? Sleeper cells? GRU assassins weren't good enough? Now we're dealing with fucking terrorists?"

Kirby rubbed his tired eyes, stepped out into his living room, and sat down on the sofa. "Well, if they *were* good enough, I'm sure you would have told me that by now."

"There's a bunch of dead bodies waiting to be discovered at Altman's house. Seeing how there's a shot-up Homeland Security car on West Eighty-First, I can only imagine that it's *already* been discovered."

Kirby said, "The vehicle was moved an hour ago. The bodies, as well."

Brewer continued breathing heavily into the phone. "Homeland Security is helping us?"

"I am in touch with people who can . . . provide assistance."

Finally, she said, "This isn't you running interference to cover for others. This isn't some black ops shit the D/CIA is doing for the good of the country. No . . . you're being paid through Brucker Söhne. Personally. This is about covering your *own* ass."

After a moment, she added, "You're working for the Russians. Aren't you?"

He did not reply; he just stared across his darkened living room.

"I'm going to find out, Jay. You can tell me, or Krupkin's data can. Tell me now, are you being paid off by Moscow?"

After a moment, he just said, "Not anymore."

Brewer's slow, audible breathing continued for a moment, then she said, "Go on."

Kirby stood, walked over to the bar by his kitchen, and pulled a Waterford crystal glass out of a cabinet. "I got redistricted in Congress. I went from a shoo-in to a long shot overnight. And then a savior came in the form of a producer for Russia Today, their international television network. She asked for a meeting to talk about having me appear on a show. Halfway through the meeting, she asked how much money I needed to keep my seat."

"You *had* to have known she was an intelligence officer."

Kirby poured a double shot of Lagavulin into the glass. "I had no idea. I swear, that's the truth. I assumed she was looking for inside information to report on. I knew they were pro-Kremlin, but this was a long time before President Peskov clamped down and made RT nothing more than a mouthpiece of the State."

"What happened?"

"The money showed up in one of my PACs. I spent it on my campaign, and I held my seat. My benefactor asked for nothing from me in return. Didn't even book me on a show."

"Until your next campaign?"

"By then the source of the money was hidden, but I knew it was from Russia. Who else hands over a quarter of a million dollars to a PAC anonymously without even asking for face time with the representative? I turned a blind eye, stayed in Congress for six years, then ran for Senate."

Brewer started to speak, but Kirby continued. "That time it was big money, and it came from the same woman. I know because this time she wanted to meet again.

"It was all very clandestine; our conversation was in a park in my district. I felt dirty because I knew I didn't want to get in deeper with the Russians, but I also knew I didn't want to lose the election. She promised there would never be anything asked of me other than that I continue voting my conscience when Russia was involved.

"That, I thought, I could do with no problem."

Brewer sounded exasperated. "They were just bolstering your bona fides for when they actually wanted to activate you."

Kirby nodded. "I get that. I got it *then*, to be honest, but I could see what other campaigns were spending, and I told myself everyone was taking foreign money for a shot at a Senate seat." He waved a hand in the air. "We don't talk about it, of course, but I'm sure as hell not the only one.

"Again," he said, "they have never asked for one thing from me. Not one."

Utterly exasperated, Brewer shouted at him, "They have! They propped you up through your career so that when they needed you, you would be beholden to them. That's why you, as CIA Director, are working with CIA-killing Russian spies to cover up dirty Russian money funding enemy activities here in America."

Before Kirby responded, Brewer said, "And now you've dragged me down into it, too."

"I didn't drag you *anywhere*. You saw my vulnerability and thought you could capitalize on it. And you *can*. We get that data back, you'll get the deputy directorship, and this will all go away."

"How is it going to go—"

"There are a lot of people corrupted by that money. A lot of important people, Suzanne. If the *New York Times* publishes that information, all these people . . . myself included . . . are going down." He added, perhaps unnecessarily, "The incentive is there to . . . to disappear this information. To disappear anyone who has come into contact with it."

Brewer said, "It's not just Velesky's people and Altman who know about this. The operations officer who was helping me in the Caribbean and in Europe. She's in New York now, she's with Velesky. I found her in the Homeland Security system looking at cameras in the neighborhood near Altman's home."

Kirby found himself stating the obvious now. "Well . . . that's a problem."

He shut his eyes and downed the scotch in two gulps. He walked back over to the bar, put the glass down on the marble counter, and only opened his eyes to reach again for the bottle.

With feigned nonchalance, he said, "How would you react if I said this ops officer was a loose string in this that needs tying off?"

Brewer took a moment, then replied. "I imagine that, due to my exposure here, I would react in *exactly* the way you would want me to react."

"Good." Kirby said. Brewer was telling him she had no problem killing the officer. He said, "Can you think of a way to make this happen?"

"Yes, but it will involve me working directly with the Russians and the separatists."

"I'll talk to Drexler as soon as I hang up with you." Kirby sat back down with his second scotch. "And what do you want in return, Suzanne?"

"Other than Mel Brent's office? I want an airplane. Here. Ready to go."

"Destination?"

"Some urgent job you have for me, somewhere in Europe."

"Europe?"

"I don't just want to be out of the city when this all goes down, I want to be out of the fucking country."

"Daniil Spanov loaned Drexler a GRU aircraft. It's at Teterboro in a private hangar the Russians rented for a couple of days. You can go there with him when it's all over. I'll have another business jet, one clean of Agency fingerprints, land there as soon as possible.

"Drexler will go one way, you will go another."

"Fine," Brewer said. "I need to get to work now. As you are aware, I have an increasing number of loose ends to tie off."

Kirby smiled a little. "Go get 'em, cowgirl."

SIXTY-FOUR

Angela sat next to Altman at his workstation, her SIG Sauer pistol on the desk in front of her, next to Ezra's laptop. She eyed it like it was an unfamiliar object. Six had made her put it there before he and Zoya went to bed, told her that even though she didn't think she could do much with it, she was the only one among her, Alex, and Ezra who had any training whatsoever, so she needed to provide defense for the hotel suite while the only shooters in the group slept.

Zoya had heard the conversation, and she leaned out of the bedroom and said, "If you can't shoot somebody, at least shoot the ceiling, so you'll wake us up." It was said derisively, but Angela took it as good advice.

Her only plan if someone broke down the door was to take that gun and fire it straight up, although she didn't even know if she could do that in good conscience, considering the fact that they weren't on the top floor of the hotel.

Altman had been hard at work for hours. It was nearly six thirty a.m. now, and in all that time he'd barely said a word. He'd accessed a number of databases, some no doubt of his own construction, and he jotted down indistinguishable words and figures on a notepad next to him, but he wasn't including Angela in anything he might have found.

Alex was sound asleep on the sofa, and Angela followed Ezra's lead and drank coffee nonstop, knowing that as tired as she was, she hadn't been do-ing all the fighting Six and Beth had been involved in over the past few days, so she could somehow find a way to power through.

Just as she got ready to take a quick bathroom break, her phone, lying next to the pistol, began vibrating.

As she feared, her screen read **Brewer**.

She groaned audibly, but this time Lacy picked it up and answered it, though she couldn't imagine the conversation she was about to have.

"Yeah?"

Instead of Suzanne Brewer's abrupt and aloof voice, a man with a foreign accent spoke. "Good morning. Terribly sorry to disturb you at this early hour."

"Who is this?"

The man did not answer; instead, he said, "I assume you are with Mr. Altman. May I speak with him?"

For the first time in nearly two hours, Altman looked up from his com-puter. He snatched the phone out of Lacy's hand, but she reached over and hit the speaker button before rushing towards the bedroom to wake the two assets.

Altman spoke hoarsely. "Hello?"

"Hello, Mr. Altman." The man's accent was definitely *not* Russian.

"Who is this?"

"This is the man who has been charged with the safekeeping of your family."

"So . . . you're the kidnapper."

"Oh, not at all. I am no kidnapper. I am a middleman, here to bring a positive resolution to this problem."

"I swear to you," Altman said, "if you touch a hair on any of their heads, then—"

The man talked over him; from his accent Altman thought he might have been French. "The material Alexander Velesky gave you. We want it back. It's as simple as that."

Alex Velesky was awake now, still lying on the couch but listening to every word.

Six and Beth hurried out of the bedroom behind Angela, rubbing their eyes.

"How do I know you will let them go if I do what you say?" Altman asked.

"We will perform a trade in a very public place. Somewhere you feel safe."

Lacy looked around the room at the others. Beth looked furious, Velesky looked scared, Altman looked suspicious.

But Six looked inquisitive, as if something in the man's voice or the man's words was registering with him.

"What do you want me to do?" Altman asked.

"For now, nothing. I will call you back at ten a.m. I will have a location for the exchange in mind. I just wanted to call you and tell you that if any portion of that stolen financial data makes its way into the public sphere, then unfortunately, I will not be able to help you or your family."

"I . . . I understand."

"Wherever you are now . . . just stay there and wait for my next call."

"Okay."

"Now . . . I know you are with several other people, all of whom are listening now."

"No . . . it's just—"

Again, the voice interrupted. "Just know that they do not have your family's interests in mind. Whatever they tell you, whatever they threaten to do to you, *you* are the only one who can save Sarah, Justin, and Kevin. Do you understand this, as well?"

"I do."

"Goodbye." The man hung up, and several people in the room began talking at once.

Lacy was first. "That was Brewer's phone calling. They're together. She's with the kidnappers right now."

Altman mumbled, almost to himself, "What am I going to do?"

Velesky said, "You *have* to keep working, Ezra."

Court chimed in after the others, and when he spoke, he uttered only two words.

"Sebastian Drexler."

All heads turned to him. Zoya said, "Who?"

"That man. I think his name is Drexler. He's a Swiss investigator, works for dirty governments, private banks, oligarchs. God knows who else."

Angela Lacy nodded. "A total criminal and a sociopath. I've heard of him."

Court said, "Middle-aged guy. Bad knee, right?"

She shrugged. "I said I've heard of him, I didn't say I gave him a physical."

Zoya looked to Court. "But . . . *you've* met him?"

"How do you think he got the bad knee?"

Zoya was the first to realize Court was saying he'd been the one to injure Drexler. With a roll of her eyes, she said, "Proud of yourself?"

"Not really. I should have killed him when I had the chance."

"Well, hopefully you'll get another shot."

At once, all eyes turned to Ezra Altman. After a few seconds, Angela said, "What are you going to do?"

The forensic accountant turned back to his computer. "I'm going to keep working. I didn't trust the sound of that man's voice." He motioned to his laptop screen. "*This* is my family's only chance."

Court and Zoya went back into the bedroom, and Lacy headed for the bathroom, while Alex rolled off the couch and went to pour himself and Ezra a fresh cup of coffee.

Sebastian Drexler hung up the phone with Ezra Altman, then called Daniil Spanov. This done, he stood up from his desk. He grabbed his cane and began crossing the loft apartment turned into an office space, heading over to the woman from CIA, who was standing by the floor-to-ceiling window and looking out at the morning over the city.

Drexler's ten-person team of European surveillance experts were dog-tired; they'd been working sixteen hours straight after flying nonstop from Milan, but they remained at it, now examining recorded camera footage all over the island, desperately trying to figure out where their targets had vanished to a few hours earlier.

The hostages were secure, and this was the only bit of good news Drexler had been able to give his employer in their brief phone call. The Ukrainians held the hostages at their safe house in East Rutherford, while the GRU men remained here in the city, ready to go after Ezra Altman as soon as anyone in this room got a hit on his location.

Drexler had decided to wait until ten a.m. to call Altman back, just a couple of hours before the accords were to be signed and the UN voted on the resolution. He'd then ask to trade the accountant's family's lives for the stolen information.

Brewer turned to him. "What did Altman say?"

"He said he would comply."

"We'll know in a few hours," Brewer said. "I've been reading up on Ezra Altman. How he works, how he thinks."

"And what does this research tell you?"

"It tells me I think Altman will go to his office this morning."

Clearly surprised, Drexler said, "Why on earth would he do that? He knows he's a hunted man."

"Because he *has* to. According to what I've read, the accounting software he has is incredibly advanced. Completely proprietary. He had it built by programmers from the ground up. It needs servers to operate; you can't run it from a laptop. He might have a setup at his house, I suppose; but I don't think he has the ability to render the information Velesky gave him without physically going to his building on East Fifty-Second Street."

Drexler thought it over. "You may be right. I'll have my assets go and—"

Drexler stopped speaking when the elevator doors opened and four men stepped out. They all wore coats and hats, except for one man with bright blond hair wearing a walking boot on his left foot.

Instantly Brewer knew who she was looking at.

These were GRU assassins, or what remained of them, anyway, and the man with the blond hair and the bad foot was Matador.

Drexler said, "Ah, yes, Suzanne. The people you were so insistent on meeting have arrived."

The four men stood in the center of the room a moment. The techs around them stared, then went back to their monitors; it was clear to Brewer that they knew they weren't supposed to be eyeing the assets while providing support to a running kill mission.

The blond man said something to his colleagues, and the other three headed over to the raised kitchen area in the loft and began pouring themselves coffee, while Matador limped across the room to the window.

He didn't acknowledge Brewer at all as he stepped up to Sebastian Drexler and spoke in an unmistakable Russian accent. "The Ukrainians have the Altmans secure at their place in New Jersey."

"Very well," Drexler said. "We are homing in on a target for you."

"It's been hours." Matador was clearly not pleased.

"Yes, unfortunately the vehicle in which they left the apartment on Eighty-Seventh Street entered the Park Avenue Tunnel next to Grand Central Station. There are tunnels and tracks all around there, and we saw no one leave on foot. It's possible a car picked them up there, as well. We're still checking." He added, "My people are very good, they will get a hit."

Brewer turned to Drexler. "They don't need a hit, because we know where he is going."

Matador looked to her for the first time. "Where?"

Drexler answered for her. "There is a possibility he will need to access his office to process the data, if that is his intention. If it is not his intention, if when I call him, he tells me he intends to trade the data for his family, then we will meet him at Grand Central Station at noon. He will be expecting a trade, but we will take him from there, dispose of him, his information, and his family somewhere else."

Matador said, "His people will be there."

Brewer spoke directly to Matador. "As will ours."

Matador squared up to Brewer now. "Who are you?"

"CIA. And you are GRU."

Matador raised his eyebrows. With a glint in his eye, he said, "What strange bedfellows we are."

Brewer said nothing to this, but instead, she reiterated, "At some point before Drexler calls him at ten, Ezra Altman will go to his office."

The Russian nodded after a moment, satisfied that the woman seemed to know what she was talking about. "Then we will find him there."

But now, to both his and Drexler's surprise, the woman shook her head. "That's the wrong move. You and your men should watch over the Altman family, not at a house in East Rutherford but at the hangar you have rented at Teterboro Airport.

"Do that, and send the Ukrainians to the office."

"Why?"

"The Gray Man. That's why."

"Explain."

"I know Gentry. I know how he thinks. He will go after Ezra Altman's family. I'm sure of it. I don't know if Zakharova and Lacy will be with him, but *he* is the real threat."

"He won't be able to find the hostages."

"Trust me, he is resourceful. All four of the people with him are smart. I've eliminated their ability to see intelligence material, but they might know enough, or learn enough, to track the Altmans down before the deadline."

Drexler seemed unconvinced, but Matador said, "And why the airport?"

"So we can all get the fuck out of here the second the Ukrainians do their job. You, Drexler, and your men are going to fly out on Daniil Spanov's jet. I have an aircraft inbound there; it will be here by ten." She waved around the room as she turned to Drexler. "We have to keep this surveillance going until the Ukrainians have completed their mission, but these techs can stay here and you can work with them remotely on your way to the airport. Once there, we just wait until the job is done, then we get out of the country."

With another wave to the room, she said, "Have these people break down and disappear. They can make it back home on commercial flights."

Now the Swiss man shook his head as if this idea was out of the question. "Luka and his men can get into Altman's building. But the SSB? They don't have the training."

"They don't *need* the training. One phone call and I can pull away Altman's guards and I can get the SSB access to the building. Then they just need to find an employee elevator and go up."

Luka added, "They can do it. They have been training for some sort of attack."

Brewer and Drexler both turned to him.

"What?" Brewer asked.

"They have plenty of weapons, they are well organized, and they are all combat veterans."

Brewer's blood ran cold. She knew these were agent provocateurs here in America, but she had not known that they were a well-trained combat unit. "How many are there?"

"There are eight left. They aren't Spetsnaz Alpha Group, but they are committed to their mission. I have no doubt they can find a way into an office building and shoot an unguarded man behind his desk, if that's really where Altman goes."

Drexler was coming on board now. "If they get in the building, we can help direct them with security cameras. Plus, if Altman has help, we'll be able to alert the SSB instantly."

Now Matador turned to Brewer and put his hands on his hips, a show of distrust. "What is your motivation here? It sounds like you are trying to protect me and my team."

"I'm trying to protect myself and the mission. Because whoever goes in there to kill Altman is going to die. As soon as the shooting starts, the police are going to be called. This isn't some remote mountain village in Chechnya; this is fucking New York City. NYPD will be on the thirtieth floor in numbers in less than ten minutes. Maybe less than five. And dead SSB officers in the middle of New York will play very differently than dead GRU officers. Let the DPR take the fall for this."

Rudenko looked at the CIA woman appreciatively now. His first show of professional respect.

Drexler said, "And what do we do with the hostages once the family is dead and the data destroyed?"

Rudenko spoke as if the answer were obvious. "We put them on the plane. Then we take off, throw them in the Atlantic. No trace."

Brewer could not disagree. The Altmans, every one of them, were a loose end that needed to be tied off.

Like Velesky, like Zakharova, like Lacy, like Gentry.

As *always*, like Gentry.

But for now, they needed to destroy the data before Altman could process it and distribute it.

Rudenko looked to Drexler and said, "I like her idea. The boys and I will go to the safe house, take the family to Teterboro. Mozgovoy and SSB will come back and take Altman in his office." He looked to Suzanne. "If he doesn't go to his office, they'll be there, at Grand Central, ready to take him during the meet."

Brewer nodded. "In three and a half hours, this could all be over."

Drexler thought a moment, then said, "Very well."

Brewer looked down at Rudenko's foot and pointed. "What happened to you?"

"The Gray Man."

She nodded. "Then you should consider yourself lucky. People don't normally survive hostile encounters with him."

Rudenko looked to Drexler, but Drexler did not respond.

"Is that foot going to be a problem?" Brewer asked.

He shrugged as he turned to head back to his men in the kitchen. "It's no problem at all."

SIXTY-FIVE

Just before seven a.m., Angela Lacy stood in the kitchen of the suite at the Kimberly, watching a fresh pot of coffee brew. She felt the effects of the all-nighter, but there was enough light in the sky outside to tell her she had to keep shaking it off to face the day.

Across the kitchen area in the main room of the suite, Ezra Altman stood, rubbed his eyes, and turned around.

Lacy said, "Bathroom break?"

But the big man shook his head. "Took me long enough, but I think I've got something."

She forgot the coffee and rushed out of the kitchen. "Tell me."

He shook his head. "No offense, but for this we need to tell the two of us who aren't afraid of guns."

Lacy was already heading for the bedroom where Six and Beth were resting. She banged on the door, and soon the man she'd traveled around the world with for the last several days opened it.

Six and Beth both came out, she in a sports bra and dirty jeans, bruises up and down her back and arms, he now wearing only boxers, his body even more badly damaged than hers.

She could tell they'd both fallen back to sleep after Drexler's phone call a half hour earlier, which almost surprised Angela, because they'd been sharing a bed, and the chemistry between the two hard assets, both romantic as well as sexual, was unmistakable.

Lacy said, "Ezra says he has something."

All eyes turned to the man standing there in black pajama pants and an old dark sweater. "I've got a name. He's not Ukrainian, but he's been withdrawing money from a bank in Manhattan on the fifteenth of every single month since last summer."

"What does that prove?" Angela asked.

"Nothing, except this guy has come up before in my research."

"He's working with the Russians?"

Ezra flashed a rare and very tired smile. "If you aren't working with the Russians, your name doesn't come up in my research."

Now everyone moved closer. Altman said, "Twelve accounts at First Trader's bank are being periodically replenished with Russian funds coming from Brucker Söhne." He waved his hand through the air. "Via typical offshore banking chicanery, it didn't flow directly from there to here, of course, but it was nothing I couldn't sort through."

"Go on," Court urged.

"Each account has a debit card, under the name of an LLC. Just a shell corp, but the LLC has to designate at least one person entitled to withdraw money from the bank itself or to use the debit cards, and if you have a way into their records, you can see who that is."

"How much money are we talking about?" Court asked.

"Thirty grand a month, save for the last two months, when it was nearly fifty. The name of the man on the accounts is Henry Calvin; he works at a law firm in Manhattan, and his firm was on my radar because they were proudly serving the interests of certain Russian oligarchs here in New York up until the war started and all their clients were sanctioned. Real estate deals and other legal matters.

"I locked onto them a couple of years ago, but once the feds said American banks couldn't deal with Russian money, they supposedly stopped working with their clientele from Russia."

Lacy asked, "What about the Ukrainians? The sleeper cell in New York? How much money do they need to operate?"

Ezra said, "I worked the case last year with the other SSB guys who got caught. They were getting their money directly from an SSB agent the feds picked up in D.C., but he was giving his cell fifteen grand a month."

Court said, "Okay, so the money here might be going to SSB assets here, but even thirty K a month isn't all that much."

"True, but these sleepers, they all have jobs to establish their covers. The money from Russian intelligence goes for safe houses they rent in cash, purchases of equipment, stuff like that. This isn't payroll money; whatever they're paid by the Russians is probably in some bank account in Russia for when they get back."

Ezra gave a little smile now. "And there's something else. The first time since last July that Henry Calvin didn't withdraw the money on the fifteenth was this month."

Velesky nodded animatedly. "Krupkin stole his data on January thirteenth. By the fifteenth somebody must have told everyone down the line not to touch the cash."

"Exactly," Altman said.

Zoya asked, "Any way to find out where this guy lives?"

Altman smiled again as he looked down at his notepad. "One fifty-three East Ninety-Sixth Street, apartment six fourteen."

Court cocked his head. "How the hell did you—"

"Public records. It's childishly easy searching for property that isn't hidden behind a dozen blind trusts like everything else I deal with."

"So . . . I need to pay Calvin a visit," Court said, "and ask him very nicely who he's giving this Russian money to every month."

Zoya said, "And I need to come with you."

"Wait," Lacy said. "You're not going to torture him, are you?"

Court smiled. "I prefer to call it 'tactical questioning.'"

Zoya turned to Lacy. "But it looks a little bit like torture. Don't come with us if you don't have the stomach for it."

Lacy just looked back at the Russian woman defiantly. "Let's shake him down, see what comes out."

Velesky sat down at the table next to where Ezra had been working. "I'll stay here with the genius, watch his back."

Zoya went back into the bedroom, then returned with the Smith and Wesson revolver she'd bought in the Thai market the night before last. She put it on the table in front of Alex next to the two speed loaders, each with five rounds of .38 Special ammunition. "Don't touch the gun unless you need it. If you do, point the barrel and pull the trigger. There are five bullets in the cylinder, and you can reload it with these." She pointed to the speed loaders.

Alex looked nervous, but he nodded.

Court leaned closer to him. "Remember, anything worth shooting once is worth shooting twice."

Nervously, Velesky nodded. "Got it."

Court returned to the bedroom to dress, and he saw that his phone was buzzing where it was plugged in by the bed. He snatched it up. "Yeah?"

"Good morning. It's Cathy King."

Court looked at the clock on the nightstand and saw that it was exactly seven a.m. "Are you here?"

"I'm here. Where are you?"

"Look . . . I've got to run out and take care of something. I need you to go to the Kimberly Hotel, suite 712. Knock on the door, and the two guys who answer will be the most interesting people you've ever met. Come alone."

After a moment, she said, "I'm not going to see you? This sounds incredibly fishy."

To this, Court replied, "I'm sure last time we met it all seemed a bit surreal. Trust me, this is bigger."

King sighed. "It had better be. I'm missing out on the news coming out of the summit."

Court sniffed out a laugh. "Oh, I strongly disagree." And he hung up the phone.

After telling the two men who would remain behind about the upcoming arrival of Catherine King, Lacy, Court, and Zoya headed for the door. They all had a firearm, although it was a given that if shit went wrong, Lacy couldn't be trusted to use hers.

Ezra Altman called out to them as they reached the door. "Bring my family home. Please."

"We will," Zoya assured him.

• • •

Henry Calvin walked his two young children to school at seven thirty, then dropped them off at the gate and headed east through the morning commute towards the Ninety-Sixth Street subway station.

It was cold and blustery, temperatures in the high twenties and wind that whipped through his coat and across his face, but he was a New Yorker through and through, and though he didn't love it, this was nothing he wasn't accustomed to.

He crossed Lexington and moved along with the crowd, but just steps from taking the stairs to the subway, he felt a hand on his left arm and a pressure in the small of his back.

The arm and the pressure kept him moving forward, but when he looked back over his shoulder, he saw a man there, close, his eyes locked on Henry's. Henry tried to stop walking, but the man pulled him to the left and then forward, thereby bypassing the stairs.

The lawyer stumbled a little, then said, "What the fuck is—"

Henry could feel the man's breath on his face when he softly spoke. "What you are feeling on your spine is the tip of a silencer, and it's attached to a nine-millimeter pistol. My finger is on the trigger, and I've had a *shit*-ton of coffee. Maybe you should keep walking."

The man was American, and though Henry didn't recognize him, the tone in his voice and his close and overbearing presence instantly filled him with terror.

He kept walking. "What is this?"

The only reply he received was more pressure in the small of his back.

Henry kept walking but said, "Look, I've got a little money. If you—"

"Don't worry. We'll talk money in just a second," the man said, and then he led him across the street and through a door that had been propped open with a paint can. On the other side was a concrete stairwell, and the man with a gun to his back pushed him into it.

Henry wasn't sure where they were at first, but soon he realized they were in the 175 East 96th Street Garage.

They descended two levels, then emerged in a fairly well-lit space, less than one quarter filled with cars. The man behind him had backed off a step; he seemed to be communicating with someone softly in an earpiece, and then he turned Henry to the left, leading him all the way to the corner of the garage. Here a large white Ram ProMaster cargo van was parked, its back door wide open, ominously, as far as Henry was concerned.

"Get in," the man with the gun said.

Henry looked around, then back at the man. He appeared to be in his thirties; he was neither tall nor short, neither thin nor fat. He had short brown hair and a trim beard, and he wore a dark gray coat and black pants.

"Get in," he repeated, and this time he raised the pistol to Henry's face. With the gunman's arm extended, the long silencer almost touched the attorney on the tip of his nose.

He turned and climbed inside; it was empty other than some five-gallon buckets of what looked to be white primer along the walls. There were only two seats up front, and the large rear compartment had rubberized flooring with bright speckles of paint all over. This was some sort of work truck, that much was obvious, and after more coaxing at gunpoint, he sat down on one of the buckets.

He expected the gunman to go around and get behind the wheel of the van, but instead, the man climbed in with Henry and sat on a five-gallon container on his left, closer to the driver's seat.

Almost instantly, two more figures appeared behind the van; Henry guessed they must have been waiting by the wall on the far side of it for him to enter. He was surprised and frankly relieved to see that they were both female: an attractive Black woman in a dark blue sweater and a light brown wool coat, and a severe and menacing-looking white woman in a shiny black ripstop fabric ski coat.

"Where are we going?" Henry asked the Black woman, because she looked the least threatening of the three somehow, but it was the man with the gun on his left who answered. "Nowhere. This isn't even our van, we're just going to borrow it for a few minutes."

"For what?"

The women entered the van, and they shut the back doors and sat on the containers on either side of Calvin. The white woman turned to him in the near darkness and spoke with an American accent. "You've been handling bank accounts for Russian interests in the city."

"What?" Calvin said, an air of astonishment in his voice he didn't think he'd managed to carry off very well. "I'm a lawyer, I'm not a banker."

The man seated next to him reached over now, grabbed Henry Calvin by the hair on the top of his head, and yanked his head back, slamming his skull into the wall of the paint van. The sound boomed out in the garage, and Henry groaned, bringing his hands to the impact point on the back of his head, already feeling the knot of a forming bruise.

"Jesus Christ! I don't know who all our clients are. If somebody pissed you off, you should take it up with—"

The woman in the black coat spoke again. "Are you aware of the financial data that was smuggled out of Russia the other day?"

Henry hesitated a bit, looked around, then said, "No."

The man grabbed him again, this time shoving him forward, off the bucket and across the interior of the van, where he now hit his forehead on the wall right between the two seated women.

"What the fuck!" Henry shouted, and he felt a trickle of blood drip off his eyebrow onto his cheek.

He saw the Black woman lurch back in surprise, but she quickly recovered and spoke, her voice a little shaky. "The . . . elite have their identities protected. For now, anyway. But the little people, people like you? Your name is all over that information, and that information is hours away from going public."

"I . . . I don't know what the fuck you're talking about."

Court Gentry knew one thing without a shred of doubt. Henry Calvin *did* know what the fuck they were talking about.

He said, "I tried to knock some sense into you, Henry, but I see it hasn't worked."

"What is it you three think I did?" Calvin asked.

Court replied, "All sorts of shit, I imagine. But *one* thing you did is the one thing that brought us all together today, and it's the reason you have a broken nose."

Calvin touched his forehead. "It's my forehead. I don't have a—"

Court's right foot shot out and kicked the attorney in the face, and he crumpled to the floor, clutching his nose as blood poured through it.

After several seconds he looked up at Court, and he gave a smile that Court could tell was utterly fake because the man was obviously scared shitless. "I'm going to call *all* my lawyers."

The African American woman spoke again, less nervously than before. "You don't need a lawyer. You're not in legal jeopardy now. You're in actual, real-world, laws of nature, *true* jeopardy."

Court could see it on Calvin's face. Through the blood, through the faltering smile, under the fresh sweat on his forehead, he was a defeated man.

Finally, he said, "What do you want?"

"You've been taking out thirty to fifty thousand dollars a month for the past sixth months, on the fifteenth of the month. In cash. I want to know what you're doing with that money."

"Gambling."

"You just gambled with your nose and lost. You ready to gamble with your right ankle?"

Court lifted his foot over the man's leg, held it there.

"No! Please."

Court lowered his foot back to the floor of the van. "You're paying off someone, that much we know. Who is it?"

"I don't know. I just withdraw cash every month from some LLC accounts, deliver it to a guy. That's all."

"What guy?"

"I don't know."

"When was the last time you saw him?"

"Day before yesterday. He wanted to know where the money was because he didn't get it this month."

"Because you learned from your client that there was a compromise?"

"I can't talk about my conversations with my clients. It's a breach of—"

Court raised his foot high again over Calvin's leg. The attorney cowered into the fetal position.

"Yes! I was told not to touch the accounts!"

"Told by who?"

"Our client."

"Who is your client?"

"An LLC. Based in Amsterdam. Completely legal."

"Bullshit," the white woman said now. "You've been handing money off to Russian spies."

Calvin looked like he was going to deny it, but then he looked up at the bearded man. "Listen . . . I . . . the person I give the money to, he's not Russian."

"Do me a favor and slide that ankle over here for me, Henry."

Calvin shouted. "He's Ukrainian! That's all I know!"

"So . . . money from Russia is going to Ukrainians in the USA. What do you think that's all about?"

Henry Calvin wiped blood from his face, sat back up, looked down at his coat and his suit, saw the blood. "Jesus Christ."

Court said, "Your chances of survival for the next ten minutes are slim. Really fucking slim. But maybe you can tip the scales in your favor by playing straight with me."

Calvin nodded now. "The Donetsk People's Republic. Whatever the fuck that is."

"It's Ukrainians fighting against their own nation on behalf of Russia. And you know what it is."

Calvin shrugged. "I don't watch the news."

"Your bank was flagged for working with the Russians last year. You don't get to play stupid. You knew you were passing money on to a cell of spies here in New York."

After a few seconds, Calvin just nodded. "I do what I'm told."

Court looked up at Angela and Zoya, worry on both their faces. "What's the money for?" he asked.

"I . . . I don't know."

Zoya spoke up now, speaking to Court. "He's worthless. Let's shoot him and go."

"No!" Calvin shouted. "I do know . . . I know something."

"Talk, then."

"The guy I deliver the money to. He's got a house in New Jersey."

"What's his name?"

"I don't know. We use a code-word system for communications."

"Of course you do. Go on."

"I call him Antonio. He rents this house, pays in cash, but around Christmas I got a call from his landlord. He'd used our law firm as a reference; the fucking idiot was supposed to use a shell corp we gave him but screwed up. She told me he owed six grand rent on his place in East Rutherford."

"What are they doing at that house?"

"I don't know what they are doing, and I don't care. I'm an attorney, I just fulfill the wishes of my firm's clients to the best of my ability. That's all."

"Do you remember the address?"

"Of course not."

"Shit, man," Court said. "And to think you were just about to survive the day to see your kids tonight."

"Wait! Fuck, okay, man. Windsor. Windsor Drive, something like that. I remember that much."

Lacy was already putting the street and city into Google Maps; after a few seconds she said, "There's a Windsor Avenue in East Rutherford. Only about a half-dozen homes; the rest of the properties are facing cross streets."

Court nodded. "Good, Henry. Now, how do you get in contact with your Ukrainian friend?"

"I . . . I have a phone number."

"Take out your phone and read us the number."

He did so, Lacy typed it into her phone, and a few seconds later, she said, "It's probably Telegram or Signal or some other private messaging app. Means nothing."

Court shrugged. "It means we can call it."

He turned his attention back to the lawyer trying to keep as much blood inside his body as possible. "Frankly, Henry, I would have a lot more respect for you if you'd held out a little longer before spilling the beans, but a deal is a deal. You get to leave this parking garage with your life today."

He breathed out a massive sigh of relief, blood speckling the floor in front of him from where it was expelled by his nose and mouth. "Thank you . . . thank you. Thank you so much."

Court shook his head. "I wouldn't thank me, and I wouldn't tell anyone about us. In fact, you have twenty-four hours, tops, to get your dumb ass to a non-extradition country, or else, better yet, jump in front of a moving subway train, because your name and your affiliation with Russia and the terrorists will be all over the news by this time tomorrow."

"But . . . I gave you what you asked for."

"My only promise was that you'd walk out of here with a heartbeat. After that, ace, you're on your own, and frankly, you're fucked."

Zoya knocked the man down on the floor, then deftly hog-tied him. "This will keep you occupied for a few hours."

"You can't leave me here like this!"

Zoya opened the back door of the van and slid out; Court followed behind her without another word to Henry Calvin.

Lacy remained on her five-gallon drum for a moment, looking the man over. Finally, she said, "When you get free, you need to either start calling prospective lawyers or start calling prospective pallbearers." As she slid out the door, she said, "If I were you, I'd do both. Cover all my bases."

SIXTY-SIX

Catherine King sat in the suite at the Kimberly Hotel, motionless, a pen hovering over a notepad almost exactly where it had been for the past thirty minutes. She'd jotted furiously at first, but then it had just been too much, too fast. She'd switched to shorthand, but then even this couldn't keep up. Alexander Velesky was hopped up on coffee, and he talked nonstop about his job funneling Russian money to the West, his meeting with a financial advisor from Moscow, and the information he took involving Kremlin espionage activities.

She learned the circumstances of the dead CIA officer in Zurich; this had been widely reported, but without a suspect or a motive mentioned by authorities. Velesky talked about the train trip from Milan to Geneva, and of course Catherine knew about this. She'd been following the investigation into several dead Russians very carefully, at least one of them a known GRU assassin, in case it affected the ongoing talks between Moscow and Western nations in New York.

Her knowledge of some of the things Velesky discussed aided his credibility, but when Ezra Altman began speaking, she began to wonder if this was all some sort of crazy hallucination.

Altman had talked about the attack on his home the night before, right here in the city; the mysterious phone call from the Swiss man named Drexler; and the fact that someone very high up in the CIA named Suzanne Brewer was both here and directly involved.

King knew Suzanne Brewer, mostly by reputation. They'd met a few years back in D.C., and she'd kept an eye on the woman as she'd moved up the ranks at the Agency. She was now special assistant to the deputy director for operations, Mel Brent, which made King wonder if Brent was involved in whatever this was, as well.

If any of whatever this was, was even true.

While Altman spoke to her, he'd faced away, his attention split between telling his story and his computer monitor, and when she asked what he was doing, he revealed he was compiling the disparate data from Krupkin's phone, although King hadn't seen one single piece of the data yet herself.

So far she was only certain that she'd just met two intense men who looked exhausted but told a compelling and desperate story, connected somehow to a man she knew to be reliable.

It was enough for her to be here, but it certainly wasn't enough for her to begin typing up an article.

She explained as much to the men when they were done regaling her with all the details, and Altman shrugged his big shoulders. "I can't give you any proof until Six and Beth get my family back. Then . . . it's all yours."

She looked past him to his monitor. On it were databases and spreadsheets, dozens stacked upon each other, making for a confounding display. She said, "*What's* all mine? That raw data?"

Now Altman looked her way. "No. I've got to go in to my office and run this through my servers. It will create a user interface suitable for media." He said, "Six said I should give you an exclusive, but only if you promise to put it online immediately and to contact the accused for comment."

"But . . . why me?"

"I think because you're the only one Six trusts."

Velesky chimed in now. "Look, if people in Homeland Security and the CIA are involved, then it's not impossible that journalists could be on the take from the Russians, as well."

King said, "If you saw my little apartment and eleven-year-old car, you'd clear me of any wrongdoing pretty quickly."

Before Velesky could respond, Altman said, "I'm going now. My office is just a few blocks away. I'll get everything into one large document with my conclusions, attach all the raw data, link corroborating source material, and email it to you."

"How long will that take?"

"I'll need at least an hour, but I don't know if I have that much time. I can generate something with *some* of the names of parties on the take from Moscow. The low-hanging-fruit stuff."

Additionally, he said, "Remember, this is all predicated on Six and Beth and Angela getting my family back."

Velesky stood now. "I will come with you, Ezra, and watch your back."

King stood, as well. "Me, too."

But Altman shook his head. "They can tap into cameras. If they see me and Alex there, they will come and stop us, but if they see a reporter for the *Washington Post* at my office, they're just going to kill my family."

King breathed out a long sigh. "I know people at NYPD. I know feds who work here. I can call—"

Both Velesky and Altman shook their heads. "No cops," Velesky said. "The people after us are going to know it the second we start talking to authorities in any way."

King looked to Altman now. "You're going in to work dressed like that?"

He looked down at himself. "Yeah . . . I guess I have to."

She reached into her purse, pulled out a wallet, and handed him a credit card. "No, you don't. There's a Target over on Tenth that opens at eight." She shrugged. "I'm here a lot doing the news shows, and more than once I've had to do a mad dash for fresh clothes first thing in the morning."

He took the card, promised her he'd email her the second his family was safe, and King said she'd return to her hotel and await news, determined to do her own work confirming the information around the data before she even got a look at the data itself.

The three of them shook hands at the door a minute later. Catherine was first to leave, while Ezra packed up his laptop and prepared himself for what he knew would be the most important day of his life.

...

Petro Mozgovoy climbed out of his East Rutherford, New Jersey, basement with a large canvas duffel bag hanging from his shoulder, right behind Arsen Ostopenko, who labored carrying a similar bag.

The five other male members of his cell were upstairs already with their own bags, unzipping them on the living room floor, taking out the contents.

The black bags had been hidden behind a large piece of particle board, placed and painted to appear to be the back wall of the closet, but accessible with only a minute's work with a screwdriver.

Two bags remained in the closet, because two of his men, the massively strong but not terribly bright Barabash and the older of the Bondarenko brothers, Taras, had been killed early this morning, their bodies recovered from Altman's home. They were then driven away and weighted down with sacks of concrete wrapped to them with rope and thrown into the Hudson River along with a GRU officer Petro never even caught the name of.

It was all a fucking mess, Petro lamented to himself, but he knew he needed to keep his cell engaged because they still had work to do.

The cell had gotten word that they'd be going back into Manhattan, and the Russians would be arriving shortly to take control of the three hostages currently bound to heavy furniture in the main bedroom upstairs. What the Russians would do with the three Americans, none of these SSB operatives had a clue, but Petro was glad they wouldn't be his problem anymore. He had two boys of his own, and the thought of shooting a sixteen-year-old and his fourteen-year-old brother had been hanging over him since they took control of the three Altmans several hours earlier.

He'd killed before, killed boys not much older than these, he was certain, fighting in his nation's civil war. But these Jewish American boys, tied up with their mom, didn't have anything to do with his fight that he could see, so the fact that the Russians were going to deal with them made the prospect of Petro engaging in an assassination of an accountant in Manhattan considerably easier to swallow.

The men began undressing in silence, their minds focusing on the work at hand. They'd planned for a specific mission, but this wasn't it. Originally they were going to infiltrate a construction company working on some floors at the Millennium Hilton at the UN towers with the goal of assassinating the foreign minister of Ukraine, who was in town not to attend the summit itself but to speak to the UN General Assembly in protest of America's proposal to stop arming Ukraine in exchange for a cease-fire.

That plan seemed to be out the window—for now, anyway—and this new mission had replaced it.

After a few minutes spent changing clothes, all seven of the men were now dressed in the garb of construction workers, and they each had a smaller satchel with tool belts, hard hats, radios, and other gear, all purchased at wholesale from the hardware store where the late Taras and his younger brother Evgen worked. They looked the part they would need to play today, and they all had one more tool they each stored in a small personal backpack.

The SIG Sauer Copperhead was one of the tiniest subguns in existence, and with its single-shot configuration and collapsible arm brace instead of collapsible stock, the small lethal weapon was legal to purchase with only a fifteen-minute-or-so wait for a background check in many states in the United States.

The SSB cell had acquired ten of these 9-millimeter weapons in New Hampshire; they accepted a thirty-round magazine, and when fully collapsed, they were only fourteen and a half inches in length.

Having spent their military careers using the larger Kalashnikov, the team had driven to West Virginia four times over the winter to train with the smaller weapon, and by now, every man was proficient in its use.

The seven surviving male members of the cell were ready, and this greatly relieved the one woman in the group, Kristina Golubova, who had been impatiently waiting on the sofa for a half hour while the men worked over their plans, double-checked their weapons, and then finally donned their disguises.

Kristina wore a dark blue business suit; she sipped tea and looked at an iPad showing the layout of the building on East 52nd Street where Altman Globus Accountancy LLP was located. She knew the location well enough, having studied it for the last hour, but their original mission at the hotel she had been studying for months, so this was very much a change to her plans.

Kristina did not carry a Copperhead like the rest of her cell; instead, she had a Taurus GX4 micro-compact pistol in her purse, along with the same brand of radio as the rest of the team. She'd trained with the pistol, but she was only to serve as the lookout today, and she knew that if she had to pull out her pistol and use it, then something had gone horribly, horribly wrong with the operation.

Once all the men were dressed, their weapons stowed in packs, lunchboxes and hard hats under their arms, there was a knock at the door.

Alarmed, all the men quickly scrambled to get their Copperheads out and aimed; they spread out in the hallway, the dining room, the living room, and the kitchen, and Antoin Zhuk covered the back door with his weapon in case this was a coordinated attack by the FBI.

With a nod from Petro, Kristina pulled her pistol from her purse, went to the door, and looked through the peephole.

"It's the Russians," she said as she reached for the dead bolt.

Petro stood in the center of the hall and cursed. "Sukha. He was supposed to text me. Why can't they do anything—"

As the door opened, Petro stopped talking.

Luka entered with his three surviving men; they held no weapons but were nevertheless intimidating by their presence, even with the man with the spiked blond hair wearing a big boot on his foot.

Petro and his men lowered their weapons, and Luka regarded the cell leader. "Much better this time," he said, clearly referring to his last visit here, when he and his men bum-rushed the team and completely surprised them.

The SSB leader addressed the rest of his team. "Pack everything back up." Then he turned to Luka. "You were to text when you were out front."

"I must have forgotten."

He hadn't forgotten, this Petro knew, but he let it go.

Luka asked, "Where are the captives?"

"Upstairs. Secured."

Without waiting to be told, two of Luka's GRU men headed for the staircase.

He then turned back to Petro. "You can go. Good luck to you."

"You will stay here with the prisoners?" Petro asked.

Luka walked up to him. Petro could see the man was moving with ease now, so unlike when he saw him before, when he limped and winced with every step.

Luka said, "Worry about your mission. Everything relies on you."

Petro's eyes narrowed. "We are not cannon fodder. You told me before you would be there with us when we acted."

"Operations change. We won't be with you, but we expect an attack to recover the Altmans, and I've been impressed by what our adversary has been able to accomplish."

"There will be a lot of police in that building we're going to have to hit."

Luka shrugged. "Your operation is spoon-fed to you. You have assets watching security cameras, you have the target's security being ordered away once you get there. Just shoot all the targets in the head, recover the data, and leave." When Petro said nothing, Luka added, "If you can't handle shooting an accountant behind his desk, then maybe I—"

"We will complete our mission." The Ukrainian puffed his chest up, raised a fist in the air, and shouted loudly, "Arise, Donbas!"

The rest of the team called out in unison, "Arise, Donbas!"

Luka seemed bored, but he raised his fist, as well, and replied, "Mother Russia is with you."

These were lyrics to the DPR's unofficial national anthem, and while Luka didn't appear to Petro to give a shit about the DPR, he at least gave them the courtesy of a callback.

Petro gave Luka the two remaining Copperhead personal defense weapons, and extra magazines, to augment the pistols all the GRU men carried.

The Ukrainians left through the kitchen door a minute later and packed into a pair of work vans parked in the detached garage that sat at the end of the drive behind the little clapboard house, and a minute later they pulled out onto Windsor Avenue, turning to the south.

As they made a left onto Randolph Avenue, headed for Route 3, a red Nissan Armada turned off Hoboken Road and onto Windsor, two blocks to the north.

The occupants of the Armada did not see the vans, and the occupants of the vans did not see the Armada.

SIXTY-SEVEN

Court Gentry sat behind the wheel of the stolen red Nissan Armada, the keys of which he'd found after sneaking into a valet booth at a hospital parking lot in Midtown Manhattan. Next to him sat Zoya Zakharova, and behind her was Angela Lacy, who had spent the half-hour drive concentrating on the GPS app on her phone.

Zoya did most of the talking. She and Court had two whole hours of sleep and a lot of coffee after that, and their various aches and pains meant it was hard to just sit back and relax.

Court didn't say what he was thinking, however: that it was pretty clear to him Zoya had done a line or two of coke when she'd stepped into a bathroom at the garage while Court hunted for car keys. She'd been much more animated since they'd climbed into the Armada, and he didn't know what to do or to say, so he neither did nor said anything the entire drive.

Once they got on Windsor, they all began looking at the houses. As Angela had told them from her check of the satellite image, there were just a few homes with addresses on the street, because all the corner houses actually faced the cross streets.

They knew they were looking for a Windsor address, however, so they evaluated the five homes they saw with mailboxes on the avenue. All the homes were small but neat, two stories, with tiny front yards and driveways that extended to the back of the property. Court saw garages out back of each one he passed, all with the doors closed.

They crossed the first intersection, and on the other side Court saw a white Chevy Tahoe backing out of a drive in front of him.

Angela saw it, too. "That's a rental. Three rows. You can fit a lot of dudes in there."

"Yep," Court said, and he kept driving, continuing on past the driveway while the truck stopped, waiting to back out.

Now Court was in front of the vehicle, and it turned out of the drive and in the opposite direction.

"All eyes forward," Zoya instructed, and then she adjusted her rearview to try to get a surreptitious look behind as the truck headed the other way.

Behind her, Court heard exasperation from Angela, clearly annoyed to be getting tradecraft tips from a Russian spy. "Damn, I was just about to spin around on my knees and press my face to the glass."

Zoya said, "I don't know what you were about to do."

"Please, guys. Not right now," Court muttered.

They neared the end of the street; the white SUV behind them made a right, so Court turned left, trying to stay parallel to its path as he checked his navigation screen in the car.

Zoya said, "It's them."

"What did you see?"

Court was certain Zoya had snorted coke by the way she talked. Slightly more rapid, slightly more dramatic. He even thought he heard a twinge of her Russian accent creeping in. "At least four pax inside. The windows are tinted, couldn't get an accurate count. But I'll tell you what I *didn't* see. I didn't see any other vehicles on that street big enough to move a terrorist cell."

"There were garages, Beth," Angela pointed out.

Zoya spun around. "Were there? Oh, great. Let's go back to Windsor, park there, and see if a garage opens sometime in the next few hours and a bunch of DPR assholes pull out in armored cars, while letting the one fucking vehicle on the street big enough to hold a crew of operators drive off towards Manhattan. That's your plan?"

Jesus Christ, Court muttered to himself.

Angela conceded the point. "Fine." Then she turned to Court. "How you keep from shoving your pistol in your mouth every day with her, I don't know."

Zoya said, "You could shove your pistol in your mouth, but we all know that wouldn't do any good, because you won't pull the trigger."

Court did not speak up this time; there was nothing he could say to ease this situation. He made a left and then, seconds later, found himself in traffic behind the white Tahoe as it turned north on Route 17.

Lacy said, "You have to go south to get to Manhattan. Where's he going?"

"I hope this isn't a wild-goose chase," Court said. "Ezra and Alex are on their own, and we're following some random truck."

Zoya said, "It's them, guys. Relax. They're going somewhere, and we're going to follow them."

She looked to Court. "How many rounds in your magazine?"

"Nine."

She turned back to Angela now; her moves and her speech patterns remained altered. "Give me your gun."

"What?"

Zoya said, "Give him seven rounds. If we confront these guys, we need to do it with full mags. Your SIG has thirteen, and we sure as hell know it's fully loaded, don't we? We'll leave you with six."

Lacy just looked at Zoya for several seconds. Finally, she said, "Are you . . . are you hopped up on something?"

"The gun, please," Zoya said, holding out her hand.

Angela drew her pistol, dropped the magazine, and began fanning hollow-point bullets out of it. "I'm not giving you *another* loaded gun, you're dangerous enough as it is. You're on something, sister, and that is really fucking unprofessional, especially right now."

Court said, "Angela. Let it go. Please."

Zoya spoke with menace. "Good advice."

Angela fumed but passed all seven rounds up to the woman she knew as Beth, eyed her malevolently, and then slid the mag back into her SIG and reholstered.

Court handed his weapon off to Zoya after thanking Angela, doing his best to defuse the deteriorating situation. Zoya loaded him up and handed his HK back.

And then, right in front of them in the gray morning, a private jet rose into the sky.

Court and Angela said it at the same time. "Teterboro."

"Shit," Zoya said. "They're going to the airport."

"Do they have the Altmans?" Court asked, rhetorically. "If they do, then that doesn't make any sense. They want to trade them for Krupkin's phone. Why would they leave with them?"

Lacy held up her phone. "Unless there *is* no plan to trade. Maybe we just call the cops. Give them the tag number of that vehicle and tell them there are armed men holding hostages."

Zoya shook her head. "It will take the cops a half hour to muster a SWAT team around here, and if those are Ukrainian terrorists in that van up there, then anything short of a SWAT team is going to get wiped out, and then the Altmans will be killed. We need to keep this covert."

Court agreed. "I'd love to bring in some help, but we don't know they won't just make the situation worse."

Angela Lacy thought about it a moment, then said, "Okay. I'll check Teterboro for scheduled flights out." She dialed a number while Court concentrated on staying far enough back from the Tahoe without losing it.

Ezra Altman entered the front door of his building on East 52nd at eight forty a.m. He wore a light gray suit with an open-collared button-down and new shoes, all purchased at the early-opening Target store on Tenth Avenue.

He even had a small faux-leather folio under his arm holding his computer, Krupkin's phone, and peripherals he'd borrowed from Lacy.

He wasn't particularly well put together, but he thought he looked close enough to any other day that he would avoid any undue scrutiny, other than the fact that he wasn't wearing his yarmulke like every other time he'd walked through these doors in the dozen years he'd worked here.

Alex Velesky walked along with him. He, too, had purchased cheap business attire at Target, and he, like Ezra, looked presentable if not polished.

Ezra stepped up to the guard at the desk in front of the elevators, with Alex trailing a half step behind. "Hey, Marcus."

The sixty-something man in a blue blazer looked inquisitively at Altman's attire, but he quickly smiled. "Morning, Mr. Altman."

"Yeah . . . Left home without my wallet." He hefted his shoulder bag. "Walked out the door with just this."

"No worries. I'll print you out a day pass."

"And one for my visitor, too, please."

Alex passed over his Swiss driver's license; Marcus took his and Ezra's pictures and then printed out a pass for them both.

A minute later they entered the elevator; they got out on thirty and began walking up the hall. Ezra purposefully did not look up as he passed under security cameras that he imagined had the resolution to pick up the sweat dripping from his brow, but he waved to the two guards at the entrance to his office.

They showed no surprise in seeing him, and no particular interest in the man walking with him, and he took this as very good news.

"Morning, guys," he said.

They nodded in return. These two had only been with him a couple of weeks; the Department of Homeland Security had changed out his detail multiple times of late, and while he didn't trust that he wasn't being watched or even bugged, he thought these two guys were just doing their workaday jobs, guarding a hall to the office of an accountant that the government called on from time to time for matters involving dangerous parties.

Once inside, he greeted his other two guards, who returned his greeting with the same aloofness he'd grown accustomed to, and then he waved to his staff, a dozen people in cubicles or small offices, and though he kept walking and did not introduce Alex, he did his best to act like this was just any other day. It was clear to him it was just that for the rest of the people here, and soon he made his way to his private office in the back of the long, narrow space.

The phone in his pocket began ringing as he put his bag down. He prayed it was good news.

He answered with, "Altman."

"It's Six."

"My family?"

The tone of the man's voice instantly told him he'd gotten his hopes too high.

"We're tailing some people in New Jersey. We're not sure who is in the vehicle, but suspect it's the Ukrainians. We think they're heading to Teterboro Airport. What's happening there?"

"I just got to my office. I'm going to—"

"Your *office*? You weren't supposed to leave the Kimberly."

"The only way I can process this data in any form the media can use quickly is to do it here. If this information doesn't get out soon, then it won't get out in time to stop the accords from being signed."

"We can't protect you from fucking New Jersey."

"Alex is here, he's armed."

Six did not sound reassured. "The guards there at your office? How are they acting?"

"Completely normal. Everything feels like a regular day."

"Trust me, somebody on the other side saw you go in there. You need to be ready to barricade your—"

Ezra had already sat down at his computer. "Look, I've got a lot to do, I have to get to work. This is me, living up to our bargain. Please, you have to live up to yours."

"Just be careful."

"You, too. Call me the second you have good news." Altman hung up, plugged his laptop into jacks on his workstation, and got down to business, while Alex Velesky sat on a couch by the closed glass door that led to the rest of the office so he could eye the room.

Suzanne Brewer rode in the back of a Mercedes sedan with Sebastian Drexler, heading down Tenth Avenue through morning traffic towards the Lincoln Tunnel. Drexler sat in the front seat; he had been talking very softly to someone while one of his team members drove next to him.

She wondered if Drexler was speaking with Matador, or maybe even to Daniil Spanov himself, but eventually she told herself she really did not want to know, so she just looked out the window, stressing about everything that had already happened, and everything that was still to come.

The rest of her life hinged on the next hour; this she knew without reservation.

Just as she closed her eyes to take a few calming breaths, her phone rang in her hand. Her eyelids snapped open, and she brought it to her ear quickly.

"Brewer."

It was one of Drexler's technicians, the German/Turkish man she'd heard called Franz. "I am trying to reach Herr Drexler, but he's not answering."

"He's with me, but on a call. What's going on?"

"Subjects one and two have been located."

"Velesky and Altman? Where?"

"They are in Altman's office. Arrived less than five minutes ago."

Brewer nodded with satisfaction. Ezra Altman wasn't just sitting in some drab hotel somewhere waiting for a phone call at ten a.m. so he could hand over the data and get his family back. No, he was at work, no doubt doing something to the data that Velesky had handed over. This made her even more sure Violator was on a mission to recover the man's family, because otherwise there was no way Altman would have taken the risk to go to a known location.

She asked, "Who else is there?"

"Same office staff as yesterday. Same two guards out front, same two in his lobby.

After a moment, she said, "Okay." She hung up, then dialed the number Drexler had given her so she could speak directly with the leader of the SSB cell.

There had been so many points of no return in Brewer's career that she didn't know how to quantify the magnitude of this one, but something about directing a cell of foreign terrorists on U.S. soil felt dirtier than most anything else she'd done.

On the other hand, she *had* essentially murdered a predecessor at the Agency once, so she didn't dwell on the morality of this moment, only the expediency.

A voice answered in accented English. The man sounded Russian to Brewer, but she knew he was actually Ukrainian.

"Yes?"

"Altman's location has been fixed."

There was a brief pause. "Who is this?"

"I work for the same person Luka works for."

This time there was no pause. "Where is he?"

"As we expected, he is at his office now. Velesky is with him."

"His guards?"

"His guards will be gone by the time you get there. I'll see to it. How long till you arrive?"

"Twenty-five minutes."

"Speed it up if you can."

"If I could speed it up, I wouldn't have told you it would take twenty-five minutes."

Brewer hung up. "Dick."

SIXTY-EIGHT

One minute after the white Chevy Tahoe that Court had followed from East Rutherford pulled up to the guard shack next to a driveway entrance to a fixed-base operator on the general aviation side of Teterboro Airport, Court slowed his stolen red Nissan Armada to a stop alongside Riser Road, one street parallel to the fence. He was out of view of both the shack and the FBO now because a thickly wooded drainage ditch separated the two streets.

There were only dead brambles and a few brown leaves on the trees in January, but there was enough coverage to make an approach towards the airport fence undetected, at least until they would have to cross two-laned Fred Wehran Drive where it passed along the fence on the other side of the woods.

It was silent in the Armada for a moment while Zoya and Court tried their best to peer through the foliage to where they had last seen the Tahoe. They detected nothing at first, but soon they saw fresh movement. The Tahoe rolled into view in the distance and almost immediately disappeared around the side of a building. It didn't come out on the other side, so Court assumed it had either stopped in back or rolled into the first of three massive white hangars, this one attached to the smaller building.

Angela spoke up from the back seat. "I feel like I should remind everyone that we don't know for certain that the SUV we've been following for the past ten minutes has anything to do with—"

Zoya started to turn around to face her; Court assumed an argument would soon ensue, so he put his hand on her arm. "Angela, I think Beth is right. There were multiple people in that vehicle. That's probably going to be the Ukrainians in there, and although we don't know they have the hostages, we're going to have to check it out."

Zoya kept looking through the woods towards the FBO. "There are two of us. We don't know how many we're up against, but it could be a lot."

Lacy corrected her. "There are three of us."

Zoya just sighed, but Court said, "I need you out here, Angela, reporting what you see."

They climbed out of the car, looking to make sure there was no activity around, and then they all entered the thick brush. Court led the way, and soon a small but strong limb dug into his right arm where he'd been knifed in Switzerland, and he stifled a cry of pain.

He worked his way no more than ten feet down a hill before he found himself at the edge of a sheet of ice. It was the ditchwater, frozen, and it was easily six feet across.

He put a foot on it gently, then slowly placed more weight down.

The ice held, he stepped forward with his other foot, and slowly he crossed the ditch, immediately grabbing on to the thin trunk of a tree on the other side. He turned and extended a hand to help the others over, but both women had each taken their own path, and no one took his hand while they crossed.

They all lowered down as they climbed up the thick brush towards the road that ran along the fence, and then they lay flat as they looked across towards the hangar.

They saw a single-story building that looked to be a tiny private terminal, and it was connected to one of at least three hangars on the property, each one a couple hundred feet in length and three stories tall. Maintenance trucks and fuel trucks were arrayed behind the hangars, but no more than a few employee cars were parked in the lot directly in front of them, almost as if the facility were closed.

Between the three hangars they could catch narrow glimpses of tarmac on the other side. Court tallied one private jet, one Cessna Grand Caravan, and then what looked to him to be some sort of replica of a World War II fighter plane.

He saw no activity around any of the aircraft, but the vast majority of the tarmac, and all of the interiors of the three hangars, were out of view, so he still didn't have much in the way of the lay of the land here.

Zoya leaned close to him. "That fence is child's play. Spiked, but only six feet high. You could vault me over it."

Court looked over at the guard shack now. He couldn't see inside, didn't know if there was one sleepy old coot or four jocked-up Rambos, so he looked back to the wall of the hangar on the other side of the fence.

"Cameras," he said.

"Yeah, but distant. They will only be set to detect motion on the inside of the fence, because otherwise every car on that street would set it off. If we're quick about it, we can make that run and get in a building without anyone at the guard shack noticing."

"So I vault you over and then I do . . . what?"

Zoya turned her head to him. "Really? You don't know how—"

Court did know how. "I just climb the motherfucker at one of the fence posts and try to not lose a nut on those spikes."

"Exactly."

Lacy said, "What about me?"

"What *about* you?" Zoya asked.

Court took the Nissan's keys out of his pocket and handed them over Zoya's back to Angela, who took them.

He said, "Everybody put your ears on, we'll have a call going the whole time. Angela, if you see anything, let us know."

All three put their earpieces in and Court initiated a conference call. Court knew Angela wouldn't consider herself much of an asset if it came down to a hostage rescue, so staying here would be the prudent thing.

It was eighty yards or so to the guard shack; Court felt relatively confident they could make it over and into the parking lot, behind one of many work trucks and tugs parked there on this side of the hangars, even though it was after nine a.m. on a gray but otherwise bright day.

A car passed leaving to the north, and then everyone tested their earpieces one last time. Soon, Zoya and Court climbed to their knees and took off at a sprint, crossing the street in seconds, then racing across a narrow strip of brown grass to the black iron fence.

Court spun quickly and put his back to the fence, and Zoya leapt up onto him, landing both feet on his bent thighs. He put his hands on her hips, and then he knelt deeper and then exploded off his legs. Zoya pushed off in unison with his momentum, and then she launched over the fence, landing in the grass on the other side in a roll.

Court turned back around; with both hands he grabbed the top of the fence at one of the steel four-by-four vertical posts with the small spiked posts running vertically between them, and he used his feet to climb up.

His hands ached with the effort of holding the icy cold steel, but in just seconds he was at the top, where he kicked his legs sideways over the spikes and let go of the post.

Court dropped down onto the grass flat-footed, then began running for the parking lot behind Zoya, rubbing his bandaged right arm as he did so.

The fixed-base operator had been rented in full for three days by one of Daniil Spanov's front companies here in the United States, and this meant it was empty other than Spanov's two armed pilots, already preflighting their aircraft inside an open hangar, and a small local ground crew who were told to wait in the otherwise empty terminal next door until called upon.

The facility was new, brightly lit, and spotless; a thirty-thousand-square-foot hangar, three stories high, that held private planes, along with a complete repair shop on the hangar floor. There were overhead catwalks, a second-floor business office and conference space, warehouse and storage facilities along the wall, and even a basement facility reached by stairs where fuel and other hazardous chemicals were stored.

As soon as they climbed out of the Tahoe, GRU officers Mischa and Stepan walked the three members of the Altman family across the shiny white floor, past a white Gulfstream G450, one of three aircraft on the hangar floor, along with a refueling truck, mobile APUs, aircraft fuel testing carts, and several massive aviation toolsets, even electric engine hoists, and they took a metal stairway up to the second floor. Here the family was placed in an office, and each sat down at a swivel chair. The two Russians ignored the Altmans' protests and zip-tied their hands behind their backs.

The boys began pushing away, earning Justin an immediate slap across the face from Mischa.

Sarah Altman screamed at the man, and he raised a hand towards her, but the older brother lunged at him, heading him in the chest and knocking him back into the chair.

Stepan pulled his pistol and swung it down in an arc, smashing it down on the sixteen-year-old's head.

Kevin Altman fell to the ground and lay on his side, still tied to the swivel chair and now groaning in pain, but when his mother and brother both tried to get up and come to his aid, the Russians ordered them to stay where they were.

While this was going on, Luka Rudenko was out in the hangar with Leonid. The major sat in a chair in front of a desk against the wall of the hangar floor, his wounded foot up on the desk and his walking boot off and lying on the floor next to him.

From his backpack he pulled out a vial of lidocaine and a syringe, given to him by the nurse in Switzerland, and he prepared a shot of the local anesthetic for his wounded foot.

Leonid had his hand on the SIG Copperhead 9-millimeter hanging from his neck while he covered the area alone, but soon enough, Stepan and Mischa came back downstairs, having secured the hostages in the office. They both augmented the security, facing out of the open hangar door towards the big airfield.

Luka had the other Copperhead on the table next to him, but he ignored it while he injected his foot right through the bandages, showing no outward reaction, though the pain he felt was indescribable. He once again fantasized about facing off against the man who had done this to him, and lamented the fact that early that morning he'd shot at him but doubted he'd hit him in the dark four stories up.

Well, he thought. *If the bitch from CIA was right, the Gray Man would be trying his best to give me one more shot.*

He reached into his backpack, pulled out a left shoe that matched his right, and slowly put it on. This time he could not help but shudder from pain. The drug would take effect within moments, but it hadn't kicked in yet.

He wanted to be as mobile as possible for the next few hours, because the next few hours were absolutely critical.

Court Gentry and Zoya Zakharova entered a locked door to the terminal building that Zoya had picked with small tools purchased by Angela the day before. As soon as they were inside, they found themselves in a hallway, and almost instantly they heard noises ahead of them.

Drawing their pistols, they approached an open door at the end of the hall, and by now they could tell they were listening to a TV broadcast.

It was cable news discussing the fact that the accords were to be signed by noon, and then the General Assembly would convene and pass the resolution, essentially legitimizing Russia's occupation of Ukraine for the sake of a resumption of most-favored-nation trade relations.

Zoya tuned it out as she dropped to her knees and slowly peeked around the corner.

She drew her head back after a few seconds, rose back up, and whispered into Court's ear. "Five guys in ground crew attire. Old and fat, mostly. Noncombatants."

Court nodded. "Bypass."

Zoya nodded, knelt back down, and held her hand up, holding Court where he stood. She peeked again around the side into the break room, and then, after a moment, waved him onwards.

Court rushed across the open door in under a second.

Zoya herself now rose, and Court knelt and looked into the room from the opposite side of the door.

He saw one of the ground crew stand and walk over to a refrigerator, and he held up a hand to indicate to Zoya that she should hold.

Seconds later the man was back in his chair and again watching the news, now with a Dr Pepper in his hand, and Court waved Zoya on.

Together they followed signs in the small and empty terminal towards hangar one. A door was closed but not locked, so Court opened it a crack and peered in.

It opened into a hallway with windows going down one side. The windows looked out over the bright hangar space, and Court saw multiple executive jets inside, along with a massive array of maintenance equipment.

He and Zoya went low again, crawled up to the window, and then rose slowly.

Within a few seconds they lowered down again.

"No hostages," Court said. "Unless they're on board an aircraft."

"That's where I'd put them," Zoya asserted, then said, "And there's something else."

Court nodded. "Across the room. That blond-haired guy with the subgun around his neck. Could be Matador."

"If it's Rudenko, then this is the GRU and not the Ukrainians. Or it could be both."

Court shook his head. "We're not that lucky. Somebody is going after Altman, I'm sure of it. Must be the Ukrainians." He sighed. "We need to scout the area and see what we're up against."

They moved to different parts of the long window to create different vantage points, taking more than two minutes to check every area in sight. The floor, the windows of the aircraft that were visible from the northern side of the hangar, the exposed areas in ground-floor offices and storage spaces, and the catwalk network that crisscrossed the entire massive space.

Finally, they met in the center of the hall under the window and Zoya gave her assessment.

"No sign of the hostages. Good news is I've only identified three armed men, plus the two pilots, who probably are not armed. The bad news is they are likely GRU, Unit 29155, and even if there are just three of them, it's not going to be easy getting through them before they kill the hostages, whose location, by the way, we don't have."

"What a shit show," Court muttered, and Zoya agreed.

Just then, Angela Lacy's voice came over the net. "Be advised. There's a black Mercedes pulling up to the guard shack."

"Copy," Court responded softly, then he looked to Zoya. "Have I ever told you about Maurice?"

"Your mentor?"

"Yeah."

"*Literally* one hundred times."

Court didn't take offense. "He used to have a thing he said to me. 'Kid, remember, it gets worse before it gets worse.'"

"Sounds like a barrel of laughs."

"He had a unique charm."

"Honestly," Zoya said, "right now we could do with less folksy wisdom and more guns. This is a big area to engage multiple people with only a couple of pistols."

Court shrugged. "Speed, surprise, and violence of action."

Zoya flashed her green eyes up at him. "I'll handle the speed."

It was a joke about cocaine, and Court didn't laugh. "Is your head right for this, Z?"

"You could always trade me out for that chickenshit desk jockey sitting outside in the bushes."

As if on cue, Lacy's voice came back into their ears now. "The vehicle pulled up to the front of the terminal. Two people got out, and then the Mercedes went to park. I can't be positive from this position, but I think one of the two in the back was Brewer."

Court and Zoya looked at each other. Court said, "They'll probably come right up this hall."

"We could grab them," Zoya replied. "Use them to get the Altmans back."

Lacy heard this and said, "You think a GRU assassin is going to forgo his mission to protect a CIA officer?"

Zoya knew Lacy was right, but she did not respond. Instead, she said, "We need to move, then."

Court and Zoya headed in a crawl down the hallway; there was a door that led directly to the hangar floor, but on their right, they passed a small conference room, visible through windows along the right-hand wall. Court found the door unlocked, and the two of them crawled inside, closed and locked the door, and then lay on the floor directly under the hallway window.

With their heads almost touching, Court said, "If the hostages are here, are we assuming they are in one of the jets?"

"Could be," she said, "but the way the catwalk is set up, I'm thinking there is a second-floor space right over our heads. Could be an office or storage up there."

"Shit, that complicates things." He asked, "Which aircraft are we betting on them flying out of here in?"

Zoya said, "That G450 could fly direct to Moscow from here without refueling."

"The other two are a Citation and a Falcon, and the Falcon has an engine removed, so it's not going anywhere. The Citation doesn't have the range to get to Russia, but we also don't know that they're heading to Russia, either."

They heard footsteps in the hallway to the hangar, right on the other side of the wall they lay next to, and after the footsteps passed, Zoya rose to her knees and looked through the glass. She could see across the hall and through the window there into the hangar.

"Brewer and a guy with a cane, walking with the two pilots."

Court nodded. "That's going to be Drexler." He thought a moment, then said, "No more Russians, at least, so that's good. Don't know if Brewer is armed. How do you want to do this?"

"You're asking *my* advice?" Zoya whispered. "*That's* new."

Lacy came over their earpieces now. "If you were talking to me, I'd suggest finding a way to disable that aircraft, then search the building for the hostages."

Zoya looked up at Court, then tapped her earpiece three times to mute any transmissions. "She's not wrong. When this all goes loud, one of us needs to take out both the front tires of the Gulfstream and the Citation. We do that, and they aren't going anywhere."

Court reached over and tapped Zoya's earpiece, reopening the line between all three of them.

Court said, "So . . . with the pilots, the three Russians, Drexler, and Brewer, we have seven targets that we know of, at least three of which are armed. Plus, we have to take out the two front tires on two aircraft, and we also need to both locate and rescue the three hostages. Am I missing anything?"

Zoya blew out a sigh. "Maybe we call the cops. Roll the dice that it doesn't go up high enough to where more guns come in here to stop us instead of to help us."

Court thought about this. "I don't see that we have the time. With Altman at his office right now, the enemy will move on him. Once they have him and the data, then they won't need the family, and they won't need to hang around in the U.S. any longer."

Lacy spoke up again. "I'm coming in."

Both Court and Zoya responded in unison. "No." Court said, "Just sit tight. We're going to do this on our own. If we don't succeed, that means the Altman family is dead. You'll have to call Ezra and tell him, and just hope he releases the information because he has nothing else to lose."

Zoya popped up and looked out the window again but almost immediately dropped back down.

Looking at Court, she said, "You want the good news or the bad news first?"

"Good news."

"The pilots are doing their inspection on the Gulfstream. *That's* the aircraft."

"Fewer tires to shoot. I'd call that 'okay news.' What's the bad news?"

"One of them took his coat off. He has a pistol in a shoulder holster."

Court closed his eyes a moment. "Keeps getting better and better, doesn't it?"

"My pistol carries nine bullets. Yours has seventeen, and a silencer."

Court pulled his HK. "Let's trade."

"Why?"

"Are you going to make me say it?"

Court was the better shooter, and Zoya knew it. With nine rounds, he could very likely score himself another weapon from a fallen enemy.

She drew her Shield 9-millimeter and traded with him, and while she did this, she said, "We don't have time to wait around. We've got to move."

SIXTY-NINE

Alex Velesky stood at the door to Ezra Altman's inner office, looking out onto the office floor, all the way up to the lobby, some twenty-five meters away. The office staff went about their duties; Altman had told his executive assistant he was not to be disturbed, so Alex had locked the glass door in front of him.

Behind him, he heard Altman furiously typing at his workstation, occasionally letting out gasps, but there was little interaction between the two men. They both knew there were a number of ticking clocks counting down. The signing of the accords would be within a couple of hours, Six and the others had to rescue the hostages before then, and they were all but certain the enemy already knew they were here at the office.

Still, Altman plugged away, and Velesky stood watch.

One of the two security guards in the lobby was visible from here, and he talked on his cell phone. Alex didn't focus on him directly; he kept scanning the others around the office, but soon the double doors opened and the two other Homeland Security officers stepped in and conferred with both of their colleagues.

After no more than ten seconds, all four guards walked out of the double doors without even looking back.

Alex called out to the man behind him. "Altman?"

"Not now."

"The guards. They just left."

The clicking of keys echoing through the office stopped. "Shit."

"Keep going," Alex urged, then said, "But . . . your staff."

"Get them out of here. Tell everyone to go home."

"They aren't going to listen to me, they don't even know—"

Altman kept working but said, "Pull the fire alarm. They'll sure as hell listen to *that*."

Alex left the office without another word, walked halfway up the hall towards the lobby, past conference rooms and offices full of people who paid him no attention, and pulled the alarm.

Instantly the ringing began, and he turned, retreating back to Altman's office, where he again locked the door.

The staff in Altman Globus began filing out the double doors within thirty seconds, with Alex mentally urging them on. Ezra's administrative assistant came to the door and he opened it for her, and the man behind the desk just politely told the sixty-five-year-old woman that she should get her purse and go downstairs to the street, and he'd be seconds behind her.

It took over two minutes for the office to vacate, but as soon as it did, Alex ran the length of the space, locked the double doors, and then pushed several chairs and even a couch up in front of them.

It wouldn't slow anyone down for long, but at this point, Velesky knew every moment would count.

Back in Ezra's office, he again locked the door. "How much more time do you need?"

"More than I've got" was the terse and disheartening reply.

"Do your best, Ezra."

There was more clicking of keys, but at the same time Altman said, "Do you really trust Beth, Charlie, and Angela to save my family?"

Velesky did not hesitate in his response. "I trust Beth with my life, and she trusts that man. They'll get them back; you just do your part, and you will have done a great thing."

Petro Mozgovoy and the rest of his team had just entered a locked side entrance from the parking garage, after Kristina Golubova entered the building, slipped past guards, and found access for the team, holding the door open till they arrived.

Kristina went left, back towards the main elevators, but the rest of the team turned right, then began walking down an unadorned hallway, at the end of which was an employee-only elevator. Their construction attire seemed to be working; a few people from the skyscraper's maintenance and physical plant passed them by without so much as a second look.

As the elevator began to ascend towards the thirtieth floor, the men took off their packs and unzipped them, leaving the subguns inside but easily accessible, holding the bags in their hands.

Petro turned to the team now. "This is not the job we trained to do, but this is the job we *will* do, and our training will ensure our success."

Just as he said this, however, the elevator slowed, then stopped on the twenty-second floor.

The doors opened, and immediately they heard the sound of the fire alarm.

Petro said, "It's them. They know we're coming." He rushed out the door. "We'll take the stairs."

The floor was one large office space, cubicles all around, and seven running construction workers did not go unnoticed by the people working there. The office staff looked on nervously as they grabbed their personal effects, thinking whatever set the fire alarm off was the reason for the men's haste.

Petro found the stairs and began moving up, but already there were a lot of people heading down. He passed a couple of NYPD officers in the crowd, but neither one of them impeded the progress of the Ukrainian separatists as they advanced.

As he climbed, he called Luka, who answered on the first ring.

"Yeah?"

"They've set off the fire alarm. They know we're coming."

"How far are you?"

"Two minutes, maybe three."

Petro heard the Russian relay this information to someone in English, and then he came back on the line. "No delay. Straight into his office. Kill them both immediately, destroy all phones and computer equipment. Burn the office down, burn the fucking building down if you can."

"Da. Understood."

Petro and his team kept pushing through the thickening crowd, passing the twenty-fifth floor, continuing their ascent.

Court and Zoya made it down to the end of the hall, cracked open the door to the hangar, and looked ahead. The vast bulk of the space, containing the three jets and all the maintenance equipment, was on their left. The hangar wall was on their right, and right in front of them were stairs going up and stairs going down into what had to be some sort of basement area.

Ahead and to their left were the massive hangar doors, open to a view of a tarmac full of aircraft, and then the runway beyond. Two men stood just outside, both armed, one distant with a small submachine gun in his hand, and the other much closer, also wielding a pistol.

Court said, "One of us needs to get upstairs undetected, and one of us has to go for the Gulfstream. We're going to have to split up."

Lacy came through his earpiece now. "I can take the Nissan and run through the gate, distract them."

"No," Court said. "You'll just bring the guards into this, and there's no telling who they'll shoot at."

"But—"

Zoya spoke up now. "We're going to disconnect if you don't shut up. There's a lot going on over here."

After a brief pause, Lacy just said, "Good luck."

Court said, "I can't fight five dudes spread out in a thirty-thousand-foot space with my pistol, and you can't make it upstairs without being seen."

"What's *your* plan?"

Court looked around a moment more, then up at the ceiling. He nodded to himself. "We need to start a fire."

"Why?"

"See those big red drums hanging down from the ceiling?"

"Yeah."

"I noticed the pipes outside. This whole hangar is protected by a foam fire suppression system. When it goes off, it will fill this entire place with about six feet of foam."

"Okay?" she said quizzically. "And that helps us . . . *how*?"

"It will obscure our approach. They'll know we're coming, but they won't be able to see us until we're on top of them."

"Then I go upstairs?"

"You go upstairs, I go for the plane. If one of us finds the hostages, the other will cover until we're out of here."

"We just have to find a fire alarm," Zoya said.

Court shook his head. "These systems won't go off by just pulling a fire alarm. These things have sophisticated flame detectors; it will take a flame, and a significant one."

"Where do we find a—"

"Follow me," he said, and he holstered his weapon, then crawled across a dozen feet of hangar floor to get to the stairs, his eyes on the two sentries facing outside. He took the stairs down, and Zoya followed close behind.

They found themselves in a machine and welding shop with equipment everywhere, and even though the lights were off down here, there was enough illumination filtering down from the hangar floor for Court to find his way around.

A spiral staircase in the back of the place led up to the main floor in the corner of the hangar, and Court took note of this as he looked around at all the equipment and chemicals in the machine shop.

Zoya held her gun up at the stairs to the main floor while Court went to work, although she didn't have a clue what he was doing.

Luka Rudenko leaned into the second-floor conference room, right up the hall from the office where the hostages were tied up. The woman from CIA and Drexler were here waiting, a phone on the table in front of them connecting them to Drexler's team still in Manhattan.

The Russian said, "Mozgovoy is attacking Altman's office now. It should be over in moments."

Drexler said, "My people say there is no sign of Gentry or Zakharova on cameras in Midtown."

Luka nodded. "Then we have to expect them to come here. How much longer? We're exposed in this building with only four of us to cover the space."

Drexler nodded. "Are the pilots ready?"

"If I tell them to be ready, they will be ready."

Sebastian Drexler looked down at his watch and saw that it was ten a.m. He held a finger up, then dialed the direct line to Ezra Altman's office, and it rang several times before it was answered.

"Yeah?" It was Altman, and Drexler could hear the fire alarm blaring in the background.

He said, "I don't know what you are doing, Mr. Altman, but you *must* know you are playing with the lives of your family."

Altman said, "I'm ready to trade. I haven't sent the data to anyone, but all I have to do is press a key and the whole world is going to know. I won't do it if you release them. I'm in my office, though you already know that. Bring them here."

Drexler looked to Luka, who was now on the phone with Petro. The Russian mouthed, *Sixty seconds*, and Drexler nodded in understanding.

"Very well, Mr. Altman. We will be there very soon."

Drexler hung up the phone and slipped it into his jacket. "He's lying about the data being ready to send, I could hear him working in the background. He will run out of time." He then said, "The only question now is the hostages."

Luka said, "Both of you, board the aircraft. Me and my men will provide security until we're out of the hangar, then I'll have one of my people come up here and shoot the Altmans last thing before we board on the tarmac."

The woman from CIA said nothing as she stood, following Drexler to the door.

Zoya had spent a full minute without seeing what Court was doing behind her, and in that time she heard the auxiliary power unit of the Gulfstream start with a low but persistent hum. She knew enough about aircraft to know that the plane needed a couple of minutes to stabilize the temperature of the APU before engine start. Over the noise she heard Court opening squeaky cabinets behind her, and she worried that if one of the Russians came close enough to the stairwell, they would be able to hear him from the hangar floor.

Glancing quickly over her shoulder, she saw that he was pulling large cans out of a cabinet, above which a sign read **FLAMMABLE LIQUID STORAGE**.

A few seconds later, as she now listened to him pry the lid off a can with a screwdriver, she heard voices above, so she turned and ran back through the machine shop, put her hand on his shoulder while he worked, and put her finger to her lips just as he pried open another can.

Court froze as he, too, now heard the voices, and he drew his Smith and Wesson, holding it down by his leg.

Zoya recognized the voice of Suzanne Brewer; she was talking to someone, but Zoya couldn't make out the words. Seconds later the voices trailed off in the direction of the purring Gulfstream.

With Zoya watching, Court grabbed the two one-gallon cans of acetone and moved towards and then past her. He climbed the metal stairs, keeping his body low, until he finally rested the cans on the top step. He then came back down, grabbed an acetylene torch, opened the valve, and then lifted the striker up to it, putting the lighter cup right in front of the nozzle of the torch.

The torch fired, and he handed it off to Zoya. "Give me this in a second." He moved up the stairs to the aircraft hangar floor, again staying as low as possible.

While Zoya looked on, Court looked around to make sure no one in the thirty-thousand-foot space was looking his way, and then he took the first can and reached up with it to the hangar floor. Slowly and silently, he poured the clear liquid out, and it ran off to the right, towards the open hangar, where it began to pool on the floor. He checked back over his shoulder and saw the two Russians still at the entrance to the massive hangar, both keeping their eyes outside. There was also movement by the Gulfstream, one hundred feet away, and more noises coming from upstairs.

When the first can was empty, he put it back on the step, then slowly began pouring the second can on the floor.

He'd only gotten about half of it out before he heard a buzz in his earpiece indicating a call coming in. He scooted back down out of sight and double-tapped the device, holding his call with Lacy and Zoya and accepting the other call.

"Altman?"

"Alex says they're here! Outside my office."

Court said, "It's the Ukrainians, not the Russians. I don't know how many there are but—"

Altman interrupted; he clearly didn't care about his safety. "Do you have my family?"

Court said, "We are within one hundred feet of them, and we have a plan. We'll have them in two minutes, I promise you." It was a promise he did not know he could keep, but he knew he had to have Altman's help in releasing the data.

He heard keys clicking in the background of the call, which he took to be a good sign.

Ezra said, "If Alex can hold them back a couple more minutes, I will get the report to Catherine King. I am putting my trust in you to save Justin, Kevin, and Sarah."

"Thank you," Court said, and then, "Good luck."

"Good luck," Ezra replied, and he hung up.

Court went to Zoya and reached out for the torch.

"You ready?" she asked.

"Ready," he confirmed. "You go upstairs, I go for the plane. Everybody who isn't an Altman dies."

She reached forward, holding the torch away from her while she took her other hand and put it in Court's hair, then pulled him to her. They kissed, and she said, "We've got this."

Court smiled. "We've got this." He took the torch, ran to the front stairs, and climbed them silently. Then he reached up and waved the torch over the floor.

Instantly he was awash in heat and light, the flames erupting to his right and streaking a dozen feet or so to where the acetone had pooled. He re-treated back down, tossed the torch, and then pulled his pistol. He and Zoya both ran to the spiral staircase at the back of the basement, and as they did, the fire alarm began bleating and echoing throughout the hangar.

SEVENTY

"Getting close!" Ezra Altman called out, startling Alex Velesky, whose adrenaline was running so high at the moment it wouldn't take much shock for him to squeeze the trigger of the stainless-steel revolver he held out in front of him, pointed through the glass door to Ezra's office and out towards the barricaded wooden double doors in the lobby.

"Yeah," Alex said. "They're right outside, trying to open the door."

"No, I mean, *I* am getting close! Keep them off me for another couple of minutes and I'll have this sent to Catherine King."

Alex looked down at his five-shot revolver and wondered how the hell he was going to do more than make a little noise. But he kept his aim as steady as he could, and said, "Thank you, Ezra. I'm sorry about everything."

Behind him, Altman said, "Thank you for waking up. Whatever it was that brought you here today, just know *you* are about to do a great thing."

Velesky thought of his sister, his parents, and his little nephew he never even got the chance to meet. Tears filled his eyes; he brought a hand away from the pistol to wipe them free, and just as he did, the double doors in the lobby burst in, knocking Alex's hasty barricade back a foot.

"They're almost inside!" he shouted to Ezra behind him, then he used a thumb to pull back the hammer of the pistol, just like he'd seen in a hundred Westerns, and he aimed at the door up the hall.

The furniture flew in even farther after another blow from the outside, and this time a figure appeared holding a small rifle.

Alex fired, shattering the glass door in front of him. He was startled by the recoil and the noise made by the weapon; he lost his sights for a moment, but then he repositioned the gun and fired again at the same man, who was now inside the lobby.

More men poured in, and he fired at them again, and this time, he saw a man fall.

But there was another behind him moving too fast for Alex to aim.

The return fire came in a cacophony, tearing through the glass door and sending Alex diving onto the couch in Ezra's office on the left. He looked back over his shoulder and saw Ezra on his knees behind his desk, but still looking at his monitor and continuing to manipulate his mouse and keyboard.

"More time, Alex!" he shouted, and the thirty-five-year-old Ukrainian pulled a speed loader out of his pocket and began reloading the pistol with shaking hands.

Both Zoya's and Court's heads and guns emerged simultaneously from the spiral staircase, just as the sixteen red foam fire suppression system distributors on the ceiling three stories above the hangar's floor began erupting. At first it was a liquid that emerged; like giant shower nozzles, they dropped hundreds of gallons, but within just a couple of seconds, thick white foam began spraying down at pressure, coating every single thing on the floor.

As Court aimed his Shield at the two Russian sentries by the hangar doors, Zoya aimed the VP9 at the Gulfstream's nose gear and fired twice with the suppressed pistol, hitting both tires just seconds before foam covered the floor there and obstructed her view.

Court fired almost simultaneously, shooting the closer of the two GRU assassins in the side of the head as the Russian looked around for a target, and then Court shifted aim to the other man, some thirty yards away.

The cascading pillars of foam obstructed his view, so he climbed the rest of the way out of the stairs and broke into a run across the hangar floor, making for the Gulfstream.

• • •

Luka Rudenko crouched by the Gulfstream's air stairs, his gun swinging in all directions while first water and then foam doused his body.

Drexler was already up on the air stairs, this Luka could see, but the sixteen columns of white around the thirty-thousand-foot space growing fatter and thicker by the second cloaked his view of the rest of the hangar.

Luka had his Copperhead up on his shoulder, trying to see through the white towards the far corner of the hangar, because that had clearly been the origin of both the flames and the gunfire. He knew his adversaries were using the foam as an obscurant, and he told himself that he was up against some very clever operators.

"Gray Man and Banshee," he said to himself, and then he opened fire blindly at the area.

Court dove to the ground when the shooting started; he was still twenty yards from the nose of the aircraft, and he landed on his chest and then slid through the foam like he was on a ride at a theme park. He heard the cracking of supersonic rounds over his head, and he thought one of the Russians must have had a fix on his position, so he began rolling to his right. Once he stopped, he climbed back to his knees through the suds, and here he saw Sebastian Drexler just as he disappeared into the cabin door of the aircraft.

He started to look for another target when a burst of gunfire, coming from near the port-side wing of the plane, sent him back down into the growing sea of foam, desperate for concealment.

His earpiece came alive with Lacy's voice. "What's going on in there?"

"Stand by" was all Court said in reply. He crept through the foam now, trying to get as close to the aircraft as possible before popping back up and shooting the Russians there, then boarding to check for hostages.

Luka reloaded the Copperhead while down on one knee, partially hidden in the growing foam, and on his right, the woman from CIA knelt next to him, also using the foam to conceal herself. "Give me your fucking pistol," she demanded.

Luka finished his reload, then pulled his HK and handed it over. She was on his side—for this, anyway—and he needed all the guns in this fight he could get.

But to his surprise, she didn't aim in the direction where the fire came from. Instead, she turned and ran towards the back of the hangar, towards the rear stairs up to the catwalk and the second floor.

Luka fired off a few more rounds blindly, and then, out of the corner of his eye, he saw movement at the staircase that went up along the wall towards the second floor. It was Banshee, and she was running full speed, a pistol in her right hand. She was heading for the hostages tied up in the office.

He raised the weapon to rake fire at her, but then he stopped himself. He only had one magazine left in his weapon, he'd handed off his sidearm, and somewhere down here, he was all but certain the Gray Man was maneuvering.

Banshee opened the door to the offices and disappeared inside.

Mischa had seen the movement on the stairs, as well, from where he had been kneeling under the starboard-side wing of the Gulfstream and scanning for a target. He fired a few rounds at the door as it closed, then shouted to his major. "Zakharova is upstairs, going for the hostages! I'll get her!"

The Russian sergeant leapt out from under the wing and into the foam, then he turned and ran for the front stairs, his Copperhead out in front of him.

Suzanne Brewer's CIA aircraft had not yet arrived, so when the gunshots began echoing through the hangar, she at first considered following Drexler up into the Gulfstream to escape. But quickly she decided against it. The Gulfstream could be easily disabled by armed attackers, and she'd be a sitting duck inside until the pilots got it out of the hangar.

No, if Gentry and Zakharova were here, Brewer knew her only chance was to get to the hostages and to use them as a bargaining chip so she could escape with her life.

To do this she'd have to beat any of the GRU men there, and even target them if it came down to it, because she was sure Luka would have already ordered them to shoot the Altmans.

She took the back stairs because it was in the opposite direction of where the shooting was coming from, but this meant she also had a lot more distance to cover to get to the hostages.

She moved as fast as she could with the pistol out in front of her, because she was well aware of the fact that down there in that insane sea of ever-expanding foam lurked two of the most dangerous people she'd ever met.

She just had to get the Altmans at gunpoint, and then she could negotiate until Jay Kirby's plane arrived and got her the fuck out of there.

SEVENTY-ONE

Alex Velesky had lost track of how many times he'd fired the revolver down the length of the hallway to the lobby of Ezra Altman's office, having already reloaded twice, but he knew he now couldn't have more than one or two rounds left in the weapon, so he crawled back towards the door.

The gunfire coming his way had slowed down. Alex waited, forcing himself not to peek around the corner, knowing that the second he did so, he'd be shot dead, and Ezra's time would be up.

He shouted in Ukrainian. "Davai!" *Come on!* "I've got a machine gun!"

A man shouted back in Ukrainian. "Then why are you using that pistol, bitch?"

It was a fair question, the banker admitted to himself, but he didn't answer. Instead, he just positioned himself next to the door, and he looked back to his partner in this.

"How much time?"

"Seconds! I just need seconds!"

Alex sniffed, stood, and then raised his gun out in front of him. He took one step to the right, found a target in the middle of the hallway approaching him, and fired.

Instantly he felt a pounding to the right side of his chest like he'd been hit with a shovel, then a sting on the right side of his neck, and he twisted away and fell onto his back.

The revolver tumbled away from his hand.

At the aircraft hangar in New Jersey, Court Gentry popped up out of the foam, and instantly he saw multiple targets. The two pilots had fled the Gulfstream at a run, twenty-five feet away, and they'd already passed his position on the way to the exit to the terminal.

Court let them go, and instead aimed at one of the GRU men straight ahead who was pushing a massive aircraft maintenance cart across the foamy floor, trying to use it for cover as he neared the plane.

The man couldn't see him, and Court held fire, swiveling around, hunting for Matador.

He didn't see the Russian killer, but he did see Sebastian Drexler climbing out of the plane, then hurriedly shuffling away towards the hangar doors through the thick white foam.

Court had four targets, but three were in the process of fleeing, so these he let go. And he knew if he fired on the GRU man pushing the cart, wherever Matador was hiding, Court would begin taking fire from him.

Fuck it, he thought. He shifted back to the cart, lowered his aim to where he thought the bottom of it would be, and then lowered his aim a little more, accounting for bullet skip.

He fired twice in quick succession into the rising foam; a man screamed out and then rose, exposing his head and upper torso.

Court already had the sights of the Smith and Wesson Shield pointed at the top of the cart, so he fired once, striking the GRU assassin in the jaw.

The man disappeared in the foam behind the cart ahead of a thick spray of blood.

Court began to shift aim to the left to look for Matador, but suddenly someone began firing his way. He caught a glimpse of muzzle flashes coming from behind the rear undercarriage of the aircraft, but Court didn't aim at it. Instead, he dove back into the thick white foam and began rolling to his right, over and over and over, trying to move himself as far away from where he'd been sighted as possible.

The shots hadn't missed by much; he'd felt the bullets whizzing close by his body, and he immediately suspected Matador had been the shooter.

The man at the Gulfstream's rear wheels expended an entire magazine, and Court began crawling forward on the floor now, again hidden by foam.

Ezra Altman knelt on the floor behind his desk and pulled up Catherine King's email with trembling hands. He attached a file folder containing every bit of his analysis of the money trail between the Kremlin and end users in the West, ninety-nine percent of which he hadn't even seen for himself, since he had no time to peruse his software's assessments and conclusions.

Still, the data had been processed completely, and now it resided in hundreds of individual files, all in one single folder. Once it attached to the email, all he had to do was press a few keys and it would instantly be delivered to—

Altman felt a powerful blow to his right shoulder, spinning him around on his knees. His face knocked against the bookshelf behind his desk, and then he fell onto his back.

Books and mementos fell from the shelf down on top of him.

More gunfire raked the area, his computer monitor jolted above him, and Ezra looked to his left and right and saw blood on his arm, on papers around him, and splattered across his chair mat.

But he wasn't worried about the blood; he was worried about his keyboard. He had knocked it off his desk as he spun away, before he'd managed to send the email, and now the attackers seemed to be targeting his computer system, trying to destroy it because Alex Velesky had managed to keep them back from entering the office.

He just had to find his damn keyboard and send the email, but when he put his right hand down to scoot back, pain enveloped him and he fell flat on his back.

Zoya Zakharova slowly entered the hallway on the second floor of the airplane hangar at Teterboro, her pistol out in front of her. She had remnants of foam on her body, and even though with each step more of it fell away, she felt like she was half-covered in soap suds.

She put her hand on the first door on her left, halfway down the hall, and she opened it. She entered behind the pistol, her finger on the trigger.

It was an empty conference room, so she stepped back outside and moved down to the next door.

She turned the latch and pushed it open with the suppressor attached to her 9-millimeter, and inside she found the room to be a small office space with four cubicles.

Against the wall she saw a redheaded woman and two handsome young dark-haired boys, all tied securely to office chairs. One of the boys was on the floor, the chair down there with him, but they were all clearly alive and apparently uninjured.

Zoya breathed a sigh of relief. Into her earpiece she said, "I have the hostages on the second floor. I'll untie them and—"

Gunfire on her left in the hallway rang out, and she dove forward into the room for cover, crashing into the ground, and her earpiece fell from her ear.

She scrambled back to the doorway, reached her pistol out, and then peered her head around.

Instantly she saw a Russian GRU man with a Copperhead pistol aiming at her. They both fired once, and then Zoya pulled her head and arm back into the room.

With the hostages tied behind her, she realized they were helpless and it was all on her shoulders. She waited a few seconds, willing the GRU man to advance on her, and then she switched her gun to her left hand and leaned out into the hall, firing as she did so. With only her head and left arm exposed to the enemy, she fired over and over, one-handed, at the man who was now no more than twenty feet away.

After four rounds she felt a blow to her left arm, spinning her back, and she dropped to her knees, now totally exposed in the hallway.

More incoming rounds whizzed by her, and she fell back on the carpeted floor, still dumping bullets up the hall one-handed as she ended up on her back.

Even here she kept shooting, firing over the top of her feet at the target that she could only now focus on.

The Russian with the machine pistol had fallen to his own knees, but his weapon was still up and belching out fire and lead.

Zoya sat up for a better angle, put both hands on her pistol, and shifted her body to switch back to a right-handed grip, but before she could do so, she felt a blow to the back of her left shoulder and a fresh hot streak of pain running all the way up her left forearm. She fought the pain and panic and she pressed the trigger on the HK pistol, hitting the Russian in the left rib cage, grazing his left temple, and then tagging him directly in his stomach.

The man crumpled forward, hit the ground face-first, lying on top of his weapon, and Zoya finished him with a shot directly between her feet into the top of his skull.

Her pistol locked open on an empty magazine, and then her head dropped back onto the floor behind her.

She was wounded, out of ammo, and the hostages were still bound. She didn't know what was going on with Court, but she knew she couldn't just wait here for rescue.

As blood drained from her body, she began trying to crawl towards the dead man with her right arm and leg, hoping to first retrieve the GRU officer's weapon and then rescue the Altmans behind her.

Court had scooted across the slick hangar floor through the foam towards the Gulfstream, all the while listening to a ferocious two-person gun battle upstairs. He couldn't call out to Zoya as he snuck up on Matador, but he listened in his earpiece with as much attention as he could muster, hoping to hear something, *anything*, from her.

He picked up his pace, knowing the hostages were upstairs and Zoya was in a fight for her life. Moving just a few feet more, he rose up suddenly and instantly realized two things. One, he was less than ten feet from the rear carriage of the jet, just on his left. And two, Matador had moved from that position, and now he was standing right in front of Court and aiming his weapon up at the second floor.

The men registered each other at the same time, spun their weapons towards their targets, and fired.

Court felt a 9-millimeter round miss the left side of his face by inches, and he squeezed his own shot off prematurely, missing Matador's face, as well.

But Court's gun was at the end of his extended arms, and as Matador swept his subgun around, the two weapons struck one another. The pistol was knocked free, into the foam, and Matador fired again with the impact, sending another round wide.

The Russian had his weapon slung around his neck, but Court got a hand on the foregrip of the Copperhead, keeping it pointed away from him. He lunged forward, removing the space between him and his target, and their bodies collided, sending them both slipping on the foam and falling to the floor.

They fought hand to hand, each man trying to take control of the weapon, but Court suddenly let go of Matador's gun, slid his hand up, and clicked open the detach buckle on the sling. Luka retook control of the Copperhead while this happened, but as he swung it back towards his target, Court grabbed the magazine and pulled with all his might, sending the Copperhead flying out of the Russian's hand and skidding away on the slick floor.

Court didn't know if Matador had a pistol, so he leapt on top of him, rained punches through the foam, and kneed the man in the groin.

The Russian finally rolled Court off him with help from a side hip throw; Court landed on his back, then pushed back deeper into the foam, trying to create a little distance in case the Russian major had either a gun or a knife.

He realized he'd lost his earpiece in the fight, so there was no way to find out if Zoya was still alive or to get Lacy in there to help. He pushed this out of his mind, telling himself there was nothing Lacy could do, and the only way he'd be able to help Zoya was by getting past this motherfucker and upstairs.

And the only way he knew how to do this was to find a weapon. He spun around on his knees, rose to his feet but stayed below the still-rising foam, now five feet high, and ran in a crouch back in the direction of the aviation maintenance cart where the man with the pistol had fallen moments earlier.

Suzanne Brewer had spent the last forty-five seconds at the top of the stairs, crouched down in the fetal position as furious gunfire raged in the hallway just beyond the door in front of her.

The fire had dissipated; she'd waited several moments more, and then she rose slowly and put her hand on the latch.

Before going inside, she looked down at the floor of the hangar. Several feet of foam covered everything, even the tops of the wings of the jets, and the fire suppression distributors on the ceiling were still dripping out the last remnants of foam and liquid. Still, she'd heard shooting down there moments earlier, so she knew her only choice now was to go forward and get control of the hostages, if they were still alive.

Opening the door, she entered the hall, saw that it went to the left for ten feet and then turned to the right. She made it to the corner, raised her weapon, and spun to her left. Immediately she came upon a scene of horror.

One of the Russian GRU men lay crumpled in the center of the hall, face-down with the top of his head split open, a six-foot splatter path of blood on the carpet behind him back in Suzanne's direction.

And in front of the body she saw Zoya Zakharova, clearly injured and lying on her stomach, blood draining from her left arm and upper back, pulling a squat submachine gun from the dead man's body with her right hand.

Brewer quickly raised the pistol Matador had given her, but Zoya saw her at the same time and hefted the subgun from her position on the floor.

Brewer did not fire; instead, she dove back around the turn in the hallway for cover.

As soon as she was there, she said, "You know what, Anthem? You look pretty shot up. I can help you. Think about it: you're more important to me alive than dead right now. Put the gun down and let me come help you."

The Russian woman's voice sounded frail, but her words were strong. "Hard pass, bitch."

Brewer smiled a little, a look of determination in her eyes. She said, "If your boyfriend's still alive, he won't dare kill me if I have you. You *must* know that much. I'm not lying. I *will* let you live, just so I can get out of this bullshit."

Zoya responded after several seconds. "Okay. Fine. I dropped the gun."

Brewer didn't believe her. She lowered against the wall to the floor, then reached out with the weapon. Once her head peered around the corner, Zoya opened fire.

Brewer returned fire as she ducked out of the way.

"You're making a mistake," Brewer shouted to the hall.

"Won't be the first time," Zoya responded, and Brewer could hear the progressive weakening in her voice. The CIA officer realized she'd already won this fight. Anthem was bleeding to death; she just had to wait the former asset out for a minute or two and then go grab the Altmans to use as leverage.

SEVENTY-TWO

After fifty feet of running through the dense foam in a crouch, Court felt his way to the cart the other GRU officer had been positioned behind before Court shot him. Here he dropped to his knees and crawled behind it, then began feeling around. He touched the leg of the dead man, then tracked up to his arm. His gun wasn't in either hand, but Court frantically dug through the foam searching for it.

"So!" He heard a voice call out behind him with a Russian accent. "You are the famous Gray Man, yes?"

Court knew this tactic; Matador was trying to get him to talk to reveal his position.

Court said nothing, he just kept feeling around, hunting for the weapon.

"Exactly the response I would expect," Matador said, a hint of mirth in his voice.

Court's hands were slick with the fire suppressant, but he kept searching desperately.

"Sounds like your dear partner Banshee met my dear friend Sergeant Semenov upstairs. Wonder how that all worked out for her."

Court cringed. Zoya had been in the process of rescuing hostages, alone; he should have been there with her, he should have found a way to help.

"Probably," Matador continued, "no better for her than it worked out for Velesky and Altman when they met Mozgovoy and his team from the SSB."

Court winced again. He had no idea if Matador was telling the truth and Altman and Velesky were really dead, but the Russian certainly sounded confident. Still, Court shoved the guilt away and concentrated on the one thing he could do to affect the outcome. He kept searching, and then his hand bumped against some sort of tool on the floor. It skidded away a few feet, but soon Court had the grip of a Heckler & Koch VP9 in his hand, and he press-checked the weapon to ensure that a round was in the chamber.

Court Gentry didn't bother to check the magazine because he was only going to need one round.

When he heard a long burst of gunfire from near the Gulfstream, he crouched behind the aviation maintenance cart for cover, waiting for it to stop.

When it did, Court rose behind the cart, aimed in on a spot well to the right of the tail of the Gulfstream, and centered his sights just above the foam there, because this was approximately the origin of fire.

It was quiet in the massive room for several seconds, the only sound being the consistent hum of the now-disabled Gulfstream. Court waited to hear the Russian say something else to get a better fix on his location, but when the GRU major still didn't speak up, Court decided he'd have to make something happen himself.

He called out into the big room. "Hey, Matador. How's the foot?"

Suddenly the maintenance cart he'd been using for cover slammed into his waist, knocking him backwards. He fired off a round from the pistol with his impact with the ground, then felt the cart slam into his legs.

Matador had snuck through the foam all the way to Court's position, and now he was just on the other side of the cart.

The gun tumbled out of Court's hands, lost again in the six-foot-high foam. In desperation he pulled open the top drawer of the cart, reached inside, and pulled out the first thing he took hold of: a large wrench.

Just then he heard a short burst of fire; it was Matador shooting over the top of the cart, just four feet away, but Court was too low to the ground to be hit by the rounds.

The shooting stopped suddenly. To Court it sounded like the Russian's Copperhead had run dry.

Court shoved the cart the other way, slamming it into Matador, then he leapt on top of it and rolled over, falling into the foam on the other side and directly onto the Russian assassin, who was on one knee, engaging his SIG Sauer Copperhead's bolt release.

Court swung the wrench as he hit the floor, striking the Russian in the left forearm and knocking the weapon away. Matador threw a punch with his right hand, hitting Court in the jaw, although the men could barely see one another in the mess of foam.

Momentarily stunned, Court dropped the wrench and fell back against the edge of the cart, spinning it around as he landed again on his back. Matador struggled to stand, and then he got over Court and reached into a drawer on the cart, pulling a large ball-peen hammer from it. He swung the hammer down at Court's head, but Court pulled a drawer open just above him, and the hammer slammed into it.

Reaching up to the open drawer, Court wrapped his hand around the first tool he touched, and he yanked it out just as the ball-peen hammer slammed down again.

Court rolled away, still unsure what he was holding other than the fact it had a plastic handle and some weight to it.

He made more space for himself by crawling around to the other side of the cart, and here he stood, his head on a swivel, desperate to find and finish his enemy before his enemy found and finished him.

Petro Mozgovoy led his team up the hall, firing bursts at the desk in view through the doorway, forcing anyone left alive to keep their heads down. Because there had been no return fire for the past minute or so, he was confident the Ukrainian speaker with the pistol was now dead, or at least too injured to fight.

But the man with the gun was not his main objective. His objective was Altman and the information he had with him, so he pushed forward closer to the edge of the office door.

This was just how they'd drilled for their attack on the Ukrainian foreign minister in the lobby of his hotel.

This mission here today in an office building was smaller scale and, frankly, easier. Yes, poor young Olek Kuzmenko had been shot to death in the doorway fifty feet behind Petro, and Yeva Nesterenko had been shot in the ankle, but he and the rest of the men were here, closing on the enemy and fighting for the glory of Donbas.

With his chest filled with pride, Petro raced into the office, scanned quickly left, then straight ahead towards the desk, and then to the right, over by the sofa.

A man covered in blood sat there on the floor, his back against the sofa and his pistol up and pointed at Petro's face, and as the Ukrainian separatist cell leader pressed his trigger on his Copperhead, he saw a flash in front of him, and then his world ended.

After a lot of searching made difficult by his gunshot wound, Ezra Altman finally found the keyboard hanging off his desk by following the coiled wire up to his workstation. The keyboard was just out of his reach, so he scooted back a foot on his left elbow, grunting from pain and effort.

He heard a brief exchange of gunfire, here in his office, and then he heard the sound of a body hitting the floor on the other side of his desk.

He reached out for his keyboard, but bullets ripped across the bookshelf behind him, forcing him lower to the floor. He couldn't make it to the keyboard without scooting again.

He did so, and as he reached for it, he looked up. He was around the side of his desk now, and he saw Alex, sitting up against the sofa. Blooms of red on his white shirt told Ezra that Alex had been shot through and through, but somehow he was still alive. Their eyes didn't meet; Alex had his pistol out in front of him, held with his left hand, as blood also gushed out of the right side of his neck.

The Ukrainian banker called out, "Have we done a great thing yet?"

Ezra Altman looked back to the keyboard dangling three feet away, and he lunged for it using his one good arm. Putting his bloody finger on the return key, he said, "We have, my friend."

Altman pressed the key, the email sent.

In front of him, Ezra Altman saw Alex as he was shot through the head.

He slumped against the sofa, the pistol dropping to the floor next to his dead right hand. Altman fell onto his back, lying there, while above him, a group of armed men converged on his position.

"Too late, boys," Altman said with a smile, just before he was shot through the forehead by a Ukrainian separatist.

The wild fighting in the hangar between Court Gentry and Luka Rudenko had cleared an area in the foam, and for the first time, Court could see the Russian plainly. The man's blond hair was soaking wet, he held the wooden-handled hammer high over his head, and he had a look of intense determination on his face.

Court also saw that the tool in his own hand was a sixteen-inch-long steel prybar, with a pointed tip at the end. It would be a decent stabbing weapon if he were close enough, but his enemy was just out of range and himself armed with a deadly implement.

Matador spoke now through labored breath. "You've already lost your mission, now you lose your life!"

Court slammed his body forward, again into the big rolling cart, knocking a surprised Matador back. Court dropped to a knee now, got his shoulder into the side of the cart, and then heaved up with all his might.

The massive loaded tool kit weighed a couple hundred pounds, but Court tipped it forward, onto the falling Russian, and it pinned the man's legs to the ground. Matador screamed in agony, threw his hammer at Court but missed high, then reached out blindly into the foam around him.

Court scrambled over the top of the cart, and just as the GRU major's hand reappeared clutching the 9-millimeter pistol, Court dove forward and down, stabbing the man through the chest with the long steel prybar.

The gun fired, missing Court's face by inches, and Matador let out a gasp of shock and pain, and Court lay on top of him fully now, feeling the last of the man's life leave him.

Suzanne Brewer hadn't heard any noises from the hallway for nearly half a minute, so she stood back up and peered around the corner.

Zakharova was on her back, the weapon on the ground next to her, not pointed in Brewer's direction. Blood soaked the carpet beneath her. Her head was up, her eyes on Brewer.

Brewer aimed her pistol at her. "Too weak to shoot, or out of ammo?"

Zoya lowered her head back on the carpet and stared at the ceiling. "I'm not too weak to shoot you."

Brewer stepped out into the hallway now. "Out of ammo, then. Good." She began walking forward, her weapon trained on the injured woman, in case she had any last tricks left up her sleeve.

But Zakharova only lay there, her eyes blinking, tears beginning to stream down her face. Blood soaked the carpet around her.

"No more shooting downstairs," Brewer said, her confidence growing with each step. She had Zoya dead to rights, and the woman looked like she would die in moments even if Brewer did nothing. "I guess that means either your person, or my people, will be up here in moments. I assume I still have hostages in that room down the hall, so I guess I won't be needing you, after all."

Zoya bit her lip and closed her eyes. She said, "Just shut up and do it, Suzanne."

SEVENTY-THREE

Court raced up the stairs to the second floor, wielding the pistol he'd scooped up next to Matador's body. He was desperate to help Zoya and to get her and the Altmans out of there.

Unless he was already too late.

He'd just put his hand on the door leading out of the hangar and into the hallway when a single gunshot cracked loudly.

It came from the other side of the door.

Panic and dread filled Court's body; he flung the door open and raced in, his weapon held high. He moved the ten feet to his left, reaching the corner, and then he spun around it in a combat crouch.

Slowly he rose as he took in the scene in front of him.

Standing in the hall was a figure wearing a light brown coat and aiming a gun in the opposite direction. Beyond this figure, a dead Russian GRU officer lay facedown on the bloody carpet.

And just beyond the dead man, Court saw Zoya Zakharova, lying on her back, her eyes closed.

She wasn't moving.

Court raised his arm to fire at the figure in front of him, but the figure lowered the gun, then turned back and looked his way.

Angela Lacy's face was a mask of both terror and disbelief, her eyes un-fixed as if she were moving into shock. The gun fell to the floor.

She then took a step to the side.

Ten feet in front of Lacy, Suzanne Brewer lay on her back, her legs folded under her torso. Her eyes were open, blinking, staring back at Court now. A bloom of shiny red blood grew quickly across her chest.

Court couldn't believe it. He moved up to Lacy, picked her weapon up off the floor, and then walked closer to Brewer. Lacy followed slowly on his heels. Brewer continued to look up at Court, and a sound came out of the CIA executive's throat.

Lacy grabbed Court by the arm.

"She's . . . she's breathing. We have to help—"

Court shook his head. "She's not breathing. That's an agonal gasp. The last sound you make before you die."

Brewer's eyes rolled up slowly as a long sigh passed her lips. Lacy looked on, transfixed and terrorized, but Court had already turned away. He rushed past the dying woman without another thought and ran to Zoya, got down on his knees beside her, and looked into her face.

She was alive. She blinked, blinked again, and then she spoke softly.

So faintly he could barely hear her, she said, "Hostages are okay. In the office."

Tears filled Court's eyes as he rolled her on her side and saw both the entry and the exit wounds on her back. The bullet had hit her left scapula, exiting through muscle just an inch from her thoracic spine, and though there was a good deal of blood, he knew she was a lucky woman.

Another bullet had run up her forearm, and a third had hit higher on her left arm, almost to her shoulder. He knew he had to get her out of here, so despite the obvious pain this would cause, he began lifting her up in a fireman's carry.

Zoya cried out, but Court knew he could always ask for forgiveness later.

Looking back over his shoulder, he saw Lacy still standing there, staring down at a now dead Suzanne Brewer. He yelled to snap her out of it. "The hostages! Cut them loose, then come downstairs. I'll carry Beth."

Lacy looked away from the body at her feet, then said, "The Nissan is parked on the tarmac, right by the door."

"Good work," Court said, which he thought was probably the understatement of his lifetime, and then he began carrying Zoya back towards the stairs.

Angela Lacy was still in a state of shock as she drove past the fire trucks coming up Fred Wehran Drive, racing away from the scene of carnage behind her.

She and the others in the vehicle with her had gotten lucky when they saw several police cars taking off after a black Mercedes leaving the scene. It was the vehicle Drexler had arrived in, and no one in the Armada knew if he was in the car or if his driver had just given up and made a run for it on his own.

Court was in the back seat with Zoya; he'd just hung up with Catherine King and was back to bandaging his patient as best he could with the very basic first-aid supplies he'd found in a roadside emergency kit in the rear of the SUV. As he did this, he called up front to Lacy.

"All her wounds are through muscle. No arteries, no bone, no major organs. I've got the bleeding stopped, mostly. She'll make it, but I'll need a lot more supplies. She's got one round in her shoulder; we'll need a surgeon to take that out."

"Where am I going?"

"Just away from here. We'll figure out everything else when we're clear."

"Okay."

Court kept attending to Zoya, but he addressed Lacy again. "How did you get into the hangar?"

"You two weren't responding. I heard all the shooting, of course, so I got in the SUV and started heading for the guard shack. I was going to just blow past the guards, but then they started running for the terminal. A couple of guys who looked like pilots came out the door, everybody started shooting at each other, and I just drove in, past the side of the terminal and around back to the hangar.

"I couldn't see anything on the floor with all that foam, but I heard shooting upstairs." Lacy shrugged as she drove. "I went in, I don't know why."

Zoya hadn't said much; she was extremely weak from blood loss, but she muttered out a soft, "Thanks."

Lacy acted like she didn't hear her. "I'm going to prison for the rest of my life."

Court sat up, looked at Angela's face through the rearview. "No. You're not."

"How can you possibly say that? Despite the circumstances, there is no way I—"

"Angela," Court interrupted. "There's a way that we can put a party hat on this pile of shit."

Lacy looked up in the rearview. "What the hell does that even mean?"

He thought a moment, then said, "You didn't shoot Brewer."

"What?"

Court said, "You didn't. *I* did."

"I was there. You weren't. I shot her."

"If you take the fall for this, you're done. They will scapegoat you, make Brewer the hero, because she was working directly for Kirby.

"If *I* take the fall for this . . . well . . . it's just another in a long line of ass-hole moves I've done, as far as the world is concerned."

She shook her head. "I can't let you—"

Court interrupted her. "You *have* to let me do it. Look. I believe in you, Angela. You could be exactly what the Agency needs. A good guy on the seventh floor. Someone who sees things the way they really are, but also someone who hasn't lost the faith.

"Don't let Suzanne Brewer destroy you like she destroyed so many others."

"But . . . what will you do?"

Court shrugged as he looked down at Zoya. She'd passed out, but he wasn't worried; her wounds were stable, and the bandages would hold till she was properly treated. He said, "Honestly, I don't think it's going to change much of anything for me."

Lacy wiped tears away now. "I don't know if I can pull off this lie."

"You're *trained* to lie, Angela. Look, we saved the hostages, Catherine King will publish Altman's findings, and you will be stronger at headquarters at the end of this. Christ, that's as close to a home run as I've ever seen on an operation. More than we have a right to expect."

"I . . . I just can't do this to you. It's not fair."

"It *is* fair. Believe me. *I* should have been there to help her. I wasn't. *You* were. *You* did what *I* should have done, so don't think telling people that I did it is a lie."

Lacy looked back in the rearview. After a moment, she smiled a little. "When she wakes up, you want me to tell her you did it? She probably won't remember."

Court smiled, as well. "I can't lie to her."

She repeated his words back to him. "You've been *trained* to lie."

But he shook his head. "She's been trained to see through my bullshit."

"Maybe that's why you love her," Angela said, and she returned her concentration to the road.

Court looked down at the injured woman in his lap. Softly, he said, "Maybe it is."

Three days after a gun battle at Teterboro Airport between suspected Russian agents and unknown members of the U.S. intelligence community, three days after the assassination of a prominent anti-Russian financial corruption advocate in Midtown Manhattan, a man looked out a window at the snowfall coating the hills around a small ranch house in Bennington, Vermont.

Seconds later, exactly on time, a black Range Rover rolled into view on the ribbonlike road and pulled up the long drive.

The man at the window went to the door.

Angela Lacy climbed out of the Range Rover wearing a business suit under a knee-length black coat, and she rushed through the snow to the front porch, then shook the accumulation off her black hair.

Court Gentry opened the door and greeted her with a hug. He wore a white T-shirt and jeans, and he took Lacy's coat and told her to go warm up by the fire.

A minute later he sat down next to her, handing her a cold beer.

She looked at her watch. "It's one thirty-five in the afternoon."

Court took a swig. "I'll slow down so you can catch up."

The African American CIA executive laughed as they clicked bottles, and then she took a sip.

"No chance you have any Cabernet, is there?" she asked after a little wince.

"No chance at all."

She put the bottle down. "How is your patient?"

"She's fine. Sleeping upstairs. The surgeon you sent checked her out. Her vitals are fine, no fragments left in her wounds, and she's both funny and grumpy, depending on the moment.

"So basically, as good as new." He added, "I really appreciate you getting everything arranged like you did."

"And I appreciate everything the two of you have done." She motioned to the house. "This is all off book, the doctor included, if you didn't guess. Private hires."

"Welcome to the dark side."

Angela laughed. "I'm afraid that ship sailed about a week ago."

Court sipped his beer while Lacy looked into the fire a moment. She said, "They think it was you who killed Brewer. I *told* them it was you."

"Good. You did the right thing."

"Sooner or later, though," she said, "they'll find you."

"There's a long list of people after me. Somebody will get me, there's no doubt." He smiled at her. "But, no offense, it's not going to be you guys."

"I hope you're right," she said. Suddenly her expression changed. "Did you see the news?"

Court looked back to the fire. "I don't like the news."

"You'll like *this* news. Cathy King is everywhere with Altman's and Velesky's information. It's all corroborated, provable. Five congressmen and three senators have been implicated so far, as well as some of the biggest news pundits in the nation, the director of Homeland Security, big shots in commerce, hell, even the DOJ. Both parties are involved." She coughed out a laugh. "Hell, half the German government was on the take from Moscow.

"Stuff is still coming out, but what's already out there is devastating."

Court was not impressed. "So now we begin the 'slap on the wrist' phase."

Lacy shook her head adamantly. "You're wrong. Not this time. This is going to make a difference."

Court sighed. "How?"

"Well, for starters, Daniil Spanov died last night."

Court lowered his beer and turned to her. "Holy shit. How?"

"They haven't released a COD yet, but I imagine he went out in the common way for those who fail the Kremlin."

Court nodded at this, then said, "He fell eight stories to his death from a basement window?"

Lacy laughed. "Something along those lines."

"Couldn't have happened to a nicer asshole."

"And speaking of assholes, not necessarily nice ones, Director Jay Kirby has turned in his resignation to the president."

Now Court sat back in his rocking chair. "Why?"

"Guess."

"You just gotta spend more time with your family."

Angela nodded, took another little sip of beer. "You *gotta*."

"Unbelievable," Court muttered.

"Three Ukrainian SSB officers, two men and one woman, were taken alive in Manhattan. They're talking to the Agency; we'll find out if they know about any others."

"They won't know shit. The Russians would have kept them compartmentalized. None of the cells knowing about any others."

"You're probably right." She shrugged. "Altman's and Velesky's funerals are both next week. I'd love to go, but . . . I'd better not."

"Yeah," Court said, thinking about the two men who'd sacrificed so much.

Angela went on with the rundown of the news Court had worked hard to avoid for the past three days. "The accords were signed anyway. The resolution passed, and the World Trade Organization gave Russia back its most-favored-nation status."

He sighed. "And I was just beginning to lose one percent of my cynicism."

"The West wants oil and grain and money. But still . . . when all is said and done, we will wreck Russian intel operations in the U.S., in Europe, in Africa. What we've done is big."

"Doesn't help the Ukrainians."

She shrugged. "Hurting Russia helps Ukraine. I think the president will continue sending Kiev weapons. Hope so, anyway. Can't say the same for

Europe." She shrugged. "Overall, we did well. You've just got to look at the big picture."

"I'll try." He looked back to the fire. "As far as Brewer. Think she'll get a star on the wall?"

There was no hesitation in Lacy's response. "I *know* she will. That's how this all works. She'll be given posthumous awards, despite the facts."

Court nodded to this. Unsurprised. "Angela, you're exactly the right person to make their way up the ladder at Langley. This is your chance, but please, use your power for good."

She flashed a toothy smile. "I very much plan to. That said, if I ever *do* lose my way, I'm pretty sure you'll show up at my house in the middle of the night to let me know."

Court smiled, reached out, and shook her hand. "May we never meet again."

Angela smiled back, then stood up from her rocking chair. "Now, sorry, but I've got to go. Feels weird here. Western Vermont isn't exactly in the CIA's jurisdiction."

"Mine, either." He added, "We'll be out of here by tomorrow."

She nodded and they walked to the door, and then she said, "Court, get away from everything for a while. Decompress. Then . . . if you want to help . . . just reach back out to me. I'm always happy to meet for coffee and a chat."

Court nodded. This midlevel CIA executive on the fast track was telling him she'd like to employ his services from time to time.

Lacy left after a hug, walked back out into the snow, and drove off to the south.

Court locked the door, then headed up the stairs of the little cabin.

The second floor was a bedroom loft. Here Zoya sat up on a bed, wearing a new white tank top along with the white bandages on her left arm and shoulder.

Before he could speak, she said, "You two guys, seriously. Get a room, already."

There was a glint of humor in her eyes that warmed him like even the fire downstairs could not. He sat on the edge of the bed next to her. "It's not like that."

"What's it like, then?"

"She wants to employ me down the road."

"I hope you're not in any big hurry to get yourself a new shit-hot fast-track executive handler at CIA. Didn't work out so great the last time."

Court laughed. "She saved your life."

Zoya conceded the point. "She did. I guess Lacy's all right." Now she looked up at him. "When do we have to leave?"

"Tomorrow. Can you do it?"

"Of course. I'll be ready to go by then. I'll make a call in the morning, get a ride up toward the Canadian border. I'll head back to Europe from there."

Court said nothing.

After a silence, she said, "What about you?"

Court looked across the dark room, out the window, and into the afternoon snowfall. He didn't speak for a long time, but when he did, he said, "I have to run, Zoya."

She waited a moment before replying, softly, "I know. I always knew this was how it would end."

After another silence, Court turned to her suddenly and took her hand; she winced with pain as he moved it, but he didn't even notice. He said, "Run *with* me."

She cocked her head. "*What?*"

"Let's go together. We'll get somewhere safe and . . . and . . . we'll figure it out."

Her face gave off no expression, though Court looked hard for one. He said, "We can watch one another's backs."

Finally, she said, "You never struck me as a man who was ready to play house."

Court held her hand tighter; she'd yet to grip his back. He said, "I'm not shooting for the moon. I know that anywhere we go, there will always be that feeling that we're just seconds away from it all falling apart. That's not playing house. That's reality."

He added, "I can handle reality. Can you?"

Her face did not falter, but soon he felt a reciprocal squeeze on his hand. He got the impression she was going to try to let him down easy.

But instead, she said, "Are you sure this is what you want?"

"This . . . this *isn't* what I want. But *you* are what I want. And if I have to keep running for the rest of my life, I'd rather do it with you than spend every night looking at the stars thinking about you."

Now Zoya's face changed; she put her right hand on his cheek, then slid it behind his head, pulled him closer.

They kissed, and kissed again.

When he pulled away, she said, "I'm still a mess, you understand that. Mentally, I'm not solid. Not yet."

"I can relate."

"I just don't want either of us to get our hopes up too high."

Court smiled. "This isn't exactly like riding off into the sunset to live happily ever after."

Zoya sniffed out a laugh. "I'd settle for a nice, quiet weekend. If that works, let's shoot for a week. If that pans out . . . who knows?"

"Let's shoot for that, then," Court said, his heart as full as he'd ever known it to be.

Zoya asked, "Where should we go?"

To this he smiled. "I have a boat in the Caribbean."

Her eyebrows furrowed. "You mean the one the CIA knows about?"

Court conceded the point with a sigh. "Shit. I *had* a boat in the Caribbean." After a moment, he said, "How about somewhere else?"

"Somewhere else is probably a good idea." They smiled at each other. "In fact," she said, "I have to go somewhere else right now."

Court cocked his head, confused. "Where?"

Zoya laughed. "To the bathroom, dummy. You mind helping me?"

He laughed himself, stood and helped her up, and they began moving across the floor.

Slowly, carefully.

Together.

ACKNOWLEDGMENTS

I would like to thank Allison Greaney, Trey and Kristin Greaney, Kyle Greaney, Devin Greaney, Joshua Hood (JoshuaHoodBooks.com), Rip Rawlings (RipRawlings.com), Jack Stewart (JackStewartBooks.com), JT Patten (JTPattenbooks.com), Don Bentley (DonBentleyBooks.com), Brad Taylor (BradTaylorBooks.com), and Joe and Anthony Russo.

Very special thanks also to Barbara Guy, Janie "The Matchmaker" Lowery, Alex Arnold, Jon Harvey, Jon Griffin, Barbara Peters, Mike Cowan, and Mystery Mike Bursaw, as well as Ava, Sophie, and Kemmons Wilson.

I'd also like to thank my agents, Scott Miller at Trident Media and Jon Cassir at CAA, along with my editor, Tom Colgan, and the other remarkable people at Penguin Random House: Sareer Khader, Jin Yu, Loren Jaggers, Bridget O'Toole, Jeanne-Marie Hudson, Christine Ball, Craig Burke, Claire Zion, and Ivan Held. Humble appreciation also goes out to my amazing copy editors and proofreaders, as well as the incredible art department at Penguin, and all the editors and staff who publish the many great foreign editions of my books.

Lastly, I wish to extend my deepest sympathies to the friends and family of my friend, the late great James Yeager. Rest in peace, James. You will be missed, but you will never be forgotten.

Photo by Claudio Marinesco

Mark Greaney has a degree in international relations and political science. In his research for his novels, he traveled to more than thirty-five countries and trained alongside military and law enforcement in the use of firearms, battlefield medicine, and close-range combative tactics. He is also the author of the *New York Times* bestsellers *Tom Clancy Support and Defend*, *Tom Clancy Full Force and Effect*, *Tom Clancy Commander in Chief*, and *Tom Clancy True Faith and Allegiance*. With Tom Clancy, he coauthored *Locked On*, *Threat Vector*, and *Command Authority*. His first novel, *The Gray Man*, was made into a major motion picture starring Ryan Gosling and Chris Evans.

CONNECT ONLINE

MarkGreaneyBooks.com

f **⊙** MarkGreaneyBooks

🐦 MarkGreaneyBook